Sign up for our newsletter to hear about new and upcoming releases.

www.ylva-publishing.com

Other Books by Lois Cloarec Hart

The Calgary Chronicles
Coming Home
Broken Faith
Walking the Labyrinth

Bitter Fruit
Kicker's Journey
Above the Tree Line
Beyond and Begone
Unstilled Voices
Yak

Stone Gardens

Lois Cloarec Hart

Acknowledgements

Walking the paths in historical cemeteries and imagining the stories behind the inscriptions on monuments is a favourite pastime for my wife, Day, and me. For us it combines art, history, and literature all in one beautiful, peaceful stroll. This is where the idea for *Stone Gardens* was born, but the book could never have come to fruition without much help. I wish to extend my heartfelt thanks to Brook Bolton of Roberts-Shields Memorial Company, Marietta, Georgia, who very kindly took the time to enlighten me on the monuments business and allowed me to poke about his shop, taking dozens of photos and asking innumerable questions. He, in turn, referred me to his friend John-Michael Weber of Superior Memorials in Kitchener, Ontario, who was equally helpful. Between these two men, I received a thorough briefing on the monuments business and heard a number of their personal stories that have found expression within these pages.

Additionally, I'd like to recognize the invaluable contributions of Michael, who is teacher, counsellor, and friend wrapped in one brilliant, frequently infuriating, but always enlightening package. It has been a journey, hasn't it?

As always, my deepest gratitude goes to my wife, Day Petersen, and my old friend Kathleen GramsGibbs, who have been editing and polishing every word I've written for many years. I couldn't do this without you, and words are inadequate to convey how much I appreciate your suggestions. I hope to keep you not-so-gainfully employed for many more books to come.

I'd also like to thank the wonderful people at Ylva, from Astrid Ohletz, who much to my continued gratitude keeps publishing my books, to Sandra Gerth, whom I have the great good fortune to call both senior editor and friend, and to Alissa McGowan, who did her usual wonderful job with the primary edits. And last, but never least, my appreciation to Glendon Haddix of Streetlight Graphics, who never fails to create a brilliant cover from my jumbled descriptions of what I'd like to convey in the cover art.

Dedication

Day,
For all the lovely hours we've spent reading the stories on the stones;
And to all the people whose stories they tell.

'I saw the angel in the marble and carved until I set him free.'

~ Michelangelo

Chapter 1

"Marcus, get out of here." Grae didn't take her gaze off Rick or Dylan as she reached down for the eighteen-inch piece of steel rebar she'd tripped over only moments before this confrontation started.

Dylan sneered. "Better do what the dyke says, fag, or we're gonna rip every earring outta your fucking head, one by one."

Marcus laid a trembling hand on Grae's back. Rick and Dylan were blocking his only avenue of escape from the top of the high-rise construction site. Grae tightened her grip on the rebar and began to circle, keeping Rick and Dylan in front of her and Marcus behind her. For a moment she thought they'd get out unscathed, but then Dylan lunged at her.

She slammed the rebar down on his outstretched arm, and he screamed with pain. She whirled and pushed Marcus toward the construction elevator, seconds before Rick roared and tackled her to the unfinished concrete. Marcus stopped his headlong rush and turned back.

"Go, Marcus! Run!" Grae didn't have time to see whether he obeyed. She fended off Rick's punches as best she could, at the same time hammering the rebar against his back. He swore and rolled away. She staggered to her feet and dodged Dylan's hardhat as it sailed in her direction. His distraction failed, and she slammed the rebar into his belly, then twisted to face Rick as he came at her again. He got in one good punch before her weapon connected with the side of his face.

Rick sank to his knees. "You fucking bitch! I'm going to kill you!"

"You're going over the side this time." Dylan laughed, his eyes crazy with malicious glee as he tried to outflank her, holding his injured arm to his chest. "Better hope you can fly, cunt."

Grae retreated. She hurt all over, and she had no doubt that Dylan meant to carry out his threat. She had to keep them from grabbing her. If she could get her back against the stairwell, she'd at least stand a chance of holding them off. *God, Marcus, I hope you're sending the cavalry.* Everyone else on the crew, including the foreman, had gone down for lunch. On Fridays they gathered at one of the pubs on street level, but Marcus and Grae always brought their lunch.

Should've known something was up when ass-face and butthole stayed behind. Rick and Dylan had been gunning for her and Marcus for months, but until yesterday they had limited their attacks to trash talk.

They feinted at her from two sides. Grae gasped for breath as she swung the rebar in an arc, fending them off. Suddenly the sound of the elevator rising caught her attention. It was the sweetest sound she'd ever heard.

Dylan and Rick glanced at each other and then at the elevator. They backed off.

The foreman emerged, followed by a uniformed police officer. "What the hell is going on up here?"

"She attacked us," Rick said. "I think she broke my fucking ribs and face."

"Broke my fucking arm, too." Dylan's face contorted as he held out the injury.

Grae winced. The arm hung at an odd angle.

The officer looked at her and put his hand on his gun. "Drop your weapon—now."

Grae let the rebar fall, and he kicked it aside.

"Hands behind your back."

She did as she was ordered. "They came after me! I was only defending myself."

The officer ignored Grae's protest, and she subsided. There would be time enough to defend her actions. For now, her bruises would barely be apparent yet, but the blood dripping down Rick's face and Dylan's grotesque arm were conspicuous evidence against her.

The plastic cuffs tightened, and she gritted her teeth against the pain.

"All of you are coming with me." The officer motioned Rick and Dylan ahead of them while keeping a secure grasp on Grae's arm.

"We gotta go to the ER, man. She broke my fucking arm."

"You'll be seen to. Now move."

The officer marched Grae past the foreman. She cringed at the look of disappointment on his face. He'd gone out on a limb to give her and Marcus jobs after weeks of her impassioned pleas. Looked as if he was regretting the day he'd taken them on as clean-up crew.

Goddamnit. Why do things always get fucked up to hell and gone? I can't catch a break.

The ride down in the elevator was silent except for Rick's raspy breathing. Grae shot his bloody face a glance and bit her lip. She hadn't meant to hurt him so badly; she'd only wanted to protect herself and Marcus.

When the door opened on ground level, Rick and Dylan exited first. The officer steered her past them and beckoned to another cop who had just gotten out of his cruiser. "Can you take these two with you? You'll probably have to run 'em to the ER first."

Marcus was talking to a third officer and a couple of the construction workers. He looked up, and his eyes widened. "No, no! You're arresting the wrong person. She was just defending me. She didn't do anything wrong."

He tried to run to Grae, but the officer he'd been talking to grabbed his arm. "Let them sort it out at the station, kid. Finish giving me your statement."

Grae shook her head. "Do what he says, buddy. And then go home—straight home. Wait for me there."

"But—"

"No buts, Marcus. Do what I say. I mean it. I'll be home as soon as I can."

"Do you want me to call your family? Your mom? Ciara, maybe?"

"No, absolutely not." Grae winced as the officer tugged her away. She twisted, trying to meet Marcus' gaze. "But call Lucy for me, will you? Tell her I have to cancel our date tonight, but I'll reschedule as soon as I can."

Grae's last glimpse of Marcus as she was stuffed in the back seat of the car was his tear-stained face. "Hang in there. It'll be okay."

"You say something?" The officer slid behind the wheel.

"No, sir."

He grunted and started the car. Grae leaned back against the seat as best she could with her hands cuffed behind her. The adrenaline of the fight had ebbed, leaving her shaky and cold, despite the warm summer day.

"Excuse me?"

The officer glanced in the rear view. "Yeah?"

"Do you know if I'll be charged, and if so, for what?"

The officer shrugged. "It's not up to me. I just file my report. Might involve a summary conviction for common assault, but if your record is clean, you could get off with probation."

Grae groaned softly. *Jesus, I'm screwed.*

"Depending on how bad the other two guys are, you'll probably be sent home with an appearance notice for Provincial Court."

Oh fuck. Screwed, blued, and tattooed. Could this day get any worse?

※

Grae was exhausted. She stumbled off the bus and shambled down the street to the tiny apartment she and Marcus shared. She felt several decades older than when she'd left for work the day before. When she unlocked the door, Marcus jumped from the couch and hurled himself at her.

"Oh, my God, I was so scared. I didn't know what to do. I kept thinking I should call someone, but I didn't know who."

Grae hugged him tightly, and his tall, thin body trembled. "It's okay, bud. Just tell me that you did call Lucy and you didn't call my family."

"Yes and no." Marcus pulled back and touched the side of her eye. "That's a helluva shiner. Did they give you anything for it?"

"A first appearance notice for Provincial Court six weeks from now."

Marcus followed her to the couch, and she dropped into her corner with a sigh.

"I tried to tell them, Grae. I said that Rick and Dylan started the whole fight and you were just protecting me."

"And myself. I don't know if they'd have actually done it, but they threatened to throw me over the edge."

Marcus stared at her in horror. "Jesus Christ! I should've stayed with you. They couldn't have thrown both of us over."

"No, you did the right thing. No point in the two of us ending up as pancakes. And if you hadn't sent the troops to rescue me, God knows what would've happened." Grae rolled her head to the side and eyed Marcus. "I'm sorry as hell you had to hear their shit, though. You didn't deserve that."

Marcus shrugged. "No worse than I heard for years from dear old Dad before he and Mumsy finally tossed me out on my ass."

"Their loss, bud. Their loss, my gain."

Marcus brushed at his eyes. "You'd think I'd believe that by now. You've told me enough times."

"And I'll keep telling you until you do believe me." Grae closed her eyes, lethargy pulling her closer to sleep. Then her eyes popped open. "What did Lucy say? Was she totally pissed at me?"

"We can talk about that later, okay? Why don't I get the mattress down so you can get some sleep."

Marcus tried to stand, but Grae's hand clamped on his arm.

"What'd she say?"

His pale skin flushed, and he looked away. "Um…"

"C'mon, bud. I'm just going to imagine the worst, so you might as well tell me."

He hung his head. "She, um… Do you want her exact words?"

Grae snorted. "Might as well."

"She said to tell you to go fuck yourself and to never, ever, call her again." Marcus peered at her from under a hank of hair. "I tried to explain it wasn't your fault that you ended up in jail, but she wouldn't listen. She said some other things, too, but I forget now."

"'S okay. I get the gist."

"I'm real sorry, Grae."

"It was only our second date. It's not like she was the love of my life."

"Still…"

Grae pulled herself upright. "Don't worry about it. Come give me a hand pulling the mattress down. I need to get some sleep, and then we need to figure out some stuff."

Marcus followed her into the apartment's tiny bedroom. "What kind of stuff?"

Grae grabbed one end of the mattress leaning against the wall, and Marcus grabbed the other. With the ease of long practice, they maneuvered it flat between the boxes stacked on both sides of the room. Once it was down, there was no room to walk, but beggars couldn't be choosers. The king-sized mattress was one of her sister Ciara's cast-offs, and she and Marcus had carried it many kilometres one Saturday to get it back to their place.

"Odds are we haven't got our jobs anymore. Not that it would be safe to go back there anyway."

"Don't you think they'd fire Rick and Dylan too?"

"No. They're union men. They get fired, they'll put in a redress. No one's going to take the word of short-time casual labourers over journeymen. That's the way of the world, bud."

"Oh." Marcus frowned. "That's just not right. We're not the bad guys. They are."

Exhausted as she was, Grae had to smile. Despite all he'd been through in his eighteen years, Marcus was still so much an innocent. "They are, and it's not right. But it's reality. We need to figure out if we qualify for Employment Insurance, and if so, get our applications in asap. If we don't, then we have to hustle to find new jobs. Only one McJob each isn't going to pay our bills." She grabbed their bedding off the top of a box and threw it on the mattress. "Hell, we have to hustle anyway. EI and Wal-Mart aren't going to support us for very long in the style to which we've become accustomed."

"I'll start looking right away. I'll go use the computer in the library while you get some sleep."

Grae kicked off her boots, lowered herself to the mattress, and closed her eyes. It was all she had the energy for. "I might have to cut your hair again."

"That's okay. It'll grow." Marcus tapped her foot, and she opened her eyes. "You might have to dye your hair back to one colour, too."

Grae ran her fingers through her multi-coloured strands. "Maybe. We'll see what you find." She rolled onto her side and tucked her hands under the thin pillow.

Marcus left the room, pulling the door closed as far as it would go. It was the last thing she heard before sinking into unconsciousness.

By the time Grae woke up, there was no light seeping around the towel they'd tacked up over the bedroom window. Dim light came from the living room, and she could smell popcorn. She smiled. There were still things that could be counted on in this lousy world, and Marcus eating his comfort food was one of them.

She rolled to her feet and stopped, hunched over. Despite the hours of sleep, her body ached from the beating she'd taken. Unlike Rick and Dylan, her injuries hadn't been considered serious. She had rejected the cursory offer of medical attention because she hadn't wanted to encounter her nemeses in the ER, but she felt the after-effects in full force now.

With painful effort, she straightened up. It wouldn't do to give Marcus any additional cause for concern. There was enough resting on his young shoulders.

She padded out to the living room. Marcus was watching TV with the headset on, a big bowl of popcorn on his lap. He looked up and removed the headset as she approached.

"Got enough to share?" Grae sat down beside him, and he offered her the bowl. She took a handful. "So, how did it go at the library? Find anything?"

Marcus shook his head. "Not a lot. There's not much we're qualified for. I submitted some applications for both of us, though, and I'll keep going back to check on them."

"Don't worry about it too much. We'll find something. We always do, right?"

"Right." The worry lines in his forehead didn't ease, though he stuffed so much popcorn in his mouth that he looked like a chipmunk.

Grae helped herself to more. It wasn't much of a supper, but they'd had worse. Marcus wiped his mouth with his sleeve, and Grae cuffed him.

"Hey, where are your manners? What would your mama say?"

He shot her a wry look. "That I'm the spawn of Satan doomed to the deepest levels of hell?"

"Yeah, well, there is that." Grae shook her head when he extended the bowl. "Nah, I'm not all that hungry."

"Me neither." Marcus popped another handful into his mouth. When he was able to talk again, he said, "So I was thinking..."

"Mm-hmm?"

He stared straight ahead. "Maybe you should think seriously about going home for a while. You know—get some legal advice, eat some decent meals, sleep in your own—"

"No."

Marcus sighed and turned to face her. "I'm not kidding, Grae. I looked it up. I might qualify for EI, but you won't. You might be in some serious shit here, and your family—"

"You're my family."

"And I love you for saying that, but we're not blood. They could—"

"Not an option." Grae's anger rose, and she fought to push it down. "We may not have come out of the same womb, but as far as I'm concerned, you're my little brother. Get that through your fucking head."

Marcus studied her for a long moment, then snickered. "What kind of language is that to use around your baby brother?"

"Fucking? Like you haven't said it a thousand times, altar boy."

"No—womb. What kind of talk is that to use around a self-respecting fag?"

Grae elbowed him and laughed. "Womb, vagina, labia—"

He stuck buttery fingers in his ears. "La, la, la, la, la, la, la."

She wrapped an arm around his skinny neck and knuckled his head. "Idiot."

She let him go and he leaned back, grinning at her. "So that just makes you the idiot's sister."

"Guess it does. Now quit hogging the popcorn."

"You said you were full."

"I lied."

Chapter 2

Grae stared at the docket list and tried not to hyperventilate. She'd planned to arrive at least thirty minutes before her scheduled court appearance, but her bus was involved in an accident with an impatient driver, and waiting for a replacement bus had eaten up her margin of safety.

"Ms. Jordan?"

She turned. A baby-faced man with a large briefcase had addressed her. "Yes?"

"I'm Grant Stark, the duty counsel for today. The clerk said you don't have representation?"

"Right."

"Okay, well I'm here to walk you through the process."

"I…don't have money for a lawyer."

Stark shook his head. "There's no charge, but I can't represent you if you choose to plead not guilty and your case goes to trial. You'll have to apply to Legal Aid for that. I'm simply here to help get you through your docket court appearance. I can speak to the Crown prosecutor on your behalf, enter your plea, or reserve it for later." He glanced at his watch. "We don't have much time, though. Do you know what you're going to do?"

"Pass out?"

Stark smiled and patted her arm. "Don't worry. You're appearing before Judge Matheny-Boyd. She's tough, but fair… But she can't stand lateness and you're first up, so let's move."

Grae opened her mouth, then shut it and trotted behind Stark, who never stopped talking as he hurried down the hallway.

"…I only had a few moments to review your case, but from what I could see it's not necessarily cut and dried."

"That's cuz it wasn't assault. It was self-defence."

Stark glanced over his shoulder. "I don't disbelieve you, but bottom line is that you used a weapon, and both men received serious injuries as a result. They have no criminal records; you do, even if it was for summary convictions. It's your choice, but you may want to consider a plea of guilty with mitigating circumstances. You're unlikely to get worse than probation, especially since your record has been clean since your last probation ended. In any case, you'll want to secure legal representation."

"That sucks. I didn't do anything but try to keep me and Marcus alive."

Stark stopped outside a door. "As I said, it's your choice, but the problem if it goes to trial is going to be lack of physical evidence to support your contention, whereas the Crown would have medical evidence to substantiate the charges."

He led the way into a crowded court. The judge was just taking her seat as Stark steered Grae into a middle row.

"Whew, just under the wire. You're first up, so when the clerk calls your name, we'll go to the front and stand in front of the judge. The charges will be read out, and if you'd like I can request that your plea be reserved for later."

"It won't come to—"

The court clerk turned to face the court, and read from a form. "Grae Jordan. Two counts of common assault." He handed a file to the judge.

Stark stood and led the way to the front of the court. Grae followed, her head down. There was a brief moment of silence as the judge scanned the file, and Grae held her breath.

"I'll be recusing myself from this case," the judge said. "Reassign Ms. Jordan to Judge Eisler's court."

There was an infinitesimal quiver in the judge's stern voice, though Grae doubted anyone else in the court had noticed. Grae avoided looking directly at her.

"Yes, Your Honour." The court clerk took back the file, made a notation, and motioned to Stark.

He shot a puzzled look at Grae, but accepted the revised form.

They exited the court by the front side door.

"Um, I'm not sure what happened there," Stark said, once they were in the hallway. "Do you know why the judge recused herself?"

"Yes."

"Want to enlighten me?"

"Not really."

Stark frowned and consulted the form the clerk had given him. "All right, your call. You're rescheduled to appear in Judge Eisler's court three months from now. Do you have any questions?"

"Nope."

Stark initialed the form and handed it over. "If nothing else, it'll give you time to consult with Legal Aid. Good luck."

"Thanks."

Stark bustled away down the hallway, and Grae studied the form. Not that it mattered. Her nightmare had come to life, and there was nothing she could do about it.

A prolonged rapping on the apartment door dragged Grae out of sleep. She lurched to her feet and padded through the living room to answer the summons, rubbing her eyes. She wrenched open the door. "Jesus, did you forget your key again—"

It wasn't Marcus.

Judge Matheny-Boyd stood stiffly in the dingy hall. "May I come in?"

Grae opened the door wider and stepped aside. "Hello, Thea. I wondered how long it would take you to show up here."

"I might've been here sooner if I'd known how to contact you." She entered the apartment and looked around.

"Sorry. We'd have cleaned up if we'd known we were having company."

"We?"

"Me and Marcus, my roommate."

Thea's eyebrows shot up. "You have a male roommate?"

Grae snorted and walked to the couch. "Don't get all excited. Marcus is the baby brother I never had."

Thea sat stiffly on the other end of the couch. "You have a perfectly good big brother."

Grae sighed. "I'm guessing you didn't come to discuss family dynamics. What can I do for you?"

"You can tell me why you didn't alert me ahead of time that my youngest daughter was going to show up in my court."

"Wasn't like I had a choice of judges. I was keeping every finger and toe crossed that it wouldn't be your court, but that worked about as well as everything else in my fucking life."

"You should've spoken to someone in the Criminal Division about a venue change."

"You're not thinking clearly, Mother dear. Did you really want anyone to know your black sheep daughter was up on charges again? You don't have to give a reason for recusing yourself. I would've had to explain why I wanted a different judge, and you can bet that juicy piece of gossip would've been all over the building in ten minutes or less."

There was a long moment of silence. "You…you were protecting me?"

Grae shot her a bitter glance. "Could you act any more surprised?"

Thea studied her. "Is that why you changed your name?"

Grae shrugged and picked at the arm of the chair. "No."

"Then why? Are you ashamed of us?"

Startled, Grae looked up, meeting her mother's gaze. She was shocked at the pain she saw there. "I think you've got things backwards."

"We've never been ashamed of you."

"Bullshit."

"Grace, I—"

"It's Grae. I won't answer to anything else."

"All right…Grae." Thea took a deep breath. "I want to help."

"I don't need your help."

"Uh-huh. Because you're doing so well on your own."

Grae straightened, trembling with fury. "I was doing fine until those assholes attacked us and threatened to throw me off the fifteenth floor of the construction site. Forgive me if I didn't stand still and let them toss me, Mom. But hey, maybe that would've made it easier for all of you. No more worrying about when the bad penny might turn up."

"Stop it! Right now."

It was her mother's judge voice, stern and commanding. Grae had been helpless against it most of her life, but not any longer. "You don't get to order me around. We're not in your court, and you have no jurisdiction over me."

A key turned in the lock, and both their heads turned to the door.

Marcus walked in, a grocery bag in hand, and stopped short. "Um, hi. Sorry to interrupt."

"Don't worry about it, bud. My mother was just leaving."

"Not until I say what I've come to say."

Fuck. I know that tone. "All right. Say it."

"I'll just get out of your way." Marcus dropped the grocery bag on the counter and hurried to the bedroom, closing the door as much as he could behind him.

Grae suppressed a smile. He might've been out of sight, but she'd bet her miniscule paycheque that he was eavesdropping.

"I read the arrest report."

Grae studied her mother. "And?"

"You do have some factors in your favour. There are witness accounts that the victims had verbally harassed you and Mr. Lyndon for weeks before the assault. Both the foreman and police officer first on the scene report that the men had you backed up against a wall. Those could be mitigating circumstances."

"What part of they were fucking going to throw my ass over the side doesn't anyone get?"

Thea shuddered and closed her eyes for a moment. "Be that as it may, if this case came before me—"

"It did, remember? That's why you're here."

Thea's gaze drilled into Grae. "I'm here because whether you believe it or not, I love you just as much as I love your brother and sister."

Grae blinked and sat back.

"And as pig-headed as you are, I'm praying you'll have the good sense to hear me out and take my advice."

"Okay."

It was Thea's turn to blink. "Okay?"

Grae gave a wry chuckle. "I may be the stupid one of the family, but even I'm not dumb enough to turn away free legal counsel. And it's not like I could afford to hire Virgil."

"Your brother would represent you for free, you know that."

"I wouldn't ask him."

"You don't have to. He's already volunteered."

"Huh."

"But there is one condition."

Grae slumped wearily and banished thoughts of competent legal counsel. "Of course there is. Tell me what it is, I'll reject it. Then you can consider your duty done and leave."

"Damn it, Grace!"

"Grae. It's Grae, Mother. If you can do nothing else for me, at least use my chosen name."

"Grae." Thea drew a deep breath. "We all want to help. Me, your father, Virgil, Ciara—"

"I can see where you and Virg might help, but what's Dad going to do—keep all his stations from featuring me on the six o'clock news?"

"Don't kid yourself. You're not important enough to make the evening news."

Grae scowled. "Don't kid *yourself*. If my name were still Grace Jordan Matheny-Boyd, you can bet your ass my arrest would be a banner headline, complete with video of me doing a perp-walk."

Thea ignored her. "You asked what your father could do, so here's the condition of our help—his, Virgil's, and mine. You accept private counselling that we will pay for until your therapist deems you ready to take on a more productive role in society."

"Might be a little difficult if I'm in lock-up."

"You won't be. Virgil will see to that. At worst you'll get probation and community service. But with your record, if you don't accept our help, we'll wash our hands of your case and you'll go to jail. Note, I did *not* say wash our hands 'of you.' We'll still be there for you when you come out of jail, but we won't step in to try to prevent you from being sentenced to prison time. You've skated too many times on lesser offences. I think that's part of your problem. So I'm offering you one last chance."

"It's not fair," Marcus said.

Grae glanced behind her. Marcus stood in the bedroom doorway, his hands clenched and his face red.

"Your daughter saved my ass on that rooftop, maybe even my life, and not for the first time. And all of you think she's guilty of something. She's not! She's the victim."

"It's okay, bud."

Marcus took several steps toward them. "No, it's not. What's the matter with your family? Do they have any clue who you really are?" He glared at Thea. "The first time your daughter saved my life was when my family tossed me out of their ever-so-God-fearing home for being a fourteen-year-old fag. I was hustling my ass on the street just trying to make enough to eat. She fed me when I was hungry, found me honest work, and took me into her home."

"Such as it is." Grae shot him a wry smile.

"Beats the hell out of trying to find someplace warm to survive a winter night. Beats the living hell out of fending off the freaks and pervs who think you're nothing more than a piece of ass, even when you're not working." Tears ran down Marcus' cheeks. "I'd have been dead by now, inside if not out. You saved me. I'll never forget that."

Grae stood and took him in her arms. They rocked together in a tight embrace, for a long moment. Then Thea cleared her throat, and they both turned to look at her. Her eyes were bright with unshed tears, but her shoulders were rigid and her expression grave.

"Marcus, believe it or not, I'm trying to do what's best for my daughter. Please, both of you, sit down and hear me out."

They sat, facing Thea.

She leaned forward and rested a hand on Grae's knee. "You took yourself out of our family. I know you don't believe me—don't believe any of us—but we never stopped loving and missing you. We did not, and would never, kick you out. Please, please, let us help."

"With therapy?" Grae shook her head. "I'm working two McJobs and barely getting by as it is, even with Marcus' help. Between my day shift and overnight shift, I barely have time to grab some sleep. No way can I work therapy into my schedule. It's not like Wal-Mart gives any benefits or breaks to shelf stockers, and I'm lucky to get a free burger and fries at my other job."

"Then quit one of your jobs and let us provide you accommodations. You know we have multiple rental properties in our portfolio. Let me look into finding you something appropriate."

"Not if the deal doesn't include Marcus. I'm not going anywhere without him."

"It's okay—"

Grae shot him a glance over her shoulder. "That's non-negotiable, now and always. You go where I go, or I don't go."

"I've always admired your loyalty to your friends," Thea said. "Of course it applies to Marcus, too. I'll even ensure that it's a two bedroom, so you can each have your own space."

Grae studied Marcus. "What do you think, bud?"

"I think... I think we're going to have to flip for who gets the mattress."

"You can have it. I'll get an air mattress. After all, I get a store discount."

"Oh, for heaven's sake." Thea slapped Grae's knee. "I'll make sure the place is furnished, mattresses and all."

"Hey, child abuse! What would people say if they knew the honourable judge beat her child?"

Thea rose to her feet. "Given the circumstances, I'm sure they'd be very understanding. You could exasperate a saint, and I am not a saint." She held out her hand. "Do we have a deal?"

Grae stood. "Who picks the therapist?"

"I do. I have the perfect person in mind, if she'll agree to take you on."

Marcus jumped to his feet, picked up Grae's arm, and waggled it at Thea. "C'mon, Grae. Shake on it before your mom changes her mind."

Grae looked sideways at him with a small grin. "You know absolutely nothing about negotiating, do you?"

"Maybe not, but I'm tired of listening to Ben gnaw on the furniture in the middle of the night."

"Ben?" Thea asked. "A boyfriend?"

Grae and Marcus laughed. "No, Mom. Ben is our resident rat. We never see him in the daylight, but we sure see the evidence that he's been around."

Marcus nodded. "He's a big pooper."

Thea shuddered. "Good lord! Why don't you complain to your landlord?"

"And give him reason to evict us?" Grae shook her head. "No thanks. Affordable housing is impossible to find in this city. We've put up with Ben for over a year now. He's practically one of the family."

"I won't be sad to leave Catie and her brood behind, though," Marcus said.

Thea raised an eyebrow. "I almost hate to ask. Catie?"

Grae grinned. This was almost too much fun. "Catie the cockroach. Actually, we're not sure which one is Catie, because she seems to have invited all her relatives in over the summer. I don't want to sound racist, but they all look alike to us."

Thea paled and began to back away.

Grae followed her. "Really though, I hate the silverfish most. Don't know why, except they keep waking me up when I'm trying to sleep. At least Catie's gang stay off my face."

"Which reminds me." Marcus walked to the counter where he'd dropped the groceries. "I found some roach spray on sale."

"Excellent. We'll get some decent sleep until it runs out, then."

Thea had reached the door. She turned the handle, then stopped. "Would you be willing to give me your phone number?"

Grae's smile faded. "I can't afford a phone. You can reach me through Marcus, though. The boy couldn't live without his cell, even if it means eating popcorn for supper three nights a week."

"587-880-2141," Marcus said. "I'll make sure Grae gets any messages."

"Thank you." Thea entered the number in her phone and tucked it back in her purse. "I'll be in touch."

She hesitated in the doorway, and Grae fought an unexpected impulse to hug her goodbye.

"Did you want me to convey any messages to your dad? Or Virgil or Ciara?"

"Sure. Tell them I said hi." It was the best Grae could do for now, but her throat closed at the look of disappointment on her mother's face.

"All right. I'll be back to you in a few days."

"Okay."

Chapter 3

Aban poked his head around the corner. "Lunch time. See you in the break room?"

Grae nodded. "Marcus is stocking shampoo. I'll just grab him, and we'll see you there." She shifted the case of toilet tissue she'd been unloading to the side. Even at four in the morning, their supervisor frowned on potential hazards left in the middle of an aisle.

She found Marcus sniffing a bottle of shampoo. "Hey, glamour guy, it's break time."

He recapped the shampoo and added it to the shelf. "Coming." He caught up with her, and they walked to the back of the store. "We have to try that new shampoo. It smells like coconut and mango, wrapped up in lotus blossoms."

Grae snorted. "Like you'd know a lotus blossom if one fell on your head."

Marcus linked his arm through hers. "Well, it beats that stuff you buy. That shit smells like tarpaper and baby poop."

"I got it on a two-for-one sale."

"Uh-huh. You either have to sniff before you buy, or let me take over responsibility for all our toiletries."

"Fine. But if you send me out into the world smelling like some frou-frou femme, you and I are going to have words."

Marcus laughed and held the door open for her. "Don't worry. It's Axe for you, and Crabtree and Evelyn for me."

"It's whatever's on sale for both of us, bud."

His shoulders slumped. "I know."

Stone Gardens

Aban beckoned to them from a table. His meal was already steaming in front of him. Grae grabbed her and Marcus' lunches from the fridge and slid in across from him.

"So, how is the world treating you, my young friends?" Aban shovelled a bite into his mouth.

Grae's nostrils flared at the fragrant scent. "It'd be treating us a lot better if you could convince Mrs. Jalali to send enough to feed all of us one of these days."

Aban stopped chewing. "You like Persian food?"

"If it all smells like that, then yes."

Marcus nodded as he bit into his peanut butter sandwich. "What she said."

"Then you must come to my home one day for dinner. I will ask Parveneh to cook for you all her favourites. You will think you are in heaven."

Grae smiled. "Our heaven or yours?"

Aban shrugged. "It's all the same neighbourhood, no?" He took another bite and murmured in contentment. "Oh, I forgot to tell you—you were right, Grae."

"I was? That's new. About what?"

"I changed my approach. I sat Nasim down and talked to him, rather than just ordering him to give up his foolishness."

"Cool. So did he change his mind?"

Aban sighed. "No. He's still set on getting a tattoo, but I begin to make peace with the idea. Perhaps in a little while, I will say yes." He glanced at Grae's arms. "Please, it is not that I think your tattoos are wrong, but it is not the custom of my family. And Nasim is only seventeen."

"No problem. I like my ink, but it's not for everyone."

Aban pointed to the most prominent design on Grae's forearm. "I like that one very much. It is bold…yet tender. It suits you."

Grae glanced at Marcus and smiled. "That's what he said when he designed it for me."

Aban's eyebrows rose. "You designed this?"

Marcus nodded.

"It is so beautiful." Aban peered at the female knight—her helmet was off, revealing multi-coloured streaks in her dark hair, and her sword tip rested on a brilliant crimson rose. He glanced from Marcus to Grae, and back to Marcus. "This is the way you see her, is it not?"

Marcus blushed, but nodded again.

"He drew it the first night he moved in with me. As soon as I got a decent paycheque from my last job, I went and had it done. It's my favourite."

"If Nasim chose something like this, Parveneh and I would not be unhappy, though perhaps a little smaller."

"Maybe you should ask Marcus to design something for Nasim."

Marcus shook his head forcefully. "Bad idea. He wouldn't want that."

"Well, not something like my knight, no, but you draw beautifully, bud. I bet if you talked to Nasim and found out what he had in mind, you could come up with something rad."

"No, I—"

"Please, Marcus." Aban extended his hand. "You and Grae come for dinner, okay? You talk to Nasim. Show him your art. I do not want him getting a skull and snake."

Marcus cast a troubled glance at Grae, but before he could answer, their supervisor stepped through the door.

"Yo, Aban! Truck's here. You're up."

Aban rose to his feet, hastily tucking the remnants of his lunch back into his bag. "I'm coming." He looked at Grae and Marcus. "Dinner soon? Okay?"

Grae answered for them both. "Sure. We'll work out a good time later."

Aban nodded and hurried away, tossing his lunch into the fridge before he left the room.

"Damn it, Grae, do you know what you just did?"

"What? I got you a new client—non-paying, but at least you'll have the pleasure of seeing your art on someone else's body besides mine. Plus we get a free meal. What's so bad about that?"

Marcus closed his eyes and shook his head. "You just don't get it."

Grae frowned. "Enlighten me."

"Guys like Nasim…seventeen-year-old boys…those are my peers. I know the way they think. I'm the last one they want to hang with. He may not be able to avoid me in his parents' house, but he's not going to be happy to have some gay boy drawing a tat for him."

"Jesus, bud, it's not like he's going to beat you up when we're invited guests."

"I didn't think he was. But it's also not fair to put him in such an uncomfortable position. What if Aban tells his son to take me to his room to look over my drawings?"

"Then you go along and behave like a gentleman, and he does the same. I don't get it, Marcus. It's not like Aban is blind to who we are. He's never treated us any differently. Why does this have you freaked out?"

"Aban's a grown man, and a good dude. His son… Well, I went to school with lots of guys like that. It wasn't fun."

"You don't know what Nasim's like. You don't know that he's a 'phobe, and even if he is, no way is Aban going to let him get on your case."

"Maybe."

The handful of workers still in the break room began to drift out. Grae folded her empty paper bag and put it in her back pocket. Marcus did the same, and they rose to leave.

"I'll meet you by the back entrance when we're done, okay?"

Marcus nodded and walked off, head down.

Grae watched him go and bit her lip. She didn't want Marcus to think the whole world was composed of Dylans and Ricks, but his fear was contagious. Maybe she'd better deflect Aban's invitation after all.

※

Grae and Marcus stood in front of their apartment building, watching traffic.

"What does your sister drive?"

Grae shrugged. "Your guess is as good as mine. It was some kind of an SUV parked there when we went to pick up the mattress. I have no idea if she's still got it. There might be some kind of rule that oil execs can't drive the same car two years in a row."

"That wouldn't have been her car, anyway. She wasn't home that day."

"I know, but they could've been out in Bai's vehicle."

Marcus elbowed Grae and chuckled. "Remember the look on the housekeeper's face when she asked where our truck was, and we told her we were carrying the mattress home?"

Grae laughed. "I thought the poor woman was going to fall over in shock."

"It was a heavy bugger. That had to be the longest walk I've ever taken."

"But we made it." Grae straightened as she recognized Ciara behind the wheel of an approaching vehicle. "She's here."

A black Cadillac Escalade pulled to the curb. Grae got in the front seat and Marcus in the back.

"Thanks for picking us up," Grae said.

Ciara checked her mirror, then glanced at Grae before she pulled back into traffic. "You're welcome."

"Um, this is Marcus." Grae jerked a thumb over her shoulder. "Marcus, this is my sister, Ciara."

"Hi. Nice to meet you," Marcus said.

"You, too."

An awkward silence fell as Ciara navigated away from their apartment and headed north. Grae cast about for a possible topic of conversation. "Um, thanks again for the mattress. We really appreciated it."

"We did, thanks from me, too," Marcus said. "It beats sleeping on the floor, that's for sure."

Ciara's lips tightened. "You're welcome."

Grae stroked the leather seat. "Sweet ride."

"It's Bai's. Believe it or not, my car is a Prius."

"Priuses are good, but I guess you could carry a lot of stuff in here when you need to."

"Uh-huh. Could've carried that mattress for you."

Grae cast an uneasy glance back at Marcus, who shrugged. "I don't know. I don't think it would've fit, even in here."

"We have a roof rack. For that matter, our next-door neighbour would've brought it over in his van. There were options. You didn't have to carry it all the way home."

"We didn't mind. We…uh…didn't want to impose on anyone."

Ciara glanced at Grae with an expression that reminded her acutely of their mother's when she was in full-on judge mode. "No, you never do."

That was the last thing anyone said until she pulled into the long driveway of a beautifully landscaped apartment building a few blocks from the river.

Marcus gave a low whistle. "Nice."

They passed a bronze sign set in a bed of colourful fall flowers: *Skyview Towers*. Grae stared out the window. It was an older building, but that didn't detract from its appearance. Dark brick and extensive use of glass gave it an airy and elegant appeal. She noted the large balconies, and the number of units that had grills, lawn chairs, and bicycles stored there.

"Are you sure this is where we're supposed to meet Mom?" Grae asked as Ciara slowed to a halt at the front entrance.

"Of course. Dad and Virgil will be here too."

Grae tensed, then relaxed as Marcus' hand settled on her shoulder. If it didn't work out, if her family tried to steamroll them, they hadn't lost anything but a ride home. They had their transit passes. They'd find their own way back to their apartment if necessary.

"Come on. They're waiting for us upstairs." Ciara parked in a guest slot, exited the vehicle, and strode toward the front entrance. Grae and Marcus scrambled to keep up.

Ciara hit the button beside 407, and they were buzzed in. She led the way to the elevators. They rode up in silence, Grae and Marcus standing together on one side, and Ciara on the other.

Apartment 407 was just down the hall from the elevator. Thea waited in the doorway. She smiled at Grae. "I'm glad you were able to make it."

"We haven't got long. We have to get some sleep before our next shift."

Thea frowned. "Haven't you given up your second jobs yet?"

Grae shook her head. "We thought we'd better see if this works out first."

"Why wouldn't it?" Ciara's tone was challenging.

Thea shot her a glare. "Your sister is being commendably cautious. Please, come in and take a look around. See what you think."

Grae edged past Ciara, who was engaged in a staring match with Thea. Marcus stayed so close he almost tripped Grae by stepping on her heels. She raised one eyebrow at him, and he mirrored her right back.

"Relax, bud. If it's not cool, we go home, okay?" Grae whispered.

"Okay." Marcus stopped short as they entered the living room.

Grae's father and brother rose to their feet.

"Marcus, this is my dad, Carter, and my brother, Virgil."

Virgil stepped forward and offered his hand. Marcus shook it. "Nice to meet you." He turned to his sister. "Nice to see you again, Grae."

"You, too." Grae almost smiled at how carefully Virgil pronounced her name. *Guess Mom briefed him.* "Hi, Dad."

He nodded, but didn't extend his hand. "Marcus, nice to meet you."

"Thanks. Nice to meet you, too, sir."

Thea and Ciara had finished their battle of the glares and moved up behind them. Thea touched Grae's back. "Why don't you and Marcus explore the apartment? We'll wait for you here."

"Okay. C'mon, Marcus." They walked down the hallway and looked into the first bedroom. It was fully furnished and next door to a complete bath.

Marcus nodded. "Nice. Guess this one would be mine, eh?"

"If you like. I don't care if you want the master."

"Your family might, and they're footing the bill."

Grae turned to face him. "It's not a done deal, bud. We don't have to say yes. If you're going to feel like a second-class citizen in your own home, then I don't want to live here."

Marcus looked around the room wistfully. "I've never had such nice digs."

"Then let's look at the rest of the place." They continued to the master bedroom.

"Damn, Grae! Look at that. You've got your own balcony. You can watch the sun come up."

"Go down, you mean. It faces west."

"East, west, who cares? You can bet your ass won't be no rat chewing on the furniture." Marcus practically danced across the room to the walk-in closet. "Double damn! You could practically fit our whole bedroom in here." He whirled and rushed to the en suite. "Oh, my freaking God! You have got to see this."

Grae laughed as she crossed the room and ducked under his arm. "Not bad."

"Not bad? Are you kidding? You could swim laps in that bathtub. You're going to feel like you're living in the Ritz-Carlton, woman."

"No, you are. I want you to take this room."

"Are you insane? No way."

"Yes, way. I'm serious, bud. I spent most of my life living in rooms like this. I'm totally cool with the other bedroom. I want you to have this one, en suite and all. Besides, my wardrobe would look stupid in that walk-in. I just need a place for my boots, jeans, and tees. You'll have room to spread out in here."

Marcus turned back to the room and spun in a slow circle, an awestruck expression on his face.

"But you have to promise me you'll keep all your shit inside this bedroom, okay? I'd like to keep our common areas reasonably clutter-free."

Marcus tilted his head. "You're a neat freak? How could I live with you three years and not know that?"

"Because we don't have the space over there to be clutter-free. We need every square inch of that dump. But here, we can do better."

He smiled. "Next thing you're going to tell me is that we're going to add veggies to our diet."

"A salad or two a week wouldn't hurt you."

"Maybe we could grow our own garden out on that great big balcony."

Grae laughed, then sobered. "I'm pretty sure management wouldn't approve, but mostly…I don't think we should get too attached to this place."

Marcus sank down on the bed. "Why? Do you think they'll boot us out?"

"I'll make sure I get an agreement for a year's residency. And I'll go along with their terms to secure that for us, but I'm not about to cede my life to anyone, no matter how much nicer this place is than ours."

"Then maybe we should just tell them no. Maybe it's better to stay where we are."

Grae shook her head. "You deserve better than that rathole we've been in. If it's only a year, it's only a year. We'll find someplace new after that. Maybe we'll even leave the city and seek our fortunes elsewhere. We can do anything we want."

Marcus studied her with troubled eyes. "If you're going to be unhappy, this," he gestured around the room, "is not worth it to me. I'm dead serious."

"I know you are, and I appreciate it." Grae took a deep breath. "Let's go talk to the parental units and see what they have to say."

Marcus shook his head as he stood. "No. You talk to them alone. This is family business."

"You are—"

"I know, but in this case, I think it's better blood deals with blood. I'll wait down in front of the building."

Grae walked Marcus to the door, then hugged him. "I'll be down in a few. Stay out of trouble, bud."

"What kind of trouble could I possibly get into?" He grinned, and she knuckled his head.

They laughed softly together, and he left.

Grae turned to find her family staring at her. "What?"

"We've just never…"

"What Virgil means," Thea shot a warning glance at her son, "…is that it's nice to see how well you get along with your roommate."

"Told you. He's my little brother." Grae brought a chair from the dining room and sat down to face them. Her mother regarded her calmly. Her father wouldn't meet her gaze. Her brother looked sad, and her sister looked mad. *Situation normal.* "The place is nice. What are the terms?"

"Trust you to cut right to the chase," Ciara said with asperity.

"And trust you to—"

"Enough. You two will be civil to each other, is that understood?" Thea asked.

Without looking at each other, Grae and Ciara nodded.

"All right. Grae, we've signed a lease for the next year. You and Marcus can move in as of the first."

"Okay."

"That's all you've got to say?" Ciara spat. "Not 'gee, thanks for rescuing me from a slum,' or maybe, 'thanks for not disowning my sorry ass'?"

Thea jumped to her feet. "Ciara! What did I just say?"

Ciara never took her eyes off Grae. "It's true, Mom, and you can't gloss over it. She's bloody selfish and inconsiderate, and you just let her get away with it. You've always done that. No wonder she turned out the way she did."

Surprised at how calm she felt, Grae looked at Ciara, and rose. "Good to see you all again." She spun and walked quickly to the door.

She was as far as the elevator when Thea and Virgil caught up to her.

Her mother seized her arm. "Please don't go. Come back and talk to us. Please?"

Grae turned and regarded them wearily. "Why?"

"Ciara doesn't speak for all of us," Virgil said. "I don't feel that way. Mom doesn't."

"But Dad and Ci do. That's fifty percent of the family."

Thea shook her head. "No, honey, it's not. It's only forty percent."

"Math? You're using math to debate me?" Grae shook her head.

"I'll use anything…anything at all that will persuade you to let us help."

Grae blinked at the fierceness in her mother's voice. The elevator door opened, and she hesitated.

"If not for us, do it for your… Do it for Marcus," Virgil said.

Grae sighed and allowed the elevator door to close. "Damn it." She lightly punched Virgil's arm. "When'd you get to be such a good lawyer?"

He glanced at their mother. "I had the best teacher."

Grae closed her eyes for a long moment. She could almost hear her mother and brother holding their breath. She opened her eyes and nodded. "All right."

Virgil grabbed her in a hug and jounced her up and down.

"Ugh, take it easy there, bro." Grae gently broke out of his embrace. "Good thing I haven't eaten yet."

He grinned and started back to the apartment.

Thea took Grae's hands. "Thank you."

"For what? You're doing me the favour—me and Marcus. We should be thanking you."

Thea's eyes glistened. "For giving us…for giving me another chance."

Grae's throat tightened. She tried to speak, stopped, and tried again. "I can't make any promises, Mom. I'm not very good at...well, pretty much anything. I don't want to disappoint you."

"You'll try. I'll try. All we can do is our best, honey." Thea released Grae's hands. "Come, let's rejoin the others."

"You're not going to make me come to family dinners, are you? There are only so many of Ciara's death-glares I can take."

Thea shook her head. "I'm not going to make you do anything except see the therapist. But maybe someday you and Marcus would like to come to dinner, of your own volition, of course. You know you're always welcome."

"Maybe." They reached the door, and Grae laid a hand on her mother's arm.

Thea turned to look at her. "Yes?"

"Thank you for...for coming after the hundredth sheep."

Thea smiled. "Always." She stepped aside to let Grae precede her into the apartment. "Good to know all those years of Sunday school weren't wasted."

Grae rolled her eyes, but couldn't suppress a soft chuckle.

Chapter 4

Thunderous knocking at the door woke Grae from her nap. Dazed, she sat up on the couch and rubbed her eyes. "Just a minute!" She shook her head to clear the cobwebs and glanced at the clock. She'd been asleep less than an hour.

She stumbled to the door and peered through the peephole. It was Ciara. "Aw, Jesus."

Totally not in the mood for her sister's antagonism, Grae wrenched the door open. "What?"

"I want to talk to you." Ciara pushed past her.

"Please, do come in. Make yourself comfortable. I'll summon the servants to bring you tea and crumpets."

"Biscuits go with afternoon tea." Ciara stalked over to the couch, took a seat, and set her purse on the floor.

Grae rolled her eyes. "To what do I owe the pleasure of this unexpected visit?"

Ciara looked around the apartment. "You really do live in a slum."

"God, I so do not need this." Grae refused to sit. "I've got an appointment with Mom's shrink in two hours, and I was hoping to get some rest before I go. So I ask again, what the fuck do you want?"

"Where's your roommate?"

Grae shrugged. "I dunno. It's our day off, so I guess he's out somewhere, doing something."

Ciara studied her. "I assumed you two were joined at the hip."

"Why? Because I like his company better than yours?"

Ciara's eyes flashed and her lips tightened. "Trust you to pick some guttersnipe to be your best friend."

Grae snickered. "Guttersnipe? Who the hell says guttersnipe these days? You've been reading way too many Edwardian romances."

"At least I read."

Grae glanced at the books she'd stacked up to be returned to the library. "And you have no idea what I do with my spare time. Which, by the way, I have very little of, so say whatever you came to say and go."

Ciara took a deep breath and locked her hands together. "I want to know why."

"Why what?"

"Why…everything. Why you left in the first place. Why you're taking advantage of Mom and Dad now." She stared at Grae, anger in every rigid line of her body. "Why the hell you are what you are. You grew up with all of the same advantages as Virgil and me, so why did you turn out to be—"

"The black sheep?" Grae fought to contain the seething within. "Every family has one, right? Better me than you or Virg."

"Every family does not have one. Most of the families I know don't have any—"

"Fuck-ups? Oh, grow up, sister dear. Some families may hide 'em better, but there are people 'like me' everywhere, even in the best of families."

Ciara shook her head. "You could've finished university. Your grades weren't great, but you didn't have to bail. You were only a couple of months away from graduating. Mom and Dad never forced you to do anything you didn't want. For God's sake, they bent over backwards for you." Under her breath she mumbled, "Which was the problem."

Grae studied Ciara for a long moment. "That's not really what you came to ask."

"Yes, it is."

"No, it's really not. You didn't give a shit what I was doing or where I was living until I ended up back in your life last week."

Ciara flushed. "You mean back in Mom's life. Do you have any idea how humiliating it was for her to have her own daughter appear before her bench? She's short listed for an appointment to the Appeals Court, and you pull this crap?"

"Pull what? Defending myself against a couple of 'phobes who were trying to kill me and Marcus? Jesus, do you live in the real world at all? Or are you just completely insulated from reality in your McMansion and executive offices?"

Ciara ignored her. "And what do you mean I didn't care? I gave you our old mattress, didn't I?"

"Then got pissed because me and Marcus carried it home. Real gifts don't come with strings."

Ciara jumped to her feet, the vein in her temple pulsing. "Strings? For Christ's sake, I hired a goddamned private detective to find you, to find out if you were okay. I thought offering you the mattress would… Was it so out of line to assume that you'd let us help you get the mattress home? You had to strut your goddamned independence through my neighbourhood by carrying that oversized mattress home yourself?"

Grae blinked. "That's what this is all about? Because I embarrassed you in front of your neighbours last year?"

"Oh, my God, you are such an asshole! No! That's not it at all. How shallow do you think I am?"

"You really don't want me to answer that," Grae said. She walked to the door and opened it. "I think it's time for you to leave. Past time, in fact."

Ciara shuddered and closed her eyes, struggling to get herself under control. When she had, she picked up her purse and strode past Grae without a word.

Grae shut the door and leaned against it, drained by the encounter. Had she really once idolized her older sister? It seemed like a century ago, before everything, including their relationship, had gone so wrong.

Grae stepped off the bus and checked the address with a frown. This was a residential neighbourhood, and there was nothing in the vicinity that appeared to be any sort of clinic. She glanced at her watch. She only had ten minutes before her appointment, and the last thing she wanted to do was get off on the wrong foot with some prissy, stick-in-the-mud headshrinker.

She left the stop and walked quickly down the street, looking for the turns MapQuest had said to make. When she came to the therapist's street, she stopped and stared down the road. It was a lovely row of older homes, with towering elms lining the sidewalks and forming a canopy of green overhead. *Maybe she has a home office?*

With only a couple of minutes left, Grae hastened to her destination. When she arrived, she passed under a wrought iron arbour and walked the cobblestone path up to the door of a yellow bungalow. She rang the bell and waited, shifting from foot to foot.

The door opened, and Grae blinked, twice.

A silver-haired woman wearing a worn cardigan over faded jeans and a T-shirt stood smiling at her, a fluffy, brindle cat cradled in her arms. "Hello. You must be Grae. Your mother described you perfectly. Please come in."

Grae followed the woman inside.

"Oh, where are my manners?" She shifted the cat into one arm and held out her hand. "Joann Reaves. And this is Maddie, who rules the roost and allows me to consider it my home, too."

Grae shook her hand.

Joann chuckled. "Why do I get the feeling I'm not exactly what you expected?"

"Um, no, not exactly."

"Well, why don't we get comfortable and talk about that." Joann led the way into her living room and motioned to Grae to take one of the leather recliners that faced the fireplace. After she sat, Joann took the other chair, still holding Maddie. A small table sat between them, and on it sat two bottles of water, a box of tissues, and a notebook with a pen.

"Is water all right? I have coffee or tea…a soft drink, perhaps?"

"No, thanks, um—what should I call you? Dr. Reaves?"

"Oh no, I'm a psychologist, not a psychiatrist. Please call me Joann, or just Jo, if you prefer." Jo laughed. "Actually, I'm a retired psychologist at that."

Grae's eyebrows shot up. "Retired?"

"Yes. Your mother didn't tell you?"

Grae shook her head. "No. She just told me your address and that I had a standing weekly appointment until I was notified otherwise."

Jo cocked her head and studied Grae. "I know it's not your choice to be here, but are you prepared to work with me to make the most of our time together?"

"I don't know."

Jo smiled. "Honesty. I like that. I think we're off to a good start."

"We've started?" Grae glanced nervously at the notebook, which Jo hadn't touched.

"Mmm-hm. Today I'd like to spend a little time just getting to know each other, if that's all right with you."

"Didn't Mom already tell you everything about me?" Jo's eyes were kind and her smile warm, but Grae fought the uncomfortable sensation that she was about to be dissected.

"When your mother approached me last week, I wasn't keen about taking on a client. I'm quite enjoying my retirement, but she can be very persuasive when she wants to be."

"Tell me about it."

"Oh, I'd much rather you tell me about it. But in any case, once I agreed, I asked your mother just to give me a brief outline of your current circumstances. I'd much rather hear your perspective on things."

"Huh." Grae stared at Jo, whose calm gaze didn't waver under the close scrutiny. "So what do you want to know?"

"I'd like to know why you're here."

"You know why. My mother—"

Jo's gaze sharpened. "You're thirty, aren't you?"

"Yes."

"And you live on your own? Support yourself?"

Grae snorted. "Not if you ask Ciara."

"Ciara?"

"My sister. She was just ragging my ass a couple hours ago."

"Why?"

"Beats the hell out of me." Grae shook her head. Ciara's visit was baffling. "Maybe she just came to piss me off. She's very good at that."

"Sibling rivalry is not uncommon, even as adults. Have you always been at odds?"

"No, that's the weird thing. We got along great when we were young, even though she was eleven years older than me. I idolized her, and she never treated me like an unwelcome tag-along. I was even the flower girl at her wedding. Mom once told me that when I was born, Ciara took charge of me like I was her kid. She'd change my diapers, feed me my bottle. Mom joked that the au pair they'd hired finally quit because she was bored with having nothing to do."

"Interesting. When did things change between you?"

Grae had to stop and think. "I'm not sure. I guess when I dropped out of university."

"Did it have anything to do with you coming out?"

"No. In fact, I came out to Ciara before my parents and brother."

"Why was that?"

Grae's throat tightened. "Because it was safe…she was safe. I knew she'd be on my side, she'd be there for me." She swallowed hard. "But that was a long time ago. Now she can't stand to breathe the same air I do."

"Are you sure?"

"Hell, yeah. After not seeing her for over two years, I've seen her twice in the last week, and both times she acted like she hated me."

"Interesting."

Grae grabbed a tissue and dabbed her eyes. "What?"

"Your phraseology. She 'acted' like she hated you."

"Yeah, so?" Grae's gaze focused on the slow, ceaseless way Jo stroked Maddie. It was mesmerizing.

"Was she just acting? Or does she really hate you?"

"Well, if it was an act, it was a helluva convincing one."

"Mmm."

Grae examined the memory and frowned. "She's fixated on the damned mattress…and Mom's career."

"The mattress?"

"My best friend lives with me. We alternated sleeping on the couch. The other person had to sleep on some towels and stuff we cobbled together."

"What's your roommate's name?"

Grae smiled. "Marcus. Marcus Alexander Lyndon."

"So, how did a mattress factor into the situation between you and Ciara?"

"I hadn't seen her for a quite a few years, not since I dropped out of university. Then one day, around my birthday, she shows up at my work and wants to take me for coffee."

"And?"

Grae shrugged. "I went for coffee. We talked a while. She asked if there was anything I needed. I was sort of joking, but I said a mattress. She said she and her husband were just getting a new one, and would I like her old one? Said it had lots of use still left in it. So me and Marcus went to pick it up. She's been pissed ever since."

"Why? What happened when you picked it up?"

"Nothing. She wasn't even there. The housekeeper let us in to get it."

"And you really have no idea what irritated your sister?"

Grae squirmed and hung her head. "I sort of know, but it doesn't make sense."

Jo set Maddie on the floor and opened the notebook. She jotted a few notes. "What doesn't make sense?"

"Best I can figure out, she's pissed because Marcus and I carried the mattress home rather than waiting for her or my brother-in-law to drive us."

Jo's eyebrow arched. "You carried it? How far?"

"I dunno. Probably about fifteen kilometres. Took us a while, that's for sure."

"I see. Why didn't you wait for her help?"

Grae scowled, started to speak and stopped.

After a few moments of silence, Jo cocked her head. "Do you know why you didn't wait for her to help?"

"Yes."

Jo smiled. "And?"

Grae stared at her boots and raised a foot. "Sorry. I should've taken these off before I came in."

"Your footwear is fine. It's dry outside. Now, about your sister and the mattress…"

"I was kinda pissed at her."

"Why? Was there something wrong with the mattress?"

"Hell, no. It looked like it had just come out of the showroom."

"Okay. But something about it bothered you."

Grae studied the quirky knickknacks on the shelves above the fireplace, mentally cataloging them as the silence lengthened. When she finally looked at Jo, expecting to meet a frown, she was startled to see a small smile flicker on Jo's lips.

Maddie jumped back into her lap, and Jo set the notebook aside. She stroked the cat as she waited out the lull in conversation. She gave no indication of being disconcerted. It was maddening.

"I...no way could I afford such a fancy mattress."

"And that bothered you?"

"No, not like that. I mean, I'm not jealous of her success or anything."

"All right."

"No, I mean it. I don't give a flying fuck that she and Virg are living high off the hog. They earned it. They did everything right."

"And you didn't?"

Grae scowled. "You could say that."

"But do *you* say that?"

"Jesus, I don't know. Yeah, okay, I say that, too. Hell, I'm sitting in your living room, aren't I? If I hadn't fucked up my life I wouldn't be here, so that's your answer."

"Mmm. Back to the mattress..."

"Why does it matter? She offered, we accepted, and we've slept well on it ever since. No complaints. Beats the old couch and a bunch of folded up towels all to hell."

"And yet you say that the sister you once idolized now hates you because...what? Because you carried her second-hand mattress home to...irritate her?"

"I'm not a charity case. I don't need her old crap."

"Okay. Yet you accepted her offer, then went out of your way to define the limits of your acceptance."

"I did it for Marcus. He deserved better than sleeping on the floor."

"If Marcus hadn't been a factor—if he weren't living with you—would you have accepted your sister's offer?"

"Nope."

"Interesting. Why is that?"

"I told you. I'm no goddamned charity case."

Jo's gaze never left Grae. "Let's set aside Ciara's reaction—"

"You mean her being a bitch of the highest order?"

Jo smiled. "As I was saying, let's set aside Ciara's anger for the moment and focus on yours."

"I'm not angry."

Jo glanced at the notebook lying open on the table. "You're not? I believe you said you were kind of pissed at her."

"She hired a private dick to find me."

"Really? Why was that necessary? Did your family not know where you were living?"

"No."

"So you weren't listed in the phonebook? They couldn't have Googled your location?"

Grae gave a short laugh. "They'd have had to know my name."

"Your name?"

"First thing I did when I dropped out was to legally change my name. Mom didn't tell you?"

"No, she didn't."

"Interesting."

Jo laughed. Grae's mimicry was dead-on. "So why did you change your name? If you wanted to hide from them, you could've left the city."

"In the age of the Internet? They'd have found me wherever I moved…if they bothered to check."

"If you think they wouldn't have bothered anyway, why go to the extreme of changing your name?"

Grae was silent again.

Jo waited her out.

"I guess…I mean, Ciara's detective found me, so I suppose she did bother to look for me. And once Mom knew my name, she had no trouble finding my apartment. Course it was on the court docs."

"Do you think Ciara told your mother your new name after her detective found you?"

Grae blinked. She hadn't considered that. "She must not have. Or maybe she did, and Mom just didn't come looking for me until I showed up in front of her bench."

"Which do you think is more likely?"

Grae absent-mindedly scratched her arm as she pondered the question. "When Mom came to the apartment after I made an appearance in her court, she said she might've been there sooner if she'd known how to contact me."

"So Ciara didn't tell her then."

Grae shook her head. "I guess not. I wonder why. I'd have thought she'd be first in line to tell my folks I was living in a slum."

"Are you? Living in a slum?"

"That's what Ciara called it today, though I'm sure the rats and cockroaches consider it fine living. Anyway, it doesn't matter. Me and Marcus are moving on up next week."

"To a dee-luxe apartment in the sky?"

Grae laughed. "Not exactly, but a pretty decent one on the fourth floor, thanks to Mom. I can't believe you caught that reference."

"I can't believe you used it. That's my generation, not yours."

"Me and Marcus like the oldies."

"Apparently. But to get back to the topic at hand, why do you think Ciara didn't tell your mother about your name change?"

Grae snorted. "Probably protecting her."

"Or protecting you?"

"No, I..." Grae stopped. Was it possible? Ciara protecting her?

"That troubles you. Why?"

"What are you—a mind reader?"

Jo chuckled. "No, just a retired psychologist and the mother of two men who were once very close-mouthed boys. Reading body language helped me get through their teens without killing them, or myself. Thank God my daughter wasn't as reticent as my sons. But back to the question: Why does it bother you that Ciara may have been protecting you and not your mother?"

Grae shrugged. "I don't know."

Jo glanced at the mantle clock. "We've come to the end of your time for today. Why don't we pick this up next week?" She set Maddie on the floor and rose to her feet.

Grae stood and followed her to the front door. "Same time next week?"

Jo nodded. "I'll see you then."

Chapter 5

GRAE WAS AWAKENED BY A delicious scent in the air. She inhaled deeply, and her eyes widened.

Marcus pushed open the bedroom door. "Supper's ready. You've got time to eat before you have to leave, so c'mon."

Grae rolled off their mattress and jumped to her feet. "Are we having steak and onions?"

Marcus grinned. "For someone who can't smell the difference between lotus blossoms and tarpaper, you're bang on. It is indeed steak… and fried potatoes, and even a salad to go with."

"How the hell can we afford steak?"

"It's our last day in this dump, so I decided to splurge since we won't have rent payments for the next year. Don't worry. I didn't go for anything really expensive. The steaks were nearing their 'best buy' date, so I got them on sale. Fried up with onions, though, you'll think you're dining at Le Cirque."

Grae followed Marcus to the kitchen. "What do you know about Le Cirque?"

"I read. I dream." Marcus dished their dinners from the single frying pan. The salads were already on the counter. He handed Grae a plate.

She took it, glanced at his, and swapped plates. "You're the growing boy. You take the bigger one." She waved off his protests, grabbed a salad, and went to the couch. "Damn, this smells good."

Marcus sat beside her. "Well, it's not exactly tartare and caviar, but it beats beans from a can."

They tore into their food. It was so good that Grae had to stop herself from asking after seconds. There wouldn't be any, and she didn't want any hint of dissatisfaction to mar the meal. She leaned back and rubbed her belly. "You are one helluva cook, buddy."

"Wait and see what I can do in our new kitchen. I'll be turning out dishes fit for a queen."

"Great, so you get to eat. What am I supposed to live on?"

Marcus grinned. "Love? Speaking of which, did you ever call Lucy?"

"What's the point? She made it very clear that she wants nothing more to do with me."

"Okay, so if not Lucy, maybe ask someone else out, maybe someone new."

Grae studied Marcus. "Why the sudden interest in my non-existent love life?"

"Because I care. You need someone in your life."

"I've got someone—you."

Marcus rolled his eyes. "And I love you to death, but I'm talking about someone who can appreciate all of you, including your lady parts, because I'm not going anywhere near those."

Grae laughed. "And I'm not going near your dangly bits, so we're even." She sat up and took Marcus' empty plate. "Maybe once we're in a place where I wouldn't be ashamed to bring a date home, but we've got a lot to do in the next few days so let's shelve the topic for now, okay? Besides, you're one to talk. You haven't exactly been burning up the dating circuit yourself."

A shadow crossed Marcus' face, and Grae could've kicked herself. "Aw hell, I'm sorry. Forget I said anything, okay?"

His eyes glistened, and Grae set the plates aside. She knelt and wrapped her arms around him. "I've got a big mouth, buddy. Just ignore me. You're doing fine, really."

"Am I?" Marcus rested his head on her shoulder. "I met a really cute guy at the library last week. We were both using the computers, and we hit it off right away. But when he asked me out for coffee, I froze. I couldn't get away fast enough."

Grae stroked his back. "Shhh, you'll date again when you're ready. You went through years of hell. It's natural for it to take some time to get over it. Don't force yourself, okay? You'll know when it's right. I just know there's someone special out there for you."

Marcus hugged her, then pushed away and brushed at his eyes. "Hey, you'd better go shower. You've got to be at the shrink's in half an hour."

Grae nodded and went to get ready. By the time she left their apartment, Marcus was his normal upbeat self, but she couldn't help wishing it were him on the way to see Jo. He'd benefit far more from therapy than she ever would.

※

Grae accepted the glass of iced lemonade. She sipped the tart liquid as Jo settled into her seat.

"So, last week we were talking about your feelings toward your sister—"

"I don't want to talk about Ciara."

"All right. We'll set that aside for now." Jo studied Grae. "You've got something on your mind. What is it?"

"Marcus."

"Your roommate?"

"And best friend." Grae rolled the damp glass in her hands. The idea had come to her on the bus ride over. Her mother wouldn't allow Marcus to take her therapy sessions, but there might be a way to get him some professional help. "I'm worried about him."

"Why is that?"

Grae bit her lip. "What I tell you—it's confidential, right?"

"It is."

"Even if I'm talking about someone besides myself, you still can't tell anyone what I say?"

"Unless you tell me something that indicates that someone is a danger to himself or others, then no. What you tell me stays strictly between us."

"Marcus would never hurt anyone else."

"Would he hurt himself?"

Grae opened her mouth, then closed it. Would he? She'd been worried about that in the early months of their friendship, but he was a lot stronger now. "I don't think so."

"Yet you're worried about him. Why?"

"Marcus..." Maybe this was a bad idea. She'd have to reveal things that he'd never want anyone to know. She glanced at Jo, wrestling with whether to trust her.

Jo met her gaze and waited calmly.

Grae took a deep breath. "Marcus went through some really bad years. His parents tried to beat the gay out of him from the time he was a little boy and they caught him wearing his mother's high heels and lipstick. They threw him out of the house when he was barely fourteen."

"I'm so sorry to hear that."

"He survived because he...because he..." She took a deep breath, then said in a rush, "He had to prostitute himself."

Jo didn't flinch. "Sadly, that's far too common with abandoned LGBT youth. My daughter began her Social Services career working with a placement agency trying to find homes for such children. I'm very familiar with such sad situations."

"The thing is, he had to do some seriously fucked-up shit." Grae's eyes filled with tears. "Today he was teasing me about dating and, without thinking, I turned it back on him. I told him he hadn't exactly been bringing any boys around either. Damn it, how insensitive can I be? To him, dating means sex for money. It's no wonder he can't bring himself to go out even when he meets a cute guy."

Jo extended the box of tissues.

Grae took a couple and wiped her eyes. "I try to protect him. We were invited to a co-worker's house for dinner and he was scared, so I made excuses for us not to go. But I want to know how to really help him."

"Help him to date again?"

"Help him get past the pain. He's only eighteen years old. He's got his whole life ahead of him. I want him to meet the right man and make a life together that will let him forget how nasty his family was, let him forget that year on the street, scrounging in garbage cans for food and selling himself for a place to sleep at night."

"How did the two of you meet?"

Grae snorted. "Sheer accident. I got kicked out of a bar one night. He was hustling in the alley behind it. I was drunk, and when I saw this fat old dude going at this skinny kid, it just...well, it pissed me off. I started throwing stones at the john, and he took off. Marcus was so mad at me. It was one of his regulars, and he hadn't been paid yet. I felt kind of bad about that, so I took him to an all-night diner and bought him a burger. The way he wolfed it down, I figured he must not have eaten in days, so I bought him another one. It vanished just as fast. We ended up smoking a joint together in the park. I have no idea why, but I offered him a place to sleep. One night became two, then three, and before you know it, I had a roommate."

"Is he still hustling?"

"No way. That was my only condition. I'd feed and house him, but only if he stopped that shit. He was happy to comply. And once he had a fixed address, he was able to get a job. Not much of one, but between the two of us, we've done all right. And tomorrow we move into our new place."

"Are you excited about the move?"

"Are you kidding? Damn right I am. Ever since I picked up the keys, I've been enjoying the thought of Marcus in our new apartment. He's going to think he died and went to heaven."

Jo smiled. "And you? How do you feel about it?"

"It's kind of complicated. I mean I'm thrilled that we'll have a nice place to come home to after work. The crap-shack we've been living in is only a short step up from being on the street. I even told Marcus that maybe once we had a place we weren't ashamed of, I'd feel better about dating again. But…"

"But?"

"But…does this put me under my family's thumb? And if so, is it worth it?"

"What do you think?"

Grae was silent for a long moment. Since her family had re-entered her life, she'd spent a lot of time thinking about those two questions and she hadn't come to any decisions. Finally she shrugged. "I guess only time will tell. For now it has to be enough that I'm providing Marcus with a decent home, even if it's only for a year. The way I see it, since I've got a year rent free, I can save up enough money to better our situation once the year is over."

"Do you think that you'll lose your new place once the year is up?"

"I think it's a strong possibility. We can't afford to take over the rent, and I certainly don't expect my parents to continue to support us. Hell, Ciara would have a stroke if they did."

"It seems to me that a lot of what you've decided, a lot of what you've done recently, revolves around Marcus. I'd like to explore that a little further."

"Sure. What do you want to know?"

"You and Marcus are both gay, correct?"

"Uh-huh."

"So there's no underlying romantic involvement in your relationship?"

Grae shook her head. "God, no. Marcus is my buddy, my little brother."

"That was my understanding. You look out for him, worry about him, provide for him."

"Of course, like a brother."

"Or a son."

Grae's eyes widened. "Son? He's only twelve years younger than me. I think that's pushing it a little, don't you?"

Jo consulted her notes. "Didn't you tell me last week that Ciara was like a second mother to you as a child? And she's only eleven years older than you."

Grae scowled. "It's not the same thing at all. Ciara was just playing dolls with a live baby. That's not me and my bro."

"Interesting."

"I'm going to start hating that word, you know."

Jo chuckled. "Then I shall be careful how often I use it. I was actually referring to your turn of phrase."

"My what?"

"I don't know if you're aware of it, but you frequently transition from proper grammar to street dialect."

"I do?"

"Mm-hmm. For example, referring to Marcus as your 'bro.' I find it fascinating."

Grae shook her head. "I'm not sure what that has to do with anything."

"It tells me that you're an educated woman who chooses to sound street-wise. And I wonder if that's related to you distancing yourself from your birth family while choosing to create a new family with Marcus."

"Huh."

"My apologies. I sometimes get off on a tangent."

Grae doubted her keen-eyed therapist ever digressed without purpose.

Jo nodded at Grae's nearly empty glass. "May I refill that for you?"

"I'm good, thanks."

"All right. Let's get back to your contention that the relationship between you and Marcus is nothing like the one between you and Ciara."

"It's not. Ciara and I don't give a damn about each other anymore. Marcus and me...and I...would die for each other."

"Yet at one time, you and Ciara were very close."

"True." Grae shot Jo a troubled glance. "Do you mean that you think Marcus and I will drift apart some day, too?"

"What do you think?"

Grae dropped her gaze to the floor. Would they? Her relationship with Marcus had sustained her since the day they'd met. Looking after him, looking out for him, fulfilled a need in her so deep she couldn't imagine life without him.

"No, absolutely not." She met Jo's gaze squarely. "I may not fully understand how or why Ciara and I got to this point in our relationship, but I would stake my life that it will never get like that between Marcus and me."

"Is that because he needs you?"

Grae considered that. "Maybe a little. Ciara certainly doesn't need me, and I was instrumental in getting Marcus away from a life that was killing him in slow increments. But that's not all there is to it. I don't have a saviour complex or anything."

Jo smiled.

Grae tilted her head. "What?"

"Listen to you—slow increments, saviour complex. Whatever would that do to your street cred?"

Amused by Jo's teasing tone, Grae relaxed. "I shall have to try to remember to leave my more complex thoughts and good grammar at your doorstep when I leave. Seriously though, my relationship with Ciara, even before it broke down, wasn't anything like the one I have with Marcus."

"What about your brother? Is it similar to your relationship with Virgil?"

"Not really. Virg and I get along well, we always have, but he's fifteen years older than me so we're not really tight. Marcus... He makes me want to be more than I am."

"What do you mean?"

"With Marcus..." Grae set her glass aside and focused intently on Jo. "For Marcus I want to be a better person. I want to stop being bad."

Jo blinked. "You think you're bad?"

"I have been. I know you told Mom not to tell you a lot about my situation after you agreed to take me on, but she must've revealed some of the shit I was involved in."

"She gave me some information, yes. None of it sounded that serious."

Grae shot her a wry grin. "You probably wouldn't say that if it was your business I'd vandalized, but in some sense, you're right. None of the charges I've accumulated have been that serious—obstruction, disorderly conduct, pot possession, trespassing, public drunkenness. But taken all together, I can see why some people might consider me a public menace. God knows sometimes I can't seem to do anything right, no matter how hard I try. Hell, all I did was attempt to save Marcus and me from a beating, and I end up charged with assault. How is that remotely fair? And more importantly, how do I stop it from happening again?"

Jo regarded her thoughtfully. "Back up just a bit. You said you can understand why some people consider you a public menace. Is that the way you see yourself?"

"It's hard not to." Grae sighed and stared at the floor. "But I want so much more. This isn't the life I envision for myself or—"

"For Marcus."

Grae met Jo's gaze. "No, definitely not for him. He's had a raw deal, but the only way I can help him is if I clean up my act for good. I'm tired of being anti-social, tired of being the continual fuck-up. Despite the potential drawbacks of accepting help from my family, I know this is a second chance and I don't want to screw it up, not this time. It's too important. It scares the hell out of me when I consider what might happen to Marcus if I'm convicted of assault and sent away. I don't think he can survive on his own, and that gives me nightmares."

"Have you formed a plan to make the changes you feel are necessary?"

"Sort of. Moving into the new place tomorrow is step one. Dealing with the charges against me has to be step two."

"How do you plan to do that?"

Grae shrugged. "I'm not exactly sure. But Virg said he'd come give us a hand moving our stuff tomorrow. He said he wants to talk to me, too, so I assume it's about my case. Maybe I'll have a better idea of how to deal once I have my lawyer's advice."

"When is your next hearing?"

"Three months. Virg told me not to worry about it, but…"

Jo's gaze was compassionate. "But of course you do."

Grae shivered, an image of Marcus as she'd first seen him flashing in her mind. "Yes. How could I not?"

Chapter 6

"Is yours the last one?" Grae lifted a cardboard box off the tailgate.

Virgil hoisted a second box and peered under the cover into the truck bed. "Looks like it. I can't believe we got you moved in just two trips. I thought it would take us most of the day."

"We could've done it in one if Marcus hadn't insisted we take absolutely everything other than the couch and mattress. I reminded him the new place was fully furnished, but…"

Virgil shot her a glance as they walked to the entrance of her new apartment building. "But what?"

Grae held the door open for him to precede her. "He thinks it's a good idea to keep things of our own for when we move again. He'd have brought the mattress and couch if we'd had any place to put them."

Virgil pressed the button to summon the elevator. "Did you leave them for the next tenant?"

"No, we gave them to Mrs. Baczkowski, next door. She's a single mom with three kids, and they have even less than we do. She'll make good use of our old stuff."

"That was kind."

Grae shrugged. "She was a good neighbour who's in a tough spot. It's the least we could do."

The elevator doors opened, and they went inside.

"A lot of people might say the same thing about you. That you were in a tough spot."

"They'd be wrong." Grae fought the tickle of irritation down. Virgil wasn't trying to anger her. "Mrs. Baczkowski was married to an abusive alcoholic who dumped her with three little kids in a city she didn't know and then vanished. *That's* a tough spot. I was born with a silver spoon in my mouth, so the situations aren't synonymous at all."

"But you both ended up in the same place."

The elevator stopped and they exited.

"Look around, Virg. I got to leave that dump behind. Mrs. Baczkowski can't. The best she can hope for is that maybe someday she'll win a lottery. I won life's lottery before I was even born."

Virgil stopped and stared at her. "But—"

"No buts, big brother. I put myself in that crap-shack. And if it had been left up to me, Marcus and I would still be living there. I'm not thrilled about how this all came about, but maybe it was the luckiest day in my life when those assholes tried to throw me off the top of a building." Grae glanced at Virgil and laughed. "You're going to catch flies if you don't close your mouth."

"I just can't believe what I'm hearing. It's so…mature, so philosophical, so—"

"Unlike me?" Grae pushed open the door to her new apartment and rolled her eyes at the sound of loud, off-key warbling. "Yo, Marcus. Give us a hand, will you?"

Her roommate jogged down the hall from the master bedroom and took the box from her hands.

"That's the last of your stuff. Virg, can you throw that one in my room?"

Virgil nodded and turned left.

"The truck is empty, bud. We're officially moved." Grae dug in her pocket and brought out a ring with three keys. "Here you go—the keys to your new kingdom."

"Queendom." Marcus set the box down and took the keys. "What's the little one for?"

"Apparently we have a storage locker in the basement. Once we get everything sorted and stored away, we may want to move some things down there."

"Good idea. I looked through the kitchen while you guys were gone. You were right. I guess we really didn't need to bring our old stuff. I'm sorry about that."

Grae shrugged. "Doesn't matter. You had a point about us needing it in the future. At first I wasn't thrilled about you being so stubborn, but since we have a storage locker, it's all good. Don't worry about it, okay?"

"Okay."

Virgil returned, his arms empty. "Do you have some time to talk? I'd like to discuss your case."

Marcus picked the box back up. "I'll go put this stuff away."

"Thanks." Grae gestured to the living room. "Let's go in there."

She took the couch and Virgil took the chair opposite her. She studied him and smiled.

"What?"

"You just put your lawyer face on. I have to say it doesn't really go with the ripped jeans and T-shirt."

Virgil laughed. "Well, I didn't think my best suit and tie were appropriate for helping my baby sister move." He sobered. "But we do need to talk about strategy. You caught a break being assigned to Judge Eisler's court. He's fair, and he's a moderate. He doesn't feel like he has to make an example of everyone who appears before his bench. He actually assesses the accused as a human being, as well as adjudicating on the merits of the case. He'll come down on the side of mercy if he thinks you're salvageable. You'd have been in a lot more trouble with some of the judicial fire-breathers."

"I guess I should be glad Mom didn't throw me to the wolves."

"She would never do that."

"I know that. But she also wouldn't compromise her legal ethics."

"No, she wouldn't, but there is some wiggle room, and I think we're in pretty decent shape with your case. I do have a suggestion, though, and I'm not sure you're going to like it."

"Tell me."

"Judge Eisler likes to see some effort on the part of the accused."

"Effort?"

Virgil nodded. "For instance, I had a client last year who trashed a community centre when he was high. By the time he came before the judge, he'd entered a rehab program and made restitution."

"What kind of restitution?"

"He went back to the centre, apologized for what he'd done, and paid for repairs. He also started volunteering there on weekends. The judge was so pleased with the pre-sentencing report that he gave my client an absolute discharge."

Grae glared at Virgil. "If you think I'm going to apologize to Rick and Dylan, you can forget it. They attacked me!"

Virgil held up his hand. "Calm down. That's not what I had in mind at all. In fact, I'm seriously considering filing a civil lawsuit against them on your behalf. With the evidence that I've gathered, I can put forward a strong case that not only were you the victim in all this, but they're the ones who should be on trial for assault. Their actions caused you pain and suffering, as well as substantial loss of wages."

"Now you're talking. God, I can't begin to tell you how good it is to have someone listen to my side and believe me."

"I do believe you. So does Mom."

"Good, but then what's with all your talk about apologies and restitution?"

"I want to hedge our bet. It's a two-fold strategy. One, we focus on your innocence by registering a not-guilty plea. Two, in the event you're found guilty, we show that despite your past misdemeanours, you're striving to be an upright citizen. You're working full-time, in weekly therapy, keeping your nose clean." Virgil eyed her intently. "You are keeping your nose clean, aren't you? I mean it, Grae. No drug use, no drunken brawls, not even smoking a little weed. Got it? You simply cannot afford any slip-ups before this litigation is resolved."

Grae fought the urge to scowl at him. He wasn't telling her anything she didn't know. "I get it. So what do you have in mind?"

"I want to show the judge that you're not only accepting responsibility for your actions, you're also committed to becoming an integral part of your community. That will go a long way toward mitigating your earlier offences, which the judge will take into consideration. We need to show him you've turned over a new leaf."

"That makes sense. But how?"

"Community service. You need to pick some worthy organization and volunteer your time."

Grae closed her eyes. "I so don't need this."

"You do need this. That's the point."

She opened her eyes and regarded him wearily. "I just barely got rid of my second job flipping burgers, and you want me to take on another one—an unpaid one, at that. That sucks. I was looking forward to maybe having a bit of a social life again. Nothing dramatic, maybe just the odd date now and then."

"I'm not saying you need to commit twenty or thirty hours a week. Go volunteer at the food bank for a few hours on a Saturday."

"Well, at least I know where that is."

Virgil frowned. "Why? Are you one of their clients?"

"Now and then. Mostly in between jobs when our cupboards were bare."

"I didn't know. I'm sorry."

Grae shrugged. "No biggie. It's not like I'm your responsibility."

Virgil shook his head. "You're family. You went hungry. That's just wrong."

"Don't worry about it. You had no way of knowing, and that's on me, not you." She leaned forward and patted Virgil's knee. "Just get me out of this legal mess, and you'll be doing me a huge favour. I won't forget it, believe me."

"So you'll think about it? Pick out some charity and start volunteering?"

"I will."

Virgil smiled as he rose to his feet. "Excellent. We'll need a statement of attendance and participation from whichever one you choose, so be upfront with the volunteer coordinator."

Grae walked Virgil out. "Okay. I'll let you know what happens."

The siblings stopped in the foyer. The sound of Marcus' singing was echoing down the hall again. They winced in unison and laughed.

"Tell Marcus not to quit his day job," Virgil said.

"I will. Are you off to pick up Caden?"

Virgil shook his head. "No, he's got a birthday party this afternoon. I'll pick him up once he's done, then I have him through until Monday morning."

"Are things going any better with Nadine?"

"Not really. The way she holds a grudge, you'd think I'd been the one who cheated and broke up our marriage."

"I'm sorry I wasn't around when it all fell apart."

Virgil sighed. "There was nothing anyone could've done, but I appreciate the thought. Just don't stop being around now, okay?"

Grae unlocked the bolt and opened the door. "I won't. Thanks again for the help moving. You and your truck were a godsend."

"My pleasure."

Virgil gave her a quick hug and to her own amazement, Grae reflexively hugged him back.

"I'll call you for an update next weekend, okay?" Virgil waved and walked down the hallway.

She stared after him. *Huh.*

***

"You're antsy this week," Jo said. "What's up?"

Grae shook her head. "I've been in your house for two minutes, and all we've done is exchange pleasantries. What makes you think I'm antsy?"

Jo smiled. "Am I wrong?"

"No. But what gave it away?"

"My super power is agitation detection."

Grae laughed. It was only their third session together, but it was startling how accurately Jo read her. "Not what I'd choose for my super power, but hey, if it floats your boat."

"It's come in handy over the years. So what super power would you choose?"

"I can't say I've thought about it much. Invisibility would be handy. I wouldn't be in this mess if I could've vanished when Rick and Dylan came after me."

"Then they'd have gone after Marcus."

Grae frowned. Even the thought of it sent shivers through her. "True. Maybe super strength, so I could've pummelled them into oblivion."

"Then you'd still be in trouble with the law."

"You are not making this easy."

Jo stroked Maddie with maddening calmness, and said nothing.

"Okay, okay. So not invisibility and not super strength." *X-ray vision would be pretty cool at times.*

Jo laughed. "I don't know what you're thinking about, but you certainly have an interesting expression at the moment."

Grae blushed. "Are you sure reading minds isn't your super power?"

"Not a super power. Just a professional skill developed over a long career."

"Flying."

Jo raised an eyebrow. "Flying?"

"Exactly. That would be my super power of choice—flying."

"Why's that?"

"If I could fly, I'd have picked Marcus up, and we'd have escaped from Rick and Dylan with no consequences and no assault charges. Besides, don't you think it would be fabulous to fly?" Grae flung her arms wide, startling Maddie, who jumped from Jo's lap. "Oops, sorry. I didn't mean to scare her."

"She's fine. What attracts you about flying?"

"Freedom. Just think about it. When people get in your face or when your boss is on your back, you could just levitate away from them and go so high that you couldn't hear anything but the birds flying next to you. You could visit the mountains without getting stuck in traffic, or buzz low over the prairies and scare the gophers. You wouldn't be restricted by road accessibility anywhere. You could be all alone in places humans have never been before."

"Interest—" Jo stopped and smiled. "I mean, intriguing."

Grae laughed. "It's okay. I've become accustomed to it. But what's so interesting about wanting to fly? Wouldn't anyone want to launch themselves into the air and go wherever they pleased?"

"Perhaps. What's pertinent is that you define freedom in terms of getting away from people, from aggravations, from life in general."

"You think I've been running away? Finding an earthbound means of flight?"

"What do you think?"

Grae chewed her lip as she considered the possibility. "Maybe. I guess my family would say I ran away from them."

"Did you?"

"Technically, yeah. But I wasn't a kid at the time, so I'm not sure it could really be considered running away."

"What did you consider it?"

"Escape from…routine. Taking control of my life. Creating my own destiny. Not that I did a very good job of it."

"Which brings us back to your concept of freedom—escape, control, the ability to leave when something or someone bothers you. Would you agree that it's been a pattern in your life?"

Grae studied Jo. "Is that so bad? When a situation drives you crazy, don't you just want to get away?"

"What about staying and dealing with the situation?"

"Like a grown-up, you mean? Yeah, I haven't done that very goddamned well, have I?" Grae looked away, the familiar anger simmering. She tucked her hands under her thighs and took a deep breath.

"Why don't we leave that alone for now? Let's get back to what had you on edge when you arrived."

Grae forced the anger down and thought back. "Oh, that. It's just I'm supposed to have something done for Virgil by the weekend, and I haven't come up with anything."

"What kind of something?"

Grae explained Virgil's strategy. "I don't disagree with him, but I'm not enthusiastic about the idea, either."

"Have you chosen a charity?"

"No. I don't have a clue where to even begin. Maybe the food bank is the best idea. Most of the charitable fundraisers were during the summer, so that's out. If it were spring, I'd volunteer for river clean-up, but I have to have something to show the judge in December. I guess I could see if I could help out at a shelter or something."

Jo was silent for long moments.

Grae regarded her curiously. "Jo?"

"It's possible…"

"What? What's possible?"

Jo stood up, her gaze steady on Grae. "Will you excuse me for a few minutes?"

"Um, sure."

"Thank you. I'll be back in a bit." She left the room.

Huh. Grae stared after her. *Wonder what that was all about.*

Jo was gone for ten minutes. Grae heard the murmur of her voice, apparently on a phone call. She amused herself playing with Maddie, and by the time Jo returned, the cat was curled up on her lap.

Jo took her seat. "I apologize for that. I had an idea, but wanted to check it out before I offered a suggestion."

"A suggestion?"

"Yes, a possible solution to your charitable dilemma. Have you ever heard of Angels Unawares?"

"I don't think so." Grae frowned. "Is it a religious organization, because I don't do religion."

Jo shook her head. "The title does actually come from the Bible. 'Do not neglect to show hospitality to strangers, for thereby some have entertained angels unawares.' But AU is a secular organization. My daughter happens to run the local chapter. I just talked to her to see if there would be a volunteer opening for you. She said yes."

"What exactly is involved?"

"AU works with hospices, shelters, and nursing homes to provide companionship for those in need. Specifically, those who, for one reason or another, are approaching the end of their lives without loved ones to care for them."

"What? You mean like people who've been abandoned by their families?"

"Sometimes. Sometimes just people who have outlived friends and family, and have no one left. It's similar to an American program called No One Dies Alone that started in Oregon in 2001."

"So what do the volunteers do, run errands or something?"

"If asked. But mostly they provide companionship for someone expected to pass within two or three days. They spend a couple of hours at a time with the patient, talking, listening—"

"Praying? Cuz I don't do that."

Jo smiled. "Could you sit and listen to someone else pray, hold their hand, and add an 'Amen' when they're done?"

"I suppose." Grae studied Jo. "I have to be the least likely candidate for something like this, though."

"I disagree. I see great compassion in the way you've cared for Marcus."

"We take care of each other."

"I understand that, but had you not initially reached out to him in that alley, he'd never have been in a position to offer compassion and companionship back to you. You took that first step. You did that, Grae. And I think you have a tremendous gift to offer others, as well."

Grae held up her hands. "Whoa. I'm not about to become some professional do-gooder. I'm just looking to make a few brownie points with the judge."

"I understand that, too. In all honesty, this may not turn out to be your cup of tea. Not everyone can handle it. Kendall's had a number of well-intentioned volunteers up and quit after just one assignment. If you find you're unable to deal with it, that's fine. There's no harm done."

"You sure your daughter's okay with this? I doubt that I'm the usual sort of volunteer."

Jo shrugged. "Do you really think that someone would object to your hairstyle or tattoos or piercings if they're all alone and dying, and you're offering them a few hours of companionship?"

"Maybe not." *Or maybe.* "All right. Give me the contact information, and I'll go check it out."

Jo handed over a slip of paper.

Grae raised an eyebrow. "That sure of me, were you?"

Jo smiled. "Sometimes I have flashes of insight, and sometimes it's only an educated guess. This just feels like it will be a good fit."

"If you say so. Look, if it doesn't work out, are we okay?"

"Okay?"

"Yes. I mean if I'm not suitable for this and your daughter gives me the old heave-ho, does that mean Mom has to find me a new therapist?"

"What do you think?"

Jo's tone was neutral, but Grae hung her head. "Sorry. Stupid question."

"No, not stupid at all, but to be clear, your relationship with my daughter and her organization, and your therapeutic relationship with me are two entirely separate things. Whether this works out with you and AU doesn't affect what goes on in this room, okay?"

"Okay." Grae glanced up at Jo, overwhelmed with relief. If the daughter was anything like the mother, this might not be the worst idea ever.

Chapter 7

GRAE TURNED IN A SLOW circle as Marcus raised one eyebrow. "What do you think, bud? Do you think I'll pass?"

"As what? A corporate wannabe?"

"Is it that bad?" Grae looked down at her crisp white long-sleeved shirt, charcoal slacks, and black oxfords. It was her standard "job interview and court appearance" attire. She'd removed most of her studs and rings, and covered the tattoos. She'd left her hair untouched, though. Hopefully Jo's daughter took after her mother and wasn't an ultra-conservative nag.

Marcus sighed. "It's fine. It's just not you."

"That's sort of the point. I'm trying to project an image here. I'm a serious-minded, responsible member of society, eager to give back by volunteering."

He tugged on a purple strand of her hair. "I've got a Ciara-clone hat to cover this up, if you want it."

She shook her head. "No. You know me and hats. They make me look dumb."

Marcus started to chuckle, and Grae joined him, releasing the stress through shared laughter. "Okay, enough already. I'm supposed to be at AU in forty-five minutes, so I'd better get going." Grae grabbed her wallet off the table and stuffed it into her pocket.

"I've got a purse you can borrow, too."

She glared at her smirking roommate. "Don't make me hurt you."

Marcus grinned and danced out of reach. "Good luck. I look forward to hearing all about it over lunch."

"Make something good, will you? I think I might need it."

Grae stood across from the old office tower on the outskirts of downtown that housed Angels Unawares. She'd been standing there for ten minutes, since she'd gotten off the bus. "Okay, this is ridiculous. If she's anything like Jo, it'll be fine."

A man glanced at her and then averted his eyes as he hurried by.

"Great. Now the whole world is going to think you're crazy."

She glanced at the piece of paper Jo had given her and tried to draw strength from the elegant script, but it only reminded her of her fear. Jo had said nothing would change between them, even if it didn't work out at AU, but Grae couldn't help worrying. *God, if I fuck this up too...*

"It's just therapy. I didn't even want to go. So what if Jo tosses me out on my ass because her daughter doesn't like me."

The light again signalled WALK, and this time Grae forced herself to move. Long before she was ready, she stood in front of the elevators and pressed the UP button.

She was the only occupant as the car groaned and squealed its way to the ninth floor.

Grae exited, glad to escape intact, and looked around. The hall carpet was worn and thin, and the walls were long overdue for a coat of paint. The door to number 905 stood open, and she took a deep breath as she entered the office.

Inside, a tall, thin woman leaned over the shoulder of a second, older woman seated at a desk. File folders were open in front of them.

"I don't know, Margie. I haven't had any luck getting one of our volunteers to agree to—" The standing woman stopped as Grae stepped forward. "Yes? May I help you?"

"I'm looking for Kendall Reaves."

"I'm Kendall Reaves."

Grae surreptitiously wiped her palm on her trousers and stepped forward with hand outstretched. "I'm Grae Jordan. Your mother talked to you about me volunteering."

Annoyance flashed across Kendall's angular face and vanished so swiftly that Grae wasn't sure she'd seen it.

"Of course. Won't you come in? Margie, I'm expecting a call from Peter DaSilva. Would you put him through immediately, please?"

"Will do."

"Please come with me, Ms. Jordan." Kendall picked up a file and led the way into her tiny office, where she gestured Grae to a chair. Before Kendall could take her own seat, her phone rang. "Sorry, I have to take this."

Grae nodded and took the opportunity to study Jo's daughter. There was a clear family resemblance in the pale blue eyes and straight freckled nose, though Kendall was taller than her mother. She even had some of Jo's silver strands scattered through her short, curly, light brown hair. But where Jo radiated compassion and kindness, Kendall projected cool reserve. Grae tried to pay attention to the one-sided conversation rather than the stern gaze focused on her.

"Peter, we've been over this a dozen times. None of my volunteers want anything to do with Herzog. Hell, your own people wouldn't accept him. I don't know what you want me to do. We're a volunteer organization. I can't insist someone come." Kendall listened for a few moments and shook her head. "You're a good man, I'll give you that." Her gaze intensified, and Grae couldn't stop herself from fidgeting. "Look, I may have a solution. Let me call you back in a few minutes, okay? All right. Talk to you in a bit. Bye."

Kendall hung up the phone, crossed her arms on her desk, and regarded Grae silently.

Grae fought to hold still, and fought even harder not to resent the intimidating stare. *I'm a fucking volunteer, for crying out loud. What the hell's her problem? It's not like I'm asking for a two-bit job.*

"So you want to volunteer with Angels Unawares, do you?"

Grae started at the sound of Kendall's voice. "Um, yes."

Kendall leaned back in her chair. "Why?"

Grae hesitated. She'd prepared a canned answer for that question, but discarded it. "I need to do some community service."

"Why?"

"Didn't your mother tell you?"

"I want to hear your explanation." Kendall's voice was flat.

Grae bristled. Who the hell did this woman think she was? She didn't have to sit still for an interrogation from some piss-ant do-gooder. "I'm up on assault charges. My lawyer thinks it'll make a better impression if I show I'm not some anti-social hoodlum. Jo thought I'd be a good fit here. Guess she was wrong." Grae stood and started toward the door.

"Oh, for God's sake, sit down."

Grae turned and glared at Kendall. "Excuse me?"

Kendall swiped a hand over her face. "Please…sit down."

Grae hesitated. She was torn between stomping out in righteous indignation, and giving Jo's daughter a second chance.

"Please?" Kendall gestured toward the chair. "I apologize. I'm having a bad day."

Grae sat down on the edge of the chair.

"Look, I really am sorry. I take what we do very seriously, and I wasn't happy that Mom palmed…ahh…sent you my way. This is tough work, and there aren't a lot of people cut out to do it. I don't want a volunteer who's only in it for themselves, or for ulterior motives. But I appreciate your honesty, and I respect Mom's judgement. If she thinks you'd be a good fit here, I'm willing to give you a try."

"Huh." Grae sat back. "Okay. So what do you want me to do?"

"How much do you know about what we're all about?"

"Jo said you work with dying people who don't have family or friends to be with them."

"Pretty close. Our mission is simple, but profound. Those who've been abandoned by family or outlived all their friends shouldn't have to spend their dying hours alone. Our volunteers go into hospices and hospitals, and sometimes private homes. Wherever there is a need, we try to fill it."

"That's pretty much what Jo told me."

"What Mom couldn't have told you is that a very difficult case hit my desk yesterday, and I've been unable to find a volunteer willing to take it on."

Grae frowned. How bad did it have to be if not even a do-gooder would accept the assignment?

"In brief, a long-time inmate named Ezra Herzog has been paroled on compassionate grounds. He's in the end stages of pancreatic cancer and has no one to visit him in his final hours. Peter DaSilva, the director of Lazarus Hospice, has asked for someone to spend some time with Mr. Herzog."

"Why isn't he in the hospice if he's dying?"

"Because Peter had a staff rebellion on his hands when he tried to arrange it."

"Why? What's so bad about this guy? Is he a murderer or something?"

"He has multiple convictions for pedophilia. He was serving his sixth sentence when he was diagnosed with end-stage cancer."

Images of the first time she'd seen Marcus flashed through her memory and Grae sprang out of the chair. "A pedophile? Are you fucking crazy? If anyone deserves to die alone and forgotten… Did you actually think I'd say yes?"

Kendall sighed heavily. "No, but I had to ask. I apologize. There's no way that I should've even broached it with a new volunteer, but I'm desperate. I've worked with Peter for years, and he's a staunch supporter of our organization. He wouldn't have made such a request unless he had good reason, and as unpleasant as the situation sounded, I didn't want to let him down."

Grae took a couple of deep breaths and resumed her seat. "Not to tell you your business, but if none of your volunteers want to touch it, why don't you do it?"

"Because I have a fundraiser to prepare for this evening, and Mr. Herzog may not still be with us tomorrow. Much as I don't want to disappoint Peter, I can't jeopardize a whole year's funding. Look, why don't you come back next week when it's not so crazy? I'll sit down with you and go through the standard intake procedures. We'll talk about our mission and some of the things you can expect. You can shadow one of our experienced volunteers to get an idea of what's involved. Then, when you feel you're ready, I'll give you your first assignment. Okay?"

Grae frowned. "How long does all that take?"

"There's no set timetable. Some people are comfortable right out of the gate, and some people take a few weeks before they're ready to fly solo. It really depends on you, Ms. Jordan."

Grae exhaled slowly. Virgil would want to see immediate progress. Maybe it would be best to check out the food bank. *Jo.* "Damn it. All right. I'll go visit the pedophile, but I'd better get an excellent report for the judge out of this."

Kendall's eyes widened. "You'll go?"

"I said I would."

"I don't have time today to go through all the usual preliminary steps. Are you sure you're comfortable with this?"

"Hell no, I'm not comfortable. But how hard can it be? I go sit by his bed, listen to him talk, and feed him some Jell-O."

Kendall frowned. "Mr. Herzog may not be our typical type of client, Ms. Jordan, but that doesn't mean you're to treat him with anything less than kindness and civility. If you can't do that, then it's better to let him die alone."

"Listen, what he did...I can't even begin to tell you how loathsome I think that is, but I'm not about to berate him on his deathbed. If he wants to talk, I'll listen. If he wants the channel changed on the TV, I can do that. If he just wants the sound of another human voice, I'll read him the newspaper." *And when he closes his eyes for the last time, I'll say, "Good riddance and tell the devil I said hello."*

Kendall studied Grae for a long moment. "God, I should probably have my head examined."

Grae waited in silence.

"According to Mr. Herzog's doctors, he has very little time left. Are you able to see him today?"

"I work midnights to eight a.m. As long as I'm home to grab some sleep before my shift starts, I'm okay with going this afternoon."

Kendall jotted some notes on a pad of paper. "How about one-thirty? I'll have Peter meet you at the front entrance of the hospital and give you a quick briefing. He won't be able to stay, but he can give you some idea of how to handle things."

Grae accepted the piece of paper Kendall held out. "Okay. How will I know how to find him?"

For the first time a smile broke out on Kendall's face, and the family resemblance was clear. "Oh, don't worry. I'll just tell Peter to look for the woman with rainbow coloured hair. I don't think he'll have any problem finding you."

"Good point. So after I spend some time with Mr. Herzog, do I come back here or what?"

"We do expect a report afterwards, but you can do that online if you like. Margie can set you up with access and a password."

Grae shook her head. "Only if you can wait until the weekend when I can get to the library. I don't have a computer."

"Oh. Okay. Well, the weekend is fine, or you can drop off a written report. Tell Margie to give you one of the formatted ones, so you know what we're looking for." Kendall stood and came around the desk. "I'm sorry this is so rushed. This really isn't the way I prefer to welcome new volunteers."

"It's all right. Just…well, I'm a little nervous about this. I want to do a decent job."

"Then treat him like a decent human being. That's really all our clients want. That, and a friendly ear and a warm smile. If you can bring yourself to hold his hand—"

"I'm not sure I can go that far, but I'll do the best I can." *How hard can it be? Dude will probably kick off from shock a minute after I walk into the room.*

Kendall held out her hand. "Thanks, Ms. Jordan. You're bailing us out of a tough spot, and I appreciate it."

Grae shrugged and shook her hand. "No worries, Ms. Reaves. And call me Grae."

"Grae, welcome aboard. And please call me Kendall."

❦

"You're the one who wanted more greens in our diet."

Grae looked up from toying with her salad. "Sorry, bud. It's good, really. I've just got a lot on my mind."

Marcus slid the milk carton across the table and filled his glass. "No kidding. You've hardly said two words since you got home."

Grae looked up at the clock. There were still thirty minutes before she had to leave for the hospital. She chewed her lip as she considered how much to tell Marcus.

"Spill."

Startled, Grae glanced at Marcus and found him regarding her with a small smile. "Pardon?"

"Something's bugging you. You never let me get away with clamming up, so spill. What's happening? Did Jo's daughter turn out to be a dragon lady?"

"No, actually she was okay. Well, not at first, but then she chilled."

"So, what's the problem?"

Grae sighed and pushed her plate away. "My first assignment. It sucks."

"Why?"

"The guy I'm supposed to see this afternoon—the dying guy? He's a loser. In fact, he was in prison, and he was only paroled because he's dying."

"What was he in prison for? Is he like some kind of rapist or murderer or something?"

"Or something. Shit, Marcus, he's a pedophile—the lowest of the low."

He sucked in his breath and froze.

Grae reached across the table and took his hand. "I didn't want to do this, bud. Christ, cancer rotting his stinking bones is fucking karma, as far as I can see. I don't even know why I said yes, except that I wanted something to report to Virgil. Ms. Reaves—Kendall was in a bind, so I thought she'd give me a glowing assessment and get me in good with the judge. But my stomach is doing somersaults at the thought of even being in the same room as that freak."

Marcus pushed his plate away. He started to say something, and then stopped.

Grae squeezed his hand. "Tell me you don't want me to go, and I'll call AU and make an excuse. Hell, I'll dump them altogether and go to the food bank instead. Jo will understand."

"No. If you can handle it, I can."

"You shouldn't have to handle it. Goddamnit, this was a stupid idea." Grae released Marcus' hand and stood. "I'm just going to call AU and tell them I can't do it."

"No, stop." Marcus circled around the table, laid his hands on Grae's shoulders, and turned her toward him. "It's okay. It really is. He's dying, right. You're sure about that?"

"Yeah. I mean, that's what they told me."

"So he'll never have a chance to hurt anyone again. Go. Do what you can to help him. You just don't have to be his best buddy or anything."

"Hell, no. My best buddy is standing right in front of me."

Marcus gave her a wan smile. "I know. It's really all right with me, honest."

Grae searched his face.

"For real. Now go. I'm going to get some of our laundry done, then catch some Z's before work." He pulled her into a hug, and left the room.

Grae looked at the phone for a long moment, then shook her head. *What the hell am I getting myself into?* Then she went back to her bedroom to put her facial hardware back in. She wasn't going to cater to some criminal's sensibilities. If he took one look at her and kicked off, too bad, not sad.

Chapter 8

Grae was barely inside the hospital entrance when a short, burly man rushed up to her with his hand outstretched and a big smile on his face.

"You must be Grae Jordan. Kendall's description was spot on, as usual. I'm Peter DaSilva, and I'm so pleased to meet you."

Peter shook her hand vigorously and grasped her arm. "Come, let me buy you a coffee while I fill you in. Kendall told me this is your first day with AU, and I'm so impressed that you'd take on this assignment. What a remarkable woman you must be."

Within moments he had steered her to a coffee shop off the lobby, and Grae was seated at a table across from him, with a steaming cup in front of her. "Um, thanks."

"You're most welcome. Really, I should be thanking you, and I do, I truly do." Peter leaned forward, his fringe of grey hair sticking out comically above oversized ears. "How much did Kendall tell you?"

"About Angels Unawares?"

"No, about Ezra Herzog."

"Oh, well, not a lot. I know he's been paroled because he's dying of cancer."

"She told you what he was in prison for?"

"Yes."

Peter sighed. "He went into a medical freefall so fast that the authorities had to scramble to make arrangements for his care. I was willing to take him into Lazarus—that's the name of the hospice I run—but my staff flatly refused. I've never had them do that before. My most senior people threatened to quit if I overruled them and admitted him. I was completely at a loss, Ms. Jordan."

"Grae."

He patted Grae's arm. "What a lovely name. Well, you can imagine my consternation. Our mission is to care for all the needs of the terminally ill and their loved ones—medical, emotional, social, psychological, and even spiritual. But how could we do that if those who are supposed to be doing the caring are so hostile that they won't even go into the room? I didn't like having to consign Mr. Herzog here, but I had no choice."

"Don't the doctors and nurses feel the same way about treating him?"

"No doubt many do. I overheard one intern scaring a young nurse with the possibility that Mr. Herzog was faking it and would threaten them all. I put a quick end to that nonsense, I can tell you. Besides, the hospital took precautions. They put him in an individual room, and a security guard makes regular checks. Plus, they made his care non-mandatory duty for staff. I heard that at least one supervisor had to take a shift because there was a shortage of volunteers."

"Sounds like a pretty lonely way to go. Does he have any family or friends?"

"He has a younger brother in the city, but his brother refuses to have anything to do with him." Peter cocked his head. "To tell you the truth, I'm rather surprised you agreed to visit."

"Because I've never done this before?"

"No. I feared anyone who remembered his last arrest and conviction wouldn't come within a mile of his bedside, dying or not. He was designated a dangerous offender for a reason."

Grae shook her head. "I don't know what you mean. Is there some reason I'm supposed to recognize his name?"

Peter blinked. "You don't?"

"No. Never heard of him."

"Oh my. I do wish Kendall had given you a more complete briefing, but I know she was pressed for time."

"How bad is it?"

Peter fidgeted with the papers he'd set on the table. "Bad. Look, you don't know me and have no reason to believe me, but it would be better if you saw Mr. Herzog without knowing his complete background. Are you open to that?"

Grae shifted in her chair. "I don't know. Why are you asking me to do it that way? Patient confidentiality?"

"Not really. I'm sure you could Google him and get his entire life story. But if I tell you right now, you're ninety-nine percent likely to walk away. As bad as his conduct has been, I'd like him to have some comfort in his remaining hours. The only way you can effectively provide that is to recognize his humanity. If you know his criminal record today, that will make it much more difficult to do. You may curse me if you Google him after he dies, but I'm willing to take that chance."

"You are, eh?"

Peter met her gaze steadily. "I am. I know Kendall only had time for the most basic briefing, and she didn't even have time to do the background check—"

Grae laughed. "If she'd done those, I probably wouldn't be here. I haven't exactly been an angel."

"Then maybe that's why you were sent. God works in mysterious ways. Besides, Kendall told me her mother recommended you. I know Jo very well, and her recommendation carries a lot of weight. If she feels you're up to this, that's good enough for me."

"Jo didn't know Herzog would be the first thing dumped in my lap."

"True. This is definitely throwing you into the deep end of the pool, but something tells me you can handle it."

Grae sipped her coffee. "You've known me for all of five minutes."

Peter grinned. "What can I say? I have good instincts about people. So, what do you think?"

"All right."

He sat up straight. "You'll do it?"

"Yeah."

"I shouldn't look a gift horse in the mouth, but may I ask why?"

"I've never done anything nearly as bad as what he has, but I've had my share of troubles. Someone recently gave me a second chance. I may never do this again, but I'll pay it forward at least once."

"Bless you." Peter pushed a newspaper and some printed material across the table. "These might help you. Kendall may have told you that sometimes our clients simply want the sound of a voice near them. Dying can be a very quiet, very lonely process when all you have to focus on is your thoughts. In Mr. Herzog's case, I imagine those thoughts are not particularly comforting."

Grae shuffled through the papers. "What are these?"

"Positive, uplifting stories, the kind seldom found in conventional newspapers. I print them from a Good News website. We've found that usually people confronting their own mortality have no desire to listen to the doom and gloom that comprises daily headlines. These articles often generate amazing conversations and break the ice, as it were. Of course, some people want to stay engaged until the last, ergo, today's newspaper as well."

"How do I know which he'd prefer?"

"Play it by ear. Herzog didn't say much, but he did seem to appreciate listening to me talk about this and that."

Grae tapped the printed material. "Did you use these? I don't want to be redundant."

"No. We mostly watched the noon news, and I helped him eat what little he could stomach. I told him you'd be by later."

"Can I ask you something?"

"Of course. Anything."

"Is he really dying soon? Like, within hours?"

Peter nodded. "He's severely debilitated by his disease and doesn't have a lot of time left, but I can't tell you how many hours or days. Death comes on its own timetable. I've found that those who are waiting for someone, or who have left something undone, often hang on longer than expected."

"Do you think Herzog is waiting for someone?"

"If he is, he'll be disappointed. His brother was notified of Ezra's condition and transfer here, but he didn't even acknowledge the information."

"I don't blame him."

Peter sighed and glanced at his watch. "Nor do I. Look, I must be going. Half my staff is out with the flu, and I need to get back to Lazarus as quickly as possible. Did Kendall give you your AU identification?"

Grae took the laminated badge out of her pocket and slipped the string over her head. "The photo sucks, but at least it's me."

"Good. Then if you go up to the Palliative Care Ward on the twelfth floor and identify yourself at the nurse's station, someone will direct you to his room. They've been instructed to keep reporters and looky-loos away, but Kendall's people are always on the approved list."

They parted ways and Grae waited in the crowd at the bank of elevators, pondering their conversation. If Herzog was so notorious, how had she missed it? Whatever he had done must have coincided with her personal turmoil, the year she dropped out of university and out of her family's life. She hadn't paid attention to anything except her own pain. It had taken another year before she was doing more than surviving from day to day. So yes, if his arrest and trial had fallen within that black hole, she knew why she'd been oblivious.

When Grae reached the twelfth floor, she was directed down the hallway to the last door on the left. She stopped before entering and took several deep breaths to settle her roiling stomach. After she schooled her face into stoicism, she pushed the door open.

The shrunken figure in the bed lay so still that for an instant she was certain she was too late. A wave of relief swept over her, but then Ezra stirred.

"You're not a nurse." The gravelly voice was barely more than a whisper, but his vivid green eyes gleamed below shaggy brows. "You must be lost." He turned his gaze back to the window.

"Um, no, I'm from Angels Unawares. Peter told you I'd be coming? I'm Grae Jordan."

He grunted, but didn't look away from the motes of dust dancing in the midday sunbeam.

"Is there anything I can get for you, Mr. Herzog?"

His laugh was as dry as a desert wind. "A beer and a cigarette."

Grae glanced at the wheelchair sitting in the corner. She grimaced at the thought of touching him. *Suck it up, Grae. You came to do a job, so do it.* "I can't help with the beer, but I can take you down to the smoking area outside if you like. Maybe someone there would give you a cigarette." *Unless they know who you are.*

Ezra wordlessly tugged back his blanket, exposing his leg where an ankle cuff and chain connected to the bed's railing. "They call it compassionate parole. It ain't really parole."

Grae's breath caught. Herzog was hooked up to several tubes and a monitor. His limbs were spindly where they jutted from ill-fitting pajamas, and his movements were feeble. He was clearly weak and dying, and incapable of attacking so much as a good meal. Restraining him like an animal seemed like overkill. She reminded herself that she, too, regarded him as an animal. The hospital administration was no doubt being cautious, and she quashed her instinctive sympathy.

"Okay. Do you want me to read to you or anything? I have today's paper."

"Is there anything in there about me?"

"I don't know. Do you want me to check?"

Ezra snorted, though the sound barely stirred the air. "It was a joke. If they wrote anything, it would be a celebration of my impending demise."

Grae had no clue how to respond to that.

Ezra rolled away from the window and gazed at her. "You could do something for me."

She tensed.

"I'd like to write a letter to my brother, but my hands shake so much I can't make out the words."

She relaxed. "I can do that. Do you have any paper?"

He pointed at the side table. "There's some in there."

Grae pulled a chair up, but not close enough to be within arm's reach. She took out a pencil and a pad of yellow legal paper. There were indecipherable marks on the top page.

"Toss that crap. I want to start fresh."

Grae tore off the marked page and sat with the pencil poised. Ezra was quiet for several long moments, and Grae waited. She wondered what she'd write to her family if she knew it was her last communication. Would she express her love? Apologize for what she'd put them through? It was easy to imagine what she'd write to Marcus. She'd tell him how much she loved him, how glad she was that he'd come into her life, and she'd give him lots of advice on how to manage after she was gone.

"Dear Jude…"

Grae blinked and hurriedly jotted down Ezra's opening. "Dear Jude."

"Yeah, I know. Sounds like that damned song. Jude hated it." Ezra's face creased in a wry smile.

"Oh, I remember that song."

"Yeah? I'd have figured the Beatles were way before your time." He sobered and stared at the ceiling. "Dear Jude. By the time you get this, I'll be gone. I wish I could've seen you one last time, but I understand why you didn't come. I shamed our family. I shamed our mother, and I know you hold me responsible for killing her. Damn near killed me that I was locked up when she had her heart attack, though I suppose it was for the best. Thanks again for letting me know of her and Papa passing."

Grae wrote as fast as she could, but it was as if a spigot had opened and Ezra's words were spilling out.

"Little brother, I hope you'll read this letter instead of just throwing it in the garbage soon 's you realize it's from me. Not that I'd blame you for that, either. Hell, I don't blame you for one damn thing. You were nothing but good to me and good for me. I know what I done horrified you. Believe it or not, it horrifies me too."

He paused and took several deep breaths. Grae caught up and waited for him to resume.

"There ain't nothing you can say I haven't said to myself. I tried to stop myself, Jude. Every time I got out of prison, I swore I'd go straight and never go within a mile of a child. But I could never find any work, and had too much time to… No, erase that. I'm not making excuses. Too late for 'em anyway."

Grae shook off the creeping revulsion and tried to focus on her task. "How far back do you want me to erase?"

"Read it back to me."

She did.

Ezra nodded. "Okay, go back to 'I tried to stop myself' and just add 'I failed.' Then write, I've been failing since we were kids, but that's the one part of my life that I can look back on with pleasure. I think of the days we spent with Papa at the shop. I remember Grandpa teaching us how to draw and cut a stencil. He never considered us good enough to work with his customers, though. Never met a man who had such high standards. Even Papa wasn't such a stickler. But I'll bet you are, aren't you, Jude? Used to piss me off sometimes, you know? I was the oldest son. I was the big brother. But you...you took to it like the stones were your own flesh and blood. I remember when you were about six and I was nine. Papa had always told me that both of us would inherit the shop some day, but I knew that wouldn't be. You were practicing sculpting a rose into a small piece of granite, and damned if that thing didn't look like it had grown on one of Mama's bushes. Even Grandpa was impressed, and that old man never praised anyone, not even Papa. But I saw the way he looked at you, and I knew—I just knew. You might've been the younger brother, but you were the golden boy. If I stayed with the family business, you'd be my boss someday."

His breath caught and he started to cough.

Grae hurriedly finished writing and set the pad down to pour him a glass of water, which he grasped with trembling hands. She steadied it, part of her mind noting that she was touching his hands despite her resolution.

"Thanks. Not used to talking this much."

She took the glass, resumed her seat, and picked up her pad.

Ezra cleared his throat. "I don't say this to make you feel responsible or anything. It's just the way it was. I took a fucked-up path, and I know I'm the only one to blame. I only wanted you to know that with all the nightmare memories I hold, the only good ones I have are of us being kids together." He stopped. "Are you getting all of this?"

"I am."

"Good." He was quiet for a long moment. "Do you like to read?"

Grae blinked at the apparent non sequitur. "Yes. When I have time."

"I had all the time in the world in prison, but I didn't like to read. 'Cept for one book."

Grae tensed again, then reminded herself that child pornography likely wasn't featured in the prison library.

"You ever heard of *Spoon River Anthology*?"

She searched her memory, but came up blank. "No, I don't think so."

"No reason you should, I suppose. It's an old book. Third time I went inside, dude who was in the cell before me left it behind. I was in segregation so my head stayed attached to my shoulders, and I was bored out of my skull. I picked it up, and it was goddamned poetry, for Christ's sake. Who'd think I'd read poetry."

"Why did you?"

"Couldn't put it down. It was a bunch of dead people, speaking from the grave. They talked about their lives, what they'd hoped for, how they'd fucked up. I could relate. It was like they wrote their own obits. I musta read that book twenty, thirty times. Took it with me when I got out, but I lost it when I went in again. Anyway, that's kinda what I'm trying to do here. Papa was never one to miss an opportunity, so he'd read the obits every day, and he'd read the good ones out loud to us at the dinner table."

"What made a good one?"

"Told a story about the dead person. Most people will write nice when a relative dies. They're not going to say he was as crooked as a Wall Street banker, or so horny no nice woman would come within ten feet of him. So you can dismiss most of what you read. But the best obits are honest. They tell you much more. For the brief span of time you're reading, that complete stranger comes alive to you, warts and all. I'm all warts, and no one will write anything nice about me when I'm gone, but this letter to Jude is my last testimony."

Grae stared at Ezra. What had Peter said? *Recognize his humanity.* She'd dismissed that as part of Peter's sales pitch, but suddenly she was uncomfortably aware that Ezra's criminal record wasn't his whole story. *Fuck this. He's a pervert, and don't you forget it.*

"I will not beg your forgiveness for all the ways I screwed up your life. I know what I done and there can be no forgiveness, not from anyone."

Suppressing her whirling emotions, Grae scrambled to catch up.

"Anyway, brother, I don't have much more to say. 'I'm sorry' could never be enough to cover all I did to you and your family, but I have to say it. I have to try. If you made it this far, maybe you'll read one more thing. I love you, Jude. Always have, always will." Ezra glanced at Grae. "I'd like to try and sign it myself."

Grae nodded, finished the last sentence, and brought the pad to him. He tried to hold the pencil, but it fell from his fingers. She picked it up, put it back in place, and wrapped her hand around his. Slowly he traced his name, then his hand slackened.

"Can you mail that for me? I don't have money for a stamp—"

Grae shrugged. "No biggie. I'll mail it. Do you have an address?"

Ezra closed his eyes. "Jude Herzog. Care of Stone Garden Monuments, 8311 Standhill Road. Can't remember the postal code, though."

She wrote the address on the bottom of the page. "I can look it up."

He looked at her. "Over a hundred years it was called Herzog Monuments. They changed it 'cause of me. Ain't that a fine legacy to leave. Jesus. I should'a never been born."

She'd been in the room less than an hour, but Grae desperately longed to leave. She didn't want to see Ezra Herzog's humanity. She didn't want to acknowledge that this miserable excuse for a human being had once been a boy with dreams and a family that loved him.

"Look, I should probably get going. Is there anything else I can do?"

Ezra scratched the coarse grey stubble on his face. "You might ask if anyone would be willing to give me a shave."

Grae tucked the pad and pencil back into the drawer and folded Ezra's letter. "I'm sure one of the nurses could help."

He grimaced. "Going by the last coupl'a days, I doubt it." Ezra looked back at the window. "Thanks for writing to Jude for me."

Grae backed away. "You're welcome."

It seemed inadequate as the last words to a dying man, but for the life of her, she couldn't think of anything to add. Closing his door behind her, she fled.

Chapter 9

Grae stood outside the hospital and stared at the letter in her hand. It would be easy to stick it in an envelope, slap a stamp on it, drop it in the nearest mailbox, and forget about it. But something held her back.

This letter to Jude is my last testimony.

She mulled over Ezra's words. It was clear he didn't expect to see his brother again, but the tone of the letter left no doubt he wished he could.

Grae shook her head in disgust. "Aw, for God's sake. I ought to have my head examined." With a deep sigh, she hauled the tattered map of city transit routes from her back pocket and figured out the route to 8311 Standhill Road.

One train ride and two bus transfers later, Grae walked along a road in an industrial park. She found Stone Garden Monuments in a modern, low-slung building. Ezra had said the family business went back over a century, so she'd expected something far less contemporary than the smart brick and glass storefront. "Must've updated over the years."

She walked up the long driveway, crunching through fallen leaves as she composed her opening lines. It was almost as daunting to contemplate talking to Jude as it had been going to see Ezra.

Inside the lobby, an attractive young woman looked up from her desk with a bright smile. "May I help you?"

Grae nodded. "I'm looking for Jude Herzog."

"Jude's out on an installation right now, Ms....?"

"Jordan. Grae Jordan."

"May I take a message, Ms. Jordan, or could someone else assist you? Mr. Grenier is available."

An employee who was passing through the lobby stopped. "Jude just called in, Ashley. He finished the installation, and he'll be back in ten."

"Oh, thanks, Rolly. Would you care to wait in our reception room, Ms. Jordan? You're welcome to help yourself to a coffee, if you like."

"Thanks, I will." Grae moved in the direction Ashley indicated and found herself in a small room. The walls were covered with flat bronze markers displaying a variety of decorations and insignias.

Grae filled a cup from the coffee urn in the corner and took a seat at the table in the centre of the room. Some of the markers were quite ornate, with intricate borders, floral patterns, and religious emblems. Others were plain, with only names and dates, though the contrasting gold and bronze lent even those an austere elegance.

Ashley came into the room with a leather binder in hand. "Would you care to see some of our designs? Our clients often find that an existing piece is perfect to commemorate their loved one, though we do custom designs, as well. Jude is one of the best. He can give you anything you'd like to see on a monument."

"Actually, I'm here to see him on a personal matter."

"Oh. All right."

Before Ashley and her luminous smile could depart, Grae said, "May I ask you something?"

"Of course."

"I thought Mr. Herzog was the owner, but you said he was out on an installation?"

"Oh, yes. Jude has been sole owner since his father passed twenty years ago, but he loves field work. Most days you'll find him either working in the shop, or out doing installations right along with the rest of the guys."

"So you get stuck with the paperwork, do you?"

Ashley laughed. "Some of it, but Jude brought his son-in-law into the business five years ago, and he's the one with the MBA. As soon as Jude had Luc trained, he turned over all the day-to-day business and went back to doing what he loves."

The front door opened, and Ashley looked over her shoulder. "There's Jude now. I'll send him in."

She returned to the lobby, and Grae drained her coffee. She wasn't looking forward to the next few minutes.

A large, dark-haired, raw-boned man stepped through the doorway, his tweed workman's cap brushing the top of the doorway. Grae's eyes widened. At first glance, this man bore no resemblance to the shrunken figure in the hospital bed, but then she noticed the familial similarity. He, too, had striking, pale green eyes.

"Ashley tells me you're looking for me?"

"Yes, sir. My name is Grae Jordan. May I talk to you for a few moments?"

He took a seat across from her. "Sure. What's this all about?"

"Your brother."

Jude stiffened and began to rise.

"Please, hear me out. I'm with an organization called Angels Unawares. We visit people—dying people—who have no one else to spend their final hours with. Your brother is my first assignment. I saw him this afternoon, and, at his request, I helped him write you a letter." Grae pushed the paper across the table.

"Does Ezra actually think I'll forgive him? That I'll come to his bedside and offer absolution like some damned priest?" He hadn't raised his voice, but its bass filled the room and his gaze stabbed at Grae.

"No, sir. He doesn't expect that at all. In fact, he doesn't know I'm here. All he asked was that I mail that letter to you. He thinks you'll get it after he dies."

"Then what the hell are you doing here?"

It was the question she'd been unable to rationalize herself. She shook her head. "Honestly, I don't exactly know. He's a very bad man, I get that. But he's only got a few hours to live, and he's so alone."

"Good! He's a goddamned predator. He's a disgrace to our family and to our faith. He deserves to die alone."

"He's also your brother, Mr. Herzog. Once you were boys together. Once you loved him—maybe looked up to him, even idolized him. I know for sure he still loves you."

Jude glared at her. "Do you know what he did? All that he did?"

"I don't know the details, but I know he's a convicted pedophile and a dangerous offender."

"Then let me fill in the blanks for you, missie, because I can tell you I'd have been doing the world a favour if I'd drowned him when we were kids."

Grae held up her hand. "No, sir. Please don't do that. For me to do my job, I need to focus on his humanity, and finding out how inhumane he's been would make it that much more difficult."

Jude leaned back in the chair and stared at her. "Why are you doing this?"

"Talking to you? I don't really know. I just felt I had to."

"No. Why are you defending Ezra? He's an animal. No, that's an insult to animals. They'd never do what he did time and time again."

"No, sir, he's not an animal. He's done terrible things and I'm not defending him, but he's still a human being and his lifespan can be measured in hours, if not minutes. If nothing else, I ask that you read his letter. It's little enough, and you can toss it in the garbage when you're done."

"I don't owe him one goddamned thing."

"No, sir, you don't. But maybe you owe it to yourself." Grae stood, her gaze locked with Jude's. "You know the only thing he asked for, other than help writing that letter, was a shave. But when I passed that request along at the nursing station, I knew not one of them would grant him even that small kindness. Think about that, and then think back to the brother who so admired the way you could carve a rose in granite. If you can't soften your heart for an hour, you can't. I'm not one to judge. But if you can—well, I think it might be as good for you as for Ezra. That's all."

She left Jude staring at the untouched letter.

※

Grae lifted the payphone, put in coins, and dialed Marcus' cell. He picked up on the fourth ring.

"Sorry, buddy. You were asleep, weren't you?"

"Yeah. Oh, it's six. Is this my wake-up call?"

Grae smiled at the sound of his sleep-fuzzy voice. "No. Just wanted to let you know that you might have to go to work on your own tonight."

"Okay. Where are you?"

"I'm at the hospital."

"You are? Why? Aren't you finished with that freak? I thought you only had to give a couple of hours."

Grae sighed. "So did I, but it turned out to be more complicated."

"Aren't you coming home before work?"

"I don't know. I hope to, but if not, it won't be the first time I pulled an all-nighter. I'll be fine."

"I don't like that at all. Without sleep, you're going to be a zombie by quitting time."

The concern in Marcus' voice touched Grae. "Don't worry about it, bud. It's not like I'm holding the key to nuclear release codes. I'm stocking shelves. The worst I might do is put the toilet paper where the paper towels are supposed to go."

"I know, but at least it keeps bread on the table, right? Speaking of which, should I bring both our lunches?"

"Would you mind?"

"Silly question. Of course not. I'll even throw an energy drink in the bag."

"Make it three energy drinks."

Marcus chuckled. "Okay, but then you'd better anchor yourself to the shelves or you're going to be flying like the laughing dude in Mary Poppins."

Grae grinned at the reference. When he was a boy, Marcus had been forbidden all secular movies, so he'd gone crazy for Disney since they'd hooked up. She'd had to re-watch all the movies of her childhood, as well as those of her parents' and grandparents' youth. But she didn't mind, even if it did mean listening to him sing along with Julie at the top of his discordant lungs.

"Go back to sleep, bud. Oh wait, did you set your alarm?"

Marcus heaved an exaggerated sigh. "Yes, Mother. I will rise at ten and be out the door an hour later."

"Good. I'll see you there if I don't get home first."

"'Kay."

Grae hung up and looked around the lobby. The hospital gift shop was doing a brisk business; patrons filled the tiny space. For a moment she reconsidered her idea, but shook her head. "It's little enough."

Fifteen minutes later, she rode up the elevator with a small bag in her hand. This time she didn't hesitate as she approached Ezra's room. It was dark, but there was a small overhead light directly above the bed.

Ezra appeared to be dozing, but he stirred as she approached. He shot her a startled glance. "I didn't expect to see you again."

"I wanted to let you know that I delivered your letter."

He blinked. "You delivered—"

He started to cough, and Grae hastened to get him water.

When he could speak again, he said, "I didn't ask you to deliver it. Just to mail it."

"I know. I wanted to talk to your brother."

Ezra grasped the bedrail. "Did he… Did you ask him…or—"

Grae shook her head. "He's not coming. I'm sorry. I thought your letter might change his mind."

Ezra slumped and his hand fell to his side. "I didn't expect it to. Thanks for trying, though."

"So, you mentioned you'd like a shave. Doesn't look like the nurses have had time to get to you, so I thought I'd pinch hit, if that's okay with you." Grae opened the bag and set a disposable safety razor and a small container of shaving cream on the side table.

Ezra's eyes widened. "You'd do that?"

She shrugged. "Sure, why not? Just don't expect barber-level expertise. The only thing I've ever shaved is my legs."

She busied herself filling a small basin with water and fetching a facecloth and towel.

Ezra watched her quietly.

She returned to his side and soaked the facecloth in the hot water, then wrung it out and awkwardly placed it over his face.

He tugged it down below his nose.

"Sorry, I really haven't done this before."

"You've never shaved your boyfriend?"

She shook her head. "Girlfriend. And no, I don't usually date bearded women."

"Oh."

He said nothing more as she removed the facecloth, then spread the shaving cream around his jaw and under his nose. Grae opened the packaging and extracted the razor. She drew it carefully down his face. She figured she had the hang of it by the time she'd gotten his cheeks cleaned up. But when she attempted to get underneath his chin, she accidentally nicked him, giving rise to a bead of blood.

"Damn, I'm sorry about that." Grae dabbed at the blood with a tissue, marvelling at how such a small wound could spread crimson so quickly.

"Don't worry about it."

"Yeah, well, I don't want to have to report back to Kendall that I slit someone's throat on my first day of volunteer work."

Ezra's dry laugh morphed into a cough, and Grae paused again to give him water. "This is nothing. You should'a seen the blood the day five guys jumped me in the showers."

Horrified, Grae stopped.

Ezra shrugged. "Lowest of the low. I never had any illusions."

She resumed work and carefully tried to navigate the corner beneath his ear. The sound of someone clearing his throat from the doorway startled her.

"I'll do that." Jude stood there. His clothes were still dusty and the cap was still on his head. He crossed the room and took the razor from her hand. "I've got experience."

For an instant Grae wondered whether it was safe to let Jude shave Ezra, given his antipathy toward his brother. But she stepped back and relinquished her spot. Ezra stared at the ceiling, his chin lifted, and Jude focused on the path of the razor. Neither looked directly at the other.

"Um, I guess I'll go then and let you two—"

"No." The protest erupted from both of them.

Jude looked at her, his eyes pleading. "Why don't you stay a bit?"

Grae glanced at Ezra, surprised that he didn't want alone time with Jude, but his expression was even more plaintive than his brother's. She pulled a chair away from the bedside so she wouldn't be in the way and sat.

She watched Jude meticulously shave his brother, and she saw the moment the silent tears overflowed and spilled down Ezra's cheeks. Her chest ached, and she fought to keep herself from crying.

Jude kept shaving, working carefully around Ezra's bobbing Adam's apple. When he was done he wiped away the excess cream and dabbed at his brother's eyes.

A choked sob broke the hush that had enveloped the three of them.

Grae dashed a hand over her eyes, unable to take her gaze off the tableau unfolding in front of her.

Jude set the towel and razor aside, and then rested his hand on Ezra's chest.

"You came." Ezra's voice was just barely audible.

"I wasn't going to." Jude tilted his head toward Grae. "You can thank that one. She made me remember that when all is said and done, you're my brother."

"I didn't think I'd ever hear you say that again. I never thought you'd come. The letter?"

"I read it."

"I'm sorry."

Jude sighed. "I know you are. It doesn't change a damned thing."

"I know. I didn't think it would, but I wanted to say goodbye. Will you bury me, Jude?"

Jude jerked, as if he had been hit by a hammer. Recovering, he nodded. "I'll do right by you."

"Cremate me, okay?"

Jude frowned and shook his head. "That's not our way. You know that."

The corners of Ezra's mouth tilted up, just a little. "You might not have noticed, but I fell away from our faith a long time ago. Nobody will sit in judgement, 'cept God. I figure he's going to condemn me to hell without so much as a hearing, so cremation ranks way low on the list of charges against me."

"It isn't right, Ezra. It just isn't right."

"Please. If you bury me whole, them that hate me might dig me up and scatter pieces of me all over. Not much scares me anymore, but that does. Please, Jude. I got no right to ask you for anything, but I'm begging for this."

Grae shivered. How horrible a life had he led that he actually thought such desecration a possibility?

Jude apparently recognized the logic of his brother's plea, as he nodded reluctantly.

"And you'll make a marker? You can make it without a name, but maybe you could put one of Mama's roses on it? I'd like that."

Jude's nostrils flared, and for an instant it looked as if he'd lash out, but he relaxed the curl of his fist and nodded stiffly. "I'll give you a rose."

Ezra closed his eyes and another tear slipped down his freshly shaven cheek. "Thank you."

Grae rose and brought a chair to Jude. He took it and sat at the bedside.

"Do you think I'll see Mama?" Ezra's voice was wistful.

Jude shook his head. "I don't know."

"She probably doesn't want to see me, anyway."

Jude shifted, making his chair squeak. "I think she would. She never stopped loving you. Never stopped grieving for her firstborn."

Ezra started to cry again. Jude took a tissue out of the box and dried his face.

"I'm so sorry, Jude. I wish I could start again. God, I'd give anything for a do-over."

"I know."

The men fell silent. Jude laid his huge hand over Ezra's, dwarfing his brother's shrunken fingers. Grae wondered again if she should leave, but it felt like she'd been drawn into something momentous and it would be wrong not to see it to the end.

Long minutes ticked by, the peace of the room broken only by the hum of equipment. Ezra's breathing grew raspy. Grae stared at the brothers and wondered what was going through Jude's mind. He had to know Ezra was in his last moments, but his features remained composed.

Then Ezra took a long, shuddering breath. His eyes flew open, and he looked beyond Jude. His eyes closed again and his chest stilled.

Jude looked from his brother to Grae with tears in his eyes.

A nurse bustled in and turned off the softly beeping monitor. "Would you like to spend some time with him? There's no rush."

Jude stood and shook his head. "No, that's all right. What happens now?"

"You make your arrangements with a funeral home, and they'll take it from there."

"Okay, thanks." He blew his nose as he moved to the end of the bed, then stopped and gazed at Grae. "I'd like to buy you a cup of coffee, if you'll do me the honour."

Grae pushed any thought of pre-work sleep aside and nodded. She followed him out of the room.

Chapter 10

They reached the lobby and Grae veered toward the coffee shop.

"I noticed a restaurant across the street. Do you mind if we go there?" Jude asked. "I don't really want to hang around the hospital a moment longer than I have to."

"Sure, no problem." Grae followed Jude out to the parking lot. "I'll meet you over there."

Jude nodded, and Grae walked briskly through the lot and across the street. By the time Jude parked his truck, she'd ordered two small coffees and was waiting for him at a corner table. She signalled to him when he came in the door.

"That was fast. I didn't even see your car leave." Jude took a seat and accepted the coffee.

"No car, I'm afraid. I just walked across."

"I could've given you a lift."

Grae shrugged. "It's okay. Walking keeps me in shape."

He nodded absently and rolled the cup between his hands.

Grae smothered a smile. It looked like a child's toy. "I'm sorry. About your brother, I mean."

"Don't be. It's better this way."

"For him?"

Jude sighed heavily. "And me, and the whole world. He wasn't always like that, you know. You were right. When we were boys, I idolized him. He knew how to do everything—fix a flat tire, change a bike chain, find the best fishing holes."

"He said you were the best carver."

"I was. It was the only thing I ever did better than him." He raised his gaze, his haunted eyes eerily like Ezra's. "Ever since the first time he went to prison, I've gone over and over our childhood. I can't put my finger on a single thing that accounts for what he did, who he became. We were both raised exactly the same way, so why did he turn out the way he did, and I didn't?"

"I don't have an answer, Mr. Herzog, but—"

"Call me Jude. And, I'm sorry, but I've forgotten your name."

"Grae. Grae Jordan."

"Grae. You were saying?"

"I was saying that—well, I don't have an answer, but I have an older brother and sister. We were all raised the same way, too. We didn't lack for anything. My brother is a lawyer and my sister is an oil executive. Me, I work the midnight shift stocking shelves, and I'm facing assault charges."

Jude stared at her. "You're up on assault?"

"Yes. I'm not proud of it, but if it matters, it was self-defence. Unfortunately, it's my word against the two scumbags that attacked me."

"Two men against one woman? Surely in such a situation the police would give more credence to your account?"

"I broke one guy's arm and the other guy's jaw with a piece of construction rebar. Plus, I have a record of petty crimes and they don't. Anyway, my point is—who knows why I turned out to be the bad seed of the three siblings. Maybe that's the way it was with you and Ezra. There isn't any logical explanation."

Jude regarded her steadily for several long moments. "I don't know you at all, but to my way of thinking, a bad seed wouldn't do what you did today."

"Don't give me any undeserved credit. I joined up with AU at the urging of my therapist and my lawyer just so I could show the judge how rehabilitated I am."

Jude shook his head. "After your visit to the office this afternoon, I asked around. I called Angels Unawares and spoke to someone there."

"Kendall?"

"I believe that was her name. All you signed up to do was spend a little time reading or talking to my brother. You didn't have to deliver that letter to me. You didn't have to give him a shave when no one else would. I stood in his doorway and watched you. You weren't skilled, but you treated him gently. I doubt anyone has touched him with kindness since our mother died."

Grae squirmed in her chair. "I didn't do anything special."

"I disagree. You treated him like a man instead of a pariah. His own brother couldn't do that."

"But you did do that."

Jude looked out the window and ran a hand over his face. "I read his letter. It made me mad as hell. I went to the hospital to rip him a new one. I was going to throw our mother's death in his face. I wanted him to die knowing he destroyed our reputation *and* our family. If you hadn't been there… If I hadn't seen what you were doing, I'd have done exactly that."

Grae stared at Jude. It had been such a little thing.

Jude turned back to her. "Ezra asked for a rose on his marker because of Mama's roses. She was passionate about them. In the summer you could smell her rose bushes from a block away. But in funeral tradition, roses symbolize eternal life and resurrection. My faith fell by the wayside a long time ago, but my father's best friend was a rabbi and they loved to argue. I remember one debate they had about reincarnation. My father said it was nonsense, but the rabbi insisted it was actually part of our religious heritage. I've been thinking about that today. Ezra screwed up in just about every way a man could, but I remember who he once was. I hope what my father's rabbi friend said was true. I hope Ezra gets another chance to do it right."

"I hope so too." Grae glanced at her watch. "I'm sorry, but I've got to get going. My shift starts at midnight. I might have time to grab a couple of hours sleep before I have to be there."

Jude raised an eyebrow. "You haven't had any sleep today?"

"It's been kind of busy. No big deal, though. I'll be fine."

"Let me give you a ride home…please."

Grae was going to turn down the offer, but the sadness and bewilderment in Jude's eyes stopped her. "Sure, if it's not out of your way."

"It won't be." He rose and dropped several toonies on the table.

On the ride to Grae's apartment, they didn't speak of Ezra.

"Do you like your job?" Jude asked.

Grae snorted. "Not in the least, but I'm a university dropout with a record and I have a roommate to support. It's the best I could do for now."

"What was your major at university?"

"Partying, mostly."

"Why did you drop out?"

Grae froze, and Jude shot her a glance.

"Sorry. Sore subject?"

She nodded.

"So do you plan to be a stock girl forever?"

"No. Marcus and I have plans."

"Marcus your boyfriend?"

"I'm gay. Marcus is my roommate—my little brother from another mother."

"Oh. So what kind of plans are the two of you making?"

"Well, we caught a break. My parents are paying for us to stay in a nice apartment for a year, so we're saving up our money, thinking maybe we'll head north to the oil patch when we're evicted. I don't want him working too long up there, though. Those are some harsh conditions and he's just a beanpole, but I can make good money."

Jude nodded. "I've lost a few employees to the oil patch. I pay a decent wage, but I sure can't compete."

"I hope to save enough to put Marcus through a culinary arts program. He's got a gift in the kitchen. He can make a five-star meal out of nothing, even though he mostly lives on popcorn. He'll need to get his high school equivalency first, but a lot of that he can do online once we can afford a computer."

"You don't have a computer?"

Grae chuckled. "No. Not even a smart phone. The bane of Marcus' existence is that he has to use an old flip phone. He's humiliated every time he has to pull it out in public. I'm saving to get him a smart phone for Christmas, but I've got a ways to go yet."

"My daughters begged and pleaded for all the latest gadgetry growing up, but my wife has very firm ideas about technology. The only reason I have a smart phone today is for the business. Course now that both my girls have kids of their own, it makes me laugh when they tell me and Elaine that we can't spoil our grandchildren with iPhones and iPads and computer games."

"Sounds like they're chips off the old block."

"Thank God not this old block, but yeah, they didn't fall far from Elaine's tree, that's for sure."

Grae liked the affection in Jude's voice when he spoke of his family. They'd turned onto the road leading to her apartment, and though she hated to bring up a sore subject, she had to ask. "Are you going to arrange a funeral for Ezra?"

Jude shook his head. "No one would come. Our entire family turned against him. But I will see him properly buried, marker and all."

"Would you call and tell me when and where?"

Jude shot her a startled glance. "You want to be there?"

"Yeah, I think so."

"Why? You've only known him one day."

"I guess…I guess I feel like my job is only half done, and I'd like to be there to pay my respects. If that's all right with you."

"Fine with me. It'll just be you and me, and maybe a rabbi if I can find one willing to say a few words, but give me your phone number and I'll let you know. It'll probably be as quickly as I can arrange it. I want to avoid any publicity."

"Do you have a pen and paper?"

Jude pulled a stubby pencil and a business card from his jacket pocket.

Grae wrote down Marcus' number. "We have a land line now, but I forget the number. You can leave a message with Marcus, and he'll make sure I get it."

Jude pulled up to the curb in front of her building and stopped. Grae put the business card on the dash and hopped out of the cab. She turned to face Jude.

He looked at her and nodded.

She closed the door.

Two days later in mid-afternoon, Grae stood next to Jude beside a neatly dug hole in a desolate corner of the cemetery.

Grae shivered as the stiff breeze swirled around them. "I don't know how you pulled it together so quickly. When my grandfather died, it took Dad a week to get everything arranged."

"It helps to have connections in the funeral business. It also helps that there are no mourners, no rabbi, and no rites to attend to."

"This isn't the Jewish section, is it?"

"No. I didn't want any of my family or friends to stumble over him when they're visiting relatives. I also didn't want anyone looking for him there. A friend let me register him with the cemetery as Leon Ezra Bruder. It's close enough to his real name and hopefully that'll throw any curiosity seekers off the trail." Jude lowered the urn into the hole, shovelled dirt on top, filled his brother's resting place, and tamped it down.

"Ezra, I finished your marker today. I'll get the foundation set soon, and you'll be properly buried. No one will bother you." Jude's soft words were carried away by the wind and lost in the grey skies above.

Grae shivered, as much from the sorrow radiating from her companion as from the cold.

"I'm going to try very hard to forget the last thirty-five years, brother. When I think of you, I'm going to remember us fishing together on a golden summer day. When you think of me, I hope that's what you'll remember too. I don't know why—" Jude choked and dug in his pocket. He wiped his eyes and blew his nose. "Well, it doesn't matter why now, does it? It's done. We can't change a thing."

Jude looked at Grae. "Did you want to say anything?"

She shook her head.

"That's about all, then. I won't promise to visit, Ezra. I didn't even tell Elaine I saw you. She would've had a fit, and I'd be sleeping on the couch for the next year." Jude started to turn away, then turned back. He whispered, "Once I loved you."

Jude strode away, and Grae hurried to catch up. She'd taken transit to the cemetery, but he'd offered her a ride home. When she climbed into the cab, she saw a small, flat granite marker on the floor of the passenger side.

"Go ahead. Take a look." Jude started the engine.

Grae picked it up. It bore the initials LEB and a single rose. Her fingertips traced the stone rose. It was exquisitely detailed and three dimensional. It appeared to be rooted in the marker, with petals bursting into the air. "He was right. You're a gifted carver."

"Thanks." Jude drove slowly along the cemetery road leading to the street, his expression pensive.

Grae studied him. "It must be hard on you—keeping this all to yourself."

He smiled wearily. "It is. I can't tell you how odd it was to share my brother's funeral with someone I'd only just met."

Grae didn't know if she should apologize.

"Don't get me wrong, I'm glad I met you. I'm thankful you were with Ezra for a bit of his last day. You put me to shame."

"That was never my intent."

"I know."

"Can I ask you something?"

"Sure." Jude turned onto the street and accelerated.

"Were you able to—I don't know—forgive Ezra at the end?"

"No. I don't think I can ever forgive what he did."

"Oh. I just wondered."

They drove on in silence, until Jude heaved a sigh. "You know the old rabbi I told you about?"

"Your father's best friend?"

"That's the one. His name was Levi. Anyway, Levi used to say that hate is corrosive, as much to the hater as the hated. I might not ever be able to forgive Ezra, but I'm going to work at not hating him anymore."

"Sounds like a start."

When they slowed to a stop at a light not far from the apartment, Jude reached through to the back seat, tugged an old cardboard box forward, and deposited it on Grae's lap. "I thought you might be able to use this."

Grae opened the box and stared at a laptop. "Oh my God."

"It's no big deal, just an office cast-off, but you said you didn't have one so I thought rather than recycle this, it could go to a new home."

"Marcus is going to freak out."

Jude chuckled, then sobered. "I have a favour to ask, though."

Grae tore her attention away from the gift. "Anything."

"Don't Google Ezra. You're probably the only person in the last few decades who doesn't hate his guts because of who he was and what he did. I don't know why that's important to me, but it is."

Grae shot Jude a troubled look. "I don't know..." She had been torn about whether she would, but didn't like having the option taken out of her hands.

"Please?"

Grae tucked the flaps of the box back into place.

Jude shook his head. "No, it's yours whether you look him up or not. It's not like I'll be standing over your shoulder checking, anyway."

"I won't promise, but I'll think about it."

"That's all I ask."

They arrived at the apartment, and Grae exited the truck with the box. "Thanks again. It's an awesome gift."

Jude shrugged. "No big deal, but I'm glad you like it. I just wanted to thank you. I didn't think I'd ever see Ezra again. When I was notified that he'd been transferred to the hospital and was dying, I wouldn't let myself feel anything. But now, I'm glad I saw him one last time. He lived an evil life. Most would call him an evil man. In the end I called him my brother, and I owe you for that. I won't forget it."

She nodded and closed the door with a bump of her hip. Jude drove off and she went upstairs, eager to show Marcus the unexpected addition to their home.

He was sleeping on the couch, so she set the box on the table and pounced on him.

Marcus squawked and half-fell off the couch as she tickled him. "What are you doing? You could give a guy a heart attack. Cease and desist, wench!"

Grae laughed and mussed his already messy hair. "Come see what our fairy godfather gave us."

Marcus sat bolt upright and rubbed his eyes. "There was a fairy here and you didn't tell me?"

Grae groaned and pulled him upright and over to the table. "C'mon."

Marcus whistled as he peered into the box. "Wow. That's some fairy godfather. I don't suppose he's looking to adopt, is he?"

"Tch. Would you leave me for material wealth and goodies?"

Marcus grinned and wrapped her in a hug. "In a heartbeat."

"You're a lousy liar." Grae extricated herself and pulled the laptop out of the box. Below it was a small mobile printer, software, and a neat coil of cords. She took those out, too.

Marcus opened the laptop. "Hey, there's an envelope inside with your name on it."

"There is?" He handed it over and Grae ripped it open. A business card fell to the floor, and she knelt to pick it up as she read the enclosed invoice. "Holy crap. He paid for six months of Wi-Fi. We just have to call and make an appointment to get hooked up."

"Ooh, Grae's got a sugar daddy. And I didn't think you swung that way."

Grae smacked Marcus' arm, and he danced away with a teasing grin. "Shut up, you idiot. He's a very nice guy. I told you about him—the brother of the AU client I saw in the hospital yesterday."

Marcus' smile faded. "The pervert's brother?"

"Yeah, but he's not anything like that, bud. He's a good man, and he was devastated by what his brother did." Grae glanced at the business card. It was Jude's. She turned it over and read, *If you get tired of stocking shelves, come see me about a job.*

Her mouth fell open. "Double holy crap."

Marcus was busy connecting wires, and didn't even look up. "What?"

"Jude offered me a job."

"Seriously? Doing what?"

"I have no idea. I mean, he's in the monuments business, but I don't know anything about that."

"You must've made a good impression. Are you going to contact him?"

"I don't know."

Marcus frowned at her. "What do you mean you don't know?"

"I like working with you."

"Oh, hell no! You're not going to turn down an opportunity to get out of minimum wage hell just because I'm stuck there. Someone has to support me in the manner to which I wish to become accustomed." He winked at her.

"So the sugar daddy hunt isn't going well?"

Marcus heaved a melodramatic sigh. "They seem to have all gone into hibernation for the winter. Maybe I'll get lucky next spring."

"Idiot."

"Takes one to know one."

Grae rolled her eyes and elbowed Marcus away from the laptop. "Let's see what my new computer can do."

"Hey, I thought this was community property."

Grae levelled a stern glance at Marcus. "It is, which means no taking it into your bedroom for some private 'me time.'"

"You have so got to get some. You're turning into a ninety-year-old in a thirty-year-old's body."

"I am not."

"You are, too. You're not getting any, and you're a regular Ms. Cranky Pants." Marcus grinned. "You know, I think I'll make it my mission to find you a girlfriend. With a computer there are all sorts of dating sites I can put your profile on."

"Not a chance. You do that, and I'll toss you out on your ass."

"No you won't."

"Pretty sure of yourself, aren't you?"

"Yup."

Grae tried to stare him down. It was impossible in the face of his gleeful impudence, and she finally gave up. "Let's get this damned thing set up, cuz the first thing we're going to do is get you enrolled in online GED courses."

Marcus' jaw dropped. "What?"

"If you're putting me into online dating, I'm putting you into high school English. You can't go to chef school without a high school equivalency, and you are going one day."

"Damn."

Grae grinned. *Chalk one up for the master.*

Chapter 11

Grae entered the offices of Angels Unawares five minutes before closing. She had her follow-up report in hand. It was the first thing she'd printed using her new computer. Margie wasn't at her desk, but Kendall emerged from her office.

"Grae, hi. I didn't expect to see you today."

"Sorry. I didn't mean to cut it so close, but I slept longer than I planned after I got off work. I can just leave this on the desk."

"No, please, come in. It's a rare day I get out of here at quitting time anyway. Here, I'll take that." Kendall took the report and gestured Grae to her office.

Grae took a seat, tried to stifle a yawn, and hoped it went unnoticed. It didn't.

Kendall smiled. "Tired?"

"Yeah. I've kind of been running on empty at work the last couple of nights."

"I'm not surprised. Jude Herzog called me twice. He was very impressed with your efforts."

Grae shrugged and stared at the worn carpet. "Just doing what you told me to do." She fought a losing battle with another yawn.

Kendall stood. "You know what, I'm starving. Are you?"

Grae looked up in surprise. "I could eat."

"Then let me buy my newest volunteer some dinner. The Blue Moon diner is next door. They do a great meatloaf, and their coffee would wake a dead man."

"Dead man?"

Kendall stuffed files and a laptop into a big leather shoulder bag. "Sorry, bad choice of words, but it's been a long day for me, too." She inserted Grae's report and then zipped the bag closed. "Let's get out of here."

Grae followed Kendall while she turned off the office lights and locked the doors. They were quiet as they rode down in the elevator, until Grae flinched at a particularly egregious squeal.

Kendall chuckled. "Don't worry. We've had our offices here for three years, and the elevator hasn't broken down once. It only sounds scary."

"Glad to hear it."

"Believe it or not, this place is actually a step up from our first office."

"I guess there's not a lot of profit in this sort of work."

"None, to be precise, ergo the 'non-profit' designation. I'm the only full-time employee. Margie works part-time. We got started with a small provincial grant, and rely heavily on our annual fundraiser as well as donations. It's getting a little easier as word spreads about the work we do. I think we'd have gone under the first year without Peter's support. He's a genius at pulling the right strings at just the right time. I swear he knows everyone in this city."

They reached the ground level and left the building. Kendall steered them to the small diner next door that had seen better days.

A waitress behind the counter looked up and grinned. "Hey, girl. You want the hump day special?"

"Yes, please, Billie, but my friend here will need a menu. She's a first-timer."

"Comin' right up."

Kendall led the way to a booth in the corner.

Grae took off her jacket and slid onto the bench. "Seems like you come here often."

"Three or four times a week. It's a lot easier than figuring out what to make for dinner when I get home, and the prices are so reasonable I probably couldn't make it myself for much less."

Billie returned with a coffee pot and a menu for Grae. She filled their cups swiftly, without spilling a drop. "Back in a few."

She hurried off as two more customers entered.

Grae perused the menu. It was basic fare, but Kendall was right, even she and Marcus could afford these prices once a week. She shook her head. "Damn, I should've called Marcus."

Kendall looked up from dumping several packets of sugar in her cup. "Marcus?"

"My roommate. We started our days off today, and I think he was going to make supper."

"So call him. Tell him he's got the night off."

Grae glanced around the diner. There was no pay phone in sight. She chewed her lip. Maybe she'd just have coffee and then hurry home.

"Would you like to borrow my phone?"

Grae found herself being scrutinized by keen eyes. "Um, if you wouldn't mind."

Kendall pulled it out of her bag, swiped, and entered a password before handing the iPhone over.

Grae tapped in Marcus' number.

He answered after just one ring.

"So, whose phone are you using this time? And when are you going to get one of your own?"

Grae sighed. It was an old bone of contention between them. "You know I'll get one when I can afford one. And I'm borrowing Kendall's phone."

"Kendall? What's this? Are you on a date? And if you are, what the hell are you doing talking to me?"

"It's not a date, and I'm just calling to let you know that I won't be home for dinner."

"You're having dinner with her?"

"Yes."

"Dinner with Kendall. Is she buying? I'll bet she's buying. Sure sounds like a date to me. Does this mean I shouldn't wait up for you? No more Ms. Cranky-pants? Praise the Lord and pass the lube!"

"I'm hanging up now, Marcus."

He started to laugh. She ended the call and handed the phone back to Kendall. "Sorry about that. My roommate can be an idiot."

Kendall smiled and dropped the phone back in her bag. "I had a roommate like that once. Drove me crazy."

"Yeah? How'd you handle it?"

"I divorced him."

"Not an option for me, I'm afraid."

Billie returned with her order pad. "So what'll you have, Kendall's friend?"

Grae handed her menu back. "The meatloaf was recommended. I'll have that."

"You got it. Want a salad to go with?"

"No, thanks."

Billie tossed a few more sugar packets on the table and winked before she left. Grae glanced at the sugar container. It was still half-full.

Kendall smiled and took a sip. "That's Billie's subtle way of making a statement on how much sugar I put in the sludge she passes off as coffee. It's a never-ending gag, trust me."

"Sounds like Marcus and cellphones. I'll get one someday, but he's a kid. He doesn't really understand economics and consumerism. If he wants something, he wants it yesterday."

"You're not exactly a senior citizen, yourself. How old is he?"

"He's eighteen."

"How did the two of you end up as roommates?"

Grae stiffened at the casual question, but forced herself to relax. "His parents threw him out. We get along well and I had room, so I gave him a place to stay. We've been together for about three years."

Kendall frowned and set down her cup. "His parents threw him out? How young was he?"

"Way too young to be out on the streets."

Kendall stared at her for a long moment. "I'm sorry."

Grae shrugged. "Not a big deal. We're fine. He's got to make up for the grades he lost, but we've got that under control. We signed him up for an online GED course."

"He's not too old to re-enroll in school. Wouldn't that be easier?"

"School was as hellish as his home. No way will he go back. Besides, until I get a better job, we both have to work full-time." Grae cast about for a change of subject. "So, you were talking about Peter's support for AU. He seemed like a really nice guy when he met me at the hospital."

Kendall's penetrating gaze didn't waver. Grae was sure she was going to ask more about Marcus, but then her expression softened.

"Peter's wonderful. He thought highly of you, too. And as I mentioned earlier, so did Jude Herzog. I'll be honest, Grae. I fully expected you to leave long before the two hours were up."

"I did. It's in the report."

"But from what Jude told me, you went above and beyond what we ask of our volunteers. He told me what you did for him and his brother. He said you even showed up for the funeral. You know we don't expect that, right?"

Grae frowned. "It's not against the rules, is it?"

"Not at all, and you're not the first to do so. But because of who Ezra Herzog was, I thought you'd bail as quickly as possible."

"I almost did. But in the end, I'm glad I didn't."

"Why?"

Grae bought herself time by taking a sip of coffee. "Whoa. You weren't kidding about potent sludge."

Kendall pushed some sugar packets across the table. "And you're avoiding the question."

Grae tore open two packets, dumped the crystals in the cup, added several creamers, and slowly stirred the coffee. "If I am, it's only because I'm not sure of the answer. I didn't want to see him. I have a particular loathing for pedophiles, and I thought I'd have to fight my urge to punch his lights out."

"We really don't recommend that to our volunteers."

Grae smiled at Kendall's dry tone. "No, I didn't think you did, and I wouldn't have. But I would've left if I couldn't handle it."

"You know, I owe you an apology."

Grae looked up in surprise. "Why?"

"My mom can be...persuasive, and I was angry with her for foisting you on me. I was even angrier when I finally had time to do a cursory background check on you after I got home from the fundraiser. I'll be honest. If I'd known about your record, I'd have turned you down flat, even if Mom did disinvite me to Thanksgiving dinner."

"Jo wouldn't do that."

"No, of course she wouldn't. My point being, I had very low expectations of you, and the only reason I wasn't furious that I'd abandoned my usual protocol and sent you in without a background check, briefings, and training, was because of who Ezra Herzog was. Then you blindsided me by doing this brilliant job with an unbelievably difficult client, first time out."

"He really wasn't, you know?"

Kendall tilted her head. "I'm sorry?"

"Difficult. Dealing with Ezra really wasn't difficult at all. It was scary at first. But all I did was write a letter for him and give him a shave. No biggie."

"That's not what Jude Herzog said. In fact, he called me yesterday morning asking for your address. It's not unusual for us to get thank you cards, but they're always sent to the office and then I pass them on appropriately. I never give out our volunteers' addresses. But Mr. Herzog was very persuasive."

"What did he want my address for?"

"He wanted to give you a gift, and needed your address for it."

"Oh, the Wi-Fi. Of course. I was so excited about it that it never occurred to me to wonder how he knew where to send it."

"I was resistant. We discourage gifts, but he told me how much what you'd done meant to him. He told me very firmly that a used laptop and six months of Wi-Fi were the very least he could do to repay you. I knew you didn't have a computer, so I finally agreed. You definitely have a big fan."

"He's a good guy." Grae toyed with mentioning that Jude had offered her a job, but put it on the backburner.

"Back to what I was saying. I'd made up my mind that even if it upset Mom, I would politely thank you for your time and tell you that our volunteer quota was full."

"You have a volunteer quota?"

"No."

Grae's heart sank. "Okay, so I guess you don't need me. No problem." *Wonder if it's too late to cancel my dinner order.*

Kendall reached over and touched Grae's arm. "You're not hearing me. What you did, and how you did it, impressed me more than I can say. I'm embarrassed and disappointed with myself, not you."

Grae blinked. "Oh."

"I looked at your mug shot."

"Which one?" It was a fair question.

"Let's see, your hair was buzzed really short, and what there was appeared to be dyed neon pink. You wore a tank and had an amazing array of tattoos. You were also wearing so much metal through your flesh that you might well have been the Tin Man."

Grae tugged the sleeve of her sweatshirt lower. "Oh, I know the one you mean. Yeah, that was my punk period, just before I met Marcus."

"I judged you harshly and I was wrong, ergo the apology."

"I don't blame you."

Kendall studied her. "You don't, do you?"

"No, why should I? I developed the look to keep the world at bay. It worked. It wouldn't make any sense to bitch about it."

"What happened to all the metal?"

Grae ran a hand over her face, surprised that she didn't miss the studs and rings. "Marcus happened. I offended his sense of fashion, so he's been working on me to tone it down a little."

"His opinion means a lot to you."

"He means a lot to me."

Billie delivered their meals and topped up their cups. Their dinner conversation turned to lighter topics. Grae enjoyed hearing stories about Jo and Maddie, and even offered a few about Marcus.

They'd almost finished when Kendall's phone rang. She answered it and raised an eyebrow. "Just a moment." She handed the phone to Grae. "I think this is for you."

"Hello?"

"Hey, sweetie. I hate to interrupt, but if you're going home with the lovely-voiced lady who answered the phone—"

Grae turned away from Kendall and cupped her hand over the phone. "Marcus, stop it. I told you this wasn't a date."

"Uh-huh. Well, just in case Ms. Sultry changes your mind, you should know that your mom called and asked that you call her back as soon as you can."

"Did she say why?"

"Nope, and I didn't ask."

"All right. I'll call her when I get home."

"I'm not sure she can wait until the morning. She seemed very intent on speaking to you."

"Marcus, for God's sake—"

"Ta-ta, sweetie. And don't forget to practice safe sex. Aw, hell. Forget safe. Just practice sex…if you remember how."

The phone clicked in Grae's ear, and she gritted her teeth.

Kendall laughed. "I don't know what he said, but the blush compliments your hair."

Grae passed the phone back. "I think I'll go home now and kill my roommate. We'll just have the judge add another count to the pending charges."

Kendall's smile faded. "About that. I will give you an excellent report, but I'm hoping that this isn't a one-time deal. I would very much like to keep you in AU, if you're interested."

Grae thought about it for a moment. "Okay. I might be changing jobs, though, so I wouldn't necessarily be available in the day."

"That's all right. Our volunteers fit visits in on evenings and weekends, or whenever they can. I would like to give you the training you missed out on. I'm happy to conduct it at your convenience."

"I don't want to impose on your time off."

Kendall shook her head. "My hours aren't exactly routine. Call me when your job situation works out, and we'll figure out a good time for you to come in."

"Okay."

When they finished eating, they declined Billie's offer of dessert. She laid the cheque on the table, and Grae reached for it.

Kendall snatched it up. "My treat, remember?"

"You don't have to do that. I can pay for my own supper."

"I'm sure you can. But it was my invitation, so please unbend enough to let me do this."

Grae glared for an instant, then reminded herself that normal people did such things. Letting Kendall pay $12.99 for the blue plate special would only damage Grae's pride if she let it. "Okay, thanks. But I'll leave the tip."

Kendall shook her head. "No, I've got it. Besides, this was dinner with a new volunteer. I'm sure I can write it off on my taxes. Don't worry about it."

Kendall paid the bill, and they parted ways.

Grae was halfway home on the bus before she realized she'd forgotten to ask how to file her reports online now that she had a computer. *Oh well. I'll ask when I see her the next time.*

Chapter 12

Jo set a cup of hot chocolate next to Grae on the table, and took her usual seat. "So, I've been hearing good things about you."

Grae blinked. "You have?"

"Indeed. I don't want you to think Kendall generally reports to me, but she raved about how you handled your first assignment."

Warmth spread through Grae's body. "I just winged it."

"Employing your super power, were you?"

It took a moment for Grae to catch the reference, then she grinned. "I did kind of fly, didn't I? And guess what?"

"What?"

"I got a job offer out of it."

"Did you? How did that happen?"

Grae related the events which had led to Jude's offer. "I don't know if I'll take him up on it, but I sure appreciate it."

"Why do you have doubts about accepting his offer? Doesn't it offer greater possibilities than what you're doing now?"

"Of course. Picking trash on a chain gang would offer greater job advancement than what I'm doing now."

"So why the hesitation?"

Grae chewed her lip. "Marcus, I guess. Ever since we met and started living together, we've worked in the same place. This would be the first time we worked apart."

"And this bothers you, why?"

"Who'll protect him?"

Jo tilted her head. "Do you think he needs protection?"

"Yes."

"Why?"

"You've never met him. He's...well, he looks exactly like what he is."

"Gay."

"Yes, and not one of those gay guys who spends a lot of time working out. Marcus is skinny and shy around strangers, and—he's just been hurt so much, you know? I can't bear the thought of him being hurt again."

"You know you can't protect him from life. What does he say about your job offer?"

"He thinks I should take it. He says I have to make more money so I can support him in the style to which he'd like to become accustomed. He's joking."

Jo smiled. "I thought as much. But I suspect he meant what he said. He truly thinks that you should accept the offer."

"I want to, but—"

"But you're afraid."

Grae shivered and nodded.

"Let's explore that for a moment. You're afraid for Marcus' safety?"

"Yes."

"What else?"

Grae shook her head. "That's all. I just worry that some asshole might get on his case at work. It wouldn't be the first time. Hell, that's the reason I'm in this legal mess."

"I understand, but I want you to look a little deeper. Taking this job offer, learning a trade under the guidance of someone who appears to have taken an interest in you—"

Grae's head snapped up. "Not like that."

"I wasn't implying that in the least. From what you told me, he seems to be a very kind man, who is grateful for what you did for him and his brother. I certainly didn't mean to convey any covert sexual motive behind his offer. Can you tell me why you leapt to that assumption?"

"It was stupid."

"Nothing is stupid in this room."

Grae said nothing.

"All right. We'll set that aside for now and return to the issue of why you're hesitating. If you accept this offer and begin making a decent wage, that would be a good thing, wouldn't it?"

"Absolutely. I could buy Marcus a smartphone and use his old one myself. He'd be thrilled with that."

"Interesting."

"What is?"

Jo stopped Maddie from poking her nose in the hot chocolate. "Your first thought is how this opportunity will be of benefit to Marcus. What about you? How will it change your life?"

"It won't really. I mean, we'd have greater security. I might even earn enough that he could quit the dead-end job and just work at getting his GED."

"Again, that's how it would affect Marcus."

Grae shook her head. "I don't know what you're getting at."

"All right. Let me come at it from a different angle. Something Kendall told me last night stuck with me. She mentioned you said that you developed your 'look' to keep the world at bay. She referred to it in the context of never judging a book by its cover, but those are your words and they're important."

Grae wondered whether she was being particularly obtuse today. "Okay. Why?"

"They're amazingly insightful."

"I guess."

"So when did you develop that look? When did you get your first tattoos and piercings?"

"After—" Grae stopped herself, appalled at what she'd been about to reveal. "Um, after I dropped out of university."

Jo studied her.

Grae's heart thudded in her chest, and her gaze flicked frantically around the room before coming to rest on the front door. *Isn't our session up yet?*

Jo rose and set Maddie on the floor. "If you'll excuse me, I think that second hot chocolate went right through me. I'll be back in a minute."

When Jo vanished down the hall, Grae bolted from her chair. Escape from Jo's questions was only a few steps away. She took those steps, was almost to the door, and froze. Her hands trembled, and she thrust them in her jean pockets. Taking several deep breaths, she made herself turn around.

She walked to the window and stood staring out at Jo's front yard. Fallen leaves filled clear jack-o-lantern bags, which lined the cobblestone walkway. Only a few strays sullied the lawn. It was so like Jo—a perfect blend of tidy and whimsical, just like her living room. The thought and the view calmed her, and when Jo returned, Grae was back in her chair, petting Maddie.

Jo took her seat and jotted something in the ever-present notebook. "All right. We were talking about you and the job offer. Have you made a final decision either way?"

Grae shook her head. "No, but I need to soon. I'm giving myself the long weekend to think about it. Oh, which reminds me, did I tell you Mom called me last night?"

"No, you didn't."

"She invited Marcus and me to Thanksgiving dinner."

"That was nice. Are you going?"

"No. I mean I was nice about it and all, but I said maybe another time."

Jo cocked her head. "Why don't you want to go?"

"Marcus has a mini-feast planned with Cornish game hens and wild rice, and who knows what else. This is the first time we can afford anything like that, and I don't want to get in the way of his fun."

"Is that the only reason?"

Grae grimaced. "Well, the whole family will be there, including Ciara. It'll ruin dinner for everyone if she and I get into a screaming match. Again."

"Can you not simply resolve not to do that?"

"I can, but she can't."

"Have you asked her?"

"I haven't talked to her since the night we first saw the apartment."

"Mmm. Do you think your mother was disappointed?"

Grae hung her head and scuffed her heel on the braided rug beneath their chairs. "I suppose. Yeah, okay, she was."

"How did you feel about that?"

"Crappy. She's been decent to us, you know. But I just…I couldn't face Ciara."

"Why?"

"Things are going really good for me right now. The apartment is sweet; Marcus loves having his own room; I might have a decent job. Virgil called me a couple of nights ago, and he's optimistic about the outcome of my case because of the people who've agreed to testify on my behalf. I don't want it all to fall apart just because my sister hates me."

"Do you really—"

Grae held up her hand. "Sorry, but I've got to tell you this before I forget."

"That's okay, go right ahead."

"It kind of ties into me and Ciara butting heads. When I went to talk to Jude, to take him Ezra's letter, he wasn't happy with me. I don't mean that he yelled at me, but he's big and intimidating, and he was not thrilled about what I was doing."

"I see."

"But I didn't get angry in return. Two months ago, I'd probably have told him he was an ungrateful SOB and I didn't know why I wasted my time."

"Very good. And why do you think you responded in such a low-key manner?"

"I don't know. Maybe you're having more of an effect on me than I thought."

Jo laughed aloud. "Now there's a glowing compliment I'll cherish."

Grae grinned. "I'm just teasing. But really, I don't know why. Maybe because it seems as if my life has turned around. Things are going so well, I'm almost holding my breath day to day, waiting for the other shoe to drop. I mean, hell, we even have a computer now. Not that long ago, I couldn't have dreamed of affording one, not even a used one."

Jo sobered. "Let me ask you something. To when do you date these life improvements?"

Grae considered that. "I guess when Rick and Dylan tried to kill me."

"Follow that chain of thought."

Grae frowned. *What's she getting at?* "Oh, you mean Mom coming back into my life. If I hadn't ended up in front of her bench, Marcus and I would still be living in that hellhole, eating popcorn for supper three nights a week, and battling the roaches and silverfish."

"Close. You allowing your mother back into your life was the crucial point."

"I almost didn't. I tried to turn her away. She's freaking stubborn."

Jo smiled.

"Yeah, yeah, I know. Acorn, tree. I got it." Grae considered this insight. Her mother had started the ball rolling. And now she wanted Grae at a family dinner. Was that asking so much?

"Is it?"

Grae blinked. "Sorry?"

"Is it asking too much?"

Grae wasn't sure if she'd spoken aloud, or if Jo had picked the thought out of her head. The odds were fifty-fifty. "I don't know. I can't bear the thought of fighting with Ciara. It's just bad ju-ju, you know? But I also don't like the thought of disappointing Mom when she's been so good to us."

"What if—and this is just a suggestion. What if you invited your mom out for coffee, or even a meal? I suspect she just wants to reconnect with you, and a family dinner offered the opportunity."

"You think?"

"Yes."

"Huh. Yeah, I guess I could do that."

Jo checked her watch. "It looks like our time is nearly up. I want to leave you with one thought, and we'll talk about it next week. Your love for, and guardianship of Marcus is laudable, but are you hiding behind those responsibilities?"

"Hiding? What do you mean?"

"You've been offered an opportunity that could very well lead to a drastic improvement in your quality of life. Marcus has said clearly that he wants you to take advantage of it, yet you hesitate. Is it possible that you do so because you're more afraid of returning to a normal life, however you define normal, than you are of going on as you have since you dropped out of university?"

The urge to flee swept over Grae again, but this time she didn't attempt to suppress it. She lunged to her feet. "I should really get going. I'll see you at the same time next week."

She ran out the door before Jo even had time to stand.

Marcus slapped at Grae's hand. "Will you stop fussing? You look just fine. And it's not like you're meeting your mom on her turf anyway. You don't have to worry about looking out of place."

Grae gave up trying to get her collar to lay flat. If she'd had an iron, it would look as sharp as a military shirt, but water and a blow dryer could only do so much. "But what if Mom feels out of place? Unless her habits have changed radically, she doesn't patronize run-down family restaurants."

Marcus rested his hands on Grae's shoulders. "Chill. You invited her out, and this is what you can afford. She wants your company, not a fine meal."

"Who are you, and what have you done with my best friend?"

Marcus laughed, dropped a kiss on her hair, and stepped back.

Grae turned away from the mirror and posed with her arms wide. "Presentable?"

"Well, duh. That's what I've been trying to tell you for the last half hour. You've got a few minutes before you leave, right?"

Grae glanced at her watch. "Sure. Why?"

"Can I talk to you about something?"

"Okay." Grae followed Marcus into the living room. His demeanour was surprisingly serious as he took a seat on the couch. She sat beside him and waited.

"I don't know if you're going to like this…"

"It's okay, bud. Spit it out."

Marcus peered at her from behind too-long bangs. "I know we need the money, but I was wondering if you'd be okay with me quitting my job."

Grae exhaled slowly. That would make it tough, even with the rent taken care of, but if they were careful—

"I have a lead on another job."

"You do? Well, why didn't you say so? What is it?"

"You're not going to like it."

"Why?"

"Because Domokos offered it to me."

Grae exploded off the couch. "No fucking way!"

Marcus shrank back into the corner. "It's not what you think, Grae. Really, it's not. I ran into him last week. He's remarried. They're having another kid. He felt sorry for me, and he offered me a busboy's gig in one of his restaurants. Plus, I'll have a chance to work my way up. There's good money waiting tables in high-end places like his."

"And what about going to school, getting your GED, and even going on to culinary school? What about your plans?"

"Your plans, Grae. I don't like school. I just want to work."

"Jesus, you can't get ahead without at least a high school diploma. Hell, these days, that's barely enough."

"I know, but that's why this offer is perfect. Domokos doesn't care if I didn't finish school. All he cares about—"

"All he cares about is keeping you on the side, just like he used to."

Marcus stood. "Do you really think I'd let that happen?"

"You mean 'again'?"

"I don't need your permission, you know. I'm an adult."

Grae stared at him. His eyes were bright with tears and his face was flushed. She spun on her heel and stormed out. What the hell was he thinking? Domokos had been the regular she'd thrown stones at the first night she'd met Marcus in the alley behind the Copper Monkey. She'd fought too damned hard to get him out of that life to let him go back. She'd kill Domokos before she'd let that happen.

Standing in front of the elevator, she slammed her fist against the button, then decided it was taking too long. She took the stairs down to the ground floor two at a time. Too riled to wait for the bus, she started walking, but covered the ground so fast she was almost running. By the time she arrived at the restaurant, she was sweating and breathing hard.

Her mother waited in front of the door.

Grae shook her head. Of course she was already there. "Sorry I'm late."

Thea studied her. "I'd have been glad to pick you up, you know."

"No, I'm good. I can always use the exercise."

Thea raised an elegant eyebrow. "There isn't a spare ounce on you, dear."

Grae tried to smile. "One of the side benefits of not owning a car." She pushed the door open and gestured for her mother to enter first.

The small, family-owned restaurant had seen better days, but it was a step up from the diner Kendall had introduced her to.

They were shown to a table and given menus.

Thea set hers aside, unread. "Is everything all right?"

Grae didn't look up from her menu. "Sure."

Her mother was silent.

Grae sighed and set her menu down. "I'm pissed off at Marcus. He's making a bad decision, and there's nothing I can do about it."

Thea regarded her with a small smile. "I sympathize. Would you like to talk about it?"

"No. Yes. I don't know. I had a job offer that I'm probably going to take. Maybe that's why he wants a new job, too."

"I want to hear all about your job offer, but isn't it a good thing for both of you?"

"Normally I'd say yes, but…" Grae debated how much to tell her mother, the judge. Then the glimmer of an idea hit her, and she sat up straighter. "But hey, let's not let it ruin dinner, right? We've got lots to catch up. And Mom, I'm really sorry about Thanksgiving dinner. Maybe by Christmas things will be better, and we can come over."

"I'd like that, very much. I'm glad you suggested tonight as an alternative."

"So am I."

Dinner was unexpectedly pleasant. Thea listened attentively as Grae related her experience with AU. She grimaced when Grae mentioned Ezra's name, but nodded approvingly at Jude's offer.

"Are you going to call him, dear?"

"I am. In fact I'm going to do that tomorrow, and as long as Jude's offer is for real, I'll put my notice in at work."

"I'm sure it will be. From what you've told me, he sounds like a good man."

"Yeah, that's how he struck me, too. Guess I'll find out soon enough."

When they finished eating and the cheque arrived, Grae grabbed it. Thea shook her head. "Let me get that."

"No, it was my invitation, Mom. I know it's not Magellan's, but I enjoyed seeing you."

Thea beamed. "I enjoyed it, too. You know I was just in Magellan's last week, and their food is as good as ever."

"Yeah? Man, I still remember the way their steaks melted in my mouth. I dream about those sometimes."

"Then let me take you and Marcus there soon."

"I'd really like that, but can we keep it to just you and me?"

"Of course, but I thought…well, I thought you'd want to bring Marcus along."

"We might actually see him there. He's hoping to get on as a busboy with the Magellan chain."

"Was this the job you didn't want him to take?"

"I'm sure the job will be fine. I just wanted him to finish his GED first. I don't want to see him stuck in minimum wage hell all his life."

"That's commendable, dear. I'm so proud of you for looking out for him."

Grae dropped some bills on the table and followed Thea as she left the restaurant.

Damn right I'm going to look out for him…whether he likes it or not.

Chapter 13

THEA STOPPED HER CAR IN front of Grae's apartment. "Thank you again for inviting me to dinner. I enjoyed myself."

"So did I, Mom. I look forward to doing it again soon."

"Wonderful. I'll check my schedule and call you tomorrow." Thea started to add something, then stopped.

Grae cocked her head. Her mother rarely had trouble speaking her mind. "What?"

"Would you mind if I invite your father to join us at Magellan's?"

Grae sighed. "I don't think he'd want to. Why don't we leave it for a bit, let him get used to the idea that his youngest isn't a complete loser before we all start socializing again."

"He doesn't think that, dear."

"Yeah, he does, but he has a right to. Let's just take baby steps, okay? I figure by my next birthday, we should all be able to sit in a room together without wanting to haul out the machetes."

Thea chuckled, but it wasn't a cheerful sound. "Even Ciara?"

"I don't know. You'll have to ask her that." Grae leaned over and kissed her mother's cheek. "Thanks for the ride. I'll see you soon."

"I look forward to it."

Upstairs, Grae paused before she unlocked the apartment door. She and Marcus rarely fought, and she hated it, but Grae loathed the idea of Domokos making Marcus his rent boy again. Taking a deep breath, she went inside. Marcus stood in the foyer, his thin arms wrapped around himself.

They both spoke at once. "I'm sorry."

When Marcus started to say something else, Grae held up her hand. "You're right. You're an adult. But it drives me crazy to think of Domokos getting his hooks into you again."

"That's not going to happen, I swear. First hint that he's even thinking that way and I'm out of there, I promise. You have to trust me, Grae. You have to believe in me. You're the only one who ever has. I can't do this without your support."

Grae's throat tightened at the fear in his eyes. *When will I learn?* She opened her arms, and he stepped into them. "I'm sorry. I'm a goddamned asshole, and my only defence is that it's just because I love you so much."

"I love you, too. And yes, you're an ass."

Grae chuckled through her tears.

Marcus tightened his grasp, resting his cheek on the top of her head. "Are we okay?"

"We're absolutely okay."

"Thank God!" He pulled back and dried his eyes on his sleeve. "I'm just not cut out to be a drama queen."

Grae laughed. "Yeah, right, RuPaul." She hooked her arm through his and led him to the living room. "I do want to talk to you, though."

He stiffened. "About what?"

They each took their traditional spots on the couch.

"I know you think you don't need your GED, and I get that you want to work. But will you at least consider spending some of your off hours on the courses? I'm happy to help you all I can, you know that. And I promise I won't bug you about going on with culinary school or anything else, as long as you at least get your high school certificate. It gives you options, buddy, options that aren't open to you right now."

Marcus sighed. "Okay. But I hated school."

"You hated what was done to you at school. This isn't like that. No one's going to bully you in the bathroom. No one's going to punch you in the hallways and dump food on your head in the lunchroom. This is just you and the computer, and me, if you should need some help. You're smarter than they ever gave you credit for, bud. I want you to show that to the world."

He blinked at her. "You think I'm smart?"

"Hell, yeah, I do. Who survived on the street when he was barely fourteen? Who kept himself sane and together, even when the whole world was throwing shit at him? Who had the good sense to share some primo weed with the weird metal-face who ran off his best customer?"

"And who can set up any electronics without even looking at the directions?"

"Exactly. You don't have the formal education yet, bud, but you have the street smarts and the brains to get that diploma and make more of yourself than your parents and teachers and classmates ever thought you'd be. I know you can. I just need you to know that, too."

A slow smile brightened his face. "You sure give a helluva pep talk, metal-face."

"Maybe I should've joined the Army, eh?"

Marcus laughed. "With that hair?"

"I've actually been thinking of losing the colours."

Marcus sat bolt upright. "What? You're serious?"

"Thinking about it. I haven't decided for sure."

"Wow, I can't imagine you without the rainbow. I don't even know what colour hair you were born with."

"Kind of mousy brown."

He shook his head. "That won't do. If you're going to go with just one colour, we're going to choose something glamorous. We'll pick up some dye when we get off work. It'll be a good way to celebrate your last day in that dead-end job, and maybe mine, too. We're starting new, you and me together. Maybe I should get a haircut too."

"Whoa, I didn't say I was committing to it. I'm just thinking about it. Besides, I don't do glamorous. You know that."

Marcus jumped to his feet. "I think you should go bold, either a Marilyn Monroe blonde, or an Elizabeth Taylor dark brown. With your dark eyes, you could go either way and it would look spectacular."

Grae grinned as she watched Marcus pace back and forth, expounding on the merits of each possibility. *We're good.*

The following Tuesday, Grae stood at the foot of the driveway leading to Stone Garden Monuments, and mentally ran over her checklist. Hair,

Elizabeth Taylor brown. Check. All metal except for single earrings gone. Check. Clothes Jude hadn't already seen. Check.

She'd asked her mother if any of her old clothes were still stored at her parents' house. They weren't, but Thea had immediately insisted on taking her shopping. Grae had allowed it, but only on the condition that she pay her mother back. But when Thea had told her to consider the spree as gifts for all the birthdays and Christmases she'd missed, Grae hadn't missed the subtle quaver in her mother's voice. She'd accepted with good grace.

Now Grae had enough serviceable clothing in her wardrobe that she could go almost anywhere with confidence that her appearance would be appropriate. She'd even sprung for a cheap iron, though she wasn't going as far as investing in an ironing board until she felt secure in this job. In the meantime, a towel spread on the countertop worked just fine.

Grae took a deep breath. The only job she'd fought for since she'd dropped out of university was the one on the construction crew, and look where that had gotten her. She was accustomed to applying for work in which employees were interchangeable and their employment short-lived. But she wanted this job as she'd never wanted any of them.

She glanced at her watch. Jude had said she should be there at 9:00 a.m., and it was 8:55. *Time to get moving.*

As she approached the building, Jude opened the front door.

"Good morning, Grae."

"Good morning."

"Come in. We'll talk in my office."

Grae nodded and followed him inside. Ashley, in her customary spot at the reception desk, gave her an encouraging smile.

In contrast to the well-appointed foyer and private room for the bereaved, Jude's office was barebones. Aside from a large photo of a grouping Grae assumed was his family, there were no other personal touches. It was clean and functional, and she doubted that he spent much time in it. The only thing that distinguished it was the overly large desk chair that creaked alarmingly when he sat.

Grae took the chair across from him and waited.

Jude pushed some papers across to her. "So to start with, fill these out and give them to Ashley."

A man stopped at Jude's door. "Hey, Pop. Are you handling the Tyndall order, or is Rolly running point?"

"Give it to Rolly or Tyson. I'm going to be tied up for the day. Oh, and Luc, I want you to meet our new employee. Grae Jordan, meet my son-in-law and the head honcho around here, Luc Grenier."

Luc laughed and crossed the office to offer his hand to a stunned Grae. "Don't believe him for one minute. I'm strictly the numbers and admin guy. This whole place would go under it if wasn't for Jude."

Grae stood and shook Luc's hand. "Very nice to meet you."

Luc turned to Jude. "Are you still going to do the Friedman marker?"

Jude nodded. "I thought it would be a good way for Grae to get her feet wet. She's going to shadow me for the next little while."

"Good. You're in excellent hands, Grae. Jude trained all our guys, and there's no one better. He'll have you working stone like butter before you know it."

Luc left the office, and still shocked, Grae turned to Jude. "I'm hired?"

"Yes."

"But...but no interview or anything?"

"What would I ask you?"

"I don't know. What I can offer the company, maybe? Or what kind of wage I'd expect?"

"You can offer me integrity. I can teach you everything else. As to wages, I pay minimum plus five to start, with regular raises depending on how quickly you learn. Time and a half when we have to do weekend jobs. You good with that?"

Grae's mouth dropped open, then snapped shut. "Yes, sir. I am."

"Good. Fill out the employee paperwork so Ashley can put you on the books, and then we'll get started. Meet me in the back when you're done, and I'll show you around the shop floor. Then you'll come out with me. I won't let you do anything but watch for now, but in a couple of days, you'll get to try your hand at it and see if you like the work. If you do, great. If you don't, that's fine too. It doesn't suit everyone, but I have a good feeling about you."

"Thank you. Just...thank you."

Jude smiled. "You're welcome. I'll see you in a few minutes. Ashley will direct you." He left the office.

A new job with a living wage! "Goddamn." Grae pinched herself and flinched. No, she wasn't dreaming. She hastened to fill out the forms and get them to Ashley, who in turn pointed her to a door marked "Shop. Employees only, unless accompanied."

Grae grinned. She could hardly wait to call Marcus.

※

"So, what do you think so far?" Jude asked as they climbed in his truck, which now had a portable air compressor connected to the rear.

"It's amazing, also sort of overwhelming." Grae's mind was awhirl with all Jude had shown her in a quick overview of the shop. Stacks of granite slabs and foundations; machines to engrave, carve, saw, and polish; the Sand Handler, which took up half a room with its large sand blasting compartment and sand recovery system; and monuments that ranged from modest to magnificent—it was almost more than she could absorb.

"Don't worry about it. Each thing I showed you will become familiar as you start to use it. And you won't be working with anything unsupervised until I'm satisfied you know what you're doing."

"That's a relief."

Jude chuckled, then sobered. "So, I told you we were going to do the Friedman marker this morning."

"Yes."

He glanced at her. "We're also going to install Ezra's foundation and marker, but I don't want anyone else to know about that."

Grae nodded, warmed that he trusted her with something so personal and painful. "I won't say anything."

"I knew that, or I wouldn't have brought you in."

"Do markers normally get placed this fast? It took months for my dad to decide on Grandpa's headstone."

Jude shook his head. "No. Though sometimes the deceased has previously made their own arrangements. It's not that uncommon for older people who are well aware that their lives are drawing to an end. But more often, and particularly if it's a sudden death or that of a young person, it can take months before a family decides on the monument they want. It's also a cultural thing. For example, funeral rites in my community are very specific."

"Your community?"

"The Jewish community. I'm about as lapsed as you can get, but even I'll conform with our traditions when my time comes—no cremation, and the unveiling is when the marker is placed within the first year after death. It's almost like a second funeral rite, but without the rabbi."

"So Ezra—?" The words were out of her mouth before Grae could stop them. She winced at her insensitivity. "I'm sorry."

"'S okay. It's like my brother said, though—in his case, security and anonymity are more important than communal ritual." Jude glanced at Grae. "Did you Google him?"

"No, I haven't. I didn't even tell Marcus your last name so he couldn't look him up either."

"Thank you. You must've been curious, though."

"Yes and no. I guess I felt like… I don't know. You were straight with me, and you offered me a way out of minimum wage hell. I felt like it'd be dishonourable to go against your wishes, even though you have no way of knowing whether or not I'm telling you the truth."

"I know you are."

"Oh. I'm glad." His quiet certainty warmed Grae's heart. *I think I'm going to like this job.*

When they got to the cemetery, Jude drove past a section of flat markers and pulled up alongside an area of upright monuments. The Friedman monument was close to the road, but Jude walked past it and stopped in front of an elegant monument with the name "Frayne" emblazoned near the top, and "Howard" and "Ruth" below that.

While Grae kept a respectful distance, Jude took off his hat. His lips moved silently for a few moments, then he took a small stone out of his pocket and set it on top of the monument. He turned around, and Grae joined him at the Friedman monument. She'd already seen the stencil he'd prepared before leaving the shop. Ann Friedman had outlived her husband, Norman, by a decade.

Jude glued the stencil onto the monument, checking to ensure it was precisely placed. "Remember what I was saying about cultural norms?"

"Uh-huh."

"What strikes you about this monument as compared to that one?" He pointed to one on the other side of the road that featured a cross.

Grae hurried over to look, and then came back to compare. "The wife's name and birthdate on that one are already in place. It just needs the date of death. But this one only has the husband's name."

"Exactly. Good eyes. That's because Christians don't mind if both spouses are listed on a marker even if one is still alive. We do. You never put the living spouse on a marker. Ever. I've had Jewish clients shudder when they see our display of sample markers done up with living spouses."

"Oh. I didn't realize that. There sure is a lot to know about this job."

"Yup. You have to know the regulations of a particular cemetery, too. Some permit both uprights and flat markers, but only in specified areas. Some are more flexible. You have to steer the client so they don't select something that can't be installed."

Jude finished peeling the letters out of the stencil, then put on goggles and ear protection. "Best stand back. This is the messy, noisy part."

Grae stepped back a few feet as Jude started the air compressor and began to sandblast the letters into the granite.

When he was done, she stepped forward and ran her hand over the new letters. "Amazing. It looks a little newer, but it's perfect."

Jude gathered up his equipment. "The letters will weather. By next summer, you won't be able to tell the difference. And you'll still be able to read them hundreds of years from now. The art of engraving has come a long way since hammer-and-chisel days. Plus, granite lasts a lot longer than marble. Marble tends to sugar over the years and makes lettering a lot more difficult to read."

Grae helped Jude tidy the area and store his gear, and then they drove to the isolated corner where Ezra was buried. She was relieved to see nothing out of place, not that she had really expected it to be. She helped dig the hole for the foundation, and assisted Jude in settling it into place. He put a thick bead of adhesive around the edge, then carefully lowered the flat marker onto the base.

When Jude was done, he rose to his feet and stared at the marker. "The Kaddish will never be said for you, Ezra, but I've done my best to bury you with dignity. Goodbye, brother."

Jude turned on his heel and walked to his truck without a backwards glance. Grae followed him. They were quiet as they drove out of the cemetery.

Jude cleared his throat. "So, what do you think of your first morning on the job?"

"I think I'm going to love working for you."

A smile lightened Jude's somber expression. "I'm glad."

"Can I ask you something?"

"You can ask anything. It's the best way to learn."

"You left a stone on the Frayne monument, and I saw stones on other monuments, too. What was that all about?"

"Ah, that was just me signalling I'd been by to see my grandparents. Whenever I'm working near my parents, grandparents, or aunts and uncles, I do that."

"Will you do it for Ezra?"

Jude shook his head. "No."

"Oh. I'm sorry."

"No need to be. I don't mind your questions. You're the only one who knows about Ezra's final resting place, aside from me. It's kind of ironic."

"What is?"

"I once thought about taking my maternal grandparents' surname for my own. I even talked to Elaine. I asked her how she'd feel about being Mrs. Frayne instead of Mrs. Herzog."

"Because of Ezra?"

"Yes. We were changing the name of the business anyway. I figured we might want to make a complete change to protect the girls."

"I take it Elaine didn't agree?"

"Nope. She said she'd married Jude Elijah Herzog and she was proud to call me husband, no matter what her brother-in-law had done. Mind you, when the girls married, she certainly didn't urge them to retain their maiden names, but I give her credit for her courage. She always had more of that than I did. When the reporters came to our door, I'd hide in the basement, but she'd literally shoo them away with her broom." Jude laughed, then sobered. "It means stranger, you know."

"Sorry?"

"My maternal grandparents' name. I always thought that was so appropriate for them since they came to Canada as immigrants not knowing another soul. And then after Ezra's first arrest, it seemed appropriate for my family, too. He destroyed the familiar, the comfortable, the name my paternal grandfather built his business under. I was a stranger to my own world."

"Are you glad you kept it—the name, I mean?"

"Most of the time. Those who know me don't hold Ezra's crimes against me. There have been some ignorant people along the way, but their opinion didn't mean jack-shit to me. I think I built up calluses, you know? With each of his arrests, it got easier to distance myself from him and what he'd done. He became a stranger who just happened to share the same last name."

"I understand."

Jude nodded. "I believe you do. So, are you hungry? Why don't we stop for lunch before heading back to the shop?"

"Sounds good."

Chapter 14

THREE WEEKS LATER, GRAE WAITED in front of Magellan's flagship restaurant downtown. She had dressed with more care than she had done in almost a decade. Grae wanted to be seen and acknowledged as the judge's daughter.

When Thea emerged from her car, they greeted each other with a hug.

"You look wonderful, dear. Just wonderful."

Grae grinned. "You don't miss the rainbow?"

Thea stroked Grae's hair. "It was unique, but this looks more like you."

"You can thank Marcus for that. He chose the colour. Though if I hadn't put my foot down, I'd be a brassy blonde right now."

Thea laughed as the valet took her keys and the doorman opened the door. "I can thank Marcus for many things, but I can't even imagine you as a blonde."

"Me neither, ergo the putting down of the foot."

The maître d' stepped forward. "Your table is ready, Judge."

"Thank you, William. And how are you this evening?"

He led them to their table. "Very well, madam. And may I say it's a pleasure to see you again. Will Mr. Boyd be joining us?"

Thea took the seat William held out for her. "Not tonight, I'm afraid. He has a business meeting."

As Grae waited for William to seat her, she was pleased to see the small approving nod from her mother. William snapped thick linen napkins across their laps, settled leather-bound menus in their hands, and departed.

"So Dad's in a business meeting, is he?"

"If you consider going to the Flames game as business, then yes."

They shared a smile.

"Some things never change."

"True. Your father will be a diehard fan until they carry him from the Saddledome, feet first."

"I think it was the heartbreak of his life that Virgil showed absolutely no aptitude for hockey."

Thea sobered. "No, dear. Whether you believe it or not, the heartbreak of his life was losing you."

Grae reached across the table and rested her hand on Thea's arm. "I'm sorry, Mom. I really am. For the longest time, all I could think about was myself. I was so consumed with my own pain that I was incapable of recognizing anyone else's."

"Do you think you'll ever be able to tell me what happened?"

Grae's hand flexed convulsively, and Thea winced.

Grae pulled her hand back. "Sorry."

Thea rubbed her arm. "Goodness, your new job has given you a grip like a stonemason."

Grae was grateful for her mother's sensitivity in changing the subject. "Well, it's not like I'm physically responsible for lifting monuments or anything. We have equipment to do the heavy stuff."

Their waiter approached, and conversation was put on hold. While Thea ordered, Grae surveyed the restaurant. Her breath caught as she spied Domokos schmoozing with some of the customers. It was a full house, but it would only be a matter of time until he worked his way over to the judge. She slowed her breathing and reviewed her plan. All she needed was an opportunity.

Their waiter departed as the sommelier arrived. Grae left the selection of the evening's wine to her mother.

"So, dear, you mentioned that Marcus might be working as a busboy here. Did he get the job?"

"He's working for Magellan's, but in their south side restaurant. Apparently even busboys have to earn the right to work in this one."

"Is he enjoying it?"

"He is. He said he's working even harder than when—uh, working harder than ever before. But he's happy that even busboys get a percentage of the tips, so it's worth it."

"I'm pleased to hear that."

"Oh, and he's made some new friends. I think he has his eye on one in particular."

"Does he now? How do you feel about that?"

Grae raised an eyebrow. "I'm not his mother. He can see anyone he chooses."

Thea smiled. "You may not be his biological parent, dear, but I know he looks up to you and craves your approval."

"I guess. I haven't actually met this Frederico guy yet, but the way Marcus raves about him, he must walk on water. I don't know if I should be worried or ecstatic."

"Why would you worry? Do you think this new friend is a bad influence?"

Grae shook her head. "Just the opposite, actually. Marcus was dragging his heels about his online schooling, but since Frederico came into his life, he's gotten his ass in gear and is actually studying."

"That's wonderful…isn't it? What's putting that furrow in your forehead?"

"Marcus is—he has a complicated history with guys, Mom. He had to do whatever he could to survive on the streets, and it left him scarred. I'd like nothing better than for him to have a healthy relationship with Frederico or anyone else, but it scares me too. What if Frederico just ends up using him?"

"There's always that risk, but we have to let our children make choices for themselves, even if we doubt the wisdom of those choices."

Grae smiled. "Why do I get the feeling we're not talking about Marcus anymore?"

Thea took a sip of her wine. "I'm sure I have no idea to what you're referring."

"Uh-huh. Sure you don't, Judge. So other than the single stupidest decision of my life to drop out my old life—school, family, and all—did I make other choices of which you disapproved?"

"Well, it would've been nice if you'd brought the same girl around to the house more than once."

Grae grimaced. She couldn't refute her mother's gentle indictment, and chose silence as the better part of discretion.

Thea patted Grae's hand. "Let me make myself clear. I'm not criticizing you, dear. We all do things in our youth that make us shake our heads when we get older. Your father and I were never unclear as to why you preferred living in residence on campus to living in your own bedroom. But I always hoped that you would find someone special during those rather…hectic years."

Grae pushed the memories back into their storage place and forced a smile. "No one special, I'm afraid. I'm not sure that's in the cards for me."

"You're a little young to give up on love just yet."

"Ciara and Virgil were both long married by the time they were my age."

"You're not your siblings, dear, nor would I expect you to be. But like any mother, I hope that love will find you one day."

Grae was saved from answering by the waiter's return with their dinners. Despite her real purpose for the evening, she couldn't help a small moan at the first bite of filet mignon. "Oh my God, I'd forgotten how good this is."

Thea laughed as she deftly opened her lobster tail. "I think I could eat here every night and never grow tired of it."

"Now that's what we like to hear from our patrons." Domokos' voice boomed from behind Grae, and she froze. "How are you this evening, Judge?"

"Well, thank you. And you, Domokos?"

"Very well, very well, indeed. It is such a pleasure to see you again." Domokos bent over Thea's hand.

Grae lost her appetite.

Thea gestured to Grae with her free hand. "Do you remember my youngest daughter, Grae?"

Domokos turned to Grae with a big smile. "Goodness, is this your little one? I haven't seen her since her feet would barely reach the floor. What a pleasure to see you again, Ms. Matheny-Boyd."

Thea opened her mouth, but Grae cut her off. "And to you, Domokos. Your food is exquisite, as always."

Domokos simpered. "Thank you, my dear. You are too kind. Well, I will leave you ladies to your dinner. Enjoy." He inclined his head and went to the next table.

Before her mother could ask why Grae had forestalled the use of her new last name, she said, "Hey, Mom, did I tell you about this new tombstone one of Jude's more eccentric clients commissioned?"

"I don't think so."

Grae grinned. "Dad would love this one. It's for a young fellow who played major junior hockey in Quebec. He was expected to go high in the draft, but he was killed in a car accident last summer. His family had Jude design the coolest monument. It's the guy's hockey locker, with his skates, stick, jersey, and helmet. And in one corner, there's a scroll with his hockey stats. Jude's doing all the design work, but he's going to let me help with the actual manufacture. It's going to be awesome."

"Oh, for heaven's sake, don't tell your father about it. I want something a little more tasteful for us when the time comes."

"Oh, c'mon, Mom. Live it up when you die. Show everyone the estimable Judge Matheny-Boyd was actually a wild woman under those robes."

Thea burst into laughter.

Grae's gaze tracked Domokos, who had stopped to talk to diners at a table near the hallway to the washrooms. "Would you excuse me for moment, Mom? I just need to use the ladies' room. You can spend the time planning something outré for your and Dad's final resting place."

Grae winked at her mother and made a beeline to the back of the restaurant. She brushed by Domokos as he bade his patrons farewell and started down the hall.

"Oh, I'm sorry." Grae laid a steadying hand on Domokos' arm. "I didn't mean to run you over."

"Not at all. Are you enjoying your dinner?"

"I am. I haven't been here since Mom and Dad brought us as children, but I've never forgotten how good the food is." Grae insinuated herself between Domokos and the dining area, keeping her hand on his arm as he faced her. "You know Mom raves about your lobster, and Dad can't get enough of your porterhouse."

Domokos beamed. "The judge and Mr. Boyd have always been very discerning clients. And they have been so kind as to steer many of their friends to our establishment."

Grae leaned forward as if she were about to impart a secret. Domokos cocked his head and did the same.

"If you ever again lay so much as a finger on Marcus Lyndon, I'll spread your perverted proclivities over every social network in the country. You'll be a pariah. After a few rent boys testify, not a single patron with any class will cross your threshold ever again. Do you understand me?"

Grae's icy threat hit Domokos like a guided missile. He gaped at her as he struggled for words.

"You are not to say a word to him, get it? And if I hear that he's being mistreated at work, the same thing goes. Everyone will instantly know of your penchant for little boys. Are we clear about that?"

Domokos' nostrils flared and his face darkened. "You have mistaken me for someone else. I am a happily married man with children. Who do you think you are to threaten me?"

"I'm the daughter of the judge, and I'm the one with photos. The alley behind the Copper Monkey about three years ago now, remember? You and Marcus, me and my cellphone camera. I threw stones at your sorry ass, and you ran out of there like the cowardly, low-life chicken hawk you are."

Panic flashed across Domokos florid features.

"So, are we clear?" Grae quietly enunciated each word.

Domokos gritted his teeth. "Clear."

"Good. Now go about your business, and I'll go about mine. But I'll be watching, believe me. He is strictly out of bounds as far as you and Tigris are concerned." Grae had saved her best shot for last.

Domokos blanched and swayed. Grae turned and strode into the ladies' room. It was a gamble, but worth it. He might doubt the existence of photos, which considering she hadn't owned a cellphone and would've been too drunk to use one anyway, was justifiable, not that he knew that. But hearing his own pet name for his junk sealed the deal. And as long as the threat kept his filthy paws off Marcus, it would be worth every disgusting moment of their encounter.

When she returned to the table, the waiter was topping up their wine glasses. Grae slid into her chair and cast a quick glance around. Domokos was nowhere to be seen. The master of the house was hiding, and that suited her fine.

"So, are you still volunteering with Angels Unawares?" Thea asked.

"I am. I've taken all the training now, and I'm shadowing Kendall again tomorrow to see how the boss does it. Then she'll start assigning me my own cases."

"Do you enjoy it?"

Warmth filled Grae and erased the acrid taste of her encounter with Domokos. "I do, actually. It got off to a rough start with Ezra Herzog, but even that turned out for the best, right? I'm in a fabulous, fulfilling job that never would've come my way if not for my meeting Ezra. And Kendall's the best. I thought she was such a hard-ass when we first met, but she's not like that at all. I really look forward to our training sessions."

"I'm so pleased. You've really turned your life around." Thea's gaze sharpened. "Your next court appearance is in mid-December, is it not?"

"Uh-huh."

"Are you worried about it?"

"Yes and no. I met with Virgil a couple of nights ago, and we went over some of the details. From what I can tell, he's assembled a solid case for me."

Thea nodded. "That's what he tells me, too. Doug Eisler is a good judge and an unbiased jurist. He'll give you a fair shake."

"That's what Virg said, too. Still, I'll be glad when it's over."

"Of course. We all will."

The rest of dinner passed in casual conversation. Domokos still hadn't reappeared.

Thea paid the bill and they left. Grae smiled to herself as the doorman summoned a valet to get Thea's car. *Mission accomplished.*

Chapter 15

Grae and Kendall left Mr. Simon's hospice room and quietly closed the door behind them. Peter was waiting to intercept them.

"I'm so glad I caught you two before you left. Do you have time for a quick coffee with me?"

Kendall nodded. "I'm available, but I can't speak for Grae. Grae?"

"Sure. It's cold outside, and my schedule is clear."

Peter beamed. "Excellent. Then let me treat you to a cup of Lazarus' finest." He led the way to the family sitting room. It was equipped with a small kitchenette and an ever ready pot of coffee. He dug out three mismatched china cups and pointed to a covered tray of cookies. "Help yourself. A local bakery donates their day-olds, and they're really good."

Grae and Kendall followed Peter's lead and collected coffee and cookies before they joined him at a small table by a window which looked out over a snow-covered patio.

"Can you believe Christmas is only three weeks away? It seems like just yesterday I was planting annuals out there."

"I know. I had to buy a heavier jacket for work," Grae said.

Kendall smiled at her. "Do you work outside a lot in the winter?"

"I can't speak for any other winter, because this is my first one there, but I think Jude's half Inuit. He doesn't care how cold it is. When he's got engraving to do or a monument to set, we're off and running. Funny, the other guys at the shop prefer the indoor work right now, but I like hopping in the truck with Jude and getting outside. It's fun."

"You really love your job, don't you?" Peter observed.

"I do, and I have both of you to thank."

Peter shot Grae a puzzled look. "You do?"

Kendall laughed. "It's no use trying to argue with her. I've told her until I'm blue in the face that we didn't do her any favours assigning Ezra Herzog to her, but she insists she owes us big."

Peter shook his head. "Kendall's right. You took on the most difficult case I've ever encountered, and I've been in the hospice business for decades. You were the one who created your own opportunity. We may have played a tiny part, but you were the one who put the puck in the net."

Grae dropped her gaze, but didn't try to hide her smile.

"You're embarrassing her, Peter."

Kendall's soft, amused tone caused Grae's blush to deepen, and her face to hurt from the width of her grin.

"Well, I certainly wouldn't want to do that. So, how did it go with Mr. Simon?"

"Very well. Grae even had him laughing."

Peter's eyes widened. "No. Really? Mr. Abe Simon, who couldn't do sweet if his mouth was full of sugar?"

"That's the one. We promised him we'd come back tomorrow afternoon, didn't we, Grae?"

Grae nodded.

"That is so kind of you. I know he's no Ezra, but I think there's a reason none of his family come around to see him." Peter sighed. "It always makes me sad when our patients are abandoned, but in his case, I think he is sadly reaping what he spent his whole life sowing."

"That was the impression I got as well," Kendall said. "I thought our two hours were going to drag like a dental appointment, but with Grae as my ace in the hole, the time just flew by. I wish I could clone a dozen of her. It would make my job so much easier."

Grae hid behind her oversized coffee mug as the other two smiled at her. She had no idea how to respond to Kendall's unabashed admiration, even as she basked in it.

"So are you ready to strike out on your own now?" Peter asked as he brushed at the powdered sugar on his face.

Grae glanced at Kendall. "I guess. Whatever the boss says."

Surprisingly, Kendall lost her smile. "She's certainly more than qualified. She has a real gift for this work."

"Wonderful. Then no doubt we'll be seeing a lot of you around here." Peter looked up as a nurse approached. "Yes, Peggy?"

Peggy's gaze flicked from Kendall to Grae. "You're needed in room 108, Peter."

Peter sighed. "Again?"

"I'm afraid so."

"Okay. I'll be right there."

He turned back to Kendall and Grae with an apologetic grimace. "Sorry, duty calls. I've got to go head off a son who thinks his dying father should rewrite his will, cutting out his stepmother. I'll see you soon."

He stood and hurried away.

Grae studied Kendall. "Is something wrong?"

"No, of course not. Why do you ask?"

"Because when Peter asked if I was striking out on my own, you looked like you bit into a lemon."

Kendall toyed with the crumbs on her napkin. "It's not what you think. You really are one of the best volunteers I've ever had. You've taken to this work like a duck to water."

"Then what is it? You think I need more experience before I solo?"

Kendall gave a wry laugh. "You haven't actually needed any of the experience you've gotten the last two weeks."

Grae frowned. "Okay. Then—?"

Kendall looked around the room, refusing to meet Grae's gaze. "God, this is so embarrassing."

"What is?"

"Can we walk out to the car while we talk?" Kendall was on her feet gathering her coat and gloves before she finished the sentence.

Grae hastened to follow while she shrugged into the thick down jacket that Jude had recommended. She trotted after Kendall, whose long stride had them out the door and over to her car before Grae could say another word. The icy wind tossed Grae's hair, and she hurriedly tugged a toque over her ears as she waited for Kendall to unlock the car door.

When they were both inside, Kendall turned on the ignition.

"So, what's going on, Kendall? You're happy with my work, but you don't think I'm ready to do it alone? I don't get it."

Kendall half-turned to face Grae. "You're ready to see people on your own. I knew that the first time you shadowed me."

Today was the sixth time Grae had shadowed Kendall. "So, then—?"

Kendall covered her face with gloved hands and shook her head. "I cannot believe I'm being this unprofessional. I swear it's never happened before."

"Never happened…" Grae's eyes widened. *Surely not.* "Um, Kendall?"

"Yes?"

"Did you keep me shadowing you because you…"

"Enjoy your company, yes. I'm sorry. I never meant to use my position to—"

"You haven't done anything wrong."

"Excuse me?"

Grae shrugged. "You're not my boss. You don't have supervisory control over me."

"I sort of do."

"No, you don't. I'm a volunteer in an organization you happen to run. No fiduciary leverage at all."

"Fiduciary leverage?"

Grae grinned. "That's right. And just so you know, I've enjoyed shadowing you. In fact, I may need to shadow you a few more times so I'm sure I've got all the nuances down."

Kendall snorted. "What nuances? I just spent two hours watching you make a cranky old man, on his deathbed no less, laugh, and even play checkers with you."

"He killed me. Tomorrow I'm going to insist on Chinese checkers and make him jump his own marbles. With his palsy, I might stand a chance of winning."

Kendall laughed and shook her head. "You're terrible."

"Sometimes. So can I buy you an early dinner at our favourite diner?" Grae held her breath, hoping this wasn't a step too far.

"You know, I'd like that. We can work on our report together."

"Sounds good to me."

Grae pushed her empty plate aside. The Brunswick stew had been just what the doctor ordered. Her tummy was warm and happy, though she also considered the possibility that her general euphoria might be from the company she was keeping.

When Billie approached with a coffeepot, Kendall pushed her cup to the edge of the table. "Don't you ever take a day off?"

Billie snorted as she topped up both their cups. "Are you kidding? If I take a day off, I might have to spend it with my old man. I'd rather work."

Kendall laughed and glanced at Grae as Billie hurried away. "Don't let her fool you. She's been married for over thirty years, and she's still crazy about the old coot."

"What about you?" Grae regretted the words as soon as they were out of her mouth.

"Pardon?"

"Sorry. None of my business." She was confused about the definite pull between the two of them, since Kendall had been married to a man, but she couldn't bring herself to ask.

Kendall studied her for a long moment. "You want to know about my marriage?"

"As I said, it's none of my business."

"It's okay. Long story short, he cheated on every business trip he took, and he took a lot of them. After one of those trips he brought me home an extremely unwelcome gift. That finally opened my eyes. I divorced the cheating son of a bitch, and got the townhouse, half our portfolio, and part of his pension in the settlement."

"Pension? How old was he?"

"Almost thirty years older. We met when I was in university, and I was blinded by his silver mane, blue eyes, and worldly status. Little did I know how many other women were just as smitten." Kendall shrugged, but it wasn't difficult to read the pain that lingered in her eyes.

"I'm sorry."

"Eh, it happens when you're young and dumb. I'm much older and wiser now."

"And since then? I mean, have you met anyone else?"

"No. It's only been a couple of years since I tossed his cheating ass out the door, but I haven't even looked."

"Why?"

Kendall was quiet a long time.

"I'm just being nosy. Sorry about that. Forget I asked."

"No, it's okay. I just never met anyone else I was interested in, or maybe I didn't trust my own judgement. After all, I've never been able to figure out why Derek even asked me to marry him. He never had any intention of being faithful, so why bother? Was it just because I was so young that he didn't think I'd see through his act? He must've known that the dewy-eyed hero-worshipper was going to wise up sooner or later."

"Maybe he wanted to settle down and start a family."

Instantly, tears filled Kendall's eyes.

"Oh damn, I'm sorry." Grae hastily wrenched a couple of napkins from the holder and held them out.

Kendall took them and dabbed her eyes.

"I'm so sorry. I obviously put my big fat foot in it."

Kendall gave a shaky laugh. "You have to stop apologizing."

"I didn't mean to hurt you."

"You didn't. I wanted children, desperately. But after three miscarriages, Derek decided they were all my fault, and he didn't even fake being a faithful husband anymore. As much as he blamed me, I blamed myself even more. It didn't make for a happy home. And still I couldn't end it until my doctor told me why I— I suppose I should be grateful he didn't bring home anything worse. A double dose of antibiotics and I was fine again, but I had to accept that our marriage wasn't. I hired a private detective, got the evidence, and sued for divorce. He didn't even try to contest it. I think he was as glad as I was that the sham was over. Derek's company transferred him to Texas before the ink was dry on the writ, and I haven't seen him since. No loss, I assure you. But enough about me, tell me about your love life."

"Pretty scant for the last eight years."

Kendall cocked her head. "Really? I'd have thought the girls would be all over you. You've got such a sexy androgynous thing going, even without the multi-coloured hair."

Grae reminded herself to breathe slowly. "I dated in university. I haven't really had time for anyone but Marcus since then, and he's not exactly dating material."

"Surely you haven't sworn it off."

"No, but I spend my days in cemeteries or covered with granite dust, and my evenings in the company of my little brother or in hospice wards. I doubt I'll meet any suitable dates under any of those circumstances."

Kendall smiled. "Oh, I don't know. You might run into a really cute zombie who'll sweep you off your feet."

Grae was pleased to see the pain had faded from Kendall's eyes. "It couldn't be just any zombie. If the good parts are eaten away, I'm not interested."

Kendall chuckled. "I'm not even going to ask what the good parts are."

"Her arms, her legs. I like to dance, or at least I used to. What were you thinking of, Miss Potty-brain."

Kendall laughed harder. "Exactly what you were thinking, and don't even try to tell me you weren't."

Billie brought their check, and Grae grabbed it. When Kendall tried to protest, Grae shook her head. "Nope, you bought the last couple of times. I just got paid, and this one is on me."

"Money burning a hole in your pocket?"

"Yes and no. I'm off to the mall to spend some tonight, but I've banked most of it."

"What are you looking for? Anything specific?"

Grae set out a handful of bills and coins. "I want to get Marcus' main Christmas present. I'm looking for a phone like yours."

"Really? Could you use a consultant? I go through phones like I go through my mom's Christmas cookies. I might have an idea or two."

"Absolutely. I'd welcome some well-informed consumer advice. I don't want Marcus running to the store for an exchange five minutes after he opens it."

Kendall stood and gathered her things. "Well, he'd probably have to wait until Boxing Day, anyway."

Grae snorted. "You're assuming I can actually wait until Christmas to give it to him."

"I was assuming that. Silly me."

"Silly you, indeed." Grae grinned as she followed Kendall out of the diner.

Marcus got home from work at midnight. He yawned as he ambled in from the foyer, and stopped short when he saw Grae, who sat on the couch waiting for him with a big grin.

"Hey, what are you doing up so late?"

"Counting the minutes until you got home. Come, sit." Grae patted the couch.

He slouched down beside her and yawned again. "Okay. What's going on? You're not going to chew me out for not finishing my English assignment, are you? Freddie said he'd come over tomorrow and help me with it."

Grae sighed dramatically. "I've been replaced as your tutor, haven't I?"

"Well, not that I don't appreciate your help, sweetie, but Freddie has a way of, um, rewarding my efforts that would not be appropriate coming from you."

"Hey, I could reward you with chocolates."

Marcus grinned, and Grae was struck by how much older he looked in his white shirt, black pants, and short hair.

"Grae, I love you, but let's just say Freddie is sweeter than any chocolate you could give me."

Grae's eyes filled with tears. "I can't begin to tell you how happy that makes me, bud."

"Me too."

"So why are you home then?"

"Freddie's parents are visiting from Vancouver. No sleepovers tonight. Speaking of which, I called here around five. I thought you'd be here by then."

"Oh. No, Kendall and I went for dinner after we left Lazarus."

Marcus straightened up and poked Grae. "Another date? Whoo-hoo. What does that make? At least half a dozen in the last couple of weeks.

You dog, you." He whipped off his loose tie. "Here, we'll start using this as our signal when one of us needs some private time in their bedroom."

Grae cuffed him. "They weren't dates. We were working on AU stuff."

"Ooh, is that what they're calling it now?"

"Keep it up and I'm not going to give you what I got for you today."

Marcus sat upright and folded his hands in his lap. His eyes twinkled as he grinned mischievously.

Grae rolled her eyes. "You make the worst fake choir boy I've ever seen." She pulled the wrapped box from behind the cushion. "Here. I decided not to make you wait until Christmas since I figure you'll be spending it with Freddie."

Marcus halted mid-paper rip and regarded Grae seriously. "I want to spend it with you." He tried to hand the gift back.

Grae shook her head. "No, it's okay. I've got some other things for you to unwrap on the big day. I really do want you to have this early, though."

"You're sure?"

"I am."

"Okay, but I don't want you to ever think anyone can replace you in my heart, okay?" Marcus' gaze was intent.

"Ditto, bud. But I'm still glad you and Freddie met. Go on, open it."

Marcus proceeded at a slower pace. Before he unveiled the contents, he stopped. "What would you think of me making dinner on Christmas Eve, and we can invite Freddie and Kendall?"

"Kendall and I aren't dating." *At least I don't think we are.* Grae shook her head. She was still confused about the vibe she was getting from Kendall, but it certainly wasn't unpleasant.

"But she's your friend, right?"

"Yeah, I guess. Sure."

"So it'll be a dinner to introduce our friends to each other. Please say yes."

Grae stifled her grin. "Aw, geez, you're giving me the puppy dog eyes."

"Is it working?"

"All right. I'll see her tomorrow so I'll ask, but she's probably got plans with her family."

Marcus grinned and ripped the rest of the paper off in a flourish. Then he squealed in delight. "Oh, my God! An iPhone! You got me an iPhone!" He flung his arms around Grae and squeezed her so hard that she couldn't breathe.

"Yo, bud, you're killing me here."

He released her and tore into the box.

"Um, you might want to save the—" Grae stopped. It was useless.

"Look at the killer apps you've already got on here. You rock!" Marcus was instantly lost to his new toy.

Grae smiled indulgently and began to pick up the mess.

"Oh, here." Marcus pulled his old flip phone out and handed it to her. "Now I'll be able to reach you all the time."

"If I remember to turn it on."

He pasted a glower on his face. "I'm going to run daily drills to make sure you don't leave home without it being active and in your pocket."

Grae laughed and accepted the phone. Once she'd deposited the wrapping paper in the garbage, she sat down on the couch to look it over. It was a model that would've been basic even the last time she'd owned a phone, and it didn't take her long to pull up the phone book. The only listings were their home number, Frederico, and Magellan's. She found the loose piece of paper she'd been recording numbers on and began to add listings—Marcus' new number, Jude, Stone Gardens, her mother, Jo, and Virgil. She hesitated over her father and Ciara, but decided to put them in there, too. She added AU's number and Kendall's personal cell, and then sat back.

Gazing at the screen, she almost had to pinch herself. Was it only a few months ago that none of those numbers would've been in her list of contacts?

Grae smiled contentedly.

Life was definitely picking up.

Chapter 16

Jude glanced at Grae, who was working on a stencil using the computer design software. "So what's the big grin about? Did you have a good weekend?"

"I had a great weekend." She had spent much of it with Kendall. For a moment, Grae tried to tame her irrepressible grin, but it was impossible.

"So, do I take it you're not too worried about tomorrow?"

Grae's smile faded. "I am, actually. And I was going to ask you if I could leave at noon so I can go home and get cleaned up first."

"Your court date is at what—three o'clock?"

"Yes, but by the time I get home, shower, change, and catch the bus downtown—"

Jude shook his head. "Not why I asked. I was going to suggest you bring your court clothes in with you and you can get ready here. You know you're welcome to use the shower. We'll just tell the guys it's off-limits for half an hour."

Grae had initially been surprised to find that the company had a small shower room, but once she'd ridden home a few times in her work clothes, she understood why.

"I'll get you to the courthouse on time," Jude said.

"Oh, I can catch the bus, but it's a good idea to bring in my good clothes. It'll save time, and I can work longer."

"You're missing the point. I'm going to the hearing anyway, so you might as well ride with me."

Grae blinked at Jude. "With you?"

He gave her a lazy grin. "Yup."

"But why would you be going—?"

"Didn't your lawyer tell you? I'm going to be a character witness. He said it'll carry a lot of weight with the judge that you're gainfully employed and learning a trade."

Grae's eyes filled with tears. "You'd do that for me?"

Jude snorted. "Silly question."

Ashley stepped into the shop. "Jude, we have some clients here. Luc's out, so you're up."

"Be right there." Jude jerked his head at Grae. "C'mon. It's time you started learning to handle clients, too."

Still stunned that Jude was going to vouch for her in court, Grae trailed him to the reception room where two older women sat.

One of the women stood and extended her hand. "Mr. Herzog, I don't know if you remember me, but it's nice to see you again."

Jude shook her hand. "Jude, please. And it's Ms. Glenn, isn't it?"

"It is, and please call me Lee." Lee rested a hand on the shoulder of the woman seated in the chair next to her. "This is my partner, Gaëlle Germaine."

"And this is my apprentice, Grae Jordan."

They shook hands all around, and Jude and Grae sat.

Grae smiled to herself as Lee took Gaëlle's hand under the table before starting to speak.

"In four months it'll be two years since my wife, Dana, died. At the time I had you make a plain marker for her. I always planned to do something bigger and better, but to be honest, I wasn't in a very good place and I couldn't deal with it." Lee shot Gaëlle a glance and got a warm smile in response.

"That's not uncommon for our clients," Jude said gently. "Many wait for years before settling on a design for their loved ones. Have you something in mind now?"

"I do." Lee dug in her jacket pocket and came out with a piece of paper. "I'm hoping you can do something like this." She pushed it across the table.

Jude opened the paper and ensured that Grae could see it too. He studied it and nodded. "That shouldn't be a problem, at all."

Stone Gardens

As Grae looked at the drawing, she was already planning how it would go on the monument. Design was one of her favourite aspects of their work.

"I don't want it on a typically shaped monument, either. I want the labyrinth to almost fill the face of it, and for Dana's name to be in the centre, along with a single rose."

"We can do that. May I show you some options?" Jude nodded at Grae, who went to get the design books.

They spent the next half hour designing the monument. Jude took the lead, but encouraged Grae to contribute. She was delighted when Lee and Gaëlle chose to go with her suggestion of an asymmetric, tear-shaped, rough-edged black granite.

Grae pointed to the example she'd sketched. "We could do the rose in pink granite so it really stands out. And you might want to consider putting the flower at the peak here, and leaving the centre of the labyrinth solely for your wife's name and dates."

Lee nodded. "I'd like that. Can we put words underneath the labyrinth, too?"

"Of course," Jude said. "What did you have in mind?"

"'Where there is love, there is life.' It's one of Gandhi's sayings, and I've come to appreciate it a lot this year."

Grae shivered at the look Lee bestowed on Gaëlle; it was clear that Lee had found love at least twice in her life. Grae would be happy to find it just once, and she wanted nothing less than someone who would look at her with the devotion with which Lee looked at Gaëlle. Her mind flashed to Kendall, but she instantly shut down that avenue of thought. It was far too soon.

They wrapped up the design details, and Jude escorted the women to Ashley's desk to take care of the deposit.

Lee and Gaëlle left, and Jude joined Grae in the shop. "Do you know if Rolly and Blair did the Hampson baby's installation yet?"

"I don't think so. I think they were doing the Burney monument first. Why?"

"Because I want you to do the Hampson one."

Grae's eyes widened. "By myself?"

"Yup. You're ready."

"Sure." Inwardly Grae did a mental jig, but outwardly she kept a sober face. After all, they were talking about a memorial for a baby. She had helped Jude construct that one. It was a tiny, traditional monument, with a lamb on top. "Jude?"

He was working on the hockey locker monument, which was taking impressive shape at almost six feet tall. "Yeah?"

"Do you ever have trouble when it's a child's monument? I mean emotionally?"

Jude stopped working and stared pensively at the wall. "Sometimes, yes. I was a young father when I had a couple come in to order a stone for their baby. He'd died of SIDS, and the mom couldn't stop crying. I kept choking up, and it took them forever to settle on what they wanted. You know, for a long time after that, I got up twice a night to check on my girls. I probably drove Elaine crazy, but she never complained."

"When did you stop checking on them?"

Jude grinned. "When they got married."

Grae laughed. Given how protective Jude was of his family, she didn't doubt it.

He regarded her seriously. "Never forget we often see families at their worst moments, and we need to be conscious of that. If they dither, don't ever get impatient. They're trying to honour and memorialize loved ones to the best of their ability, but they're fighting their own pain while they do it."

Grae's heart ached, and all she could do was nod.

"One time, I had an elderly woman come in. Her daughter lost her husband and two teenagers in a car accident. The daughter was so devastated that she couldn't even leave the house, so the grandma was trying to ease her burden by doing the preliminary work on selecting a single monument for the whole family. The grandma did all she could, and then the daughter came in to finalize things. She leaned on her mama's arm like it was all she could do to put one foot in front of the other."

"How do you deal with a situation like that?"

Jude shot her a wry glance. "Stay kind, stay professional, and then bawl your eyes out after they leave."

Grae was silent for a long moment.

"What are you thinking?"

"I'm thinking that what we do is really important."

Jude nodded and returned to his work. "It is."

Jo studied Grae. "So tomorrow's the big day. How do you feel about that?"

"Scared…a little. Optimistic…a little."

"That's not a bad combination. Could you elaborate?"

Grae shifted in her seat, and wished Maddie was in her lap rather than Jo's. "Virgil tells me we're in good shape, and Mom has encouraged me to have a positive outlook."

"But?"

"But…I've just got so much to lose this time."

"Interesting. So you didn't feel you had much to lose any of the other times?"

"Not really. At least not before Marcus came into my life. I cleaned up my act a lot once we started living together."

"Let's set aside the possibility of loss, and examine what you think you could lose."

Grae shook her head. "Everything. If I go to jail, I literally lose everything—Marcus, my home, my job, my family, Kendall—I mean working with AU."

"All right. Let's start with Marcus."

"I guess I wouldn't really lose him. I know our friendship is solid enough that it would survive if I were incarcerated. Hell, he'd probably bring me home-baked brownies in prison every weekend. But I worry about leaving him on his own."

"I thought you said he was doing much better. Didn't you tell me he enjoys his new job and that you approve of his boyfriend?"

"I do, and he is, but…" Grae didn't know how to put her amorphous fears into words. "He's so…vulnerable, you know?"

"I don't actually. Tell me what you mean."

Grae chewed her lip, torn as always over how much to reveal about Marcus' past. "I've told you a little about his parents, right?"

"I know they threw him out at a terribly young age and left him to fend for himself."

Grae's fists clenched. "They threw him out like he was a bag of garbage, like they hadn't given birth to him and raised him for fourteen years, like he didn't matter anymore than last night's fish bones."

"And that still makes you angry."

"Damn right. Sometimes I picture myself marching up to their front door and punching their lights out."

Jo arched an eyebrow. "I trust that is merely the stuff of imagination."

"It is. I wouldn't really do it. But I wouldn't pull them out of the path of an oncoming bus, either. They don't have a fucking clue if he's dead or alive, and they don't care."

"Are you sure?"

"Hell, yeah, I'm sure. No one has ever tried to find him. No one. I caught Marcus checking online for information about his family. His brother, Gideon, has a Facebook page, and Marcus was reading it. His brother talked about everything under the sun, except the fact that he has a missing brother. Marcus looked so dejected that I wanted to put a fist through the screen."

"I have a question for you."

"Sure. What?"

"In today's session you've talked about punching Marcus' parents and not pulling them from the path of a bus. And you've mentioned wanting to put a fist through a computer screen. When was the last time you actually did anything remotely violent?"

The encounter with Domokos flashed through Grae's mind. "Do words count?"

"No. I'm talking physical violence."

"Um..." Grae quickly ran through the last several months in her mind. "I guess not since the run-in with Rick and Dylan."

"Yet physical violence is still part of your lexicon. Have you considered why that's your go-to mode?"

"Well, I didn't actually mean any of those things—except maybe the bus part."

Jo smiled. "I know. But I think it's important to understand why you developed such a linguistic habit in the first place and whether you still need it."

"I hate to tell you this, but it wasn't that long ago that it wasn't just a linguistic habit. I settled a lot of things with my fists."

"Exactly. But you no longer do that, do you?"

"I guess not. Huh. So you're telling me that I'm not that person anymore."

"Actually, you're telling me that you're not that person. When you speak of your affection for Marcus, for your job, for Jude and your family, you're telling me that you're no longer the violent construct you erected as a defence against life."

"I still can't guarantee I won't pop Ciara in the nose if it's warranted."

Jo chuckled. "And if you did?"

"Hell, she'd pop me right back."

"So…food for thought?"

"Yes."

"You mentioned fears about losing your home. Were you speaking about your apartment, or your parents and siblings?"

"Actually I'm getting along really well with Mom and Virgil right now."

"And your father and Ciara?"

Grae shrugged. "I haven't seen either of them since the first night we went over to the apartment."

"Have you made any attempt to do so?"

"Not really. Mom suggested that Dad join us at Magellan's for dinner last week, but I shut her down."

"Why was that?"

Because I had to threaten Domokos, and I wanted to have as few witnesses as possible. "I just want to rebuild my relationship with Mom before taking on the really difficult stuff."

"And you term your father and sister 'difficult'?"

Grae considered that for a long moment. "I'm not sure, to tell you the truth. Mom said that the greatest loss of Dad's life was when I left the family."

"Do you believe her?"

"I didn't."

"Do you think she would lie about that?"

Grae slowly shook her head. "Mom doesn't lie, about anything."

"That's a bit unrealistic, don't you think? I read a recent study that showed on average, people tell ten lies a week."

"Not Mom."

"Even your mother. Our world would be hell if everyone told the unvarnished truth all the time. White lies are the lubrication of a civil society. Did your mother ever comment on your hair, or tattoos, or facial hardware?"

"All she ever said was that my rainbow was unique, but that she preferred one colour because it was more like me—the old me."

"And do you think she actually didn't mind your rather wild look?"

Grae shook her head. "I expect she hated it, but Mom can do diplomatic better than anyone I know. Huh, I guess that means she is the master of white lies after all. I never looked at it that way. But I know Dad and Ciara couldn't be tactful if their lives depended on it."

"And Virgil?"

"Way less blunt than Ciara, not quite as diplomatic as Mom."

Jo glanced at her watch. "We're almost out of time, and speaking of Virgil, I want to ask again if you have any issues to bring up ahead of your court appearance."

"Not really. I didn't tell you—Jude is going to be a character witness. Can you believe that?"

"Why would I disbelieve it? I'll be there to testify too."

Grae's mouth fell open. "You will?"

"Of course. Virgil has lined up a number of witnesses to speak on your behalf. Why does that surprise you?"

"It wasn't that long ago that I didn't think anyone but Marcus would even stop to pick me up if I were lying in the street."

Jo gave her a gentle smile. "Perhaps you need to understand that time has passed. You have friends and family who care about you more than you know."

"I do, don't I?" *Well, I'll be damned.*

Chapter 17

Grae sat next to Virgil and tried to slow her breathing as they waited for court to be called into session. The row behind her was filled with supporters. Jude and Jo were chatting like old friends. Kendall had positioned herself at the end of the row so it was easy for Grae to catch her eye when she glanced back. Marcus and Freddie, dressed in their working garb, sat with their heads together, whispering. Her father and Ciara sat stiffly next to them.

Grae's eyes widened as three newcomers walked into the courtroom. The foreman from her old job was sporting an ill-fitting suit, and two of his construction crew, Eddie and Phil, flanked him. She held her breath and waited to see if they would sit behind the prosecution or the defence. She shuddered in relief when they sat behind Kendall.

"Is Mom coming?" Grae asked Virgil, sotto voce.

He shook his head. "It wouldn't be appropriate. Mom's a stickler, as you well know, and even her presence could be construed as an attempt to influence Judge Eisler. But I have strict orders to text her immediately after the hearing concludes."

"Okay."

Jude leaned forward and tapped her on the shoulder. She half-turned to face him.

"Jo, here, tells me there's a fine Irish pub a couple blocks from here. Halligan's, isn't it?" Jude glanced at Jo, who nodded. "We're getting everyone to meet up there afterwards for a celebration."

"A celebration?" Was he that sure, or just trying to bolster her confidence?

"Damn right."

Grae forced a smile. "Then I'll be there with bells on."

Jude winked. "First round is on me."

The court clerk called the court into session, and everyone rose as Judge Eisler entered. Virgil glanced at opposing counsel and frowned.

"What's wrong?" Grae asked.

"His witnesses aren't all here."

Grae had been so nervous that she hadn't noticed the absence of her nemeses, but Virgil was right. Rick and Dylan were nowhere to be seen. "What does that mean?"

Virgil shook his head. "I'm not sure, but we'll deal with it."

Judge Eisler eyed the Crown Attorney. "Mr. Salinger, are you ready to call your first witness?"

"Yes, Your Honour. I call Constable Allary to the stand."

The police officer's testimony was quick and dry. He'd been on beat patrol and when the 911 call came in was on the same block. He recited the details of Grae's arrest and booking, and the condition of Rick and Dylan, who had been taken to the ER for treatment.

Virgil only had one question on cross-examination. "Did my client exhibit any injuries when you took her into booking?"

The constable nodded. "She had a black-eye and some minor cuts and bruises. She was offered an opportunity for medical treatment, but refused."

"Thank you. That's all."

The judge dismissed the officer and looked at the Crown Attorney. "Call your next witness, Mr. Salinger."

Salinger rose, quickly glanced behind him, and shook his head. "Your Honour, Mr. MacIsaac and Mr. Toylen aren't here yet. I'm sure they're caught in traffic and will be here as quickly as possible."

The judge scowled. "Unacceptable. You know better than to pull that in my court."

Grae almost felt sorry for the Crown Attorney, who gulped audibly and whispered to his assistant. The assistant hurried out of court.

"Mr. Matheny-Boyd, are you prepared to begin your defence?"

Virgil rose to his feet. "I am, Your Honour. I call Alfred Thompson to the stand."

Grae's former foreman rose to his feet, advanced, and was sworn in, then seated.

Virgil moved to address him. "Mr. Thompson, could you please tell us of the events of the day in question."

"We'd broken for lunch. Most of the boys went across the street to eat. I was at ground level talking to one of my suppliers when Marcus came flying out of the elevator, yelling that Rick and Dylan were going to kill Grae, and somebody had to stop them."

"What did you do?"

"Called 911 and got my ass up to the roof as quickly as possible. Damn elevator was acting up or I'd have been quicker. Fortunately, Constable Allary was Johnny-on-the-spot, and he came with me."

"Were you surprised at what Mr. Lyndon had said?"

"No, sir. Rick and Dylan had been riding those two pretty hard for a long time. I'd had to have words with them only the day before."

"What kind of words?"

"I told them to back the fuck off or I'd can their asses, union or no union."

Virgil glanced at Grae. "Do you know what their issues were with Ms. Jordan and Mr. Lyndon?"

"Yeah, they 'hated queers.'" Thompson glanced at the judge. "Sorry, Your Honour. That's their language, not mine."

Judge Eisler nodded. "Go on."

Virgil continued, never missing a beat. "When you say they didn't like gay people, what do you mean?"

"I mean they were always ragging on those two, saying nasty things and making their lives miserable."

"How did Ms. Jordan and Mr. Lyndon react?"

"Well, Grae, she always looked out for Marcus. Ran interference, you know? But they pretty much just kept to themselves and tried to stay out of Rick and Dylan's way."

"When you and the police officer reached the roof of the building, what did you find?"

"Grae was backed up against the stairs, holding a piece of rebar."

"Was she attacking Mr. MacIsaac or Mr. Toylen?"

Thompson shook his head. "Nah. Looked to me like she was just trying to keep them from attacking her."

"One more question, Mr. Thompson. What is the size difference between Ms. Jordan, and Mr. MacIsaac and Mr. Toylen?"

"Dylan and Rick are big boys, taller 'n me and probably thirty or forty pounds heavier."

"So, it wasn't a fair fight?"

Salinger rose to his feet. "Objection. Calls for an opinion."

The judge raised an eyebrow. "I believe Mr. Thompson can offer an objective assessment in this case."

"Yes, Your Honour." Salinger sat and fiddled with his tie.

Virgil cocked his head. "Mr. Thompson, would you answer my question?"

"Hell, no, it wasn't a fair fight. If either of those boys had landed a fist on her, they'd have torn her head off."

"Thank you. One more question, Mr. Thompson. Are Mr. MacIsaac or Mr. Toylen still in your company's employ?"

Thompson shook his head. "No. MacIsaac dragged out his sick leave until even the union was fed up and let us can him. I heard Rick went to work for his old man in Fort Mac. He never even came back for his gear."

Virgil turned to the Crown Attorney. "Your witness, Mr. Salinger."

The Crown Attorney attempted to get the foreman to say that Grae was a troublemaker, but Thompson would have no part of it and held his ground. Finally Salinger gave up, and Thompson was dismissed. As he walked back to his seat, Grae tried to convey her gratitude with her eyes. He smiled and gave her a slight nod.

Virgil called Eddie and Phil in succession, and their testimony supported Thompson's account. Rick and Dylan were agitators who incited each other's worst tendencies. They had alienated almost all of their co-workers, and not a one was sad to see them go.

"What about Ms. Jordan and Mr. Lyndon?" Virgil asked. "Was anyone sad to see them go?"

Phil nodded. "Yeah, they were good kids. Worked hard, kept their noses clean. The jerk wad that replaced them can't find his ass with both hands." He glanced at Thompson. "Sorry, boss."

When Virgil was finished questioning the members of the construction crew, he called Marcus to the stand and walked him through the events of the day.

"When Ms. Jordan was brought down in handcuffs, what did you do?"

"I tried to tell the police that they'd arrested the wrong person—that Rick and Dylan had attacked us and Grae was just trying to save our lives."

"Did you genuinely feel your lives were at risk?"

Marcus nodded. "Yes, sir. It's just like Phil said. They'd been talking smack for weeks, threatening to throw us off the edge of the building. Grae called them on it, and they said they were just kidding, and if we couldn't take a joke we should get off the site."

"So what did you do?"

"Well, the day before they attacked us, Rick tripped me, and I fell so close to the edge that I thought for sure I was heading for the street on a one-way trip. Grae was so mad that she went right to Mr. Thompson. He read Rick and Dylan the riot act. Things were quiet for the rest of the day, and we hoped that the worst of it was over." Marcus looked at Grae, his eyes shining with tears. "We were wrong. When they came after us, I was terrified. I thought we were both going to die, but Grae told me to run. I should've stayed. I should've tried to help her."

Grae shook her head as they locked gazes. *You did the right thing, buddy.* Her silent encouragement appeared to buck Marcus up. He wiped his eyes and sat up straight, as Virgil wrapped up his questions. When Salinger half-heartedly cross-examined, Marcus spoke firmly, and never wavered on his testimony.

Jude, Jo, and Kendall were just as impressive as character witnesses, and Salinger's cross-examination was perfunctory.

Grae's hopes soared.

By the time Salinger's assistant reappeared and whispered into her boss' ear, and Virgil rested the defence, Grae was confident that she'd be exonerated.

Judge Eisler looked at Salinger. "Have you any further witnesses to call, Counsellor?"

Salinger rose. "No, Your Honour."

"All right. I'm ready to render my decision. The defence will rise."

Virgil and Grae stood.

"Ms. Jordan, your record is not at all impressive, and normally I'd not be inclined to extend leniency. But your employer, volunteer coordinator, and therapist have all submitted glowing reports to the court. By all appearances, you have converted to the side of the angels in the last several months. That alone would not be enough to see these charges dismissed, but your lawyer has presented a very strong case in your defence." The judge peered over his glasses at Salinger. "I cannot say the same for the prosecution."

Grae held her breath.

"Ms. Jordan, if you ever appear in my court again, I'll take a very dim view of your presence. Keep your nose clean and don't make liars out of all these good people who appeared on your behalf."

"No, Your Honour. I won't."

"Good. I'll hold you to that. Case dismissed."

Grae sagged in relief. Virgil smiled at her, and Marcus ran around to hug her. She was quickly lost in the midst of congratulatory hugs and pats. When she could get free, Grae made a point to go up to Thompson and extend her hand.

"Thank you. Honestly, I can't thank you enough for your testimony. You saved me."

Thompson shook her hand. "Nah, you had a good lawyer. I just told the truth. Phil and Eddie, too."

Grae shook the hand of each of her former crewmates. "Thanks, guys. Look, we're all going to Halligan's. If you'd like to come along, I'd love to buy you a beer."

"Can we take a rain check on that?" Thompson asked. "We've got to get back to the site. We're on a deadline, and head office will have our balls if we don't finish up the interiors on time."

"It was really kind of you all to come, especially being under deadline."

Thompson shook his head. "You got a raw deal, and it was the least we could do. It was the least *I* could do. I should've canned Rick and Dylan the first time they threatened you. That's on me, so if today helped you out, I figure the scales are balanced."

They parted with promises of sharing a beer in the near future. Grae knew the odds were long that would actually happen, but she was feeling so good that she'd have happily promised them the moon.

An arm slid around Grae's shoulder, and she looked up into Kendall's beaming face.

"So did I hear you're buying beer?"

Before Grae could answer, Jude intervened. "Nope, first round is on me. Second round is on my apprentice."

With laughs all around, the group left the court. When they reached the hallway, Ciara and Carter hung back.

Grae stopped. "I'll catch up with you guys, okay? Save me a seat."

Marcus opened his mouth, but Freddie hustled him away, and they followed Virgil, Jude, Jo, and Kendall out of the courthouse.

Grae faced her father and sister. "You guys are welcome to come, you know. I think Virg said that Mom's going to join us once she's finished work."

"Thanks, but I have to get back to work," Carter said. "Let's plan to have dinner soon though, okay? Your mother says you really like Magellan's, and we'd be happy to treat you to a celebratory dinner."

"That sounds good, Dad. I'll be in touch."

"Good." Carter turned to walk away, then turned back. "I'm very pleased with the outcome here today."

"Me too."

Her father walked briskly down the hall, and Grae was left facing Ciara. "Would you like to join us?"

"Were you serious about what you said?"

Grae canted her head. "Um, about what?"

"That we…that I'm welcome to come."

"Of course."

"There's no 'of course' about it."

"No, I guess there isn't, but the invitation is genuine."

Ciara studied her for a long moment. "Then I accept."

They walked out of the courthouse and down the street together.

"Some of what I heard today was pretty eye-opening," Ciara said as they waited for a crossing light.

"Yeah? How so?"

"They all spoke so highly of you."

"Kind of belies the total screw-up, eh?" Grae tried to keep her tone light, but couldn't help the bitter undertone.

"Can you blame me?"

Grae bristled, but bit back the sharp words that sprang to mind.

Ciara shook her head. "Seriously, I'm not trying to start a fight here. I really want to know. Put yourself in my shoes for a moment, okay? You have a little sister you've adored since the day your parents brought her home from the hospital. And then one day she's just gone and you miss her so badly that it's like an open wound that won't heal. Can you really blame me for being so disappointed, so hurt at what you did with your life up until recently?"

Grae matched her sister stride for silent stride as she considered the question. "You were hurt?"

Ciara took Grae's arm and pulled her to a halt. "Of course I was. How could you think otherwise? Since you uttered your first sentence, you'd been coming to me with all your secrets and to ask me for advice. Then suddenly you drop out school, drop out of the family, and drop out of life in general, without a single word of explanation. I gave you all sorts of time and space to sort out your life, but I finally had to hire a private investigator to find you."

Grae's ire rose again. "And when you did, you got pissed at me for accepting the gift you offered me."

Ciara laid her hands on Grae's shoulders and stared at her intently. "Can we never, ever mention that damned mattress again? Please?"

It felt like something of great import hung in the balance of their interlocked gazes.

Finally Grae relaxed, and her body lost its stiffness. "Sure. It's a deal."

Ciara closed her eyes for an instant. "Thank you. And just so you know, I really enjoyed hearing what everyone had to say. I was proud of you…proud of the woman they all spoke so highly of."

Warmth surged through Grae. "Really?"

"Really."

Ciara linked arms with her, and they finished their walk to the pub.

"So, can I interest you in a free beer?" Grae asked as she opened the door.

"You can interest me in two."

Grae looked around the table with lazy contentment. Empty pitchers and empty platters bespoke the boisterous celebration they'd been enjoying. Kendall sat to her right, and Marcus and Freddie to her left. Jude and Jo, across the table, were still chatting like they'd known each other all their lives. Virgil nursed a beer and listened to his elders. Ciara, who had been surprisingly good company, had departed, but not before wangling a promise from Grae that they would get together for coffee the following weekend.

Freddie nudged Marcus. "We have to get going, or we're going to be late for work."

"Okay." Marcus stood and wrapped his arms around Grae's neck. "I'm so happy for you, sweetie. I promise you a dinner of your choice from the Lyndon-Jordan kitchen."

She grinned. "When did it become Lyndon-Jordan instead of Jordan-Lyndon?"

"When you cook more than scrambled eggs and hot dogs, you can have first billing." Marcus kissed her head and waved to everyone as he and Freddie left.

Kendall turned to Grae. "They're such a sweet couple."

"They are, aren't they? Freddie's a great guy." Grae shot Kendall a smile. "Damn, life is good, isn't it?"

"It is. And what are you going to do now that you're a free woman. Have I seen the last of you at Angels Unawares?"

"No way. Why? Are you trying to get rid of me?"

Kendall leaned over. "No way."

Her soft words, breathed right into Grae's ear, sent a delicious shiver through her body.

Just then, Virgil looked past Grae and waved. "Hey, Mom, we're over here."

Grae twisted and saw her mother approaching. She jumped to her feet. "Mom, did you hear?"

Thea's wide smile and hug answered. "I did, indeed. I'm so pleased, Grae. And so relieved."

"Virgil had the judge in the palm of his hand."

Thea shook her head. "No one gets Ben Eisler in the palm of his hand, honey. Your case was solid, and that's why he dismissed the charges."

"Hey, wait a minute," Virgil protested. "She also happened to have a damned good lawyer."

Those around the table laughed, and Thea regarded her son indulgently. "She had the best."

"Damn straight. Now sit down, Mom. You've got some drinking to do if you're going to catch up." Virgil pushed Ciara's empty chair back, and Thea sat. She refused a beer, but ordered an appletini.

"Great idea, Mom. I think I'll have one of those too." Grae held up two fingers to their waiter. "What about you, Kendall? Can I buy you a green drink?"

Kendall laughed. "No, thanks. I think I've had my limit. Someone has to stay sober enough to drive you home."

Grae waved off the waiter and turned to regard Kendall. "So, you're offering…to be my chauffeur?"

A tiny smile flirted with Kendall's mouth. Grae stared at her lips.

"I'm offering."

If Thea hadn't just arrived, Grae would've taken her leave at that instant. But manners compelled her to remain at the table. After all, she was the guest of honour. But it was impossible to ignore the frissons of desire that rippled through her each time Kendall leaned close. Finally Grae furtively checked the bar's clock. Five more minutes, and they would leave.

Her pocket vibrated, and she jumped.

Kendall chuckled. "I think your pants are calling you."

Grae bit off a ribald reply and flipped open the phone. Marcus' number popped up on the screen. "Hey, buddy. What are you doing calling me? You on a coffee break already?"

"Grae, it's Freddie. You have to get down here."

Grae sat bolt upright at Freddie's shaky tone. "Freddie? Where are you? Where's Marcus?"

"We're in the Foothills ER. We were attacked by four guys on the way to work. You have to hurry."

"Marcus!" Grae jumped to her feet. "Is he okay?"

Freddie broke into sobs. "No. He's not okay."

Chapter 18

"I'll be there as soon as I can! Hold on, Freddie. It's going to be all right." But it wasn't going to be all right. Grae could scarcely breathe as she frantically looked around the table. She stepped back, and wrenched her coat off the chair.

"Grae! What's going on? What's wrong?"

Kendall's words barely registered. She had to get to Marcus. She started for the door, but Kendall stood and blocked her path.

"Grae, sweetie, look at me. Tell me what's going on."

"Marcus is in Foothills. He and Freddie were mugged on the way to work. I have to get there."

The others around the table surged to their feet, their words an indistinguishable babble.

Grae broke away. "I have to go."

Kendall grabbed her coat and purse. "I'll take you."

"No, I—"

"Hush. I can get you there faster than any bus or cab. C'mon."

"Text me when you know something," Thea said. "And anything you need, just call me."

Jude nodded. "Don't worry about work tomorrow. Take care of Marcus, and I'll see you on Thursday, if he's out of the woods."

"Thanks." Grae stumbled blindly in Kendall's wake. A chorus of encouragement followed them, but Grae was deaf to their optimism. *Marcus. Oh, God, please let him be okay.*

When Grae pulled back the curtain to the exam cubicle, she almost passed out. Kendall's arm slid around her shoulders as Grae stared at Marcus' bloodied, stitched, and bandaged face. His eyes were closed, but she wasn't sure whether it was because he was asleep or unconscious, or because they were so swollen he couldn't open them. A cast encased his left arm from elbow to fingertips, bandages wrapped his torso, and leads ran from his thin chest to beeping machines.

Freddie stood on the far side of the bed. He clutched Marcus' uninjured hand as he described the attack to the police officer taking down notes. "It couldn't have been a robbery. They didn't take our phones or our wallets. It had to be a case of mistaken identity. They must've thought Marcus was someone else."

The officer looked up. "Why do you say that?"

"Because one of the guys beating him up said something like, 'Tell your old lady to keep her nose out of the boss' business, or we'll be back to finish this.'"

Grae's mouth dropped open, and her gaze flicked between Marcus and Freddie. *It can't be!*

"The guys holding me never hit me, even when I was screaming at them to stop before they killed him. They just kept punching and kicking Marcus until he was unconscious."

"What did they do then?"

"They dropped him on the concrete and took off. I ran to Marcus and near fainted when I saw all the blood."

Grae bolted down the hallway for the washroom. She barely made it before she vomited her celebratory dinner into the commode. *Oh my God. What have I done? What have I done?*

A cool hand settled on the back of her neck, and a damp paper towel was pushed into her hand. "He's going to be all right."

Grae shook her head, tears pouring down her cheeks. "No. No. He's not all right."

"Not yet," Kendall said. "But he will be. He's young and strong. A few broken bones aren't going to stop him."

Broken bones. That she was responsible for. She had no doubt who the thugs worked for. *Domokos.* The message was for her, delivered in the most visceral way possible.

Grae's thoughts spun in confused agony. Should she tell the officer of her suspicions? Not only did she have no evidence, she knew Domokos would've covered his tracks. She couldn't even speak up without admitting to her culpability in the assault. *Oh God.* Marcus would hate her. Not only for the beating, but he'd know she hadn't trusted him to handle Domokos on his own.

Her empty stomach twisted again, and she gagged, spitting out what little had escaped the initial eruption.

Kendall backed out of the stall, and returned moments later with more damp paper towels. She helped Grae to her feet and put the towels in her hands. "Get cleaned up, and we'll go back. Marcus will want to see you when he wakes up."

No he won't. But Grae just nodded and went to a sink to rinse her mouth and splash water on her face. She grabbed some dry towels, and wiped the water off her face as she stared in the mirror. For an instant she saw her 22-year-old self, and she started to shake.

"It's happening again. I can't do this. I can't do this again." She darted past Kendall for the door.

"What the— Grae! Where are you going?"

Grae ran down the hall, desperate to escape both past and present. She burst through the double doors and out into the cold night. She didn't pause to think where she would go; she just ran. When she finally came to a halt, she doubled over. Her breath came in steaming gasps as tears congealed in frozen slivers on her face. When she could breathe again, she looked at the houses surrounding her without a clue as to her location.

Grae shivered. The temperature had fallen considerably since their triumphant walk from the courthouse to Halligan's. She looked around for a bus stop. There was one down at the end of the block. It might take a wait, but she'd get home tonight, which was more than she could say for Marcus.

She plodded down the street, her head lowered. Why was this happening again? Fresh tears rolled down Grae's face. Another innocent had paid the price for her mistakes. She had tried so hard to distance herself from that woman, and just when she thought she'd finally put her past behind her for good, here she was—full circle.

A car wheeled to a stop at the curb next to Grae, and the driver's side door flew open. Kendall jumped from the car and hurried to her. She grabbed Grae's shoulders. "Why the hell did you leave? What's going on?"

Grae stared at her dully. "It's my fault."

"What's your fault?" Kendall softened her tone and brushed her glove over Grae's cheek. "Come on. You're half frozen. Get in the car, and we'll talk."

Kendall steered Grae around the front of the car, and opened the passenger door. Grae slid in, vaguely appreciating the warm interior. She'd gotten cold once she'd stopped running and the sweat had dried.

The heat that poured from the dashboard vents did nothing to thaw the ice that had settled around her heart, though. It was time to go again, and this time she'd leave the city, not just her life. She could lose herself on the streets of Vancouver. Lots of people did.

Kendall twisted to face Grae. "I don't know where you are right now, but the look on your face is scaring the hell out of me."

"Thank you for coming after me. Would you mind dropping me at my apartment?" Grae could feel Kendall's gaze on her, but she stared out the front windshield, numb to anything but the need to run. The sooner she got to the apartment, the sooner she could pack a bag and consult the outbound bus schedule.

Kendall put the car in gear and drove. Lost in plans of how to execute her disappearance, Grae paid no attention to the passing streets. When Kendall pulled up in front of Jo's house, she stared.

"What the—? This isn't my place."

"No, but it's the place you need to be right now. I don't know what's going through your mind, and you don't have to tell me. But I'm going to walk you inside, and you are going to talk to Mom."

Grae shook her head, released her seat belt, and reached for the door handle. She knew where she could catch a bus from here.

Kendall seized her arm. "No you don't. You're not running—from Marcus, from me, or from your life."

"I'm just going home."

"No, you're not. I don't know why I know that, but I know it, and I'm not going to let you."

Grae looked at Kendall and shook her head. "Why would you even care?"

"Are you kidding me?"

"No, I'm not. I don't know what this is between us, but if you have any sense at all, you'll let me out of this car and forget you ever met me. Believe me, you'll regret it if you don't."

Kendall cupped Grae's face and kissed her passionately. It took a long moment, but Grae began to respond. Kendall's kisses softened, until she pulled away and rested her forehead against Grae's.

"Don't run away before we even figure out what this is. Give us a chance."

"I can't." But Grae's words were half-hearted. Could she? What she'd done to Marcus…and to Melissa…wouldn't she do that to Kendall, too? She couldn't risk that. Not again.

Kendall pulled back a little. "I don't know what's going on in that convoluted brain of yours, but will you please just talk to Mom? I'll wait for you, and then I'll take you home afterwards, okay? We don't have to talk if you don't want to, but I'm asking you to talk to Mom. Will you do that for me? More importantly, will you do it for yourself?"

"I'm not sure I can. You don't know—"

"You're right, I don't. But what I do know is that I care about you more than I've cared for anyone in…forever. And I'm pretty sure that if I took you home right now, I'd never see you again. So I'm begging you, if you care anything about me at all, please talk to Mom."

Kendall's plea finally fractured the ice around Grae's heart. "What if it doesn't do any good?"

"It will. I have faith in Mom. And I have faith in you, Grae."

Under the power of Kendall's simple words, the ice cracked completely and fell away.

"It might take a while. It's a very long story. I can catch the bus home."

Kendall shook her head. "I'll wait in my old bedroom."

Grae studied Kendall's expression as it warred between determination and desperation. "Why does it matter so much to you?"

"God, don't you get it? Because *you* matter so much to me. I haven't felt like this in more years than I can remember. I thought you were starting to feel the same way."

Stone Gardens

"I am... I was," she amended hastily.

"So fight for us, damn it! Get your ass in there and talk to my mother."

After a long moment, a smile curled the corner of Grae's mouth. "Your seduction technique is really weird."

Kendall burst out laughing. "Hey, I'm rusty. Cut me a break here."

A tiny flicker of warmth spluttered to life in Grae's chest. "All right. Let's go see what Jo has to say about us barging in on her in the middle of the night."

"It's not even nine. Mom's a night owl. She won't mind. Now come on."

Kendall jumped out of the car and met Grae on the sidewalk. She took Grae's hand as they walked up the path. The front door swung open as they approached. Jo stood framed in the doorway with Maddie in her arms. There wasn't a hint of surprise on her face.

"The hot chocolate is almost ready."

She went into the kitchen, while they took off their boots and hung up their coats.

Kendall drew Grae into a hug. "Thank you."

Grae returned the embrace. "For what?"

"For giving us a chance." Kendall touched her lips lightly to Grae's. "Take as long as you need, and call me when you're done."

Kendall left Grae and passed Jo returning to the living room with two cups of hot chocolate. "I'm just going to grab a cup, too, and I'll be in my room."

"That's fine," Jo said. "Your bed is made up, if you want to take a nap."

Kendall yawned. "Just might do that. Thanks, Mom."

Grae automatically took her usual seat. "Should I even ask how you knew we were coming?"

Jo smiled. "Kendall called me when you ran away from the hospital. She said she was going to look for you, and if it took all night, she'd find you. My daughter is as stubborn as her father was, so I knew she'd find you eventually. Maddie and I decided a pot of hot chocolate would be just the thing in case you wanted to drop by. And if you didn't, that was fine, too. Hot chocolate is just as good heated up for breakfast."

"You—both of you—are amazing."

"We both care. Now, would you like to talk about what happened tonight?"

Grae sighed. "How much did Kendall tell you?"

"Just that Marcus was in really bad shape, and it freaked you out so terribly that you ran out of the hospital. But I suspect that's not the whole story."

"No, it's not." Grae closed her eyes. Could she really tell Jo what she hadn't told anyone, even Marcus?

"Shall I ask a few leading questions?"

Grae nodded wearily. "Go ahead."

"Whatever happened tonight, is it related to whatever originally drove you to drop out of your life eight years ago?"

"How did you know?"

"Because whenever we even come near the source of your disappearance, you panic. It sounds like you panicked tonight."

"Seeing Marcus—"

"Would of course distress you. But your normal response would've been to stick to his side, not to run. So, what happened? What made you flee like all the hounds of hell were after you?"

"Freddie told the officer what the bastards said."

"What did they say?"

"As those animals beat my best friend to a pulp, they said, 'Tell your old lady to keep her nose out of the boss' business, or we'll be back to finish this.'"

"And what did that mean to you?"

"That I caused them to go after Marcus. It's my fault he's lying in the hospital beat up so badly he's barely recognizable."

"Why are you taking responsibility for that?"

"Because it was my attempt to protect him that actually made him a target instead."

"All right, start from the beginning and tell me what you're talking about."

It's was Jo's no-nonsense, time-to-tell-the-truth voice, but Grae hesitated. Telling her about Marcus and Domokos would lead to telling her about Melissa. She didn't know if she could do that. Her gaze flicked to the door.

"No, Grae. Not this time. You stopped yourself the last time. We need to explore why your first instinct is to run. Yesterday you sat in that chair and agreed with me when I told you that you have friends and family who care about you more than you know. It's past time you believed that."

Grae looked away. "They wouldn't if they knew what I did."

"Do you think I wouldn't?"

"Maybe." Grae shrugged. "I don't know."

"Then let me reassure you of something you should already know: This is a safe space. We can discuss anything and I'm not going to judge you, I'm not going to dismiss you, and I'm not going to abandon you. I am going to help you help yourself. You've made tremendous progress over the past few months, but you are never going to find the peace and stability you long for until you deal with why you withdrew from everyone who loved you and constructed a suit of armour to keep the world at bay. For a long time Marcus was the only one to find a way inside that armour, but now there are a lot of people who would like to rip it away so you can live a full life again. I'm asking you—is that what you want? Do you want to be rid of that armour that imprisons you more than it protects you?"

Grae didn't answer. She was so tired. She had been tired for a long, long time. Finally, after what seemed like an eternity, she summoned up her last vestiges of energy. "I do."

Jo exhaled softly. "Good. Then let's talk."

Grae was silent for a long moment, then she took a deep breath. "My senior year in university. I'd been living in residence since I started. I told my parents I wanted the whole experience of being a student, but really I wanted the freedom."

"Freedom?"

Grae shot Jo a shame-faced glance. "I wanted to be able to bring women back to my room."

"That's not unusual for students. They're learning to live out from under their parents' wings and frequently explore their sexuality."

"Well, I kind of got carried away exploring. I didn't do relationships, but the women I dated didn't care. They weren't into long-term relationships either, so it was all good. At least until Melissa came into my life."

"And who was she?"

Grae dug her nails into the arms of the chair and struggled to suppress the rising panic. She hadn't said Melissa's name out loud in more than eight years. "She was just a kid, a freshman, who had the fucking misfortune to develop this massive crush on me."

"And why was that a misfortune?"

"Because it cost her her life."

Chapter 19

Eight years ago

Grace was in the library stacks, trying to find an obscure volume on computational finance, when someone called her name.

"Hey, Grace, have you finished Patterson's assignment?"

Grace turned to see Andi walking down the row toward her. "Are you kidding? I haven't even started it. That's why I'm here."

Andi slipped her arms around Grace's neck. "So, you want to work on it together?"

Grace raised an eyebrow. "Do you really want to work on the assignment?"

Andi nibbled at her neck. "Depends. Is Michelle going to be gone to her boyfriend's place tonight?"

"When isn't she? I don't think I've seen her in our room for more than fifteen minutes at a time since New Year's."

"Good. See you at seven?"

"Make it six. I'll leave the door unlocked in case you get there first."

Grace grinned as she watched Andi sashay away. Andi was such an accommodating—

"Hi, Grace."

Melissa, her arms full of books, stood at the end of the row, eying Grace with her customary shy smile. Inwardly, Grace sighed. She usually half-enjoyed the freshman's unabashed admiration, but it was becoming a little tedious. Melissa's invitations had become more frequent, and she hated to keep letting the kid down, but she also didn't want to give her false hope.

"Hey, Missy. How's it going?"

"Good. Um, I was wondering if you wanted to go to The Den tonight? It's student appreciation night. Half price drinks, and I'm buying."

"That's really sweet, and I wish I could take you up on it, but I've got an assignment due in a week. I really have to stay in and get it done."

Melissa's face fell. "Oh, okay."

"Don't you hate when work interferes with fun?"

Melissa stared at her feet. "Maybe another time."

"Absolutely. Let me get caught up, and I'm all yours." Grace regretted the words the instant they were out of her mouth.

Melissa's face lit up like sunshine. "Great! Well, I'd better be going. Talk to you later."

As she walked away, Grace groaned quietly. *Goddamnit. When will I learn?* Melissa seized on the tiniest sliver of encouragement and magnified it into a full-blown fiction. It had been flattering at first. Three weeks into her senior year, Grace's friends had pointed out that Melissa popped up almost everywhere she went, even though they took no classes together. Grace had recognized the signs of a giant crush, and it had amused her.

Her friends had teased Grace about her devoted acolyte, even suggesting that Grace just take her to bed so Melissa could get it out of her system. But Grace sensed that Melissa wasn't a one-and-done kind of girl. This kid wanted a relationship—toaster oven, matching rings, a U-Haul, and canine children. Grace didn't do relationships, so she'd been politely brushing Melissa off for months.

"Maybe I have to stop being so gentle."

Ryan poked his head around the corner of the stacks. "You say something, Gracie?"

"Nah. Just talking to myself."

Ryan grinned. They were old friends from their days in Earth Sciences 101, when Grace had coached her new buddy through the entire semester. "They can treat that now, you know. You don't have to be crazy."

"In this place, it helps. So, shut up and let me tell you about my plans for tonight."

"Ooh, do tell. Who's the lucky lady, and can I listen in?"

"Pervert," she teased.

"Takes one to know one. Hey, you want to get a coffee? You can tell me all about the girl-du-jour over a latte. And since I don't have anyone waiting for me in my room, you're buying."

"Not sure how you figure that, but since Dad gave me my allowance last weekend, I'll pick up the tab."

Ryan snorted. "With the allowance your old man gives you, you can afford to buy me the thickest steak in Calgary."

"Dream on, lover boy."

"Oh, believe me, I am. I am."

※

Grace traced circles on Andi's damp back as they both recovered their breath. Andi had been particularly athletic during this encounter, and Grace had been a grateful recipient.

Once their breathing returned to normal, Grace tugged gently on Andi's hair. "Hey, it's still early. You want to go to The Den tonight? Half-priced pitchers of beer and fifty-cent wings. Beats having pizza again."

Andi rose up on her elbows, and her breasts brushed enticingly on Grace's. "Wish I could, but I actually do have to do some work tonight. I have a deadline tomorrow, and since you lured me into your bed instead of us working on Patterson's paper, I've got that due for next week, too. You are such a bad influence."

"Jesus. You've got one tomorrow? And you're here with me? You're going to be pulling an all-nighter, for sure."

Andi lowered her head and nibbled on Grace's breast. "Which is precisely why I came here before going to the library."

Grace arched her back. "Not that I object in the least, but I don't get the connection."

"Just releasing a little stress first. It'll help me focus." Andi's hand moved between Grace's legs.

"Damn, I don't know about your stress levels, but you're doing wonders for mine."

※

It was the usual Thursday night insanity at The Den, and Grace stumbled her way through the crowd. It was her turn to pay for the next pitcher of beer, and her party had grown tired of waiting for their server. She didn't mind. She'd noticed an old friend leaning on the bar.

Grace moved in behind Maggie. "Mags, how're you doing? I haven't seen you in forever."

Maggie turned and wrapped her arms around Grace's neck. "Hey, stranger. How've you been?"

"Mmm, missing this, that's for sure." They indulged in an enthusiastic reunion before coming up for air, then turned to wait for the bartender's attention. "So, what have you been up to now that you're a wage-slave?"

Maggie groaned. "I've been working way too hard for way too little."

"Really? I thought you got a good job after graduation."

"More like a glorified secretary. But hey, my day just got way better. You here with anyone?"

"Just Ryan and the gang." The bartender stopped in front of them and Grace ordered a pitcher of beer. "Anything for you, Mags?"

"No thanks. I think I've had enough for now." Maggie eyed Grace speculatively. "So no one's waiting back in your room?"

Grace grinned and lowered her lips to Maggie's ear. "Not that I know of. Why? You interested in a little auld lang syne?"

"As long as I don't have to drive."

"Oh, baby, don't you worry, I'll do all the driving. Just let me drop this beer back with the gang, okay?"

Grace paid for the pitcher and led the way back to her table. Maggie slapped Grace's ass as she leaned over to put the beer down, and Ryan hooted.

Grace winked at her friends. "See you later, guys. I've got a better offer."

A round of laughter and catcalls followed Grace and Maggie as they left. They walked back to the dorm, stopping frequently to make out on the unusually warm spring evening. By the time they got to her room, Grace could hardly wait to get Maggie inside. She went to put her key in the lock, but the door opened. *Michelle must've been here. I gotta remember to tell her to lock up next time.*

She backed into the room, and pulled Maggie with her. She had Maggie's shirt halfway off when Maggie suddenly clutched it closed over her chest.

"Whoa, cowgirl! I don't do threesomes."

Grace frowned. "Threesomes?"

Maggie pointed over her shoulder. "Your bed is already occupied."

Grace whirled around, and her jaw dropped. A very naked Melissa was sitting in her bed, the sheets artfully draped about her. Dismay was clear on her face.

Grace turned back. "Oh, shit. Mags, I didn't—"

Maggie shrugged her shirt into place. "I'm going back to The Den."

"But...but wait. I didn't—"

Maggie fled, and Grace wheeled around. "What the hell, Melissa?"

Melissa pulled the sheet over her chest and mumbled something.

"Goddamnit. What the fuck were you thinking? Did it ever occur to you to wait for an invitation before you climbed into my bed?"

"I saw you at The Den tonight, and I decided—" She took a deep breath, and then said in a rush, "I just got tired of waiting and I decided to go for it."

"Well, for Christ's sake, did you maybe think there was a reason I hadn't asked you into my bed? It wasn't like I didn't know you'd jump at the chance." The alcohol was making Grace intemperate, but she didn't care. This had gone too far. "You're not my type. Get that through your thick skull. And stop following me around like a goddamned puppy. It's embarrassing to me and humiliating to you. People have been laughing at you for months. Hell, I've been laughing at you for months."

Tears filled Melissa's eyes and spilled over.

"Jesus." Grace glanced around the room. Melissa's jeans and red sweater were neatly folded on her desk chair. She grabbed the clothes and threw them at her uninvited visitor. "Go. Just get dressed and go."

Sobbing, Melissa clambered from the bed.

Grace watched her struggle to get dressed, and guilt surged through her. "Aw, shit. I'm sorry. Look, Melissa, stop."

Melissa dragged on her pants and fumbled with the zipper.

"C'mon, Missy. Just stop. Let's talk, okay?"

Melissa stopped, her small breasts heaving with sobs.

"Aw, crap." Grace reached out and took the girl into her arms. "Shh, I'm sorry. I didn't mean it."

She soothed Melissa, who burrowed against her neck. "It's okay. It's okay." She caressed Melissa's naked back. "Everything's going to be all right. Shh."

When Melissa was calmer, Grace just held her, hands moving in lazy circles as she pondered what to do next. Maybe she should take her for coffee so they could talk this over. She'd try to be compassionate. After all, there was a time not long ago when she'd had a big crush on—

Melissa reached for the buttons of Grace's jeans and started twisting them open.

Grace grabbed her hand. "Whoa, not a good idea. I'm half-wasted as it is. You should just go back to your room. Maybe we can have coffee tomorrow and talk, okay?"

"I don't want to talk. You were going to fuck her. She's gone, I'm here. Fuck me."

Grace blinked. Hearing that word from Melissa's innocent mouth sounded so incongruous, but it was also undeniably erotic. "Uh, you still want to—?"

"Damn right." The determination in Melissa's face was supported by the nimble fingers that undid Grace's buttons. She plunged her hand down the front of Grace's pants.

Her libido reignited and Grace sucked in a breath. "Jesus."

Melissa swivelled them in a half-circle, and Grace stumbled against the bed.

Melissa's hand kept moving between Grace's legs as she struggled with Grace's shirt. When it was open, she dropped to her knees and wrenched Grace's jeans down. Grace's eyes widened as Melissa's tongue slid roughly over her clit.

"Holy crap!"

Her balance was already off, thanks to multiple pitchers of beer, and when Melissa thrust her fingers home, she toppled onto the bed. Grace barely got out a squawk before Melissa swarmed all over her.

"Whoa, whoa, slow down there, girl. We've got all night." Grace extracted Melissa's hand, and pulled her up into her arms.

Melissa stared at her, and a smile broke over her delicate features. "We do?"

"Absolutely."

Grace helped Melissa push her jeans off, and removed the rest of her own clothes. It wasn't how she'd planned to spend the night, but now that Melissa was naked in her bed, she wasn't averse to giving the kid what she'd obviously wanted for so long. She was about to remind Melissa that this was just a one-time thing and she didn't do relationships, when Melissa slid down her body and picked up where she'd left off. Her tongue and hands quickly had Grace rising to a climax.

"Oh God, yeah. Right there. Good girl. Good—" Grace clamped her hand on the back of Melissa's head and thrust wildly against her mouth. "Jesus, Jesus…"

She exploded rapturously, then slumped to the bed. Damn, if she'd known how good the kid was, she'd have given her a chance sooner.

Melissa rested quietly with her head on Grace's pelvis. When Grace recovered, she pulled Melissa up beside her on the bed. She slid one arm around her shoulders, and brushed back her long blonde hair.

"I don't know who taught you your moves, but wow. Just wow."

Melissa smiled up at Grace. "No one taught me. This is my first time."

Grace reared back. "Your first—? Are you serious?"

"I am. I wanted you to be the one to… You know."

Oh my God. A fucking virgin. Grace didn't know if she should jump Melissa's bones, or haul ass to the nearest confessional.

Melissa took Grace's hand and glided it down her belly. When Grace's fingertips rested at the top fringe of her pubic hair, she whispered, "Please?"

Grace hesitated, but Melissa's wide eyes pleaded with her. Finally she slid her thigh between Melissa's legs and lowered her mouth to her breasts. *A virgin. Damn. That's a first. No way Ryan's going to believe this night.*

Grace winced at the morning light coming in through the window. Her head pounded fiercely and her mouth tasted like an iguana had died inside. She fumbled blindly for the water bottle she usually left on the nightstand for such occasions and knocked her harness off onto the floor.

"What the—? Oh, shit."

She rolled over, but her bed was empty and Grace heaved a sigh of relief. Melissa was gone. Thank God she'd caught a clue and cleared out early.

Grace sat up, and rested her head in her hands. "Jesus. Feels like the goddamned Army is doing maneuvers in there."

She groped in the drawer of her bedside table for the bottle of aspirin, and dry-swallowed four in rapid succession.

The door swung open and Melissa walked in, a big smile on her face. She carried a brown bag and two cups of coffee. Grace's stomach lurched, and she scowled at the unwelcome visitor.

Melissa plopped down on the bed and held out a coffee. "I thought you'd need this. Black, two sugars, just the way you like it."

"Thanks." Her surly mood was lost on the overly-perky Melissa. "Look, I don't think—"

"And I got you your favourite—a cranberry almond muffin with cream cheese, not butter." Melissa passed the muffin over on a napkin and tore the top off the tiny container of cream cheese. "They were out of knives, but I thought you could spread it with the end of the spoon."

"Melissa, stop."

Melissa's hand dropped, and she stared at the floor. Her shoulders were tight and braced.

It was hard to be civil with a vicious hangover wracking every molecule of her body, but Grace tried. "Look, I'm glad you came over last night, I really am. I had a good time."

Melissa shot her a shy glance. "So did I."

"That's good. That's really good. Everyone's first time should be memorable. It isn't always, you know."

"I've heard."

"Okay. So, we can maybe do it again sometime if you want, but you can't just show up unannounced, okay? You gotta talk to me first."

"I tried to talk to you."

"I know, I know. And that's on me. I will talk to you, I promise. But you gotta know that I don't do relationships, right? I'll probably be back at The Den tonight, and I don't have a clue who I'll go home with. I'm not a one-woman woman, okay?"

Melissa's head was bent. Her hair curtained her face, but Grace didn't miss the tear that hit the plastic cover on the coffee cup she was holding. That tear irritated the hell out of her. It wasn't like she'd invited Melissa to her bed under false pretences. Hell, the kid had practically ravaged her when she was just trying to be nice. And after Melissa had driven Maggie away, too. Grace's temper began to rise.

"You do get that it was sex and nothing more, right? It's not like we're having a relationship. So if that's what you're thinking, you can forget it."

Melissa raised her head. Her gaze fell on the discarded harness. "I thought—"

"Aww, Jesus, Missy. We had a good time. I enjoyed myself, really. I hope you enjoyed yourself, too. But I've been as clear as I can that I'm not into relationships. I like to have fun. That's all. Don't limit yourself to me. Go meet some other girls. I mean, damn, you're good in bed. Once word gets around, you'll have your pick of—"

Melissa jumped to her feet and her coffee spilled. Hot liquid splashed over Grace's naked chest.

Grace yelped and used the pillow to blot the coffee. "Goddamnit!"

"I hoped it meant something to you. I hoped *I* meant something to you."

"Aww, shit."

Melissa whirled and dashed for the door. Grace jumped to her feet, only to crash to the floor as the entangled sheets tripped her up.

"Christ on a crutch!"

She stumbled to her feet and hurriedly searched for her jeans, finally locating them where they'd ended up under the bed. She dragged them on and grabbed the nearest sweatshirt. Her feet were still bare when she ran out of the room.

The stairwell door was just closing, and she raced down the hall. Inside the stairwell, she could hear the clatter of footsteps several floors below. Grace took the stairs as fast as she could, but had to halt at the second landing when her stomach threatened to spew all over the passageway. At a slower pace, she descended the rest of the stairs.

She emerged from the ground floor exit and instantly closed her eyes against the brilliant sun. "Sonuvabitch." Grace covered her eyes and peered out through her fingers as she adjusted. The squeal of hard-used brakes caused her to wrench her hand away, and she stared in shock.

"Oh God, no! Stop!"

Melissa glanced back over her shoulder at Grace as she darted across the road. The driver of the oncoming pick-up didn't have a prayer of stopping in time.

The impact threw Melissa into a retaining wall, and she crumpled to the ground.

Grace froze as people ran to Melissa. Through the crowd she caught a glimpse of bright red. Melissa's sweater? It had to be, didn't it?

A scream erupted from the first girl who'd reached Melissa's side. The din of people yelling rose to a crescendo. Several people were already on their phones, their faces distorted with horror.

Grace fell to her knees and puked until she couldn't breathe.

Chapter 20

Jo held out the tissue box, and Grae plucked several before settling back in her chair. She mopped at the tears that had been running down her face since she'd begun her account. Without a word, Jo stood, moved to Grae's side, knelt, and hugged her. Grae clung to her until her sobs turned to hiccups.

Jo released her. "Are you okay?"

"I don't know. It's like…"

"Like a dam finally broke and the waves overwhelmed you."

"Yes." Grae accepted a few more tissues and dried her face before adding them to the overflowing trashcan.

Jo returned to her seat. "Are you up to telling me a little more?"

"What more is there to tell? I acted like a Grade A bitch, and poor Melissa paid the price. Just like Marcus did."

"Let's separate those two instances for a moment. You had no intention of harming either, and I think you've more than paid your penance for Melissa. Correct me if I'm wrong, but wasn't that the impetus for you abandoning your former life?"

"Yes. The guilt sickened me. I couldn't eat, I couldn't sleep, I started skipping classes and not handing in assignments. I was only months away from graduation, and my grades nose-dived so bad, it was questionable whether I would've even passed. I didn't bother to stick around to find out. One day it got so bad that I was either heading for the roof to throw myself off, or I was leaving. I chose to leave."

"And you left everything."

Grae uttered a short laugh. "Yeah. I never was one for half measures. When I screwed around, I screwed half the female population on campus. When I dropped out of my life, I dropped off the edge of the world. When I messed up Marcus, I—" She choked.

"Enough." Jo's voice was kind, but firm. "Tell me why you think you're responsible for Marcus being mugged."

Grae related her threat to Domokos and her certainty that it had led directly to Marcus' beating. When she was done, Jo's expression was dark with anger. For one terrible moment, Grae thought that anger was directed at her. Instinctively, she began to rise.

Jo held up a hand. "No. I'm not mad at you. It may not have been the smartest thing you've ever done, but you were trying to protect someone you loved. The fault lies with Domokos, not you."

"No, it is my fault. Just like with Melissa."

Jo leaned forward and fixed Grae with a compassionate gaze. "Let's examine that."

Maddie chose that moment to jump into Grae's lap. She wrapped her arms around the cat and cuddled it to her chest, with her face in Maddie's luxuriant fur.

"Did you chase Melissa into the street?"

"No. But she was running from me. If she hadn't been so upset, she'd have seen that truck."

"But her safety was her responsibility, Grae. She should've looked both ways, whether or not she was upset."

Grae's brow furrowed. "That's pretty harsh. She was just a kid. A kid who was crying her eyes out because of me."

"You said she was a freshman."

"Yes."

"So she was at least eighteen."

Grae shivered as she relived that terrible day. She squeezed Maddie tighter. "Nineteen—at least that's what the obituary said."

"We let nineteen-year-olds drink and vote and drive, and yes, even have sex with whomever they choose."

"I know that."

"Did you feel responsible for yourself at nineteen?"

"Yes, but—"

"Would you have resented anyone insinuating you were anything less than an adult at that age?"

"Yes, but you're not—"

Jo fixed her with an intense stare. "At barely twenty-two, you left everything you knew behind and made your own way in the world without one of the advantages with which you were born."

Grae scowled. "And a bloody fine job I did of it, too."

"You not only survived probable PTSD, you rescued Marcus."

"What are you driving at?"

"There isn't a lot of difference between most nineteen-year-olds and most twenty-two-year-olds. My point is that you've been denying Melissa's responsibility in what was, in all respects, an accident. You've treated her as if she was some child you wronged. She wasn't a child. She was a young adult who should've known better than to run across a busy road without looking, no matter what her state of mind."

Grae stared at Jo, who sat quietly under the scrutiny.

Finally, Grae shook her head and looked away. "I couldn't handle the memorial that students built up against that goddamned wall. It was right outside my dorm. I'd go clear around the other side of the building to avoid it, but when I looked out my window, there it was. The day I left school, I saw her parents there. Her mom was small and blonde, like Missy. She wore all black and clung to her husband's arm like she wouldn't be able to stand without him. I watched them look over the flowers and cards and candles. But when she picked up a teddy bear and hugged it, I lost it. I collapsed and bawled my eyes out. No one else knew why Melissa was dead, but I did, and I couldn't stand it one more second. I had to get out of there. I threw some clothes in a backpack and left. I walked out of my life and never looked back."

"Until now."

"And look what I did…again. I hurt everyone I care for. I'm not fit for human company."

"Don't say that."

The words came from behind Grae, and she twisted.

Kendall stood in the doorway, tears in her eyes. "Don't ever say that."

Jo glared at Kendall. "You know better than to come in here when I'm in session."

"I'm sorry, Mom. I heard Grae crying. I couldn't—"

Grae held out her hand to Kendall. "It's okay. I don't mind."

Kendall knelt by Grae's side. "I really am sorry. Mom's right. I do know better, but this was…this was you, and I couldn't stand hearing you cry for one second longer without doing this." She wrapped Grae in a warm hug.

Grae laid her head on Kendall's shoulder, and an unexpected peace soothed her battered soul.

Jo cleared her throat and rose to her feet. "I'll let you two talk. But Kendall, you and I will be discussing this further."

Kendall didn't stir from Grae's embrace. "I know."

Jo left the room.

"Please don't say you're not fit for human company. If you'll let me, I plan to spend a lot of time in your company, and I'm very human. Just ask Mom."

Grae smiled. "I didn't mean to get you in trouble."

"It wasn't the first time, and it won't be the last. Mom takes her professional responsibilities very seriously. You should've heard the lecture I got when she found out you and I were dating."

"Are we? Dating?"

"I hope so. I want to…if you do."

Grae caressed Kendall's cheek. "I'm a fucked-up mess. You know that, right?"

"I know you think you are. No one else does."

Instead of all the things Grae wanted to ask, she said, "I can't remember the last time I was this tired. Could I impose on you to give me a ride home?"

"Why don't you stay here tonight, and we'll pick this up in the morning." Grae and Kendall turned at the sound of Jo's voice. She was leaning against the doorjamb. "Since my daughter already broke the rules, why don't you stay, Grae? I'll feed you breakfast in the morning, we can talk some more, and then I'll take you to the hospital to see Marcus."

Grae stiffened, but forced herself to relax. "Are you sure?"

"I am." Jo levelled a stern look at Kendall. "And you, my dear darling heart, are going home."

"Mom—"

"No. I know you want to support Grae, but this is not your home at the moment. This is Grae's safe space. She's not ready to deal with what you bring to the table, so you have to step back. I'm not saying forever, I'm just saying for tonight."

Kendall scowled.

Grae suppressed a laugh as she imagined how often a much younger Kendall had probably glared at her mother in the same way. She cupped Kendall's chin and turned the pouting face toward her. "It's okay. Seriously. Your mom's plan is a good one. I do want to talk with her some more before I see Marcus. I can't begin to tell you how grateful I am that you came after me when I bolted out of the hospital, and we will talk soon, okay? But for now, you really should go home."

It was clear Kendall wasn't thrilled about the idea, but finally she nodded. "All right. Walk me to the car?"

"Sure."

They donned their outerwear and went out to Kendall's car, hand in hand.

"Kendall?"

"Mmm-hm?"

"I'm confused."

Kendall leaned against the passenger door. "About?"

Grae gestured between them. "Us. I don't understand— I mean, I knew something was going on. If I had any doubts, your kisses removed them. But, well…you were married."

"And you figured that made me straight. I get it. Makes sense, right? It might seem strange, but I wasn't surprised when I started having feelings for you. It's not the first time I've felt romantically for another woman. Truth is, I married Derek before I ever worked up the nerve to ask a woman out. So, this is the first time I've allowed an interest to get beyond imagination, and actually explored and acted on what I feel."

"I haven't let myself feel much of anything in a long time."

Kendall gently drew Grae into her arms. "I figured that. I know we have a lot to talk through before this goes any further. I'm just asking that you not run away. That you give me…that you give *us* a chance. I think we could be really amazing together."

This time Grae initiated the kiss. When they finally drew apart, she echoed, "Amazing." Then she added, "I agree. Now go home before I forget all about my therapist's excellent advice and go home with you."

Kendall's eyes shone. She walked around to the driver's side and gazed across her car, a playful grin on her face. "So will you dream of me while you're lying in my old bed?"

"Maybe your mom will put me in your brothers' room."

"Nah. After they left home, Mom turned Brandon and Jake's room into her meditation space. Unless you want to sleep on the mat beside the Buddha fountain, you're better off in my bed."

Grae winked. "You might be right. Only time will tell." She walked away with a little swagger in her stride.

"Hey."

Grae turned, and walked backwards as she relished Kendall's grin. "Yes?"

"Mom keeps a pair of my pajamas in my old room. Feel free to borrow them."

"What if I prefer to sleep naked?"

Kendall's mouth fell open, then snapped closed. She banged her forehead on the roof of the car. "You're killing me."

"Then my work here is done. G'night, Kendall."

"Sleep tight, Grae. And thanks for just making my sleep all the more difficult to come by."

Grae winked, though she wasn't sure Kendall could see it in the dark. "You're welcome."

By the time Grae re-entered the house, her weariness had lifted a touch, and an unprecedented lightness filled her heart. Whether it was unburdening herself of her long-held guilt, or Jo's compassion, or Kendall's confession, she couldn't say. But when she saw Marcus tomorrow, she would confess her culpability. Whatever happened, happened. No more running. She was ready to face the consequences of her actions.

※

The following morning Grae woke to the scent of bacon. The smell reminded her of Marcus' Sunday morning brunches, and her dawning smile faded. *Marcus.* She would see him today, and she'd make her confession. Would he hate her?

"Wouldn't blame him if he does." Grae sighed and pushed back the covers. *Time to face the music.*

She noticed a bath towel, sweatshirt, and sweatpants on the chair next to the door. They hadn't been there the night before. "Damn, I was really out of it." She hadn't even heard Jo slip them inside her room, but she was grateful for the thoughtfulness.

Grae took a hasty shower and donned the fresh clothes. From the length of the sleeves and pant legs, these must've been some Kendall had left behind. The thought made her smile.

She went to the kitchen and found Jo at the stove. The kitchen table was set for two.

"If you want some coffee, help yourself."

Grae poured herself a cup and took a seat. "Anything I can do?"

"No, everything's ready." Jo pulled two plates from the oven and added omelets to the bacon and hash browns.

"Wow, Jo, you didn't have to do all this."

"You look surprised. What were you expecting?"

"To tell you the truth, I took a peek into your meditation room when I was done with my shower."

Jo smiled. "So you thought surely we'd have granola for breakfast."

"Well, I did smell the bacon, but…"

"Expectations are funny things, aren't they?"

"What do you mean?"

Jo took a seat across from Grae. "Go ahead—eat."

Certain that her aborted therapy session was about to resume, Grae nevertheless dug in. She wasn't disappointed.

"I imagine that when people first met you over the past eight years, they had certain expectations of you."

"Because of how I looked. Sure."

"Exactly. You constructed that look as a defence. Do you know why?"

Grae took a sip of coffee as she considered her answer. "Maybe…I had such a low opinion of myself that I expected everyone else to feel the same. By looking so radically different from the norm, I made sure people felt that way. No one knew me from my old life, so no one knew the pre-Melissa me. I made sure I never ran into family or friends. No, actually, I did run into an old friend one time."

"Did you? What happened?"

"It was about four years ago. Remember I told you about my friend Ryan?"

"Yes."

"I walked past him on a downtown street. He was in a business suit and talking on his phone. He looked right at me and didn't blink. I don't think he had a clue who I was."

"How did that make you feel?"

"Invisible. But happily so."

"In what way?"

"I was glad I was invisible. Ryan was the world I left behind. He and I were tight for four years. If he couldn't see me, then no one could. I was safe."

"Safe from what?"

Grae considered that as she ate. Finally she set her fork down and crossed her arms. "Safe from judgement."

Jo nodded. "Whose judgement?"

"Everyone's. If they knew I'd killed—"

"Uh-uh. Try again."

Grae studied the pattern of the tablecloth for a long moment. "They didn't know I was responsible for her death. No one knew."

"We'll be talking more about the fact that Melissa was responsible for her death, but follow that thought."

"Since they didn't know, they couldn't judge."

"So who could?"

"Me."

"Yes. And you judged yourself so harshly that you gave yourself a life sentence. Or it would've been, if not for…?"

"Marcus."

"Yes. In saving him, you saved yourself."

"And look how I paid him back." Grae pushed her plate aside. She'd lost her appetite.

"Which brings us back to expectations."

"How?"

"Other than Marcus being assaulted, things have gone extremely well for you recently. Would you agree?"

"I would, but—"

"I know. What happened to Marcus is terrible. But I can't help wondering if you were expecting it."

Grae stared at Jo. "Expecting? I would never have deliberately put Marcus in danger!"

"That's not what I'm saying. Correct me if I'm wrong. Or more specifically if Kendall got the wrong impression, but when she called me last night, she told me she was sure you were going to run away. Were you?"

Grae hung her head. Her powerful impulse to flee seemed distant now, but she couldn't deny it. "I was."

"Did you have a plan?"

"I was going to pack some clothes, take my cash out of its hiding place, look up the bus schedules online, leave the key for Marcus, and catch a bus out of town without leaving a forwarding address."

"You have a hiding place for money?"

"Yeah. I mean I have a bank account, too, but I always keep some cash at home, just in case."

"Just in case of what?"

"I don't know. Marcus might need something, or we might run short on grocery money."

"Or you might need it to leave town?"

"I guess, though I never thought of it like that."

"Perhaps not consciously. Considering that everything played out in such a short span of time, your plan to flee was well thought out."

Grae stared at Jo. "What are you getting at?"

"Do you think it's possible that even when things got better for you, even when you had a great job, Marcus was in a good spot, you'd reconciled with your family and beaten the charges that had been hanging over your head, a part of you still thought you couldn't possibly deserve this and it was all going to come crashing down on you?"

"Well, it did, didn't it?"

"Did it? Marcus was certainly badly injured, but you have the love and support of your friends and family. Jude expects you back at work tomorrow. What, other than Marcus' injuries, has changed?"

"Everything!"

"Explain, please."

"I got Marcus hurt. It was my stupidity that has him lying in a hospital bed right now."

"Really? So when you spoke to Domokos, you knew he would send men after Marcus?"

"Of course not. I wouldn't have done it, if I didn't think it would help—"

Jo smiled. "No, you wouldn't have, would you? And when you found Melissa in your bed, didn't you try to tell her to go back to her room?"

"Yeah, but I was such an asshole about it, I made her cry."

"And when she cried, you tried to comfort her."

Grae squirmed and looked away. "Sure, but I ended up having sex with her."

"Which, from all you've told me, she initiated and was rather forceful about pursuing."

"I could've said no."

"You could've. Were you inclined to?"

"I…I thought I was." Grae frowned. *Why didn't I?* "We just sort of got caught up in the moment, and one thing led to another."

"That's hardly surprising, is it? You'd been drinking. You returned to your room with a woman you thought you were about to have sex with. And there was another naked woman in your bed, waiting for you. It seems to me that sex with someone that night was almost inevitable."

"Huh."

"And yes, you could've handled things better the next morning, but I suspect if Melissa hadn't run out in front of that truck, you'd have caught up with her and convinced her to talk things out."

"Maybe."

"Probably?"

"I guess. I chased her because I felt so bad about making her cry again. I just wanted to talk to her—"

"Exactly. You wanted to talk to her. You didn't want her to be hurt. You certainly didn't want her to be killed. It was a terrible accident. When you talked to Domokos, you were trying to keep a predator away from your friend, to protect your little brother as you'd been doing for three years. You didn't expect it to rebound on Marcus. You certainly didn't put Marcus in the hospital. Domokos did. Just because you may have expected bad things to happen, doesn't mean you caused them to."

Grae rubbed her forehead. There was a distinct throbbing behind her eyes. "I swear you could talk an Inuit into buying a deep freeze."

Jo chuckled. "I'm not trying to talk you into anything. I simply want you to get past your sad assessment of your life and expectations of disaster, and see things as they really are."

"That might take a while."

"And that's fine. As long as you don't run away, you'll have all the time you need to deal with your issues."

"I sort of promised Kendall I wouldn't run." It was a non-verbal promise, but those kisses had spoken unmistakably of a future.

Jo sighed. "About that."

"About Kendall?"

"Yes. I feel that we should clear the air about you and my daughter."

Grae stiffened. "Okay."

"To be honest, the last thing I thought when I referred you to Angels Unawares was that you and Kendall would end up being attracted to each other."

"You thought she was straight, too?" Grae was surprised at Jo's laughter.

"I watched my daughter and her crushes on other girls from puberty right up until she met Derek. I always thought she'd eventually come out, but I'm afraid Derek made mincemeat of her good sense. So no, it comes as no surprise to me that she would be interested in another woman."

"So I was the surprise."

"Yes. Under normal circumstances it wouldn't be an issue, but because of our clinical relationship, we do need to draw clearly defined boundaries. As your therapist, you may talk to me about anything, and that includes your feelings toward Kendall. But when I take off the therapeutic hat, and I'm simply Kendall's mother, we can't cross-pollinate our talks. Do you understand?"

Grae nodded slowly. "I might end up seeing you more socially as well as professionally, and I have to keep those two Jos separate."

"That's right. In an ideal world, I would ask you and Kendall to suspend your relationship until you'd finished therapy. But given how my daughter sounds when she talks about you, I suspect that you'd quit seeing me before you'd quit seeing her. And I'm not sure that's a good idea."

"It isn't. I trust you. I can work with you, and I know I'm making progress."

"You're making excellent progress. So we'll give this a try and see how it works out. If we find it's not working, then I can recommend an excellent therapist to take over."

Grae shook her head sharply. "I don't want that."

"But you also don't want to stop seeing Kendall, right?"

"Right. Jo, I really like her. I've dated one girl in the last eight years and that was only one date. Lucy dumped me when I got arrested."

"We can deal with your prolonged period of celibacy at another session."

Grae groaned. "Do we have to?"

"What do you think?"

"I think—painful or not—I'm going to be talking about my non-existent sex life."

Jo smiled. "It may come up. Now, how about we get these dishes done and then I'll drive you to the hospital."

Chapter 21

They were still several blocks from the hospital when Jo asked, "Would you like me to come up with you?"

Grae had been focused on answering all the texts she'd found after she finally turned on her cellphone. She shook her head. "No, thanks. I think I need to see Marcus by myself."

"All right, but you know I'm here if you want to talk afterwards."

"I really appreciate that, thanks." Grae held up her phone. "Would you believe there are five texts from Ciara?"

"Why is that so hard to believe? The two of you looked like you were getting on very well at Halligan's."

"We were. I guess I'm just not used to believing she cares."

"She does, you know."

Grae chuckled. "Yeah, I get that feeling. In message number four she says that if she doesn't hear from me soon, she's re-hiring the private detective to find me."

"Did you hear from your mother?"

"And Jude and Dad and Virg."

"And Kendall?"

Grae smiled. "There was one or two from her."

Jo pulled into the drive that wound around the parking lot and past the hospital. "It is okay to drop you at the front door?"

"Of course, and thank you very much for the ride. And for…what you said this morning."

"I only ask the questions."

"No, you do a lot more than that. I know I've never said this, but I'm really grateful that Mom found you for me."

Jo glanced at her. "It wasn't hard. Your mother and I were very good friends once. She's about the only one I'd have come out of retirement to help."

Grae's mouth dropped open. "You and Mom were close?"

"I knew her long ago, yes."

"But...why didn't I know you?"

"Because the last time I saw you, you were about seven or eight years old. I certainly wouldn't have recognized you as an adult. You actually played with Kendall while your mother and I visited. Though, as I recall, you were more interested in Jake's GI Joe than Kendall's pink princess castle."

"But—"

Jo stopped the car. "They won't let me linger in passenger unloading, so ask your mother if you want to know more. And good luck with Marcus. Remember he loves you and will accept that what you did, you did with his best interests at heart."

Stunned, Grae clambered from the vehicle and Jo drove off. *Mom and Jo were best buds once? How did I not know that?*

She wasn't sure whether or not she should be angry that she'd been unaware of their friendship. If Jo hadn't seen her since she was eight, though, there had to be a reason. Maybe they'd drifted apart over the years.

Grae shook her head and entered the hospital. She asked for Marcus' room number at the admissions desk, then took the elevator to his floor.

He was in a ward with three other patients. The others had their curtains drawn. Marcus' bed was nearest the door and Grae stopped short as she entered the room. Kendall stood on the far side of the bed, laughing at something he'd just said. She looked up as Grae approached, and her expression softened.

"Hey, stranger."

"Hey, yourself. I didn't expect to see you here."

Kendall held up her AU identification badge. "Official business. I was just up on the Palliative Care Ward and decided to drop in and see how Marcus is doing."

It wasn't until Marcus cleared his throat that Grae realized she hadn't even looked at him. "Sorry, bud." She scanned his face. Last night's wound dressings were all in place, but she found a clear spot to kiss. "How're you feeling?"

"Like something big ran me over." Marcus' voice was raspy, but he smiled. "You didn't happen to get the licence number, did you? I scared Freddie so badly that he forgot to snap a photo of the truck that hit me."

Kendall patted Marcus' shoulder. "On that note, I think I'll leave you two alone to talk." She rounded the bed and stopped in front of Grae. "Call me later, okay?"

"I will."

Kendall hesitated. For an instant Grae wondered if she was going to kiss her, but Kendall contented herself with squeezing Grae's arm before she left the room.

When Grae turned back to Marcus, he was studying her.

"Something's changed."

"What do you mean?"

"You and Kendall—something's changed." Marcus' eyes widened. "Grae Jordan, you dog. You didn't. You did! Sit down and tell me all about it."

Grae pulled the visitor's chair up in the cramped space next to his bed, and took his uninjured hand. "It's not what you think, and there's not really all that much to tell. Freddie called and Kendall insisted on driving me here."

Marcus started to shake his head, but grimaced and stopped. He took long slow breaths and detached his hand from Grae's so he could press the button on the patient-controlled analgesia machine. He closed his eyes while Grae stared at him.

Finally he opened his eyes. "Don't worry. I'm still among the living. I don't know what gremlin is hidden in that machine, but I was overdue for a visit."

Grae hung her head. "God, I'm so sorry, Marcus. If I could just go back—"

"And do what? I know you're convinced it's your job to protect me, but you wouldn't have stood a chance against those muggers."

"I'm the reason they came after you."

"What do you mean? How could that be?"

Grae forced herself to meet his puzzled gaze. Marcus deserved no less than the entire sordid story. "Do you remember me meeting Mom for dinner at Magellan's?"

"Sure."

"I went there on purpose, bud. I wanted Domokos to see me as the daughter of an esteemed judge."

"Okay. Why?"

"So that when I told him to keep away from you, he'd know I had powerful connections and take me seriously. But it backfired."

"You told him to keep away from me?"

Grae nodded. "I told him if he didn't, I'd use social media to spread information about his liking for little boys all over town."

Marcus snorted. "You won't even set up a Facebook page."

"Yeah, but he didn't know that. I think I really did scare the hell out of him, but obviously as time wore on, the fear was replaced by anger."

Marcus struggled to sit up. "We have to tell the police. Call them."

"We can't, bud. I wish we could, but I don't have any proof at all."

"Maybe it wasn't him, then."

Grae shook her head. "No, you probably don't remember this, since they were kicking the shit out of you, but Freddie told the cops that one of the thugs yelled that you'd better tell your old lady to keep her nose out of the boss' business, or they'd be back to finish the job."

"My old lady?"

"Exactly. Anyone who knows you well enough to put a hit on you knows you don't have an old lady. Your mom's not in the picture. You'll never have a girlfriend, let alone a wife. So the only possible 'old lady' in your life is me."

Marcus stared at Grae. A smile grew on his battered face, then he broke out in laughter.

Grae's eyes widened. "Jesus, bud, what kind of drugs have they got you on?"

"Good ones, believe me. It just struck me as funny—you being my old lady."

To Grae's amazement, Marcus' hilarity was contagious. She started to laugh and gathered Marcus in a gentle hug. He winced, but returned the hug as best he could with one arm. When Grae sat down again, she felt as if a hundred-pound anvil had been lifted off her back.

Marcus regarded her with a smile. "So what are we going to do if we can't prove Domokos is responsible?"

Grae's bonhomie vanished. "Nothing. There's nothing we can do. It's the way of the fucking world. The guys with money, power, and position get away with this shit. I stand up for us against a couple of bullies who want to kill us, and I'm the one that ends up in court on charges."

"Charges that were dropped. Don't forget that part."

Grae sighed. "I won't, but it doesn't change the fact that Domokos is going to get away with hurting you unless the cops pick up his hit-men and one of them rolls on him. Not a damned thing we can do about it."

"Well, there's one thing I can do. Quit."

"But you love your job."

Marcus snorted. "Not enough to keep working for the sadist who signs my paycheque."

"Good. And don't you worry about a thing. I make enough to support both of us until you're better. Hey, you can use this time to study, bud. I know using the computer will be a bitch until your hand heals, but you can still work on your GED."

"Did anyone ever tell you that you have a one-track mind?"

Grae laid her hand on Marcus' forearm. "It's even more important now. You have to—"

Marcus stared past Grae, eyes wide and mouth agape. She turned to see a candy striper standing just inside the doorway. The teenager's fingers gripped the handle of her amenities cart so tightly that every knuckle was white.

Marcus swallowed audibly. "Rebecca?"

The girl burst into tears. She abandoned her cart and fled the room.

"Buddy? Marcus! Are you all right?" Grae snapped her fingers in front of his eyes.

He blinked and focused on her.

"Are you okay? Who was that?"

"I think it was my little sister. She's grown a lot since I last saw her."

Grae's mouth dropped open. "Holy shit! Do you want me to run after her?"

"No. She knows where I am. If she wants to talk to me, she'll come back. I don't expect her to, though." He closed his eyes. A tear slipped out and rolled over his swollen cheeks.

Grae snatched a tissue and dabbed delicately as more tears followed the first. *Damn, damn, damn.* The girl looked to be about thirteen or fourteen, which meant she hadn't seen Marcus since she was a child. Who knew what their parents had told her and her siblings to account for the disappearance of their oldest brother. She may well have thought she was seeing a ghost. Grae caressed the least damaged side of Marcus' face. *A really messed up ghost.*

She sat quietly at his side and used up half a box of tissues to dry his eyes. It wasn't unusual for Marcus to cry—sentimental commercials could start his waterworks—but she'd never witnessed such silent and prolonged tears. He was usually a messy and melodramatic weeper, which occasioned much teasing on her part.

When the tears finally abated, Grae touched his unblemished hand to her lips. "I'm sorry, bud. That had to be a shock."

"She's so grown up now. The last time I saw her she was in pink footie pajamas with a kitten in her arms."

"I wonder why she's here on a school day."

Marcus tried to smile. "Home-schooled. My parents believed in one day a week of giving back, so I assume this is Rebecca's charity day. You don't really think my parents would allow their children to be corrupted in public school, do you?"

Grae poked him gently. "So how'd you end up corrupted then?"

"Bradley Givens. We grew up next door to each other. His parents were in the same church as my folks, so we were always hanging around together. We used to borrow comic books from other kids and hide them, because our parents didn't approve of us reading what they called trash. Then one day I realized I was more interested in Bradley than in comic books. Not long after that, I figured out he was more interested in me than comic books, too. A couple of weeks later, his dad caught us together in the tool shed. That was the night my parents threw me out. I don't know what happened to Bradley. I never saw him again."

"I'm sorry. Makes what I went through pretty penny ante."

Marcus regarded her steadily. "Are you ready to tell me about it now?"

"Now?" Grae frowned. "Did Kendall—"

"All she told me was how badly you took it when you saw me last night, and that you ended up talking to her mom. She didn't tell me what you said."

"She doesn't know. But you deserve to know."

"I'm always happy to listen, but why do I deserve to know?"

"You're lying in that hospital bed because of what I did eight years ago."

"I doubt it, but hit the PCA again and then tell me what happened."

Grae didn't know if the machine would deliver another dose of pain medication so soon, but she pressed the button again, just in case. Then she began to tell Marcus the same story she'd related to Jo. She didn't spare herself blame or sugar coat any of the details, and by the time she was done, she was emotionally wrung out.

"Come here," Marcus said.

Grae leaned close.

He wrapped her in a one-armed hug. "I'm so sorry that happened to you, sweetie, but it wasn't your fault. Not then, and not now."

Grae sniffled and grabbed a tissue. "That's what Jo said."

"Wise woman. So we'll both tell you over and over until you believe us. Besides, I think there's one thing you're forgetting."

Grae wiped her eyes. "What?"

"Without you, I'd have been lying on a mortician's slab long ago, rather than lying in a hospital bed getting sponge baths from handsome orderlies."

"You've been in here less than a day. I highly doubt you've gotten a sponge bath from anyone yet."

"Freddie promised me one before I made him go home to get some sleep this morning. And I saw a Teutonic-looking orderly with muscles on his muscles, so I have high hopes for later today."

Grae responded to Marcus' jest with a smile, but his words had sunk in. "If I hadn't killed Missy—"

"Uh-uh. You didn't kill her. It was an accident." Marcus' tone was unyielding. "But if you hadn't run from your life, you wouldn't have been in that alley to save mine. Remember that the next time you're kicking your own ass, okay?"

"I will. Marcus?"

"Yes?"

"I hate what happened to Missy, and I don't know if I'll ever forgive myself, but I wouldn't change a thing if it meant not being in that alley that night."

Marcus beamed. "Love you, too."

Grae stared at the floor. "I almost ran away again, bud."

His smile faded. "When?"

"Last night. I was so sick about what I'd done to you that I was going to leave you the keys to the apartment and take off."

"To where?"

"Probably Vancouver. Maybe Toronto. Basically wherever the next bus was going."

"Jesus, Grae. What the hell were you thinking?"

"That I'd destroyed your life just like I killed Missy."

Marcus struggled again to push himself higher on the pillows.

Grae laid a restraining hand on his chest. "Whoa there, cowboy. You're going to mess up the doctor's fine work."

"I don't care." But he stopped moving and drew in several shallow breaths.

Grae watched him closely, worried that she'd made things worse with her confession. She was about to apologize, when he pointed a finger at her and glared.

"I'm going to tell you this one more time so you can get it through your thick head, okay? You. Saved. My. Life. I was spiralling into hell on the streets. I hated what I had to do to survive, and suicide was all I thought of from the moment I woke up to the moment I went to sleep. I'd been raised since birth to believe in God, Jesus, and the angels. I sang hymns, and I could recite biblical verse with the best of them. But I stopped believing in God the night my mom told me I was evil and she wasn't going to let me near my brothers and sisters ever again. I stopped believing in the goodness of the Universe when my dad literally picked my skinny ass up and threw it out the back door. I stopped believing in kindness when the porch light went off, and I heard the lock turned to bar me from the only home I'd ever known."

Tears were running down Marcus' face again, but Grae couldn't move. She'd never heard Marcus say these things before, and she knew they were coming from deep within his soul.

"In the alley that night, a multi-coloured, hard-ass punk with metal all over her face reached out to me. When you took me in and didn't want one damn thing from me, I couldn't believe it. And when you proved yourself my friend, over and over and over, I knew you were a gift from God, and the angels I'd long ago stopped believing in. So there is nothing—*nothing*, that you could ever do that would make me think I was better off without you in my life. You saved me. And maybe I helped to save you, too. I hope so. So if you ever try to run away again, I'll come after you. I don't know how, but I will. I'll search every damn street in every damn city until I find you and bring you home. That's a promise."

Grae was crying openly now, too. They reached for each other's hand. With her free hand, Grae pulled the tissue box between them. Marcus gave a choked laugh and let go of Grae to grab several tissues.

Grae did the same. "Aren't we a pair?"

"We are, sweetie. We really are. So, do I have your word you'll never run away again?"

"Yes."

Marcus exhaled softly.

"I'm glad Kendall found me last night."

"Once I can use both arms again, I'm going to cook that woman the best meal she's ever had."

Grae smiled. "I think she'd like that, bud."

A noise at the door drew their attention. Rebecca had returned with a thin, grey-haired woman wearing a hospital volunteer pinafore in tow.

"Hello, Mother." Marcus' tone was flat.

"You don't get to call me that, boy. I may have given birth to you, but I am not your mother."

Grae jumped to her feet, but Marcus grabbed her sleeve. "It's okay, sweetie. She's not staying."

Mrs. Lyndon advanced into the room, with Rebecca close on her heels. "Doggone right, I'm not. When Becky told me you were in here, I just had to see what kind of mess you'd gotten yourself in."

Grae tensed.

"I was mugged on my way to work." Marcus' voice was shockingly calm.

Mrs. Lyndon sniffed and glared at him. "Work, eh? And what kind of work does the likes of you do?"

Grae had had enough. She tore herself from Marcus' grasp and lunged toward the woman.

Rebecca gasped and pulled on her mother's arm. "Let's go, Mom. Please?"

"What kind of work did you think a fourteen-year-old boy could get when you threw him out? Everything that happened to him, everything that put him in that bed right now, is because you dishonoured the words of the God you swear you worship. Do you think Jesus would've pitched Marcus out into the cold night and locked the door on him? Do you think God approved of your cruelty? Do you think St. Peter will be waiting for you at the Golden Gates because you abandoned a helpless boy to whatever fate you consigned him to? Hell, no. Satan is so eager to get his hands on you goddamned sinners that he's rubbing his hands in gleeful anticipation of your arrival."

Mrs. Lyndon recoiled, then her nostrils flared and she thrust her face so far forward that Grae could smell her sour breath. "That boy is evil. We raised him right, and he willingly went down the path to Sodom. We had to cut the cancer out, and that's what we did."

Grae's fury escalated. "Cancer? You fucking well call this magnificent human being a cancer? Who the hell do you think you are? You sit in judgement of him? I'm telling you right now, lady, your God is going to sit in judgement of you one day, and he's going to bring hellfire down on your ignorant, nasty, bigoted head like it was spring rain in June."

"What is going on in here?" The large orderly Marcus had been admiring earlier stood in the doorway. "We can hear you two floors away. What on earth are you yelling about?"

Grae spun and pointed from Marcus to Mrs. Lyndon. "We're yelling because this miserable excuse for a mother threw my friend out of his home when he was fourteen years old, and this is the first time she's seen him since then."

The orderly scowled at Mrs. Lyndon, who shrank back and took Rebecca's arm. "Why on earth did you throw him out?"

"He's a faggot. We caught him kissing and touching another boy. We couldn't tolerate that kind of behaviour in our God-fearing home. He'd have been molesting his brothers before we knew it, so we had to throw him out. Didn't have any other choice."

"Is that right? Well, when my older brother came out to my parents and me, we had a choice. And we sure didn't make the same one you did. In fact, we're all going to my brother's wedding in three months. I can hardly wait to hug the grooms and welcome his husband into our family. So you picked the wrong room to throw this shit around, lady. Take your bigotry and get the hell off my floor. And stay away from my patient. If I see either of you around here again, I'll inform the administrator that we have vermin on the ward and we need an exterminator."

There was loud applause from the hidden residents of the other three beds. Rebecca bolted from the room, and Mrs. Lyndon edged her way past the orderly until she was out the door. The clatter of heels could be heard fading into the distance.

The orderly glanced at Marcus. "You okay?"

Marcus nodded. "Just tired. I wasn't expecting a family visit."

"I think I'll go make sure they've left. They won't bother you again."

"Thanks." Marcus closed his eyes.

Drained, Grae returned to his side and took a seat. She rested her head on the edge of the bed. Marcus put a hand on her hair, and they stayed that way for a long time.

Finally Marcus tugged on a lock of Grae's hair, and she sat up. "Gleeful Satan? Raining hellfire? Where'd you get that stuff?"

"I dunno. It seemed appropriate. Should I apologize for insulting your mother?"

"You heard her. She's not my mother. She's just the woman who had the misfortune to give birth to me." Marcus' voice was wearier than Grae had ever heard it. "I am sorry about Rebecca, though, and the others. These are the beliefs they're being raised with. Unless something radical happens, they'll never have any idea that they can break free and think for themselves."

"Maybe *you're* that something radical."

"I doubt it. Did you see how fast Rebecca ran from the room? I'm sure my parents have brainwashed all of my siblings."

"Yeah. Sorry about that, too."

Marcus shrugged. "It's not like I've had a family for years."

"Hey, what am I? Chopped liver?"

Marcus mustered a smile. "No, sweetie. You're the best family a man could ever ask for. But let's talk about something else, okay? Now about you and Kendall… What's the 411?"

Chapter 22

Grae shook her head. "There's really not much to tell, bud. It's like I told you—I freaked and rabbited out of the ER last night. Kendall tracked me down, and she made me go talk to her mother."

Marcus studied her. "I could feel the heat between the two of you when you first got here today, so don't tell me there's nothing going on."

"I think there is, but I don't know exactly what. She kissed me like she meant it—"

"Kissing, eh? Kissing is a good start. Tell me more."

"I swear, that's all there is to tell." Grae chuckled at Marcus' disappointed expression. "Okay, she really, really kissed me."

"What does that mean?"

"I mean she kissed me so hard that my clothes practically disintegrated."

"All right! Now we're getting somewhere. So you were nearly naked…"

Grae rolled her eyes. "Metaphorically speaking, you idiot."

"Sure, sure. But metaphorically can lead to physically, so when do you plan to actually get naked with her? You know, the doctor told me this morning I'm in here until at least the weekend. The apartment is all yours. You could even use that beautiful big bed of mine."

"Uck, no way. It's got boy cooties all over it."

"Well, I would expect you to change the sheets. And just so we're clear, that's before and after. I don't want girl cooties on them." Marcus grinned broadly at her.

Grae was grateful that his mind was off the encounter with his family, however temporarily. "There was one thing…"

He arched an eyebrow. "Do tell, even if it is the PG version."

"After she kissed me senseless, she said something that really hit home. She told me not to run away before we figured out what was happening between us. She asked me to give our relationship a chance."

"Oooh, I like it. I like her."

"Me, too. It's just kind of scary. She said that she cared for me more than she's cared for anyone in a long time. Well, she actually said 'in forever.'"

"Damn, Grae, you have to give this woman a chance to sweep you off your feet. Hell, she's half-swept me off my feet by proxy."

"I think I want to, but…"

Marcus' expression softened. "But you're terrified. I get that now. I could never figure out why you loved the ladies on one hand, and they scared the crap out of you on the other. It all makes sense to me now."

"Pretty lame, huh?"

"No, not at all. Can I tell you something?"

"Anything, anytime. You know that."

"I really like Freddie."

Grae snorted. "Jesus, tell me something I didn't know. But for what it's worth, I really like him too. He stuck right with you last night. That's more than I did."

"Whole other situation, sweetie, but yes, it almost made up for the pain to wake up and see him sitting there. The way his whole face lit up when I looked at him—" Tears brightened Marcus' eyes.

Grae wordlessly handed over the nearly empty tissue box.

He dried his eyes and smiled at her. "My point is, he's really special. I've known that since our first meeting, but it wasn't until last week that I could…you know."

"Um, yeah, got it."

"He was really patient, and you know he could have anyone he wants."

"He is pretty damned good looking."

"I know, right? I could melt in those black eyes of his." Marcus fanned his face with the tissue box.

Grae chuckled. "Okay, Romeo."

Marcus sobered, dropped the tissue box, and reached for her hand. "We're survivors, you and me. Jo would say this a whole lot better than I can, but I'll bet there's something in both of us that is always going to question whether love is going to turn around and bite us in the ass."

"You had it way worse than me. Your parents threw you out. Mine just didn't know where to find me. I rejected them. They didn't reject me. And I didn't love Missy, I just slept with her."

"And a few hours later she was dead, and you blamed yourself. It doesn't take Freud to figure out how you mixed those two things together, sweetie. Sex and death. They put you on the streets just as much as my sexuality and my metaphorical death to my family held me on the streets. It's pretty powerful stuff."

Grae nodded and squeezed his hand.

"So all I'm saying is to be kind to yourself. Just because I tease you doesn't mean I'm pushing you into anything you're not ready for, okay? If it's right for you and Kendall, then sweet. I'll be the one designing your wedding dress some day."

"Dress?" Grae reared back in feigned indignation. "Can you really picture me in a dress?"

"So she'll wear the dress, and you can wear the tux. My point is that you don't have to rush into anything. If she's the right one—the woman who's going to break this eight-year drought—then she'll wait until you're ready. If she's not willing to wait, she's not the right one."

"She feels like the right one."

Marcus strained to hear Grae's whisper, then beamed. "I'm so fucking glad for you, sweetie."

She looked him in the eye. "Yeah. Me too, bud. Me too."

Grae was at Stone Gardens by mid-afternoon.

Jude looked up in surprise when she entered the shop. "Hey, I thought you'd be with Marcus all day."

"I just came from there. He's so tired that he booted me out of the room so he could sleep."

What Grae didn't say was that Marcus had begun to mentally replay his encounter with his mother and sister. He'd grown quieter and less responsive, and his gaze had grown distant. She'd tried to jolly him out of his introspection, until he'd finally asked for some space. He'd insisted that he was all right, so she'd reluctantly left, but had promised to return after she got in a few hours of work.

But before Grae had reached Stone Gardens, he'd texted her to tell her that Freddie was coming by after dinner. He'd said that he would see Grae the next day and suggested that she call Kendall. They'd argued back and forth by text, until she'd finally yielded. Freddie would be with Marcus all evening, and she did want to talk to Kendall later.

"How's he doing?" Jude asked.

"Well, considering he looks like he got beat up by a Transformer on a rampage, not too bad. His spirits were mostly okay, at least until his mother showed up."

"His mother? I didn't think his mother was even in the picture."

"It was purely a coincidence that she was at the hospital, and she didn't stay in the picture any longer than it took to spew a bucket of vitriol at her son and then leave."

Jude frowned. "That's harsh. Talk about kicking someone when they're down."

"Yeah, well, I kind of kicked back on his behalf."

"I'm shocked. Shocked, I tell you."

Grae couldn't help but chuckle at Jude's dry tone.

"Just tell me that I won't have to bail you out on an assault charge."

"Nope. Never laid a finger on her. We just yelled insults back and forth until a friendly orderly, who happens to have a gay older brother, tossed her out on her ass."

"Did he now? The world is definitely improving."

"In some ways, yes. So, did Rolly finish the Herman monument?"

"No. He left it for you. He said no one does an angel like you do. He put it next to the sandblaster."

"Good. I'll get right on it."

Grae worked past the normal quitting time. She wanted to compensate for the hours she'd missed over the previous two days. She was putting the finishing touches on Wanda Herman's angel when Jude stuck his head in the shop door and whistled.

She looked up.

"Got a couple of visitors here for you, Grae. Okay to send them back?"

"Visitors? For me?"

Jude grinned. "That's what I said. Did you forget to wear your ear protectors today?"

"No, of course not." Grae set aside her precision tools and dusted off her clothes.

Jude swung the door wide and gestured for Ciara and Virgil to enter.

Grae blinked. They were perhaps the last people she'd expected. "Hi. What are you guys doing here?"

Virgil waved as they started across the shop floor, winding their way through stacks of granite slabs and rows of finished monuments. "We decided to pick up our little sister and take her out for dinner."

Ciara stared around the shop. "These are gorgeous. Did you make any of them?"

Grae nodded. "Jude lets me handle the easier ones myself now. And he's teaching me the more intricate stuff as we go along." She indicated the angel she'd been fine-tuning. "This is one of my current projects."

Virgil gave a low whistle. "Damn, Grae, you do nice work."

"It's beautiful. So lifelike." Ciara lightly ran a finger over one of the wings. "It's like I can feel each feather."

Grae beamed. She couldn't remember the last time her siblings had praised her. It felt good. "Thanks. I never thought I could draw my way out of a paper bag, but the CAD program does the technical design stuff."

"CAD?" Ciara asked.

"Computer-assisted design. When Jude started in his grandfather's shop, all the design was done by hand, and he's still got the skills. But nowadays we use a computer to turn a customer's request into the final product. We can play around with ideas, alter things to fit the way we need them to, and produce a photo-like rendering of the final concept. We can even simulate how sunlight will fall on a monument, given its placement, so if we need to rotate something for full impact, we can. CAD will show us how a monument will look head on, or from the side, or from above and below. Not that I think anyone would look at it from below, but we could check that out too, if the customer wanted it."

Ciara studied her. "You really love this, don't you?"

"I do. It's such an amazing sense of accomplishment to take an ordinary slab of marble and turn it into a beautiful tribute to someone's lost loved one. It's satisfying for me on many levels."

"What are you doing now?" Virgil asked.

Grae raised her blade. "Putting on the finishing touches. We sandblast most of the design in, but Jude always says that nothing beats a craftsman with a steady hand. This is the stage where we turn a monument into a piece of art."

"Amazing." Ciara smiled. "So, Michelangelo, are you going to let us take you out for pizza?"

"Sure. Just let me get washed up."

When Grae returned to the lobby, she found Jude, Ciara, and Virgil in animated conversation.

"I'm ready."

Jude nodded approvingly. "It's about time you quit for the day. You were making me look like a plantation owner with the hours you're putting in."

"Um, I—"

"Just teasing you, Grae. Go enjoy your dinner. I'll see you tomorrow morning."

"Did you want to join us?" Virgil asked. "You're certainly welcome."

Jude shook his head. "Thanks, but Elaine has supper waiting for me. Nice to see you two again."

"You too."

Jude shook hands with Virgil and Ciara, and gave Grae a friendly pat on the shoulder. "Don't let them keep you out too late. We've got three new clients coming in tomorrow."

Grae nodded. "I'll be here as early as the buses start running."

The siblings left and climbed into Ciara's Prius.

"So, to what do I owe the pleasure of your company tonight?" Grae asked from the back seat.

Ciara and Virgil exchanged glances.

"Uh, oh. Should I be worried? Is something wrong?" *Should've known this wasn't just a social occasion.*

"Nothing's wrong," Virgil reached a hand back to pat her knee. "We were just concerned about you."

"You were? Why?"

"Because of Marcus, of course." Ciara studied Grae in her rear view mirror.

Grae met her gaze. "Really?"

Ciara sighed. "Really. You need to get used to having us in your life again. I stopped in to see Marcus after work. Freddie was there so I didn't stay long, but Marcus told me you'd been there earlier. He did not look in good shape, so I knew you'd be distressed. I called Virgil and suggested that he and I pick you up for dinner."

"She bribed me with Toledo's," Virgil said. "And besides, I had something I wanted to discuss with you anyway."

Grae perked up. Toledo's had been their favourite pizza place as children. It was where their parents had taken them when they'd gotten straight A's or won an award. "Awesome. I haven't had a Toledo's pizza in forever."

Virgil shot her a puzzled look. "Why not?"

"Time, money. From where Marcus and I used to live, it took three transfers to get there, and it's not the cheapest place in town to eat." Grae didn't miss the exchange of glances between her siblings.

"Well, I'm driving and Virgil's paying, so the only thing you have to decide is whether we eat in or take it home."

"Can we take it to my place? I'm too tired to go formal."

"Sure, but I wouldn't exactly call Toledo's formal dining." Ciara sped up the ramp to enter the heavy rush hour traffic, and immediately had to slow down. "I'd say we could call ahead, but I'm not sure how long it will take us to get there."

Grae pulled out her phone and texted Kendall to let her know she would be dining with her siblings. Kendall's return text arrived within moments.

Call me after they leave?

Grae smiled. It was how she'd hoped Kendall would respond. *Will do.*

Good. If it's not too late, maybe I could come over?

A shiver ran through Grae, and her fingers fumbled as she texted, *I'd like that.*

Grae was pleased that her siblings were concerned enough to come check on her, but by the time they got back to her apartment, all she could think about was how soon they'd leave. Still, she was a good hostess, and brought out plates, napkins, and cold drinks.

Soon they were gorging on Toledo's trademark Southwestern pizza. From her spot on the floor next to the coffee table, Grae put away four pieces in quick succession before she had to stop. Virgil matched her piece for piece, but Ciara restricted herself to two.

"Damn. That's every bit as good as I remember it." Grae wiped her mouth and eyed the two remaining pieces. They would make an excellent breakfast if Virgil didn't finish them off.

He laughed and pushed the box toward her. "Keep them. I haven't forgotten how you like cold pizza in the morning."

Ciara rolled her eyes. "Which is so gross."

"It is not. Are you sure, Virg?"

"I am. I have Toledo's pretty much every weekend when I have Caden. It's his favourite, though I usually have to have plain old pepperoni. He doesn't have his father's sense of culinary adventure."

Ciara snorted. "I wonder why? Nadine's idea of adventure is to get a massage instead of just a mani-pedi."

She shot Grae a look, and Grae nodded imperceptibly. Neither of them had liked Nadine, but they'd made a pact not to tell him. However, now that she had cheated on their brother, broken his heart, and taken his son away in a caustic divorce, all bets were off.

Virgil held up a hand. "I know she's not your favourite person, but she's still the mother of my son, okay? So we're not doing a Nadine-bash tonight."

"You're a bigger man than I am," Grae said. "If any woman did to me what she did to you…"

Ciara leaned forward with a smile. "Speaking of women doing things to you, you seemed very cozy with Kendall at Halligan's last night."

"Was I?"

"Don't give me that. You know you were. Are you two dating?"

Grae exhaled slowly, unsure of how to describe what was going on between her and Kendall. "We're not exactly dating—yet. We're sort of in the 'exploring-the-possibilities-of-maybe-someday-dating-if-everything-goes-well' phase."

Ciara and Virgil stared at her.

Finally Virgil shook his head. "How on earth do lesbians ever hook up?"

Grae flashed back on her university days, and was shocked not to feel the usual stab of guilt and pain. "Um, we manage somehow. But hey, I have a question for you guys. Jo recently told me that she and Mom are old friends, and that's why she came out of retirement to take me on as a client. Did you guys know that?"

Virgil shrugged. "I remember her coming around sometimes, but it was a long time ago. I didn't pay much attention to Mom's friends."

"They were," Ciara said quietly.

"So they aren't now?" Grae asked.

Ciara refused to meet Grae's gaze. "Well, Jo did as Mom asked, so they must be at least friendly acquaintances."

"Ciara—?"

"I don't know. I remember having picnics with Jo and her kids, but that was a long, long time ago."

"So you don't know what happened between them?"

"Probably nothing. Mom's career was advancing, they both had families to raise. I'm sure they just drifted apart."

Ciara was hiding something, but Grae knew that unless and until her sister wanted to reveal it, she wasn't going to find out. "So, what did you want to talk to me about, Virg?"

"Oh, right. I think you should pursue a civil suit against Dylan MacIsaac and Rick Toylen."

"I know you mentioned that before, but I really don't want anything more to do with those assholes."

Virgil leaned forward with a serious expression on his face. "I know you don't, but I want you to consider a few things. They almost got away with ruining your life."

"I'd been doing a pretty good job of that on my own."

Virgil shook his head. "Not recently. That's why I was able to make such a good case for the defence. You'd straightened up, and you were making an effort to fly right. If they'd gotten away with it, they might've killed you on that roof, or at least had you sent to jail on such serious charges that they would've crippled your employment chances long after you got out. At the very least, I can go after them for lost wages, and pain and suffering, and something thrown in just for being such homophobic dicks."

"Listen to him," Ciara said. "I know you don't want anything to do with them, and I don't blame you, but Virg found out that they're both making top dollar up north. They should have to pay for what they did to you. You can't tell me you couldn't use the money. You don't even own a car, for crying out loud."

"I don't really need one, but maybe…" Grae's mind turned to Marcus' education, and she smiled. Wouldn't it be karmic justice if Dylan and Rick ended up funding Marcus' way to a better life. "You know what—let's do it. Oh, wait. How much is this going to cost me?"

"I'll take it on a contingency basis, and give you the family discount. You only pay me if we win."

"Awesome. I can live with that."

"Excellent. With all the testimony and evidence I amassed for your criminal case, I expect any decent lawyer will tell those two to settle out of court."

"So I won't have to see them?"

"That's what you have a lawyer for, baby sister."

Grae high-fived Virgil and settled back with a grin. Wait until she told Marcus that culinary school might be courtesy of Dylan and Rick. He was going to laugh himself right out of his hospital bed.

Half an hour later, Ciara got a call from Bai. She assured her husband she was on her way, so Grae waved off their help cleaning up and walked them to the door.

"Thanks for all of this. I really enjoyed myself. I'd like to do it again sometime soon," Grae said as her siblings put on their cold weather gear.

Ciara leaned in for a hug. "Me too."

"And you didn't even have to hire that private dick again."

Ciara shot Virgil a guilty look.

He shook his head. "Tell her, Ci. She should know."

Grae looked between them. "Know what?"

"Okay, but don't be pissed, all right?" Ciara asked.

"First I have to know what you're talking about."

"There was no private detective. We always knew where you were, pretty much from the moment you dropped out of school."

Grae's jaw dropped. "Even after I changed my name?"

Virgil chuckled, though there was little humour in it. "Mom's a judge. How hard do you think it was for her to find out your new name and track your addresses, especially since you kept getting in trouble with the law. You left a paper trail a mile long."

Grae was stunned. She had been so certain that none of her family knew where she was. "So the whole time...?"

Virgil nodded. "We knew where you were. But it was obvious you wanted nothing to do with us, so we left you alone and waited. It broke Mom's heart, and this one," he elbowed a sheepish Ciara. "She finally couldn't stand it anymore, so she made contact and told you she'd hired a private eye to find you."

"Huh."

"Don't be mad at us." Ciara took Grae's hands. "We were out of our minds with worry at first. You wouldn't believe how many family councils we had on what to do. We thought of interventions or kidnapping you to rehab facilities. Mom even called Jo, and that was a huge deal for her. But Jo told us that until you were ready to renew a relationship with the family, you'd resist any attempts to pull you back into the fold. She also pointed out that you were an adult, and even a screwed up adult has the right to live her life on her own terms."

"Damn."

Ciara pulled Grae into a hug. "I know it's a lot to think about, but please don't push us away again, okay? We've just found you. Please?"

"Yeah, no worries. We're good." Grae returned the embrace tentatively. She had a lot of things to talk over with Jo at their next appointment.

Ciara and Virgil left, but Ciara kept casting worried glances back over her shoulder as they walked down the hall. When they punched the button for the elevator, Grae closed her door and leaned against it. *They knew where I was? The whole time?*

The sound of an incoming text brought her out of her reverie, and she hastened to the living room where she'd left her phone.

Have they left yet?

Grae hesitated over Kendall's text. Then the memory of those kisses made her shiver, and she quickly tapped out a reply. *Just now.*

So can I come upstairs?
Grae blinked. *Where are you?*
In visitor parking.
Grae grinned as her fingers flew. *Then get your ass up here.*

Chapter 23

Grae buzzed Kendall in, and ran down the hall to the bathroom. She hurriedly swished mouthwash, wishing she had time to clean her teeth. Toledo's Southwestern pizza had a distinct aftertaste. Her sleeve inched up as she reached for the tap, and she stopped short. The base of her lady knight tattoo protruded below her sleeve. Grae stared at it.

Kendall, for all that she could be a goofball in private, projected intellect and sophistication to the world at large, much like her mother. *What if she thinks I'm just trash?* For an instant, Grae regretted allowing Kendall to come upstairs. Then she remembered Kendall's comment about her booking photo the first time she'd taken Grae to her favourite diner.

"*Let's see, your hair was buzzed really short, and what there was appeared to be dyed neon pink. You wore a tank and had an amazing array of tattoos. You were also wearing so much metal through your flesh, you might well have been the Tin Man.*"

Grae smiled. Kendall had seen how she looked at the nadir of her punk phase, and still wanted to spend time with her.

"Wait until she sees the dragon." That tattoo started on her left shoulder. The dragon's tail curved around and between her breasts, and ended up curled around a diamond so beautifully inked that it almost illuminated the flesh above her right nipple. The thought of Kendall tracing the dragon with her mouth or fingertips sent Grae into a fantasy that dissolved abruptly in the wake of a loud knock. She hurried to the door and swung it open.

"I know you said just to get my ass up here," Kendall said. "But the rest of me insisted on coming along."

"I'm very glad. As gorgeous as your ass is, I like the whole package." Grae gestured her in.

Kendall closed the door behind her and pulled Grae into a relaxed embrace. "Gorgeous, eh?"

Grae pushed Kendall's open peacoat off her shoulders and ran her hands lightly over the body part in question. "Absolutely."

There was no more need for words. Their lips met, and Kendall turned them so Grae's back was against the wall. She pressed against Grae until Grae thought she was going to burst into flames. But when Kendall's thigh slid between Grae's legs, she stiffened.

"Wait. Wait."

Kendall instantly backed away. "Are you okay?"

Grae ran her fingers through her hair, and tried to calm down, but nothing she did stopped her body from trembling.

"Oh, God, I'm sorry. I'm such an idiot. Are you all right? Can I get you a drink of water? Is the kitchen this way?" Kendall half-turned, and Grae grabbed for her hand.

"No, wait. You didn't do anything wrong."

"I must've. You're shaking like a leaf, and I don't think in a good way."

Grae attempted to smile, but Kendall's worried expression told her that she hadn't done a credible job of it. "Can we just sit down and talk…please?"

"Of course." Kendall disengaged her hand and stepped aside to allow Grae room to pass.

Grae led the way into the living room. "I'm sorry. I didn't have time to clean up yet. Ciara and Virgil just left." She hastily swept up the debris and took it to the kitchen.

"I know. I saw them." Kendall took a seat at the far end of the couch.

"How long were you waiting down there?"

"About half an hour."

Grae thrust the plates into the dishwasher. "You should've called. There was extra pizza."

"I didn't mind. I did some work while I waited."

"Crazy woman. It's cold out there."

Kendall laughed. "I'd just filled the gas tank. I was good."

When Grae returned from the kitchen, she wavered. She wanted to sit next to Kendall, but was unsure of herself. One freak-out per night was enough, and she didn't want to scare Kendall away for good. Grae sat at the opposite end of the couch and leaned forward, not looking at Kendall.

"You probably think... Hell, I don't know what you think. I don't know what I'd think if I was in your shoes. One minute I've got my hands on your ass, and the next I'm telling you to stop. I'm not really a tease, I swear."

"I know that. I tried to rush into something you weren't ready for, and I apologize."

Grae's head jerked around. "You have nothing to apologize for."

Kendall's gaze was remorseful. "I do. I really do. You've been through so much this week. I don't know what the hell I was thinking of—throwing myself at you like that. It was about as insensitive as I could get, and I am so sorry. It won't happen again."

"It won't?"

"Not until you're ready...if you are. If you're not..." Kendall sighed deeply. "If you're not, then I would like us to be friends, if you'll allow it."

"I want much more than that."

Kendall brightened. "You do?"

"God, yes. I'm sorry if I gave you the impression that I don't. I just... I just..."

"You just need to slow things down."

"Yes. And I need to tell you why."

"You don't have to. Seriously, Grae. If this is something you and Mom are dealing with, you don't owe me any kind of explanation."

"It affects us. You asked me to give you a chance, to give us a chance to figure out what's going on between us. I want to do that. With all my heart, I want to do that. But I want to come to you with a clean slate, or at least make you understand why my slate isn't, and maybe never can be completely clean."

"I'll listen to whatever you want to tell me. I won't judge."

Grae hung her head. "I wouldn't blame you if you did."

She took a deep breath and launched into her story. She told Kendall everything, and just as she had with Marcus and Jo, took full responsibility for Melissa's death. When she was done, she waited.

Kendall studied her. "So, since that time, you haven't dated at all?"

"I tried a few months ago. I met a woman named Lucy at a bar. She was a freak, too, but cool as ice. She invited me home with her. I barely got through it. If she hadn't been as high as Everest, she'd have realized I was struggling to force myself to touch her. She didn't care that I couldn't let her touch me, and I got out of there as fast as I could. I don't know what I was thinking. I guess I so desperately wanted to be normal after over eight years of being celibate, that when she called me, I agreed to go out again, but it was the night when I got busted because of Rick and Dylan. Ironically, I was sitting in the cell, and the only silver lining I could come up with was our blown date. When Marcus told me that he called Lucy and she said to tell me to fuck off, I was actually relieved."

"Don't you think you've punished yourself long enough?" Kendall reached out a hand.

Grae stared at it.

"I'm not asking for anything you're not ready to give, but I would like to put my arm around you, if that's okay with you. No expectations, I promise."

"I thought you'd run."

"No, Grae, I'm not running—not away from you, anyway."

Grae's eyes filled with tears, and she reached blindly for Kendall's hand. Kendall met her in the middle of the couch. Grae rested her head against Kendall's shoulder and enjoyed the security of the arm wrapped around her. They sat quietly for a long time.

Finally Grae stirred. "I'm sorry. I didn't even ask if you wanted anything. I'm a lousy host."

Kendall chuckled. "I don't need anything. I'll actually have to go pretty soon. I'm the guest speaker at a Lazarus-sponsored breakfast meeting. I should get home, review my speech again, and get a good night's sleep."

"I'm sorry—"

"Shh." Kendall kissed the top of Grae's head. "You have nothing to apologize for."

"I doubt this is how you expected this evening to turn out."

"Believe it or not, I had no expectations. I seriously just missed you and wanted to see you."

"I missed you—"

The phone's buzzer sounded from the lobby, and Grae jumped. Had one of her siblings forgotten something?

She reached for the phone. "Yes?"

"I'm sorry I didn't call ahead, dear, but may I come up and talk to you? It's important."

"Mom? Yeah, of course. Come on up." Grae entered the access code and turned to Kendall, who rose to her feet.

"I heard. Guess that's my cue to go."

"I'm sorry, really. I have no idea why she's here. Unless... Listen, do you know why our moms were close friends once and aren't anymore?"

Kendall's expression sobered. "I do, but it's not my story to tell."

Grae heaved a frustrated sigh. No one would tell her anything.

"It really isn't my place to talk about this. Can you trust me on that?"

Grae scowled. "Okay, but I feel like I'm the only one in the dark here."

"I'm sorry. Will you walk me to the door?"

"Of course."

Kendall's peacoat lay in a heap in the hallway, where their feverish embrace had left it. Grae picked it up and held it while Kendall slipped her arms into the sleeves.

Kendall buttoned the front and knotted the belt. "No pressure, but Peter called me tonight with a client he thought you'd be perfect for, if you're interested."

"Is it a felon of some sort?"

Kendall chuckled. "No. In fact, she has family. But apparently they can't stand her and have pretty much abandoned her in the hospice. Peter asked if you could come around after work tomorrow night."

"Sure. When you see him at the breakfast, tell him I'll come over as soon as I'm done. Just text me the name."

"Thanks."

Kendall leaned over to touch her lips to Grae's. Grae slid a hand behind her neck, and when Kendall started to pull away, Grae held her close. A knock at the doorway separated them, and they stared at each other.

Kendall took a big gulp of air. "Okay, then. I'll, um, call you tomorrow, if that's all right with you."

"Sure." Grae couldn't take her eyes off Kendall. A second knock sounded, louder than the first. She started, then hastily turned the deadbolt and opened the door. "Hi, Mom."

Thea entered, and stopped short when she spotted Kendall. Her eyes widened. "Oh, I'm sorry. I didn't mean to interrupt."

Kendall smiled. "Not at all. We were just talking, and I was just leaving. Grae, it was wonderful to see you again." She brushed her lips against Grae's cheek and departed.

"I'm sorry, dear. I didn't know you had company."

Grae smiled. "It's been my night for it. Ciara and Virg took me for pizza earlier." She extended a hand for Thea's coat. Thea gave it to her, along with her purse and gloves, all of which Grae put in the hall closet.

"That's why I'm here, actually. Ciara told me— Well, she told me you had some questions about Jo and our…friendship."

Without waiting for Grae, Thea entered the living room and began to pace in front of the windows. Grae followed, took a seat, and watched her mother's unusual behaviour. Thea had long ago mastered the art of inscrutability, but her steps now were rapid, almost frantic.

Thea slowed to a stop, crossed her arms over her chest, and faced Grae with an uncertain smile. "So, does Kendall visit you often?"

"Tonight was the first time."

"Is there something going on between you two?"

"I don't know. Maybe. It's too soon to tell." Grae studied her mother. Something was off. "Mom, what's going on? This isn't about me and Kendall, is it?"

"No, of course not. She seems like a lovely woman. She was a good kid, so I'm not surprised in the least. I didn't know she was gay, but—" Thea dropped her arms and took a deep breath. "Ciara also told me she'd confessed our awareness of your whereabouts. May we talk about that?"

"Sure. So you always knew where I was and what I was doing—the whole eight years?"

Thea sank onto the couch and shot Grae a wry smile. "Yes and no. We didn't know your every move, but I always knew when Grae Jordan had gotten into another scrape. And early on, your father privately assigned one of his best investigative journalists to get information on how you were living. It wasn't pleasant reading. That was when I asked Jo to consult with the whole family on how to handle matters."

"So Jo knew about me long before she took me on as a client?" Grae wasn't sure how she felt about that. Her heart fought against believing that Jo had lied to her, but her head was having issues with Jo acting as if she was a stranger when they first met. They would be discussing that at their next session.

Thea shook her head. "She did advise us, but she hadn't seen you since you were about seven, so it would be a long shot to say she knew you. She basically told us not to force you back into the family, to stay at arm's length until you were ready to allow us closer."

"It was good advice. I would've shut you out in the early years. But you did finally come to me."

"I had to. My hand was forced when you showed up in front of my bench on such serious charges. I couldn't let it to go any further without trying to help."

"And when you called Jo?"

"She very graciously agreed to take you on as a client."

"She told me that you were the only one she'd have agreed to come out of retirement for. Why, Mom? From what I can tell, your friendship had ceased to exist a long time ago. So why would Jo make an exception for you? What compelled her?"

Thea looked away. "Love."

Grae's eyes widened. She'd envisioned blackmail or a debt owed, but not this. "Excuse me?"

"Once…long ago, Jo loved me."

Grae's mouth dropped open.

Thea smiled ruefully. "I know. It shocked me, too."

"Holy crap."

"I think I need to tell you the whole story. Will you listen, knowing it doesn't paint a pretty picture of your mother?"

"Uh-huh."

"You know you were born prematurely."

Grae nodded. Thea had only been twenty-seven weeks along when her youngest had decided to enter the world.

"Thirty years ago, that was much more dangerous than it is with all of today's medical advancements. You were such a little scrap of a thing, but you were a fighter. I named you Grace because I always felt it was only by God's grace that you survived and thrived. I was with you day and night in the NICU. Kendall was three and also in the children's ward, with pyelonephritis—a serious kidney infection. When it is acute rather than chronic, it's curable, but Kendall had complications and was in the hospital in for a quite a while. Jo and I bonded as worried mothers in the coffee room. We really hit it off, and after you and Kendall were released from the hospital, Jo and I made an effort to continue our friendship. I was there for her when her husband died of an aneurism when Kendall was only eight, and she was there for me when—well, when your father and I were having some serious problems in our marriage."

"You and Dad had problems? I don't remember that."

"You wouldn't. You were very young, and we were careful to keep our fights as private as possible, though Ciara knew."

"Virg?"

"Totally oblivious. He'd met Nadine by then, and they were young and in love. She was all he could think about."

Grae shook her head. "That's my brother. So Jo counselled you and Dad?"

"No. I did ask, but she refused. I begged her to reconsider, but once Jo makes up her mind, it stays made up. It wasn't until later that I found out why."

"Because she was in love with you."

"Yes. And she knew it would be unethical to offer any advice. She did hear me out as a friend and provided a shoulder to cry on, but she never did anything inappropriate."

"Then why did your friendship break up?"

Thea averted her gaze. "Because…I did something totally inappropriate."

"You? Oh, my God! You cheated on Dad with Jo?"

"Yes."

Grae stared at her mother. "Jesus Christ."

"It wasn't Jo's fault, dear. It was all mine. I was so unhappy. I knew how Jo felt about me, and I also knew she'd never do anything unethical like press her attentions on me. So one day when I'd gone to her in tears over Carter's affair—"

"Dad had an affair?" Grae's voice pitched so high it broke, and she coughed several times.

"We weren't perfect. We were human. We still are."

"But you're together, so you must've worked it out somehow."

"We almost didn't."

Thea turned to stare out the window and a tear trickled down her cheek. It shocked Grae almost as much as her confession. She dug an unused tissue, leftover from visiting Marcus, out of her pocket and passed it over.

Thea dried her eyes. "May I have a glass of water?"

"Of course." Grae jumped to her feet and hurried to the kitchen, relieved to have a break from the string of revelations. *Mom and Jo slept together? Dad had a mistress?* All she thought she knew about her parents had been overturned. *Mom and Jo?*

She returned and handed Thea the glass of water. Thea drained half of it in one gulp, then cradled it in her hands, staring at the water.

"I'm probably telling you far more than you want to know, but Ciara said you were asking questions, and I wanted you to hear the truth from me."

"Jo wouldn't have told me. She said I had to ask you if I wanted to know."

Thea looked up with a weak smile. "She always was stronger than me."

"What happened?"

"We had a brief, very intense affair. Then Carter left his mistress and begged me for another chance. I broke it off with Jo. Your dad and I went to couples' therapy and made it work through exhaustive hard work."

"So Dad knows about you and Jo?"

"No. I never confessed that, not even in counselling. He knows I had an affair, but he assumed it was with another lawyer in my firm who'd been sniffing around me for months. He banned the poor fellow from ever being in my company alone again. We weren't even allowed to work together on cases, which made it very awkward at times. But that was Carter's condition to continuing the marriage."

"And you? What was your condition?"

"He had to fire his secretary and hire a new one."

"Sucks to be the secretary."

Thea's eyes flashed. "Then maybe she should've thought twice about sleeping with her married boss."

Grae held up a hand. "Don't take it out on me. I haven't really slept with anyone in eight years, let alone my boss."

"Well, I can hardly imagine you sleeping with Jude."

"Uh, no. That would never happen." Grae's mind flashed to Kendall and their sizzling kisses. *Kendall isn't my boss, and Mom doesn't need to know any more.*

"I imposed one other condition, but on myself, not your father." Thea's voice broke, and she dabbed the sodden tissue to her eyes.

Grae suddenly understood. "You loved her. That's why you had to end the friendship as well as the affair."

"Yes. And Jo never said a word. She just let me go back to your father without protest. We've seen each other now and then at professional women's meetings, but we've never been alone since."

Grae's estimation of Jo returned to its usual lofty height. "When you called her for help about me?"

"She only asked if I was sure I wanted her involved. I was desperate, and even after all that time, there was no one I trusted more. So I said yes. I needed her help. And she gave it willingly and without conditions. It's who she is."

Grae nodded. "It is. Mom, do you still have feelings for Jo?"

Thea met her gaze. "I think I always will."

"Wow. And she feels the same?"

"I don't know. It's been a lot of years and a lot of water under the bridge. I'm sure she's had other relationships. She's too special not to be loved and appreciated."

Thea's voice softened, just as Jo's had when she'd told Grae to talk to her mother if she wanted to know how they knew each other. Grae wasn't entirely sure that Jo's feelings for her mother had evaporated with time, either.

"But when I was frantic and reached out to her, when I was so scared that I'd lost you to the streets, she was there for me, for the whole family. She kept me at arm's length, but she met with us several times, and once we'd accepted your choices as best we could, she backed off."

"Until you called her again and pulled her out of retirement."

"Yes." Thea's gaze searched Grae's face. "Do you think I'm a coward?"

Grae frowned. "A coward? I've definitely never thought that."

"I was afraid, so afraid."

"Of what? Being outed?"

"I couldn't bear to think of the consequences twenty-odd years ago. This is a very conservative province. Ciara and Virgil were young adults, but there was you and your father…and my career. By then, I knew that a judgeship was in my future. I'd been assured of that by those with the power to make it happen."

"So you chose the bench over Jo. Do you think you'd still make the same choice under today's conditions? After all, we're equal under the law now. We've even been marrying for years now, coast to coast."

"This isn't Quebec, dear. Attitudes aren't nearly as progressive."

Grae shook her head. "I know, but…"

"When you're young, it's easy to put love above everything else. I had so much to lose if I'd chosen Jo."

"And yet, you still cry over that decision. I doubt this is the first time, either."

Thea raised her gaze to the cold night sky, where stars shone brilliantly in defiance of the city's lights. "No, it's not."

Chapter 24

Grae closed the door to Mrs. Branson's room, walked part way down the hall, and slumped against the wall with her eyes closed. Even Ezra Herzog hadn't been as difficult an assignment.

"Grae? Are you all right?"

Grae's eyes flew open at the familiar voice. Kendall was staring at her with uncharacteristic worry lines on her forehead.

Grae smiled. "Hey, you. What are you doing here? And how is it you're always around when I need a hug? Is that your super power?"

Kendall's brow furrowed. "Super power?"

"A joke between your mom and me. Did you not hear the part about the hug?"

Kendall stepped forward with arms extended. Grae burrowed into her, drinking in the warmth and the light citrus scent that was so much a part of Kendall.

"I want you to know I'm not a stalker. When we were at the breakfast meeting, Peter told me more about the woman you were seeing tonight, and I was worried. So I asked an old friend on the evening shift to text me when you got here."

"I don't care if you're Stalky McStalkerville. I'm so glad you're here."

"Good." Kendall nuzzled Grae's hair. "So you don't mind if I offer you a ride home?"

Grae stayed where she was. "I'm not going home right away. I tried to postpone my weekly appointment with your mom, but she was adamant that we simply reschedule for after I finished up here. She can be very persuasive."

"You're telling me? Mom personifies benevolent dictatorship. She used to do this thing with my brothers and me when we were little that drove me crazy. But I could never figure out countermeasures."

Grae pulled back far enough to see Kendall's expression. "What did she do?"

"None of us liked drinking milk, so she'd coax us to just drink half a glass. And then half of a half. Then half of a quarter. Even knowing exactly what she was doing, most times we still ended up drinking the whole glass." Kendall rolled her eyes. "And the worst part is, if I ever have kids, I'll probably use the same tactic."

"Because it worked?"

"Uh-huh."

They laughed as they started down the hall toward the lobby.

"So can I give you a ride to the benevolent dictator's house?"

"I'd like that, thanks."

Kendall waved to the woman at the nursing station. "Thanks, Teresa. Give me a call if you and Libby still want to go out for dinner next Wednesday, okay?"

Teresa nodded. "You know I will, girl. We just gotta get Libby to unlock lips with her new boy toy and come out with us for once."

Kendall laughed. "I leave that entirely up to your powers of persuasion."

"That and promisin' her a bucket of margaritas should work. And if that ain't enough, I'll kidnap her."

"Works for me."

Kendall and Grae retrieved their coats from the closet in the lobby and left the building.

Both shivered when they emerged into a light snowfall and a swirling breeze.

"Ugh. Good day to be curled up next to the fireplace with a hot toddy." Kendall swept her arm over the snow on her windshield.

"Or a hot woman." Grae hadn't thought Kendall would hear her, but Kendall flashed her a big grin.

"I couldn't agree more, but the benevolent dictator awaits, and you better not even think of ditching her."

"Even for her daughter?" They gazed at each other across the hood of the car.

"Especially for her daughter. She'd go up one side of me and down the other for keeping you from your appointment."

"Well, we wouldn't want that, then. We'd better get moving."

They got into the car and Kendall started the engine. Grae cranked the heat as high as it would go, and they waited for the windows to defrost.

Kendall put the car in gear and backed out of her space. "So, you look pretty ragged. Exactly how bad was Mrs. Branson?"

Grae blew out a long breath. "I understand why her family doesn't want anything to do with her. Have you ever met someone who is so unrelentingly negative that they seem to suck all the life and optimism out of the room like they're an emotional black hole?"

"That bad, eh?"

"Worse. I'm not sure I can manage a second visit with her, Kendall. I'm sorry."

"It's okay. I have someone else I can ask. He's very good with the problem cases."

"I hate the thought of letting you down."

Kendall reached for Grae's hand and held it as she drove. "You're not, and I mean that. Sometimes it's not a match between a volunteer and a client. Sometimes there's a good reason our clients are alone. For the most part, it's just a matter of the way someone's life has worked out that they end up dying alone. Maybe they never married or had children. Maybe they've outlived friends, siblings, and other relatives. Maybe they're living far away from everyone they know. I had a woman once who'd moved to Calgary to be with her only daughter, but then her daughter died in a car accident and the woman got terminal cancer. She couldn't afford to leave here, and what family she had left couldn't afford to visit for any length of time. She was a sweetheart, and we spent a lot of time together. I introduced her to Skype so she could see and say goodbye to her loved ones in Newfoundland. That meant the world to her, and to them."

"What a great idea. I'll have to remember to suggest that if it would be helpful."

"I've found that modern technology can greatly improve our clients' lives. I've helped some find relatives or wartime buddies that they long ago lost track of. It's incredibly rewarding to bring a smile to a dying man's face when he can swap tall tales with someone who was in the trenches with him sixty years ago. But Grae, there are also people like Mrs. Branson."

"You mean royal pains in the ass?"

"Yes. But our mandate is not to judge why a person is dying alone. It's to try and ease that process. Even the most miserable outcasts are human. In their final days, no matter how they've lived their lives, it's a gift to them and a reward to us to ease their way with kindness. But then, I'm preaching to the choir, aren't I? You took on Ezra Herzog when no one else would."

"I know you're right. But Mrs. Branson feels like one of those Harry Potter Dementors, you know?"

Kendall laughed and took her hand back as she steered through a slippery patch. "Were you warding off her soul-sucking kisses?"

"Oh, trust me. I doubt Mrs. Phillipa Branson has kissed anything but her bank book in over seventy years. She told me all about her brilliant investment strategies, and then cackled that her so-called ungrateful children wouldn't see a damned cent of her wealth, because she's leaving it all to some fundamentalist preacher she adores. I don't think she had a clue I'm gay because, among other things, she ranted on about the homosexual agenda until I finally had to excuse myself before I puked, and I backed on out of there."

"Oh, Grae, I'm so sorry. If I'd known that, I definitely wouldn't have asked you to see her."

"Aw, don't worry. I feel sorry for her, actually. She has all the money in the world, and it didn't seem that she's spent one thin dime to make her life, or anyone else's, better."

"Except for the preacher."

"True, but let's talk about something more pleasant. Hey, I spoke with Marcus earlier today, and the doctor has cleared him to come home Saturday afternoon."

Kendall reached over and rested a hand on Grae's thigh. "That's wonderful. Can I take you to pick him up and bring you both home?"

"I can't ask you to do that. This week to the contrary, you're not my personal chauffeur. I'll get a cab to bring him home."

"Don't be silly. I don't have any plans for the weekend. Maybe we can pick up some Chinese on the way and welcome him home in style."

"Are you sure?"

Kendall glanced at Grae. "What part of 'I'd really like to spend time with you' is going over your head?"

"You would, would you?"

"Yes. In fact, I am officially asking you out on a dinner date Friday night."

"You are?"

"I am." Kendall's voice turned serious. "I'm not asking for anything else, okay? I just want to take you for dinner and spend some time with you. That's all."

Grae raised Kendall's hand to her lips. "Yes."

"Yes?"

"I want to spend time with you, too."

"Excellent." When Kendall smiled at Grae, her eyes shone.

Grae hated to end the lovely moment between them, but she had to know. "Can I ask you a question? Well, actually two questions."

"Sure."

"Do you remember playing with me when we were kids?"

"I didn't know it was you until Mom reminded me, but I do remember one time when you and your mom were at our place. I was about nine. I wanted you to play dolls with me, but all you wanted to do was play with Jake's dinosaur collection. You made his T-Rex eat my Barbie's head. I was so mad at you that I stormed out to Mom and demanded that you go home right away, or else."

Grae grinned. She didn't remember that, but it was consistent with her childhood patterns of play. "Or else what?"

Kendall shot her a rueful glance. "That's basically what Mom said before she marched me back to my room for a timeout."

"Was that the last time we played?"

"Maybe. I don't recall you coming around after that, though it might've traumatized me so much that I blocked it from my memory."

"Second question?"

"Fire away."

"Did you know our moms were lovers?"

Kendall gave a short whistle. "She told you, huh?"

"Yeah, last night."

"And?"

"And…I honestly don't know what to think about it. I'm stunned, obviously. I had no idea Mom and Dad ever had such serious trouble in their relationship. And I never, for an instant, thought either of our moms were lesbians."

"I don't think they actually are."

Grae studied Kendall's profile by the passing streetlights. "They did sleep together, and I got the feeling that, at least then, they had very strong feelings for each other."

"I know," Kendall said.

"So, what? You think they're bi, or something?"

"What I think is, had they met each other as young women today, they'd have fallen deeply in love and lived as a lesbian couple. But I also think that their love was specifically for each other, not for women in general."

"Huh."

"Do you disagree?" Kendall asked.

"No, not necessarily. I've never thought of Mom as anything but a happily married heterosexual, that's for sure. Though what do I know? I was out of the picture for a lot of years."

"Well, I can tell you I've never seen my mom date any other woman. She rarely dated at all, unless it was to attend a wedding or something. She did have a gay friend for a long time. He was a fellow shrink, and sometimes she would accompany him places as his date, but it wasn't real."

"Their friendship was."

"Oh yes, but that's not what I meant. I think Mom gave her heart twice, and didn't have it in her to give it again."

"How do you know all this stuff? We were pretty young when they had the affair, and from what Mom said, it didn't last long."

"Several years ago I was helping my mother clear out the basement. We were moving old boxes and such, and I came across some letters someone had written to her stashed away in a cookie tin. When I held them up and asked if they were to go in the keep or trash pile, she started to cry. The only other time I can remember her crying is when she told me and my brothers that Dad had died."

"I'm sorry. I didn't mean to bring up bad memories."

Kendall waved a dismissive hand. "Long, long ago. My point being that Mom rarely lets anyone see her cry, so it made a huge impact on me. I took the boxes out of her hands, and we went upstairs and cracked open the first of several bottles of wine. The letters were from your mom. We spent the rest of the day talking, about her and Thea, and me and Derek. It was an eye-opener. By that time, my marriage had been in trouble for a few years, but I wasn't quite able to quit it, or him, even though I didn't even like him anymore. But seeing the sorrow in my mother at her loss of someone she truly loved made me realize I didn't want to settle. I wanted more—so much more."

"I'm glad. I wouldn't want you to settle, either."

"That's the day I started my journey to you."

Grae's eyes widened at Kendall's quiet words. They weren't an explicit declaration of love, but they came damned close.

Kendall wheeled into the curb in front of her mother's house, threw the car into park, and turned to Grae. "I'm sorry. That was wrong of me. I swear I don't mean to pressure you. It's just that my heart is overflowing right now, and my feelings keep bubbling up. I promise I'll put a cork in it. We can forget about tomorrow night, if you'd rather. I'll still give you and Marcus a ride on Saturday, I just won't hang around."

Grae pushed the release for her seat belt and reached for Kendall. "Shut up for a moment, will you?" She proceeded to quiet Kendall with fevered lips and hands.

When she finally pulled away, Kendall stared at her. "Jesus, woman!"

"What I was going to say, if you'd given me a moment, was that I couldn't be happier that your path led to me. I'm not ready for some things yet, but I promise I want to be. If you'll just give me some time—"

Kendall leaned forward and kissed Grae lightly. "I'm not going anywhere."

As much as Grae wanted to linger, she had to leave the car before she started unbuttoning Kendall's coat. "I've got to get in there before the benevolent dictator finds me making out with her daughter."

Kendall laughed. "Tell old BD that her daughter says hi, okay?"

"Will do." Grae pushed the door open. "Let me know when and where for our date tomorrow, okay?"

"'When' is as soon as you're free to see me. The 'where' I haven't figured out yet, so I'll surprise you."

"Sounds good."

Grae closed the door and walked up the path, acutely aware that her every step was being watched. She turned at the door, waved, and rang the bell. Jo opened the door, motioned her in, and waved at Kendall, who pulled away from the curb.

Grae knelt to unlace her boots. "Your daughter says hi to—and I'm quoting here—'old BD.'"

Jo chuckled. "She dug out that ancient chestnut, did she?"

Grae stood and hung her coat up. "Yup."

She followed Jo to her regular seat. Maddie was snoozing in it, so Grae gently lifted her onto her lap. *What the hell? I might as well point out the elephant in the room.*

"So…you're a lesbian. Who knew?"

"What? The cat and the cardigan didn't give it away?" Jo's tone was light, but there was a guarded wariness in her gaze that Grae had never seen before. "I take it you spoke to your mother?"

"Yes. She came over last night."

Jo sighed. "Would you prefer to end our sessions? I can recommend someone else."

Grae shook her head. "No. That's definitely not what I want."

"What do you want?"

I want to get well enough to love your daughter the way she deserves to be loved. Aloud, Grae said, "I want to continue working with you. I trust you. I don't want to have to break in anyone new."

"You know I have to put the subject of your mother and me off-limits."

Grae shrugged. "I figured. It's none of my business anyway. What happened twenty-odd years ago has no bearing on the way I fucked up my life. So let's talk about me, me, me, me, me."

Jo responded to Grae's smile with a tentative one of her own. "All right. Then let's discuss how things went when you saw Marcus yesterday."

Grae gathered her thoughts.

Jo held up her hand. "Wait. This isn't fair to you or our therapeutic relationship. And I'm not even certain about the ethicality of it. Do you have any issues with the history between your mother and me? Is there anything you want to discuss or clear the air on before we continue?"

"Well, unless you have a technical explanation for why my gaydar rusted out so badly over the last eight years, we're good."

Jo brushed off Grae's lame jest. "I'm serious. I need to be sure that you are okay with what you learned about us, and that you're very clear it was long in the past and there is nothing between us now."

"Nothing but memories." The words were out of Grae's mouth before she considered them, and she winced at the almost imperceptible flash of pain on Jo's face.

It was swiftly replaced by Jo's usual noncommittal professional expression. "Forgive me, but I think I do need to postpone our appointment after all. Please allow me to pay for a cab home for you."

Grae shot Jo a worried glance. "Are we okay?"

"We are, but I need to consult a former colleague before we continue."

"Why?"

Jo rose to her feet, and Grae followed.

"I may be retired, but I still adhere to a professional code of ethics. I need an outside opinion on our situation. I hope you understand."

"I do, but I want you to understand that I won't go to anyone else. If you feel you can't work with me any longer, then I'll get by with what you've given me so far."

Jo shook her head. "No, that's not what I want. We're not finished here by a long shot. I have a wonderful therapist in mind for you—"

"No, Jo. I'm not trying to change your mind. I'm not trying to influence your decision. I'm simply telling you where I stand on this. I will honour your decision if you no longer wish to work with me because of something that happened when I was a little kid, and something that doesn't impact me one way or another. But if that's your choice, mine is that I'm done with therapy. And thanks for the offer, but I'll catch the bus home."

Grae put on her winter wear and zipped her jacket.

Jo regarded her with a troubled expression.

"Don't worry, okay? I'm feeling really good these days, despite Tuesday's melt-down being evidence to the contrary. And if this is the last time we see each other professionally, I just want to thank you for all you've done for me. I'm not anywhere near to being the mess I was the first time I walked in here, and that's all due to you. You have my undying gratitude."

Grae waited a moment. When Jo said nothing, she left and quietly closed the door behind her.

Chapter 25

GRAE PINCHED HER THIGH AND bit her lip in a desperate attempt to avoid laughter. She didn't dare look at Jude, who maintained a professional expression as he gathered up the papers that had been strewn about during the course of their hour-long consultation. He took a very long moment to straighten the edges of the stack, then looked across the table at their client.

"I think we have a clear vision of what you wish for William, Mrs. Ferber. We'll contact you with the final design in a few days."

Their elderly client grasped her cane and struggled to her feet. "Thank you, Mr. Herzog. My cousin was right. You do lovely work. I know you'll create a worthy monument to dear William."

"Absolutely." Jude went around the table to offer her an arm. "At Stone Gardens we strive to incorporate all the love you hold for your lost…ah…loved one into his monument. When you visit William in years to come, this will be a fitting way to remember him."

Mrs. Ferber nodded. "It will. He would approve. He would, indeed."

Jude shot Grae a warning glance, and walked Mrs. Ferber to the lobby. Grae buried her face in her hands, but despite her best efforts, giggles escaped between her fingers. When Jude returned and carefully shut the door behind him, Grae gave up the losing battle and erupted in mirth. Jude joined her, his booming laugh echoing off the walls of the consultation room.

Grae's sides hurt. "So, when did you figure out that 'dear William' was a hound, not her husband?"

Jude eased into the chair opposite her. "I did think referring to her husband as a 'noble breed' was odd, but I thought maybe he was a distant descendent of some European nobility. What about you?"

"It was when she referred to William as an outstanding stud. My brain translated that to 'stud muffin,' and for one confusing moment I thought it was just her pet name for hubby. But when she started to talk about how he loved to lie on the rug in front of the fire as he got older, I finally put the pieces together. You?"

"When she added the dates to our drawing. I thought she'd gotten them wrong, because it made William out to be fourteen, but when I drew her attention to the birthdate, she insisted she had it right. When she pulled out William's kennel papers to prove it, the puzzle was complete."

"I knew I was going to lose it when I saw the expression on your face. I pinched myself so hard that I'm sure my thigh is black and blue."

"I couldn't look at you."

"I couldn't look at you, either."

Jude chuckled. "It's a good thing Mrs. Ferber was satisfied at that point, or we'd have disgraced the good name of Stone Gardens."

"Have you ever been asked to design a pet's headstone before?"

"Sure. But I'd always been told in advance that it was for an animal, not a human. Mrs. Ferber seemed to assume we knew that her late, dearly beloved had four legs, not two."

"She did, didn't she?" Grae's laughter erupted again as she recalled Mrs. Ferber's fawning description of "dear William's" sterling character.

"I just hope that when the day arrives that Elaine comes to you to design my memorial, she describes me as lovingly as Mrs. Ferber described William."

"Comes to me?"

"Sure. You don't think Rolly could do justice to all this, do you?" Jude grinned and tapped his chest.

Grae was touched. She loved the thought that not only would Jude trust her with designing his own monument, but he expected her to still be working at Stone Gardens decades hence. "I'll do you proud, boss."

Jude sobered. "You already have. So, I'll let you get started on this. I'm going to be out for a couple of hours, but we'll go over what you have when I get back."

Grae picked up the stack of papers and stood.

"Oh, Grae, before I forget, I've been meaning to tell you our holiday schedule for next week. We close from Christmas Eve to Boxing Day, and then New Year's Eve and New Year's. I'll cover any calls during Christmas, but since you're low man on the totem pole this year, you'll have to cover New Year's. You don't have to be in the office. You just have to check the answering machine two or three times a day to make sure we don't have any time-sensitive requests. Ashley will give you the access code."

Grae's eyes widened. "Christmas."

"Yeah. Christmas. I assumed you and Marcus celebrated the season. I apologize if I'm wrong, but even if you don't, you still get paid time off."

"I mean that I forgot it's the end of next week."

"How could you forget? You can't even watch the evening news without seeing twenty Christmas commercials in a row."

"Well, since we didn't know what would happen at court, we didn't want to jinx anything by buying Christmas stuff until we'd heard the judge's decision. And then Marcus—"

"Of course. I understand. Well, you said he's coming home tomorrow, right? Maybe you can pick up a little tree to decorate or something. And you still have time to get gifts."

Grae ran a hand through her hair. "Time, just no ideas. Shit."

"You need to get yourself a wife who's happy to take over all holiday preparations. My daughters are both in mixed marriages, so they celebrate Christmas and Hanukah. Elaine makes the family favourites, organizes who's hosting what, and buys the gifts for the grandchildren. All I have to do is show up wearing my bright red bow tie, and pay the bills in January."

"And that works for you?"

Jude winked. "It has for thirty-seven years so far."

"Elaine doesn't have any eligible sisters, does she?"

He laughed. "All married with multiple kids, I'm afraid. Well, I've got to get going. I'll see you later."

"Yeah. See you later."

Grae rode the elevator up to Kendall's office. Jude had sent her home early, after approving the work she'd done on the "dear William" monument. A blizzard was forecast, and he'd advised her to go straight home. She didn't tell him that she wasn't going to miss her date with Kendall for anything less than a Category 5 hurricane. She'd taken transit to Angels Unawares, instead.

Kendall's face lit up when Grae entered the office. "Hi! I thought I was going to pick you up at your place."

"Jude let everyone go early because of the storm."

"It does look like a bad one. I told Margie to go home about an hour ago."

They came together in a hug that lasted until Kendall tipped Grae's head back so she could kiss her. "I wasn't sure if you'd want to cancel our date because of the weather. I've been keeping my fingers crossed."

"I definitely don't want to cancel, but I thought maybe we should just grab a bite at the Blue Moon and go back to my place after, if that's okay with you."

"Sure. I made reservations at Cicero's, but I'll cancel. Give me a moment, okay?"

Kendall hurried into her inner office. Grae perched on the corner of Margie's desk and smiled as she remembered that first day. She'd been so worried that Kendall would reject her and Jo would cancel their therapy because of it. Her smile faded. She might've lost Jo's services anyway. She'd checked her phone multiple times, but hadn't heard from her today.

Kendall returned with a coat half on and her bag under one arm. "Why the sad face?"

"Long story. I'll tell you over dinner. Were you able to cancel the reservation?"

"Yes. They didn't sound at all surprised. I expect the weather has many people cancelling their plans for tonight."

"It was already snowing and blowing when I got off the bus. Maybe we should get something to go."

"Sounds like a plan. Let's get moving before we have to trade my car in for a dogsled."

As it was, their take-out was ice cold by the time they arrived at Grae's building. The blizzard had progressed into near white-out conditions, and accidents littered their way. Kendall drove with supreme caution, while Grae rode white-knuckled in the passenger seat.

"Park in the garage." Grae passed over her key as they pulled into the snow-drifted driveway. "We have two spots assigned, and we're not using either. There's no point in you parking outside when you can be underground and out of this mess."

"Thanks. I have a shovel in the trunk, but underground sounds much more appealing."

Both heaved a sigh of relief when the garage door closed against the howling winds.

When they reached the apartment, Grae walked over to the window. She couldn't even see the street below.

"I hope the snowplows get around to us sometime tonight. Marcus is not going to be happy if he can't get home tomorrow. He was already bitching earlier about having to stay there tonight." Grae didn't add that his complaining had come to an abrupt halt the moment she mentioned her date with Kendall. "Hey, I've got some beer left over from pizza night. Would you like one?"

Kendall finished storing her winter gear in the closet. "I would, but I'd better not. I may have to leave soon or I won't get home, and I'll need my wits unclouded."

"I don't think you should go home tonight."

"Um, okay. Do you think Marcus would mind if I borrowed his bed?"

"Well, he did say something about girl cooties on his sheets, but I'm pretty sure he was just joking."

Kendall chuckled. "I'll change the sheets before we go to the hospital to get him then."

Or you could sleep in my bed. Grae couldn't quite bring herself to say the words, even though the thought had been dancing in her mind since she'd walked through the gathering storm to get to Kendall's office.

Kendall held up the brown paper bag with their cold supper. "How about we heat this while we still have electricity?"

Grae led the way into the kitchen. "Do you think we'll lose power?"

"I hope not, but this is the worst I've seen it in a long time. Actually, I'm going to call Mom, if you don't mind."

"Not at all. Let me take the food, and you go call her." Grae took the brown bag and tried not to eavesdrop when Kendall went into the living room.

She returned a few minutes later, staring at her cell. "Well, that was weird."

Grae put the first plate in the microwave. "What?"

"Mom's fine, but when she asked if I was, too, I told her I'd taken refuge in your apartment."

"That upset her?"

"Not exactly, but she had this really weird tone in her voice." Kendall cocked her head at Grae. "Is everything okay between you two?"

Grae sighed and handed the warmed plate to Kendall. "Cutlery's in the drawer beside you."

"Grae? What's going on?"

"Let me get this heated up, and then I'll tell you. I'll meet you at the dining room table."

Kendall backed out of the kitchen with her gaze fixed on Grae, who stared off into space as she waited for the microwave's done signal. *Déjà vu.* Once she had feared Jo's response if she and Kendall hadn't gotten along. Now the shoe was on the other foot.

Arms wrapped around Grae's waist. She leaned back against Kendall and absorbed her warmth.

"Tell me what's wrong."

The microwave beeped, but they ignored it.

"I told your mom that I knew about her and my mom."

Kendall turned Grae around to face her, but didn't relinquish her embrace. "And?"

"And Jo doesn't know if she can keep working with me under the circumstances."

"So?"

Grae studied Kendall's face. All she saw was puzzlement. "So, I guess..."

Kendall arched a brow. "You thought that would affect our relationship?"

"I hoped it wouldn't, but I wondered whether it might."

Kendall bent her head and kissed Grae. "Then let me set your mind at ease. What's happening between you and me is completely separate from your relationship with my mom. Got it?"

"Got it."

The microwave beeped insistently, but Grae and Kendall were lost in a kiss that went on long after the machine ceased its reminders. When they emerged from their blissful interlude, they had to reheat their food again.

They were almost finished with the meal when Grae related the story of Mrs. Ferber and dear William. Kendall laughed so hard that she choked, and Grae ran around to pound her on the back.

"Ouch, ouch. Stop, woman. I can breathe now." Kendall seized Grae's hand, turned her chair and pulled Grae into her lap. "There. That's much better. Damn, you've got strong hands."

Not at all in a hurry to leave her comfortable perch, Grae examined her hands. The months at Stone Gardens had strengthened them.

Kendall took one and kissed a callus. "I like strong hands."

Grae rested her head against Kendall's. "I'm glad. Hey, can I ask you a favour?"

Kendall locked her arms around Grae. "Anything."

"This might not work with the weather the way it is, but I don't have any Christmas decorations at all. Do you think we could stop at a store on the way to the hospital and pick up a small tree and some ornaments? Marcus would really like that. It would be the perfect way to welcome him home."

"Of course. May I help you decorate?"

"I hoped you would."

Kendall shifted in her chair, but when Grae began to rise, she held her back. "I'm fine, and you're okay just where you are."

"This cannot be good for your back. Let's move into the living room."

Kendall snorted. "My back is just fine, thank you. But as long as you remember where you were, I don't mind moving." She released Grae, who stood up.

They cleared away their plates, and Kendall led the way to the couch. She sat and patted the spot beside her. "Now, where were we?"

Grae wrapped her arms around herself. "Not where I want to be."

"Sorry? Is everything all right?"

"Yes. No." Grae knelt on the floor and took Kendall's hands. "I want to be in your arms, but I want us naked and in my bed."

Kendall's eyes widened. "Are you sure? We don't have to rush into anything, honest."

"I know. I want this. I want you. But…and this is a big but…I have no idea how trying to make love will go. I might be fine, because it's you, or I might freak out like I've done before. I don't know. I guess I'm asking if you're willing to give me a chance, and forgive me if I completely fuck this up."

"There is nothing I could not forgive you, Grae. I love you."

Grae caught her breath. "That makes this doubly terrifying. I'm so afraid of disappointing you."

Kendall cupped Grae's face in gentle hands. "Don't be. You set the pace. You call the play. If we only make it to the batter's box tonight, so what? I'm not going anywhere."

"Me neither."

Kendall's gaze was so serene and so loving; Grae's fear subsided. She stood and offered her hand. "Come to bed with me?"

"Yes."

Chapter 26

Kendall was letting her set the pace, and Grae wasn't sure that was a good thing. So far they'd made it to her bedroom and turned on a lamp, but had gotten no further. Grae couldn't remember the prelude to sex ever being this awkward. She'd never had any reservations about who undressed who, or who took the lead, or anything else. But this was Kendall. For the first time in her life, Grae wanted to make love with a woman who mattered, someone who was so much more than a means to achieve basic physical relief. She didn't know where to start.

"I have a lot of tats. I mean everywhere." Grae blushed and stared at the floor. *Smooth.*

"I figured. It doesn't matter to me one way or another." Kendall's voice was soft and a little shy.

Grae fingered the buttons of her shirt, but didn't unfasten them. She couldn't meet Kendall's gaze.

"We don't have to do this, Grae. It's okay, really."

Grae fought her fear back, and crossed the short distance between them. "Believe me, I want to." She took Kendall's hands and rested them on her chest. "But…I need your help."

Kendall unfastened the top button and waited. When Grae didn't flinch, she opened another, and another, until Grae's shirt was fully unbuttoned. Kendall stopped and studied her. With growing excitement, Grae tugged her shirt out of her jeans and shrugged it off her shoulders. Kendall's gaze traced the dragon, still partially hidden by Grae's bra. Grae took a deep breath, unhooked her bra, and let it fall away. She was gratified by Kendall's sharp intake of breath.

Kendall reached for the button of Grae's jeans. "Is this okay?"

"Yes."

Kendall unzipped her pants and slid her hands inside, again waiting for Grae's nod before she pushed the jeans and underwear to the floor. Grae kicked the last of her clothes aside and stood in front of Kendall, dizzy with desire. Kendall's gaze never left Grae's face as she too began to undress. When they were both naked, Grae reached out, but her hand stopped short, quivering.

Kendall took Grae's hand and guided it to her breast. Grae closed her eyes and waited for the familiar panic to erupt. Instead, she was riveted by the feel of Kendall's smooth skin, the contrast with the hardening nipple that swelled in her palm. She'd always enjoyed the sensual evidence of what her touch did to another woman. She stepped closer and lowered her mouth to Kendall's breast. The softness of Kendall's skin overwhelmed her. She had missed this; missed the silky feel and warm scent of a woman's flesh. How had she gone so long without it?

Grae explored first one breast, and then the other. She moved with deliberate slowness, and revelled in the sensation of Kendall's heart beating a rapid staccato. She slipped her hands down Kendall's back and cupped her ass. When Grae traced the lower crease of Kendall's buttocks, a tremor rippled through her.

Grae drew back. "Are you cold?"

"God, no."

Grae smiled and lifted her hands to rest on Kendall's waist. "So you don't want to get under the covers?"

"Under, over. Lying down is definitely a good idea."

Grae pulled Kendall closer, and their bodies pressed firmly against one another.

"Oh, Jesus!" Kendall tightened her arms around Grae, but then instantly loosened them.

"You can hold me as closely as you want." Grae's lips grazed Kendall's collar bone. "This feels wonderful."

"Uh-huh."

The squeak in Kendall's affirmation amused Grae. She kissed Kendall's jaw, and her tongue caressed the wildly pulsing artery in her neck. "Bed?"

"Please."

Grae pulled away and flipped the duvet back. She slipped beneath the sheet and held out a hand.

Kendall touched the lamp and cocked her head.

Grae shook her head. "I'd like to see you, if that's okay."

"More than okay."

Kendall joined Grae, and they lay facing each other.

"You know I only have the vaguest idea what I'm doing here, right?" Kendall asked.

Grae blinked. She'd forgotten this was likely Kendall's first time with a woman. Her own fear receded. She slid closer and lightly pressed Kendall onto her back.

"We're quite the pair, aren't we?"

Kendall's long fingers traced Grae's temple, sending ripples of pleasure through her. "Yes…we are."

Grae began a slow exploration of Kendall's body. She relished the reassuring sounds of Kendall's pleasure, but hesitated when her leisurely path of discovery led her down to the apex of Kendall's legs. Kendall lay still and silent. As it had been since they'd entered the bedroom, it was up to Grae whether to stop or continue.

Grae parted Kendall's legs with gentle hands. For a split second, the memory of trying to do this with Lucy flashed through her mind, but there was no comparison. Lucy had been demanding, aggressive. She'd had only one thing on her mind, and Grae had laboured to provide it as quickly as possible. She hadn't been able to force herself to use her mouth. Thankfully all Lucy had cared about was the end result.

But this was Kendall, who'd given Grae all the time and space she needed. Kendall, whose whole body shook with need, but who let her set the pace. Grae sank into the experience, her constraint lost in the sensation of stroking Kendall with her tongue, of sliding her fingers inside Kendall and experiencing the explosion of pleasure as her body arched and a cry broke from her throat.

Grae slid upwards and rested her body on Kendall's. She tucked her head into the curve of her lover's neck, and listened with satisfaction to her ragged breathing.

Finally Kendall asked, "Are you all right?"

"I think so. Are you?"

"Very much so."

Grae floated in a haze of dreamy contentment. She'd done it. She'd made love without freaking out. She was normal again.

Then Kendall shifted, eased Grae onto her back, and Grae froze.

Kendall's finger followed the path of the dragon's tail, around and between Grae's breasts until she traced the outline of the diamond. "This really is amazing work. The dragon suits you—tough, but beautiful."

Grae fought to control her breathing and slow her racing heart. She battled the escalating urge to jump out of bed. *I can do this. I can do this. It's Kendall. I can do this.* Tears formed in the corners of her eyes, and she tried to figure out how to dash them away without alerting her lover.

Kendall looked up with a smile. It vanished as she met Grae's gaze. She instantly pushed away. "Are you all right?"

"No, I don't think I am. God, I'm so sorry. I thought I was fine. I thought I was…normal again. I'm such an idiot." Grae sat bolt upright and buried her face in her hands.

"Shh, it's all right. You're not an idiot." Kendall tentatively stroked Grae's back. "We knew we might not move too far just yet, and that's just fine. No pressure, remember?"

Grae hated the hesitancy in Kendall's hand, and was aware that she was watching for the first sign that she should pull back. "I'm sorry for ruining our first time together."

"Nothing's ruined. I swear. But I would like to hold you, if that's all right."

Grae flung herself into Kendall's arms and lost the battle to hold back her tears. The flood soaked Kendall's chest, but she held Grae, and caressed her back. They lay like that for a long time, until Grae had to move to get tissues. She sheepishly handed a couple to Kendall.

Kendall dried her chest without comment, and then glanced at the clock on the bedside table. "You know what? It's still early. How about we get up and watch a movie? There has to be some classic Christmas film on at this time of year."

"And if not classic, there's always Hallmark."

Kendall chuckled. "Where it unfailingly snows in the final scene of every Christmas movie."

"You noticed that too?" Grae got out of the bed and pulled on her clothes.

Kendall followed suit. "Hard not to. It always cracks me up, since the rest of the movie is so often clearly set in sunny California or a Vancouver summer."

"Yeah, right? And they set dress the green lawns with piles of fake white snow."

"Do you think they think they're fooling anyone?"

Grae shook her head. "I think they have a quota to turn out for every Christmas season, and they're not really worried about realism."

"I still love them, though. Sap-city and all."

Grae was grateful for the light-hearted small talk that carried them out of the bedroom and into the living room, where they sat together on the couch to pick out a movie. They watched two films, and Grae dug into Marcus' stash to provide popcorn partway through. At least the evening wasn't a total disaster.

When the second movie ended, Kendall checked the time. "I'd better be going. They should've cleared enough of the roads that I can get home."

Grae glanced toward the window. It was still snowing, though the wind had died down considerably. "You're welcome to stay."

Kendall was silent for a long moment. She bit her lip and finally said, "Do you want me to?"

Grae nodded. "If you do. I know I fucked up, but—"

"Stop. You did nothing of the sort. So we didn't hit a home run the first time out." Kendall chuckled. "Okay, I got to round the bases and cross home plate, but maybe next time you will, too."

"First of all, do you want a next time?"

"I absolutely, one hundred percent do. I want many more next times, and it doesn't matter if being together intimately is something we need to work on for another year. I'm not going anywhere. I told you that."

Grae held up her hands in surrender. "You did. Okay, second, what is it with the sports metaphors? Are you a secret sports geek?"

"I love fastball. It even paid for my education, since I went to the University of Washington on a scholarship. I've been playing for over twenty-five years, and I still play in a recreational league."

"Really? So this summer I can watch you worshipfully from the stands and fend off all your fans?"

Kendall grinned. "If you must worship, I won't stop you. But I've never noticed any fending off was required."

"A chick magnet like you? Now that you know you like women, I'm pretty sure fending will be a must."

Kendall's grin faded, and she took Grae's hands. "Not women, plural—you. I love you. I'm not going anywhere. Got that? We'll work it out together, I promise."

Kendall pulled Grae into an embrace. She lingered there, comforted by Kendall's warmth and strength. Grae closed her eyes and made a resolution. If Jo wouldn't counsel her anymore, she would accept her recommendation of another therapist. She had to get healthy again. For herself and Kendall.

Sunlight had begun to fill the bedroom when Grae woke the next morning. For an instant she was disoriented when she realized someone was in her bed. She relaxed when she saw a sleeping Kendall, but sadly noted the rumpled T-shirt she'd borrowed at bedtime. It had been a moment of awkwardness between them, as they'd negotiated their sleeping conditions. Kendall had broken the tension with a joke about how long red woollies would've been more appropriate, given the snow. But when Grae had donned a sleep shirt, too, it had reinforced her feeling of failure.

A wave of grief surged through Grae. Kendall had tried so hard to ease her stress. They should've made love long into the night, and been raring to go again this morning. Instead, they hadn't even been able to sleep naked together.

Grae quietly slipped out of bed to the bathroom. She indulged herself in a few bitter tears, then stared fiercely at her reflection in the mirror. "Shape up, damn it. She deserves a lot better than to wake up to you bawling your eyes out." *She deserves a lot better than you.*

When her pep talk failed to assuage her overwhelming feeling of failure, Grae turned on the shower. The hot water sluiced over her body and helped ease the ache in her chest. By the time she emerged, she was reasonably sure she could function normally. Or as normal as she usually got.

On her return to the bedroom, she was surprised to find Kendall getting dressed. "Oh, I'm sorry. Did I wake you?"

"Not at all. I'm typically an early riser. Hey, I borrowed Marcus' bathroom for a quick shower. I tried not to leave any girl cooties about, but I hope he won't mind."

"He won't, especially if we distract him with a Christmas tree and some decorations."

Kendall grinned. "Kind of like Maddie that way, is he? Just dangle a few shiny objects in front of his face?"

"Pretty much. Can I make you some breakfast? I do a decent omelet."

"That sounds good. The snow has stopped, so we should be able to go shopping and then get to the hospital without difficulty. I'm sure the plows have been out all night."

"Great. I'll text Marcus and let him know we'll be there about what—noon? One-ish?"

"Whatever works out best for him."

"Okay, I'll ask." Grae turned to leave.

"If you don't mind, though, I think I'll leave you and Marcus to do the decorating later on. I forgot that I promised Mom I'd go over there to help with her tree."

Grae rested a hand on the doorframe and didn't look back. "Sure. Look, if you need to get going, I don't mind getting a cab from the hospital."

Kendall slipped up behind and wrapped her arms around Grae's waist. "Don't do that."

"What?"

"Don't withdraw from me. That is not what this is all about, okay? Last night was just a tiny stumbling block, and we'll get past it. I promise."

"Sure." *But I can't promise.*

Kendall squeezed Grae and dropped a kiss on her hair. "We'll have a nice breakfast, go do some shopping, and pick up Marcus. All's right with our world, honest. Maybe we can plan something fun for tomorrow."

Grae eased out of Kendall's embrace. "I think I should probably stick close to home. You know, in case Marcus needs my help or something."

"Okay. Well, I guess I could catch up on some work. I did leave the office early yesterday."

Grae couldn't force one more word out of her tight throat, so she mumbled an acknowledgement and hurried down the hall to the kitchen. She prayed that Kendall would take her time coming out to breakfast. She needed to pull her ragged edges together.

※

"I think there's an open spot higher on the left," Marcus said.

Exasperated, Grae examined the tree. It was a very small tree, with far too many ornaments. There was no place left to hang the Grinch.

"Higher is already covered, bud. I think we'll have to leave this one off."

"Okay." Marcus heaved a sigh.

"All right. Give me a moment."

Grae rearranged several baubles and managed to squeeze the Grinch onto a branch with Santa, an elf, and a dark blue ornament that Freddie had given Marcus in the hospital. He swore it was exactly the same shade as Marcus' eyes.

Marcus had insisted on giving that one pride of place, and Grae had gladly humoured him. He was so happy to be out of the hospital and home that his good mood was contagious. He'd directed her on the placement of each decoration, the precise hanging of the wreath, and even where to put a sprig of plastic mistletoe. They had made a solemn vow only to engage in that tradition when Freddie and Kendall were over.

Grae's mood darkened. Kendall had helped bring their purchases upstairs while Grae had assisted Marcus, but then had refused Marcus' invitation for a glass of eggnog and taken her leave. Though they had exchanged a goodbye kiss at the door, Grae couldn't help wondering if she'd see Kendall again. She certainly wouldn't blame her if not.

"Why so glum, chum?"

Grae turned to find Marcus studying her intently.

"Your mood has been all over the map since we got home. What's going on? Is it me?"

Grae shook her head.

"Jo? Jude? Your mom? Ciara? Kendall? Ah, I just hit the jackpot. So tell me what's going on. Is there trouble in paradise? C'mon. Come over here."

Grae tried to smile. "There's nothing wrong, bud."

"Bullshit. Now get your ass over here and tell me what's going on. Don't make this invalid get up and beat it out of you." Marcus patted the couch and fixed her with a mock glare.

His threats lost any impact coming, as they did, from his bruised and battered face, but Grae yielded to the inevitable. He would get it out of her eventually. He always did.

She took a seat and hung her head. "I fucked it up."

"'It' being?"

"Kendall stayed here last night."

"Okay. I take it from your less than joyful demeanour that it didn't go well?"

"You could say that. You could also say it was an unmitigated disaster."

"Talk to me."

"We attempted to make love. I froze."

"Aw, sweetie, I'm so sorry." Marcus reached out and pulled her closer. "Was she upset?"

"No. She was so damned understanding and gentle and kind that it almost made it worse."

"How?"

"Because she's the kind of woman I could really fall for, but what on earth would she want with damaged goods like me?"

Marcus scowled. "That's crap. Kendall really likes you. She looks at you like you walk on water."

"She said she loves me."

"Well, there you go, then. She loves you. That's fabulous."

"Is it? For me, maybe, but not for her."

"What on earth are you talking about?"

"She's willing to give me all the time I need to get over my hang-up with sex."

"That's a good thing, isn't it?"

Stone Gardens

Grae rested her head on Marcus' shoulder. "What if I can't? What if I can never be a whole, healthy lover? She deserves better. She should have someone a lot better than me."

Marcus started to say something, and stopped. He sighed deeply. "You've only been in therapy a few months. Give it some time."

"I may be out of time. I don't think Jo will work with me anymore. I'm going to try to make more headway with whomever she recommends, but it'll be starting from scratch again with someone I don't know or trust. It could be a long, long time before I see any real progress."

"You said Kendall will give you all the time you need."

"She did say that. I'm just not sure I can let her waste that much time on me with no guarantees."

"Oh, sweetie. There are no guarantees in life. You, of all people, know that."

Grae raised her head. "How is it that an eighteen-year-old can sound so wise?"

Sadness filled Marcus' eyes. "Maybe there was too much life packed into those years."

Grae gently hugged him. "I know. I'm so sorry. I didn't mean to make your homecoming a bummer."

"You didn't. That's what friends are for, right? Now turn off the overheads, so we can see how our Christmas lights look."

"Okay." Grae went to do Marcus' bidding, but the despair that overwhelmed her erased all sense of seasonal joy, and the delight of having Marcus home.

Chapter 27

THE NEXT DAY, FREDDIE ARRIVED at the apartment just before noon and insisted on making lunch for Marcus and Grae. After they ate, Grae went for a walk to give them some time alone.

Friday's blizzard had left the world a brilliant white under deep blue skies. The air was cold and invigorating, but Grae trudged through the breathtaking landscape with her head down and her mind focused on morose thoughts. Except for a brief text that morning, she hadn't heard from Kendall.

"I blew it. The best thing to happen to me in the last decade, and I fucked it up beyond fixing!"

An older woman walking an excitable charcoal schnauzer raised an eyebrow at Grae's exclamation. She hurried past as she restrained the dog from jumping up at Grae.

"Great, now I can add insanity to my list of mortal flaws."

Grae started as her cellphone rang. Her eyes widened at the name on the caller ID. "Jo? Hi."

"Hi, Grae. Do you think you could drop over here this afternoon some time? I'd like to talk to you and resolve this issue."

"Does that mean you'll keep working with me?"

"That's what I'd like to talk about."

"Okay. I can catch a bus and be there shortly."

"That will be fine. I'll see you soon."

Grae disconnected the call and stared at the phone. *What does that mean? What has Jo decided? Is she going to resume our sessions, or is this meeting designed to let me down easy?*

"Well, you're never going to know unless you get your ass over there."

With a heavy sigh, Grae dispatched a text to Marcus and turned in the direction of the nearest bus shelter.

When she walked up the path to Jo's house, she noticed that a Christmas tree sparkled in the sunshine of the picture window. Maybe Kendall had been telling the truth about having promised to help her mother decorate. It wasn't much, but Grae would grasp any straw she could right now.

Jo opened the door as she approached.

"How do you always know I'm here before I ring the bell?"

"It's one of my super powers. No, actually, I saw you arrive. Come on in. Would you like a coffee? Hot chocolate, perhaps?"

"Water's fine, thanks."

"All right. I was just going to pour myself a cup of coffee, so I'll meet you in the living room."

From her customary seat, Grae examined the tree. Unlike hers and Marcus', there were no new ornaments hanging on the branches. All of Jo's were well-worn, and there were many that were clearly child-created. Grae wondered which were Kendall's. She guessed the hand-painted pink and lime green Santa had to be one of them. Grae made a mental note to ask Kendall the next time she saw her. *If I see her again.*

Grae struggled to suppress that gloomy train of thought as Jo handed her a bottle of water, set a cup down on the side table, and took her seat. Jo studied her for a long moment. Grae held perfectly still and waited.

"I owe you an apology, Grae."

"You do? Why?"

Jo sighed heavily. "Because you should be able to have total faith that I will always be there for you as your therapist, and I wasn't."

"That's okay. I understood why."

"No, it's not okay. I had a long meeting with my mentor yesterday. James is extremely well-respected in our field. His focus is now mainly research, but he still lectures world-wide. He and I are very different people, and that's always been reflected in our therapeutic styles. James gleefully broke the rules whenever he felt it necessary. I was more old-school, even though I'm a decade younger. I was taught that a therapist's private life was never grist for a client's counselling. During my career, if a client discovered that I was a widow with three children and had lost my husband to an aneurism, it made me uncomfortable. If clients asked for more particulars, I would turn it around as a mode of discovery for them. Why was it important that they know these things about me? Did they feel there was a valid comparison with their lives and issues?"

"Well, you've certainly never disclosed much to me in our sessions."

"Actually, I disclosed more with you than ever before. I introduced you to Kendall, and I intimated that there was a personal connection between your mother and me."

"Huh, I guess you did at that. Why?"

Jo shifted in her chair and looked away. "I've wrestled with that question more than I can tell you. Particularly after you and Kendall began a romantic relationship."

Grae frowned. "I thought the problem was your and Mom's history. Do you have an issue with me and Kendall, because that really would be a stumbling block to continuing our sessions."

"James asked me much the same thing. He also pointed out that in effective therapy, our clients share details of their lives that they've often never told anyone. Sometimes that includes things that they haven't even admitted to themselves. So he asked me a very pointed question: Why was I the one feeling exposed?"

"Good question."

Jo chuckled wryly. "James has a way of asking such questions. It's what made him so brilliant a therapist, and invaluable as my mentor."

"So, how did you answer him?"

"I told him that my relationship with your mother, though long over, was one of the most significant of my life. So while I was aware that you might learn we were once involved, I compartmentalized that possibility until your question about whether I was a lesbian meant I could no longer do so. It instantly peeled away protective walls I'd spent years erecting."

There was no mistaking the sorrow on Jo's face. She didn't even try to conceal it.

Grae's heart ached for her, but she didn't know what to do. Offering a hug might contravene Jo's personal boundaries, and she didn't want to take that chance.

"Anyway, and this does relate, James told me why he retired from accepting clients last year. I thought he simply wanted to focus on his lecture tours, but that wasn't it."

"What happened?"

"Search engines. James has always practiced a fairly open-ended therapy, in that he would reveal personal information if he felt it would help connect him to his client. Now clients were coming in with full dossiers on James' life, compiled through online research. James is well-known in academic circles, and his lectures and activities are comprehensively covered if you know where to look. But the straw that broke the camel's back was of a more personal nature. James is an avid hockey fan and had, for several years, written a blog on the Flames. It was his passion. But a long-time client of his abruptly stopped their therapy sessions when she stumbled on James' blog. When James asked her why, it was because the woman's abusive husband was also a hockey fanatic and she couldn't get past the fear that the commonality between her therapist and her husband meant that she couldn't trust James."

"Wow, that's crazy."

"Is it? Perhaps it was a trigger she couldn't handle while trying to get strong enough to break free of her husband. James has always believed that the therapeutic relationship works best in an environment of mutual trust and respect. He was deeply remorseful and he took his blog down. Even though he referred his client to a very capable therapist, James still feels guilty that his innocent avocation caused such distress."

Grae chewed her lip as she considered Jo's words. "Okay, I get what you're saying, but I never Googled you."

Jo smiled. "You wouldn't find much if you had. I've very deliberately eschewed any online presence for that very reason. You did nothing wrong, Grae. That's my point. Thea—your mother revealed our truth to you, but she only did so because I dropped the crucial hint that galvanized you to ask for the truth."

"Did you do that on purpose? Did you want me to know?"

Jo met Grae's gaze squarely. "I don't know. I wasn't conscious of wanting you to know, but I also don't believe in accidents. Something in me set these events in motion. I talked with James for several hours.

He made me see that I'm conflating what are, in reality, two separate and distinct situations."

"How so?"

"The short-lived relationship that I had with your mother decades ago is only related to our therapeutic relationship in that I agreed to counsel you because of Thea's request."

"So does that mean you will go on being my therapist?"

"If we can work through a few things, yes."

"Things like what?"

"What impact this has on you, of course."

Grae's eyes widened. She had expected Jo to simply put her relationship with Thea off-limits and make that the condition of their continuing. She'd been fully prepared to agree to that. "Um, impact?"

Jo took a sip of her coffee and grimaced. "Cold. Yes, impact. How do you feel about what you've learned about your mother and me? Are you able to separate that from my role as your therapist? Is this going to be something we need to deal with in terms of how you relate to your mother, and to your parents as a couple? You've come a long way, and I don't want something from my past to retard additional progress."

"Okay. Well, how do I feel about you and Mom being lovers? Frankly, does anyone want to think about their parents' sex lives? I've made such a mess of my life, who am I to judge Mom and Dad because they turned out to be human and flawed."

"And me? How do you judge me?"

Grae shrugged. "I made love to a girl and got her killed. You made love to a woman, and she went back to her husband and family. I'd say that in terms of destructiveness, I'm way ahead of you. I'm not going to judge."

Jo frowned. "We obviously have more work to do if you're still saying you got Melissa killed, but I'll set that aside for now. I want you to know one more thing. After almost three hours of discussion, James asked me something that really clarified this situation for me."

"What was that?"

"He asked if I could be a more effective therapist for you precisely because of our personal connection through your mother and my daughter."

"What did you tell him?"

"That I wanted to be. That I thought we'd made excellent progress up until now, and I wanted to see the process through to the end."

Grae nodded. "Me, too. But you need to answer one question for me."

"And that is?"

"Can you separate being Kendall's mother from being my therapist, because I really need to work some things out and that means talking about Kendall, even about us having sex."

Jo raised an eyebrow. "You certainly lay it on the line, don't you?"

"It's what you always encourage me to do. And my relationship with Kendall is so important to me that I need to get it right. I want to get healthy. I need to get healthy."

"For Kendall, or for yourself?"

"Both. We tried to make love last night, and I froze. I don't even know if she even wants to see me again after that debacle, but if she does, then I've got to get past freezing every time she touches me."

Jo smiled slightly. "I don't think there's any doubt about Kendall's desire for a relationship with you. She came to see me yesterday."

"I know. She said she was going to help you put up the tree."

"She did, but mostly she came to talk, or rather to plead your case."

"She did?"

"She did. She had a comprehensive argument laid out for why I should keep working with you. She informed me that I'd be breaching my professional ethics, not to mention my personal integrity, if I stopped just because of something decades in the past that did not concern you. Honestly, she should've been a lawyer. I've never seen her argue so logically, persuasively, and passionately. And believe me, I've seen her beg for everything from a new softball glove when she was ten to permission to go camping with boys when she was fifteen."

A huge weight lifted from Grae, and she was momentarily dizzy with relief. Kendall did want to be with her after all. She grinned. "Camping with boys, eh? Did you let her?"

"No, but she snuck out and went anyway. She got herself grounded for a month, but she informed me it was worth it."

Grae laughed. That sounded exactly like Kendall. "So, where does all of this leave us?"

"I would like to resume our sessions, and I won't put anything off-limits, including my past with your mother, if you feel that's something you need to process."

Grae screwed up her face. "Ew, no. I really wasn't kidding when I said I didn't want to think about that."

"Avoidance is fine in this instance, unless it has a bearing on some other aspect of your life. Then we will need to address it."

"I mostly need to talk about my own sex life."

Jo smiled. "That's quite the turn-around from not so long ago, when you practically forbade us from dealing with your, as you put it, non-existent sex life."

"That's because, as of last night, it became semi-existent again. Are we on the clock now?"

"We can be. Since your normal therapy session falls on Christmas Eve, let's do this now."

"Good. Because I really messed things up last night."

"Tell me what happened."

Grae related the events of the previous evening, but spared Jo details where she could. She focused on emotional context and her inability to allow Kendall to touch her.

Jo had opened her ever-present notepad and jotted down a few things. "Am I correct in assuming that you wanted her to make love to you as well?"

"I did...at least I thought I did."

"Did you feel pressured at all? Was this perhaps moving too swiftly for your comfort?"

"God, Kendall bent over backwards not to pressure me. She was so gentle. She let me set the pace and decide what we did. She let me know every step of the way that I could stop anytime I wanted to. I couldn't have asked for a more patient, understanding partner."

"Who initiated love-making?"

"I was the one who suggested it, and I sort of took the lead."

"When you took the lead, you felt confident and in control, is that correct?"

"Yes."

"But when it came time for you to yield control, you panicked."

"And froze. Exactly."

"Do you remember what you were thinking before and after this sense of panic assailed you?"

"Before…I was happy. I was lying in Kendall's arms, and I was just plain happy."

"Can you zero in on that emotion? You were happy. Why?"

"Because I'd brought pleasure to someone I really care about. It was gratifying."

"Anything else?"

Grae let her memory drift back. "I felt…normal. After the abortive mess with Lucy, this was more like it. This was how making love should be."

"So it was like your pre-Melissa liaisons."

"Not exactly. It was sweeter than I remember my university hook-ups being."

"Because of the emotional connection."

"Yes."

"All right. So it's your partner's turn to make love to you. How did you feel when she began? Did she move too fast and scare you?"

"God, no. I told you. She was perfect. I'm the fucked-up one."

Jo smiled. "My daughter would be the first one to tell you she's not perfect. And your self-estimation has been warped by the past eight years. That's what we're working on. So be precise about how you felt. You said you froze, and you panicked. Were you frightened of the situation? Were you afraid Kendall wouldn't stop if you asked her to?"

Grae shook her head. "No, not at all. When she saw I had tears in my eyes, she stopped immediately and backed away. It's really hard to describe, but when Kendall touched me, it was similar to being with Lucy."

"How?"

"I wanted to pop out of my body. Like I just wanted to stand outside myself so I couldn't feel anything."

Jo tapped her pen on her lips as she studied her notes. "What you're describing is not uncommon for someone who associates sex with trauma.

Abuse, incest, assault—it's very typical for the victim to disassociate in order to deny what's happening."

"But it wasn't any of those things. I was making love with someone I care about and who cares about me."

"I know that. But the last time you allowed a woman to touch you and bring you to orgasm, that woman died within hours and you plunged into an eight-year-long spiral of self-blame and despair. I would never have suggested you even attempt to make love this soon. That you were able to function as well as you did, for as long as you did, is amazing. It's actually a very hopeful sign."

"It is?"

"It is, indeed. All right. I know this session wasn't as long as normal, but I'd like to leave it there if you don't mind."

"Uh, okay. Is anything wrong?"

Jo pointed out the window with a smile. She could see past the Christmas tree to the street from her angle; Grae couldn't. "Not at all, but Kendall has been sitting out there in her car for the last twenty minutes, showing almost unprecedented patience. I have a hunch seeing and talking to her will be of greater benefit to you than finishing our session."

A wave of joy swept over Grae, and she surged to her feet. But before she could dash out, Jo held up a hand.

"Just one more thing I want you to think about between now and our next session."

"Okay."

"From what you told me, you gave your partner great pleasure last night, but could not accept any pleasure in return. We will be examining that more closely."

Grae stared at Jo. "For what?"

"For whether you are still punishing yourself for Melissa's death. Now go, before my daughter breaks down my front door looking for you."

Grae took a couple of hesitant steps. "Punishing myself?"

"Can you deny it's what you've done very effectively for the past eight years?"

"No. I guess I can't."

"Then we'll talk about it next time. Go."

Grae threw on her coat and boots so fast that she didn't even take time to tie her laces or zip her coat. She was out the door and running down Jo's path when Kendall got out of her car and rushed to meet her. They came together in a mad tangle. Kendall spun Grae in a circle as their mouths eagerly sought each other. When they parted, laughing, Grae stopped short.

Jo stood back from the window, watching them. She bowed her head and turned away. For a brief instant, sadness intruded on Grae's joy. Was Jo remembering a time when she too had eagerly awaited her lover?

Then Kendall pulled her close and wrapped an arm around her shoulders. "So Marcus told me you guys hung mistletoe. Want to show me where?"

Grae slipped an arm around Kendall's waist. "I would indeed."

Chapter 28

By Boxing Day, Chinook winds had melted most of the snow, and the streets were a slushy mess. Grae held the door open for Marcus and watched him closely as he stepped outside their apartment building. He tried to take a long stride, and winced.

"Slow down there, cowboy. Your ribs aren't healed yet, you know."

"I know. I'll take it easy. I just had to get outside. I was going stir crazy."

Grae offered her arm, and Marcus took it as they started out on a slow ramble down the street in the direction of the river.

"I know what you mean. I thought I'd be thrilled having four days off in a row, but I can hardly wait for Monday so I can get back to work."

Marcus grinned. "And here I thought the fair lady Kendall was doing a pretty good job of occupying your time."

"She is. This has been the best Christmas I can remember in a long time. You and Freddie put out a great feast on Christmas Eve."

"I can't take much credit. I mostly pointed and gave orders. Freddie did all the real work."

"I'm sure you inspired him."

"Christmas dinner with your family was terrific, too."

"I know, eh? Who knew Ciara could be such a riot?"

"She was dangerous for my health. I thought I'd spew a lung from laughing so hard."

Grae sighed as she steered Marcus around a broken patch of pavement. "It was fun, but I missed seeing Kendall yesterday."

"She invited you to join her family gathering. Was it too soon?"

Grae didn't want to tell Marcus he was the reason she'd declined Kendall's invitation. He'd encouraged her to go, but Freddie had been summoned to his family's hearth and there was no place for Marcus there. She couldn't bear the thought of leaving him alone in the apartment, so she'd turned Kendall down.

"Nah, I just knew Mom really wanted us to come over, even though she tried not to pressure me. And it turned out to be a second Christmas for both of us."

"It did. They were really generous. I didn't expect to be included in their gift giving. Thanks for putting both our names on their gifts. And thanks again for my new clothes, and the phone, of course."

"You're welcome. Freddie was a great help with the new wardrobe."

"I'm sorry I only had some small things for you. I'd planned to do more shopping, but…"

Grae blew a raspberry at Marcus. "A, you had the best excuse in the world. And B, which is way more important, the only present I wanted was you home and healthy."

"Well, I went one for two."

"You did. And before long you'll be two for two."

"I hope so. I can't even…well, you know, right now."

"I'm sure Freddie will be patient."

They walked on in comfortable silence for half a block.

"So, speaking of patience—you and Kendall. How's it going?"

Grae rolled her eyes. "Subtle, much?"

Marcus shrugged. "You did spend the night together Christmas Eve."

And it went about as well as the first time. "Still a work in progress, bud."

"Okay. No surprise there, right?"

"None, damn it."

Marcus squeezed her arm. "Don't worry. She's so much in love with you that she'll stick with you until you're in granny panties before she gives up."

Grae glared at Marcus. "Granny panties? In your dreams, wise-ass. I'll still be wearing sexy underwear when I'm ninety."

"Me too."

They laughed together.

Grae nodded at the upcoming entrance to a small park. "Are you up to a wander before we head back?"

"Sure. It's so warm we might even see a Canada goose that forgot to fly south."

"That'd be nice, wouldn't it?"

They chatted amiably about the weather and New Year's plans as they turned into the park. Halfway to the river, Grae tugged Marcus to a halt next to a bench.

He looked at her. "What's up? You want to sit for a bit?"

"Someone's been following us. No, don't look around. We're going to sit here and wait to see if he goes past."

Marcus froze. "Are you sure?"

"I wasn't at first, not until we turned into the park. Now I am. It's just one guy, bud. And he's not very big."

"But he could be a mugger."

"I've got nothing but my phone and keys on me. If he comes closer, I'm going to call Kendall and have her stand by to call the cops if needed. You get your phone out and record him, so he knows we have his picture if he attacks us."

"Jesus."

"It's all right, bud. It's broad daylight, and there are other people around. It's going to be okay. Just sit. I'm not going to let anything happen to you."

Marcus sat, his face even paler as he hunched inside his jacket. Grae hit her speed dial for Kendall.

"Hi, Grae. I was just thinking of calling you."

"We might have a problem here, Kendall. I need your help."

"Why? What's going on?"

The alarm in Kendall's voice both heartened and frightened Grae. She could absolutely rely on Kendall, but Kendall was miles away. Grae described their situation and gave their location.

"Stay on the line. I'm on my way." Kendall's words were followed in moments by the sound of a door opening and closing, and running footsteps. Another door opened and closed. "I'm in my car. Hold on, love. I'll be there as quickly as I can."

Marcus had his phone out. Grae was between him and the oncoming stalker.

"Move back a little so I can see him, Grae."

She did as he directed.

Marcus raised his phone, then his eyes widened and his jaw dropped. "Oh my God."

Grae spun around and saw that the young man was within twenty feet. Kendall was still talking, but Grae thrust the phone into her pocket so she had her fists free. She started to raise them, when Marcus grabbed her arm.

"No, Grae. It's Gideon."

Grae stared down at him. "Gideon? As in your brother, Gideon?"

"Yes. That Gideon."

That didn't mean he wasn't dangerous, but Grae relaxed a little and took her phone out of her pocket. Kendall was yelling at her.

"Are you okay? God, answer me! Grae!"

"It's okay. It's okay. False alarm. Turns out it's Marcus' brother."

"Are you sure it's okay? Given his parents' attitude, his brother could've tracked him down with malice aforethought. I'm still coming to get you."

"That's cool. I'll leave the phone on so you can listen."

Gideon held out his hands in a placating gesture. "I didn't mean to scare you. I just wanted to talk, Marc."

"How did you find me?" Marcus' voice shook.

Grae wasn't sure whether his trembling was due to the adrenaline rush of thinking they were being stalked, or the shock of seeing his younger brother after four years. She took up a defensive posture and rested one hand on Marcus' shoulder as she stood beside him.

"Rebecca. She told me she saw you. I hacked into the hospital records and got your discharge address. I've been hanging around here whenever I could get away from home. I've been trying to work up the nerve to talk to you. When I saw you out walking, I figured it was now or never."

Gideon was a few inches shorter than Marcus, with the same lanky build, sandy hair, and dark blue eyes. The family resemblance was unmistakable now that Grae really looked.

Marcus raised an eyebrow. "You know how to hack?"

"Yeah." Gideon scuffed at the sidewalk.

Marcus shot Grae a droll glance. "Home-schooling has changed a lot since my day."

"I haven't been home-schooled for a couple of years now."

"Yeah, I saw that on Facebook. I was shocked you even had a page. I was even more shocked that Mom and Dad let you into the public school system."

Gideon looked up in alarm. "They don't know about me being on Facebook. They'll kill me if they find out."

"You think I'm going to tell them?"

"No, I guess not. It wasn't easy to talk them into letting me transfer, but I want to be a doctor and then a missionary. I told them that the only way I could do God's work was to get scholarships, and to do that, I had to go to public schools."

"Interesting argument. And it worked?"

Gideon nodded.

"So Rebecca must've told you how it went down between me and Mom. Why did you want to talk to me? Cuz if you're just into throwing shade, you can take your skinny ass out of here."

Grae glared at Gideon to buttress Marcus' words. Worried about how weary he sounded, she was tempted to chase his brother away, but it wasn't her place.

"No, man. I just want to talk, okay? You ran away without a fucking word. Then four years later, Becs finds you all beat to hell in the hospital. I just want to fill in the blanks, okay?"

Marcus gave a strangled laugh. "You think I ran away?"

"Well, yeah."

"Mom and Dad told you that?"

Gideon's expression was troubled. "They did, but Becs told me what Mom said to you at the hospital. Did they really throw you out?"

"Yes."

"Are you…um…"

"Gay. Yes."

Gideon turned beet red and looked everywhere but at his brother.

"You got a problem with that, kid?" Grae put as much menace in her voice as she could.

"God has a problem with it." The words sounded like a rote response.

Grae opened her mouth to rebut Gideon, but Marcus laid his hand on hers.

"You can't argue with a closed mind, sweetie. Maybe when he gets out into the real world, but he's been living in our parents' world for seventeen years. It's all he knows."

Grae scowled. "It's ignorance."

"It's their faith." Marcus studied Gideon. "What is it you want with me?"

"To know why you chose to be like this."

Marcus and Grae shared eye rolls.

"What?" Gideon asked.

"Choose to be gay? Why would you think I'd choose something that got me punted out of my home and family when I just a kid? Do you want to know how I survived being fourteen and living on the street? Do you?" Marcus rose unsteadily to his feet.

Grae reached to support his arm, but he shook her off. He advanced on Gideon, who took a step back.

"Do you want to hear how I was fucked night after night by guys on the down low who didn't have the balls to come out and be who they truly were, so they had to pick up street kids? Do you want to know what I had to do just to have a warm place to sleep for a night? Or for a plate of food I didn't have to dig out of a dumpster? Would you like to hear all the gory details? So you tell me again that I chose this life. Go ahead. Tell me."

Gideon had gone as pale as the vanishing snow. "But, but—"

Marcus was within inches of his brother. His jaw jutted forward and his eyes blazed. "This is who I am, who I was born to be. Are you telling me God made a mistake? Cuz I can't be anything but a man who loves men. And when you get on your fucking high horse that you're so much better than me, you remember that our God-fearing parents threw me out with nothing but the clothes on my back. And this woman," he pointed at Grae, "who's also gay, took me in and saved my life. So you tell me, Gideon. Who do you think Jesus would approve of? Them, or her? Them, or me? Because I've never hurt a soul in my life, at least not intentionally, but one of those down low guys put me in the hospital with a broken arm, multiple lacerations, and a couple of cracked ribs. And he's home celebrating Christ's birthday with his second wife and fifth kid. So who do you think is the biggest fucking hypocrite?"

Gideon started to cry.

Marcus instantly backed off. "Aw, shit. I'm sorry, Gid. You get enough of this crap at home. You don't need it from me."

Gideon shook his head and rubbed his eyes on his sleeve. "S'okay."

"No, it's not. You may not regard me as your brother anymore, but you'll always be a brother to me. It's not right to get angry at you. You can't help what they made you. Go home, and someday, maybe when you're a missionary doctor, you'll understand. People can make bad choices, but they don't always get to choose. And holding that against them—well, to my mind, that's about as sinful as it gets." Marcus turned away, his shoulders slumped and his head bowed.

Grae stepped forward to support him. "Let's go, bud. Kendall's about two minutes away. She'll give us a ride home."

"Wait!"

Marcus looked over his shoulder. "What is it, Gideon?"

"For what it's worth, I think Mom and Dad are wrong about you."

They turned to face him.

Marcus gazed at his brother. "You do?"

"Yeah. I didn't know what happened to you. Until Becs told me what went down at the hospital, I really thought you'd run out on us. I've been pissed about that for a long time. I always thought I'd come across you some day and kick your ass for abandoning me…us."

"I wouldn't have done that."

"I think I always knew the truth on some level, but I couldn't understand why you left. You and me, we were tight. You were my big brother, and I looked up to you. Then one day you were just gone, and I didn't know why. I've been in public school for a couple of years now. I got into quite a few fights because of—well, the things Mom and Dad taught us. I know the world is changing, and they aren't. I get that. But it's hard, you know. When the school sent me home for fighting, the folks would be proud of me. They'd tell me I was setting an example for lost souls, and to keep standing up for God."

"So did something change your mind?"

Gideon blushed. "Yeah. Well, someone."

Marcus smiled. "What's her name?"

"Amelia. It took me forever to work up the nerve to ask her out."

"Mom and Dad vet her?"

"No. I haven't told them."

"So, what happened? Did Amelia change your mind or something?"

Gideon shot Marcus a shame-faced glance. "She busted my ass. It was our first date. We were talking, and she mentioned a cousin who'd just come out on Facebook. I didn't even think. I just—"

"Launched into Mom's talking points."

"Yeah, I guess. Amelia got so mad at me that she threw her pop in my face and ran out. Then she wouldn't talk to me at school. None of her friends would, either. It made me feel like…"

"Like an ostracized gay kid," Grae said softly. Her anger faded. The boy was obviously trying to grow beyond his conditioning, and she gave him high marks for that.

Gideon hung his head. "I don't know what to think."

Marcus smiled. "At least you're trying to think. That's what counts. Look, do you want my phone number? If you feel like talking, call me. We can even meet for coffee, if you'd like."

"I would like that, but they keep pretty close tabs on me."

"I figured. But you can contact me on Facebook, too, if you want to friend me."

Gideon's brow furrowed. "I've tried to find you a ton of times."

"Look for me under Marcus Jordan. I'm thinking of legally changing my name, so I thought I'd try it out."

"Okay." Gideon hesitated.

Grae wondered whether he wanted to hug Marcus, but still had reservations. She felt like telling him being gay wasn't contagious, but held her tongue.

"You'll always be my brother, Marcus. I want you to know that, okay?"

Marcus' eyes brightened. "Very okay."

"But I should probably tell you that the others don't feel the same way. They were all so little when you left, you know?"

"Even Timothy? Rebecca?"

"Uh-huh. I'm sorry."

The light in Marcus' eyes dimmed, but he forced a smile. "Hey, I started the morning without any siblings, 'cept for Grae, here. Now I have a brother again. It's a good day. But you'd better get going, Gid."

Gideon glanced at his watch and nodded. "You're right. When I borrowed the car, I told Mom I was going to the mall to return the ugly sweater Aunt Ruth gave me. She'll be expecting me soon."

He gave a half wave and started back the way he'd come. Marcus and Grae turned in the opposite direction. Kendall was standing halfway down the sidewalk, watching them. Grae closed her phone and dropped it into her pocket.

Marcus gave Grae a little push. "Go. I can manage to walk by myself."

Grae gave him a quick once over.

He rolled his eyes. "Go. Honestly, I'm not made of spun sugar."

She grinned and jogged to Kendall, who advanced to meet her with open arms.

Grae nestled into her embrace, and they rocked gently together. "Thank you for coming."

"Thank you for leaving your phone open so I could hear what was going on. I was going out of my mind, until I was sure that you and Marcus were safe."

Grae buried her face against Kendall's neck. "I knew you'd come."

"Always. But maybe next time you should call 911 if you're being followed."

Grae chuckled. "I doubt there'll be a next time. But isn't it awesome that Gideon hunted Marcus down?"

"It is. It's also pretty cool that Marcus is thinking of taking your name."

"Isn't it? I had no idea he'd done that."

Marcus joined them. "I haven't done it legally, yet. But yes, if you're cool with it, I'd like to."

Grae drew back from Kendall's embrace and linked arms with both her and Marcus. They set a slow pace to the parking lot. "I am absolutely down with it, bro."

Despite the grey, overcast sky, Grae was surrounded by warmth. For a moment, nothing else mattered but the two people who walked at her side. *Damn, life is good.*

Chapter 29

"Happy New Year, love."

Snuggled contentedly in Kendall's arms, Grae smiled. "Happy New Year to you."

"We were asleep way before midnight. Does that make us old?"

Grae laughed. "It probably makes us smarter than all those partiers who are going to start this year with wicked hangovers."

"Like Marcus and Freddie?"

"I don't think they made it home last night. At least I didn't hear anyone come in."

Kendall tightened her embrace. "Can I ask you something?"

"Sure."

"I don't want to upset you, but I was wondering…"

Grae tilted her head back to search Kendall's face. "You sound serious. What's up?"

"Well, it's just that last night—"

Grae tensed. They'd tried again to make love, and it hadn't gone any better than the previous times. Was Kendall getting fed up?

"Stop that," Kendall said.

"Stop what?"

"You can't think the worst every time I want to talk about us. How many times do I have to tell you? I'm not going anywhere."

Grae strove to relax, but it was a battle.

Kendall kissed her forehead. "Shhh, we're good. I swear. But I was wondering if there wasn't some way to make sex easier for you."

"How? I don't want to stop trying."

"And I don't either. I love being with you, and yes, it's a little hard that my touch still bothers you. It's even harder for me to feel as if I'm taking advantage."

Grae sat up and stared at Kendall. "What are you talking about—taking advantage? Are you nuts?"

Kendall pushed herself into a sitting position and took Grae's hands. "Hear me out, okay? It took you a long time to fall asleep last night. I know, because I was listening to you. And I was thinking about how I could help. So, if you're not ready to let me touch you, what about if you touched yourself? At least that way you wouldn't be trying to go to sleep when you're still frustrated."

"Masturbate? With you here?"

"If you want, I could go out to the living room and give you some alone time."

Grae shook her head and settled back into the bed with her head on Kendall's lap. "I'm not sure whether that's the most generous idea I've ever heard, or the craziest."

Kendall scratched Grae's back, and she undulated in pleasure. "It could be both. It also could fill the gap, until you—"

Grae couldn't help herself. "Fill the gap? Between my legs? Have you bought some toys you haven't told me about?"

Kendall swatted her. "Brat. No, but I do have a handy-dandy vibrator if you want to borrow it."

Grae curled closer to Kendall. "No thanks. I really appreciate you trying to help, but I'm content to wait for the real thing."

"Me?"

"Yes, you."

Grae couldn't see Kendall's face from her position, but she knew what her expression would be. She rolled over so she was looking up at Kendall. *Yup. That's it. Pleasure and chagrin.*

"I know you're trying to help, I really do. But it would take a lot of pressure off, if for now, you'd just let me make love to you and not worry about reciprocating, okay?" When Kendall didn't say anything, Grae slid a hand inside Kendall's nightshirt and captured a nipple. "Okay?"

Kendall squirmed and started to laugh as Grae teased her breast. "All right, already. I give."

"Do you, now? And what exactly are you giving?" Grae released the captive breast, pulled back the covers, and straddled Kendall's thighs.

Kendall's eyes widened and her breaths came faster. "Anything you want to take."

"Good answer."

Grae hooked a finger in the waistband of Kendall's panties and pulled them down. It wasn't far, but it gave her the access she wanted. Kendall spread her legs as far she could against the constricting fabric and Grae's legs. Grae lightly slid her finger over Kendall's clit. Writhing, Kendall tried to give Grae a better angle.

"I could lie down, and take these clothes off."

Grae smiled at the desperate tone in Kendall's voice. "No, this is good. Have you ever come sitting up?"

"Pretty sure I haven't."

"Then let's start this year with a whole new experience."

It wasn't long before Kendall's cries resounded in the bedroom. Grae was very glad that Marcus and Freddie hadn't come home, because she'd only just begun.

⁂

Kendall sat at the island, put her head on the counter, and extended a hand. "Coffee."

Grae pressed a full cup into her hand. "Tired?"

Kendall raised her head and took a sip. "Oh, like you don't know. Wipe that smirk off your face, woman. You're the reason I may not walk straight until Easter."

Grae leaned over and kissed her. "Maybe I'm glad you're not walking straight…anymore."

Kendall set her cup aside and captured Grae's face. "Have I mentioned I'm really, really glad you lured me from the straight and narrow?"

Their laughter was swallowed up in kisses.

When they finally surfaced, Grae continued to fix breakfast. Marcus and Freddie had prepared a virtual feast the previous evening before heading out to a party, and they'd left detailed instructions on how to ready the meal. It was a belated Christmas gift from her roommate, though she'd told him repeatedly he didn't need to worry about the scarcity of his gifts for her. Now, with everything almost ready to be heated and served, she appreciated the boys' efforts. Kendall would not be getting fresh strawberry blintzes if Grae had been doing the cooking from scratch.

Grae's cellphone rang, and she picked it up.

"Hello."

"Grae, it's Jude."

"Happy New Year, boss."

"Thanks, and to you, too. Unfortunately, it's not getting off to a good start."

Grae stopped her preparations and focused. "What's wrong? I've been checking the messages regularly, and there wasn't anything that couldn't wait."

"I know. This wouldn't be on there. Henry Zierling, the manager of Westview, called me personally. Some idiots had the brilliant idea to ring in the New Year by vandalizing headstones, and it sounds like it's a helluva mess. He asked if I could come take a look. He wants me to give him an idea of what it will take to restore them, so that he can tell the families involved. I hate to ask on a holiday, but would you come with me? I could use a hand."

"Absolutely. I'll get a bus over to Stone Gardens as quickly as I can."

"No need. I'll pick you up. Can you be ready in half an hour?"

"I'll be ready."

"Good, and thanks."

"No problem. See you shortly." Grae ended the call and looked apologetically at Kendall.

"I'm guessing that you need to go in to work?"

"I'm so sorry. Some goddamned idiots thought it would be a great idea last night to destroy a bunch of monuments in Westview. They've asked Jude to do an assessment of the needed repairs, and he wants me along to help."

"It couldn't wait until tomorrow?"

Grae shook her head. "You don't know Jude. He takes such desecrations seriously, and the quicker he can begin to make things right, the better. He feels a responsibility to the families."

"Are all the toppled monuments ones he made?"

"Probably not, but that won't matter to him. I'm really sorry. Stay and have breakfast, okay?"

Kendall set her coffee aside and stretched. "Tell you what. Let's put everything back into the fridge and have this feast for supper instead."

"You'll wait for me?"

"Sure, if you don't mind me hanging around. I've got my tablet. I can keep myself entertained."

"And here I thought that was my job." Grae grinned and waggled her eyebrows.

Kendall laughed. "It is, love. And you do it so well. However, since you can't keep me in bed twenty-four hours a day—"

"Can't? Is that a challenge, Ms. Reaves?"

"It is not, Ms. Jordan. Try that, and I won't be walking straight until Canada Day."

They exchanged a lingering kiss, and Grae almost wished that Jude had called one of his other employees.

"Mmm, that should hold me until you get home. So, may I give you a ride to work?"

"Thanks, but Jude is going to pick me up here. In fact, I'd better get dressed."

"Need any help?"

"With your kind of help, I doubt I'd be dressed and ready to go in thirty."

Kendall heaved an exaggerated sigh. "Oh, all right. Then I'll stow the dishes, and you go get some clothes on."

Grae gave her a quick kiss. "Thanks. You're the best."

Jude spun in a slow circle, a scowl on his face. "Son of a bitch. Look at this mess. What the hell were those bastards thinking?"

Grae gingerly picked her way through the mess of shattered beer and liquor bottles, and overturned and smashed monuments. "I suspect they were doing more drinking than thinking. So, where do we start?"

Jude's expression was grim. "We start by documenting everything. I forgot the camera in the cab. Grab it, will you?"

Halfway through a slow, methodical photographic sweep of the area, Grae snapped a picture of a baseball cap mostly hidden under the badly broken corner of a toppled monument.

"Hey, Jude, look at this. Do you think that cap might belong to one of the jerks who did this?"

"Maybe. Or someone visiting a loved one might've accidentally dropped it sometime before." Jude knelt and examined it.

"Still, don't you think we should tell the police?" Grae asked.

"Probably. Okay, I'll lift. You pull out the hat. Put your gloves on before you do. I have no idea if the police will try to fingerprint it, but I don't want you touching it."

"I won't." Grae had taken off her gloves to operate the camera. She put them back on and crouched next to the broken monument. "Go ahead."

Jude raised the monument enough so that Grae could tug the cap free. She almost dropped it when she got a good look at it.

"Holy crap!"

Jude grunted as he lowered the monument to the ground. "What?"

"I know whose hat this is."

"You do? How?"

Grae turned it so the insignia faced Jude. "Because how many people in Calgary do you know who wear a Tea Party yellow baseball cap with crossed Confederate and Don't Tread On Me flags? This hat haunts my dreams."

"Why? Who does it belong to?"

"Dylan MacIsaac. He got it when he was working in Texas a few years back, and even when he had to wear his hard hat, he had this stuffed in his back pocket. He never went anywhere without it. Jesus, what do we do?"

"What do you think we should do?"

Grae hesitated. There was nothing she wanted less than to become enmeshed again with Dylan. She glanced from the hat to Jude, but his expression was neutral.

"We have to tell the police, don't we?" Grae sighed. Why did it always seem that doing the right thing was so hard?

"I'm going to let you make that call," Jude said. "I'll support whatever you decide."

"We have to. He shouldn't be allowed get away with this."

"Like he almost got away with setting you up?"

"Yeah."

"If it makes you feel any better, I doubt that the presence of his hat will be sufficient evidence in and of itself, but it will give the police a direction to start looking in."

"True. Okay, maybe we can take it to the cops on the way back to the shop."

Jude nodded, and turned as his name was called. Henry Zierling approached them, accompanied by a local TV cameraman and reporter. Zierling made introductions and explained to the reporter what Jude and Grae were doing.

"Jude's the best in the business. If anyone can fix the damage, it's him."

"We're going to do a quick interview with Mr. Zierling," the reporter said. "Could I also get a quote from you, Mr. Herzog?"

"Sure, but you might have to bleep my words when I tell you what I think of the assholes who'd do something like this."

The reporter smiled and motioned his cameraman forward to set up the shot. Grae stepped out of camera range, took the incriminating cap to the truck, and continued to document the damage while the brief interview was conducted. She wrapped up just as the reporter did.

While Jude unfastened his mic, Grae reviewed the pictures she'd taken. She stopped abruptly and held her breath as she stared at one of the last photos. An angel holding a child had been battered badly with some sort of heavy instrument, but the lettering on the polished shield was still legible. Grae enlarged the image.

In loving memory of Melissa Doreen Salish.
Some people only dream of angels.
We have held one in our arms.

Grae stared at the date of death. She would never forget the day her life had imploded. Tears sprang to her eyes.

"Grae? What's wrong? Hey, what's going on? You're white as a sheet."

Grae frantically scanned the debris field. *There!* It was one of the last ones she'd photographed, when her attention had been on listening to Jude's interview. She ran to it, and brushed rubble off the face of the stone.

It was Melissa's headstone.

Grae's mind flashed back to the instant before the truck hit Melissa. Tendrils of bright blonde hair that had wisped across Grae's naked body only hours earlier blew across Melissa's face as she turned her head to look back at Grae. Their gazes locked for just a second, then came the sounds that haunted Grae—the squeal of tires and the thud of three tons of metal hitting a fragile human body. Then the second, lighter thump as Melissa hit the brick retaining wall, and an onlooker's high-pitched scream. The soundtrack of her nightmares.

Jude's hands closed on Grae's shoulders and shook her gently. "Grae…Grae. What's wrong?"

He turned her gently toward him, tearing her gaze from the accusing stone. "What's going on? Is it someone you know?"

Grae stared at him, with tears running down her cheeks. In a broken whisper, she said, "It's someone I killed."

Chapter 30

Jude shot a quick glance at the reporter talking with Henry and hustled Grae away from the badly damaged monument. He steered her to the company truck, opened the passenger door, and half-lifted her inside.

Jude got behind the wheel, and turned to face Grae. "What are you talking about? What do you mean you killed someone?"

For the fourth time, Grae related her story. The words spilled out as she bared her soul. Again, she took full responsibility for the consequences of her actions.

"It may be Dylan's fault that Melissa's monument is all but destroyed, but it's my fault that she's even in this cemetery. Of the two of us, my sin is far greater. I deserved everything that's happened to me in the last eight years. Every rotten, lousy thing, most of which I brought down on my own head."

"Do you deserve my friendship? Or is that one of the rotten, lousy things that happened?"

Shock startled Grae out of her misery. "God, no! Meeting you was one of the best things that's ever happened to me."

"And Marcus? Do you deserve his love and friendship? What about your family? What about Kendall? Is their love for you a mistake, or do you actually deserve it?"

Grae blinked in confusion. This was not the reaction she'd expected. "I…uh…"

"Since you seem to be a little confused, why don't I answer those questions for you? I listen to you talk about Marcus, and it's clear you love him like a brother. It's also clear that he feels the same about you. I know you had years of estrangement from your own family, but when it counted, they were all there for you. And from things you've told me, they'd have been there for you all along, if you'd let them. Kendall—well, all I know is that your eyes light up whenever you talk about her, and you talk about her a lot." Jude smiled. "I watched you together at Halligan's. It was like you were in emotional orbit together. You could barely look away from one another. The rest of us could've fallen off the face of the earth, and it's doubtful that the two of you would've even noticed."

"I never meant to make anyone feel like that."

"Hell, I didn't say it was a bad thing. I remember when Elaine and I were the same way. But the kids and the business, and most of all, Ezra, kind of wore that away. Don't get me wrong. We still love each other deeply, but we each have our own orbits now."

Grae wrinkled her brow. "Ezra?"

Jude sighed. "Ezra. You didn't know me back then. Your black night of the soul began the morning Melissa died and lasted for over eight years. Mine began decades ago on the night my brother was arrested and charged with multiple counts of child molestation. Do you know what ended that torment?"

Grae shook her head.

"A stranger came to my shop and challenged me to acknowledge the love for my brother that I had tried so hard to quash. I thought I'd stomped that sucker into the ground and buried it six feet deep. And then, someone with absolutely no skin in the game made me see that as much as I loathed what Ezra did and had become, I'd never stopped loving him."

"I did all that?"

"Yeah, you did. You were under no obligation to bring Ezra's letter to me. You didn't have to step out of your comfort zone and try to give my brother a shave as a final kindness in a depraved man's life. You had no dog in the hunt, and still you did a generous thing, and you made me feel ashamed of myself."

"Oh, no, Jude. That was never my intention."

"I know it wasn't. It wouldn't even have crossed your mind. That's my point. You did the right thing because that's who you are, and for no other reason. And by doing so, you changed my life."

Grae frowned. "No, you've got it backwards. You changed my life. I'm the one who's grateful to have met you."

"No, I don't have it backwards at all. Listen. I can't begin to tell you how ashamed I was to have a pedophile as a brother. I wanted to hate Ezra. I certainly hated what he'd become. Do you know that when I first learned of the charges against him, I was furious, but not at him. I was certain that the police had the wrong man, that Ezra had been unjustly accused. I went to see him in jail and vowed to get him the best lawyer money could buy so we could right this wrong together. He let me talk, and then he started to cry. He told me that he knew it would be the last time he would see me, but still he had to tell the truth. He said he was sick. He said he'd tried to stop himself, and when that didn't work, he'd tried to get help. I can remember sitting there, in utter shock, listening to him confess to those hideous crimes. My own brother could hurt a child? I'd have bet my life against it. Hell, until that moment, I'd have trusted him with my precious babies, without a single qualm."

Jude fell silent, and his gaze grew distant.

Grae laid a hand on his arm. "I'm so sorry."

He tried to smile as he patted her hand. "I could barely walk when I left the jail. When I got to my truck, I threw up right there in the street. Then I went home and stayed drunk for three days. Elaine was so worried that she called my father's rabbi friend. Do you remember me telling you about him?"

"Sort of."

"You'd have liked Levi. He, too, could focus on a soul's humanity, no matter how badly the person had messed up. So, Levi comes into my bedroom. I'm hung-over as hell, and haven't showered or shaved in three days. He throws opens the blinds, and even though it's dusk, the light just about kills me. He tells me to get out of bed and get cleaned up so we can talk."

"He ordered you around? Was he a giant?"

Jude laughed. "He was about five feet four, and probably weighed no more than a hundred and a quarter, soaking wet. Scrawny little guy with eyes that burned with a righteous fire. But he had the power of his faith, and that beat the hell out of the power of my muscles. I got my ass out of bed and did what he told me."

"Elaine must've been grateful."

"Elaine wasn't there. Levi had told her to take the girls over to visit their grandparents, and he'd let her know when they could come home. So began one of the longest nights of my life."

"What did he do?"

"Sat me down at the kitchen table with a pot of the strongest coffee you can imagine, and he talked. Some of what he said took years to sink in. Some of it didn't sink in until you showed up at my shop. Some of it is still sinking in. But I never forgot a single word he said that night."

Grae was riveted by Jude's story. Her own tears were forgotten. "What did he say?"

"It wasn't just what he said, it was how he said it. I thought for sure he was going to tear me a new one for my drunken, loutish, self-centered behaviour."

"And did he?"

"He did not. He told me what I was doing was an emotional scourging of the soul, and that it wasn't necessarily a bad thing. Sometimes a man's got to step back and examine his life, he allowed. But he told me I wasn't examining my life. I was just feeling shamed by Ezra's life, and that had to stop."

Grae shook her head. "How could he blame you for that? God, you had a right to be ashamed."

"Yes and no. You see I was taking the shame into my own soul that rightfully belonged only to Ezra. That was wrong. Ezra's shame was his alone. By making it part of my heart, I was doing wrong to those who loved me—Elaine, the kids, my parents. It was hard enough on them, and I was making it worse."

"Huh. I guess I can see that."

Jude smiled. "Old Levi could talk you into believing that a blue sky was green, but in this case, he spoke with the power of an archangel. He told me something that I'm going to pass on to you. We're all human. We're going to screw up time and again in our lives, and we have to accept responsibility when we do. But you absolutely should not take on responsibility for the things for which you are not responsible. Wallowing in guilt that doesn't rightfully belong to you is just being self-indulgent. Levi, he told me to stop doing that, or I'd destroy everyone who loved me. And I'm advising you to do the same."

"But I do deserve the guilt. Melissa wouldn't have been running across the road just when that truck was there if she hadn't been running from me because I was such an asshole."

"I get that. Here's what I don't get: How is it more your fault than the fault of the fellow who was driving the truck?"

Grae glared at him. "If Missy wasn't in the road, the truck wouldn't have hit her. And she wouldn't have been in the road if it wasn't for me."

"What if the driver had been going a little slower? He was on campus. Lots of students walking around. Maybe he was going too fast."

"You don't know that he was."

"You don't know that he wasn't."

"But...but..."

Jude tilted his head. "Why are you fighting so hard to hang onto this guilt? Do you enjoy it? Has it made your life better in any way?"

"Of course not. But it's rightfully mine—I own this."

"Here's the irony I see. Most people would've suffered some guilt, but they'd eventually have found a way to banish it, or they'd have blamed Melissa or the driver. I doubt that one in a million would've had the same reaction as you. If you'd have been that driver, and maybe you were drunk or speeding, no law could've punished you more effectively than you punished yourself."

Grae leaned back against the door. "Jo said that too."

"Said what?"

"That I was punishing myself."

"Well, hell, that's as obvious as the nose on my face. It surprises you?"

"I didn't intend to—I mean, I never thought of it that way."

Jude shrugged. "So what did you think when you dropped out of your world? If you didn't realize you were punishing yourself, were you trying to punish your family?"

"No. No, of course not. They hadn't done anything wrong."

"But you put them through years of hell."

Grae's stomach churned. *Oh, God.* "I didn't mean to hurt them."

"And maybe you didn't intend to hurt yourself, either, but you did both."

"Jesus, I screwed up."

"Past tense, Grae. Past tense. And even then, you didn't screw everything up. Look at Marcus. Look at Ezra. You were a God-given gift to both of them, and to me."

Grae started to demur and Jude held up his hand. "No. No false modesty. We've spent a lot of time together in the last few months. Even though you never once said so, I know enough from the stories you've told me that you literally saved Marcus' life."

"That's what he always told me. I always tell him he did the same for me."

"Yup, I don't doubt that. You also gave Ezra a final moment of grace that he didn't earn, but then that's the nature of grace, according to Levi. It doesn't have to be earned; it just has to be given by a generous heart. That's where you came in."

"I really think you overestimate what I did for your brother. I was probably with him less than two hours out of his whole life."

"And I spent my entire youth with him, and I wouldn't have extended him that grace, 'cept you showed me the way. I'm more grateful for that than I can ever tell you."

Grae smiled. "I'm the grateful one. You got me out of shelf stocking hell and into doing something that I love."

Jude studied her. "You do love it, don't you?"

"Yes. I can hardly wait to come to work in the morning. I didn't have a second thought when you called me today." Grae remembered the sweet softness of Kendall's body. "Okay, maybe one itty-bitty second thought."

Jude laughed. "I'm not even going to ask what's turning your face red."

Grae scrubbed at her burning cheeks with both hands.

Jude sobered. "For a lot of years, work was my redemption. To give some measure of peace to people who are experiencing some of the worst moments of their life—that's a blessing. Levi would say you need to redeem your soul by cleansing it of the guilt you've suffered all these years. If Stone Gardens offers you the same respite that it does me, I'm glad. Whether you know it or not, you redeemed me like Marcus redeemed you. I was carrying a load of anger, hatred, and guilt because of Ezra. Then you walked in his door, and mine, and you gave us one last opportunity to remember a brother's love."

"I appreciate what you're saying, Jude, but honestly, I was just looking for volunteer credits to show the judge."

"You could've gotten those easily. You didn't have to go the extra mile—hell, the extra twenty miles. I'm just telling you that the only way you can redeem yourself is to forgive yourself."

"God, Jude, I don't know. Jo's been on my case, too, though she doesn't talk about it as redemption. But the roots of this run so damn deep. I'm just not sure I can."

Jude snorted. "I'm not saying it's easy. I swear another piece of my soul felt sullied every time Ezra was charged with a new crime. It got so Elaine would automatically take the girls to her parents whenever his name hit the news. She didn't want the kids anywhere near me."

"So Levi's talk about not taking responsibility for your brother's deeds didn't convince you?"

"It wasn't the only time he tried, believe me. It was almost comical. Elaine would be heading out the door with the girls, and Levi would be coming in at the same time."

They fell silent, both lost in their thoughts.

Finally Jude sighed. "I can't convince you that what happened to Melissa was not your fault. You have to feel that in your heart."

"Do *you*? I mean, have you stopped feeling guilt and anger about the things Ezra did?"

"It's a work in progress, but thanks to you, I'm a lot farther ahead of the game than I was this time last year."

Jude's words warmed Grae to the core. "Thank you. That means a lot to me."

"You've come to mean a lot to me, Grae. I've never had an apprentice take to the stones like you have. You love them. I can tell because I see myself in you."

"Now that's a compliment."

"That's the truth. Look, you are the only one who can redeem yourself, but you're not alone. I hope you know that."

Images filled Grae's mind of all those who loved and had stuck by her. "I do know that. I've got a lot of love in my life."

"That's what matters. Levi would say it's the only thing that matters. He always said that the love of others is the only thing we can take with us when we die."

"Is he still alive? I'd like to meet him."

"No. He passed about ten years ago. Never seen so many people in one place as came to honour him. I still miss him."

"You're my Levi," Grae said sincerely.

"Well, damn. That has to be the nicest compliment I've ever received. Thank you."

"You're welcome. Jude?"

"Yeah?"

"I think you redeemed Ezra, too."

Jude shook his head. "Oh, I dunno about that."

"I do. Remember, I watched the two of you together. You were so gentle when you shaved him. When he cried, you dried his eyes. And you let him say his piece without, as you put it, ripping him a new one. You even held his hand as he died. I think you gave him the only peace he'd had since he was a boy."

"Our mother never stopped loving him. She would write and visit when she could. She never stopped praying for him."

"She gave birth to him. No matter what Ezra did, he would always be her firstborn. I'm sure he appreciated her efforts, but I doubt he was surprised by them. Other than that night in the hospital, did you ever see him again after he confessed to you?"

"No. I wouldn't even drive our mother to the prison to see him, not even after our father died and she had to take the bus two hours each way."

"So when you came to see him, you proved that there was still a little bit of love for him inside you."

Jude shot Grae a wry look. "Did you miss the part about me going down there to tear him a new one after his letter made me so angry?"

"But you didn't do that."

"Only because of you."

"Then I'm glad fate put me there at just the right moment."

"I give your heart the credit, not fate, but I'm glad you were there too. You know, my girls were never interested in the business. When they were too little to understand what I did, they used to like to visit me at the shop and play among the statues. But once they got old enough to know that my business dealt with grief and death, they didn't want anything to do with it. Fortunately Leah had the good sense to marry Luc, who's been a godsend. The girls will inherit some day, and he'll make an excellent manager, but Luc has no touch for the stones. You do. They whisper to you, just like they whisper to me."

"And that is one of the nicest compliments I've ever gotten. Thank you."

"Just telling the truth. You know, you kind of remind me of a stone."

Grae's eyebrows rose. She was unsure whether that was a compliment or criticism.

Jude grinned at her, and she relaxed.

"It's nothing bad. It's just that when we met, you had this really hard shell that you'd covered with ink and metal. You were as polite as could be when you gave me Ezra's letter, and I knew there was more to you than first met the eye, but you projected yourself as hard as a granite slab. Then, as I got to know you, I realized something."

"What?"

"Like an uncarved stone, everything you need for beauty and meaning is waiting just below the surface. It just needs to be excavated."

"So that's what you've been doing since you hired me."

Jude nodded his head. "Yeah. Do you know what Michelangelo always said?"

"I took Art History one semester, but not much stuck."

"Well, I'm paraphrasing, but it was something to the effect that every block of stone already had the statue within. It was up to the carver to reveal it."

"Huh. So you're the sculptor."

"Nah, you're the statue, the stone, and the sculptor. I can hand you the tools, but it's up to you to carve your way out and expose the beauty within."

"Damn, Jude. You're a poet."

He scoffed. "Hell, no. Though I have to say there is one other thing Michelangelo said that stuck with me from my school years."

"Yeah? What?"

"He said, 'I saw the angel in the marble and carved until I set him free.' That's what I want for you. Set yourself free. You're the only one who can do that, though you should remember that you've got a lot of people who want to hand you the tools."

Grae was quiet for a long time. As she pondered Jude's words, a sense of peace settled over her. Finally she looked up and met his gaze. "You're right."

"Of course. A wise woman showed me the path, remember?"

"Wise, eh? I think you could give Jo a run for her money."

"She's a fine woman. I enjoyed talking to her at Halligan's. We should all do that again sometime. I'll see if Elaine would like to join us. She and Jo would get along like a house on fire. They're very much alike."

Grae had only met Elaine a few times in passing when she brought Jude lunch or picked him up from work, so she didn't know her boss' wife well enough to comment. But she did like the idea of getting everyone together again. *Minus Marcus getting mugged.*

"You know, I have an idea," Jude said.

"Oh?"

"It won't be easy, but I think it'll be worth it."

Grae looked at him curiously. "What?"

"What would you think about telling Melissa's parents that we would remake her monument, if they wish? It would mean meeting with them, of course, to see what ideas they might have. They may well go with the original design, or perhaps there is something else they'd prefer now. If they accept, and if you agree, I would want you to take point."

Grae exhaled a long breath. "Wow!"

"Yup."

"I've never met them. I saw them once after Missy died. It just about killed me."

Jude started the truck. "If you're not up to it, I understand."

"I didn't say that. Can I think about it?"

"A short while, yeah, but if we don't make the offer fairly soon, they may choose another shop."

"I'll tell you tomorrow at work."

"All right."

Jude put the truck in gear and was about to back out, when Grae grabbed his arm.

"Stop!"

Jude halted the truck and looked at her. "What's the matter?"

Grae pointed to where several people were milling about the damaged headstones. "There! That's Dylan. He must've come back for his hat."

She threw open the door and took off across the field at a dead run.

He was not going to get away with this crap again.

Chapter 31

Dylan looked up as Grae ran toward him. His jaw dropped, then he shouted, "You! You fucking bitch! What the hell do you think you're doing? You're suing me? I should've thrown your goddamned ass off that roof when I had the chance. They'd still be scraping your dyke-bits off the sidewalk."

Grae slowed. She'd forgotten about the civil lawsuit Virgil had filed. Obviously Dylan had been served. "You had your one and only chance and you blew it, you loser bastard. I won't end up on any more roofs with you or Rick."

Dylan advanced, and Grae held her ground.

"I don't need a roof to mess you up. You don't have no piece of rebar this time. You broke my fucking arm. You're going to pay for that."

"No, you're going to pay for it. You were trying to kill me. If not for that rebar, you'd have thrown me off the roof without a second thought."

Dylan sneered. He was within two metres of her now, and she tensed, ready to dodge.

"We just wanted to see if you and your faggot friend could fly. Fairies can fly, right? Me and Rick, we were just conductin' a scientific experiment."

"Yeah? So why did you smash up these headstones? Were you experimenting on them, too?"

Dylan stopped short, and confusion flashed across his face. "You don't know what you're talking about."

"Damn right, I do. We found your precious yellow hat, MacIsaac. It was stuck right under a broken monument. And it's going straight to the cops. I bet they won't have any problem matching your fingerprints to the ones they'll find on broken bottles and headstones. You're going down this time for sure, you bastard!"

"Then you're going down with me," Dylan roared, and launched himself at Grae.

Jude yanked Grae out of the way and met Dylan's tackle with a block that would've done a defensive lineman proud. Dylan flew back as if he'd run into a brick wall. He staggered back to his feet, and wavered unsteadily.

A burly man who'd been watching from a short distance away strode over to Grae. "Are you sure this is the guy who smashed up my mother's tombstone?"

Grae nodded. "You heard him. And we found his hat here, under a broken stone."

The man's face went red. "And you're absolutely sure it's his?"

"I am. It's one-of-a-kind, and I can prove it's his."

"Son of a bitch!" The man whirled and cold cocked Dylan, who dropped and lay motionless.

A woman ran up to the man who had hit Dylan and waved an iPhone. "I got it all, baby. I started filming when he started yelling at that lady. We can prove he wrecked your mama's tombstone. We can sue his ass to get it replaced with a new one!"

"You'll have to stand in line," Grae muttered under her breath. Shaking from the ebbing adrenaline, she glanced at Jude, who was on his phone.

Jude ended his call. "The police will be here in a few minutes."

The other man straddled Dylan's unconscious form. "Don't worry. He's not going anywhere before the cops arrive. This fucker is going to answer for wrecking my mama's final resting place."

It wasn't until after the police arrived and took statements and custody of a dazed Dylan, his yellow hat, and the incriminating video that Jude turned to Grae.

"What the hell did you think you were doing, running at him like a madwoman? No weapon, no plan, no nothing. If we hadn't been here," he gestured at himself and the other man, "you'd have gotten yourself a helluva beating."

Grae hung her head. "I know. I'm sorry. I didn't think. I just saw him and overreacted. I'm so tired of the bad guys getting away with shit, you know? I just…I just…"

Jude sighed and squeezed Grae's shoulder. "I get it. But don't do it again, all right? I'm not always going to be around."

"Got it." They started back toward the truck. "But can I just say that I'm really glad you were here this time?"

"You should be." The heat had vanished from Jude's voice.

Grae relaxed. He'd forgiven her. "You know, that lady's video caught Dylan's confession to everything, the attack on me and the vandalism. That's really going to help Virgil's case. Wait until I tell him."

"I guess it will at that."

Grae grinned as she opened the truck door. *Maybe I can't do anything about Domokos, but Dylan the villain is going to pay for what he's done.*

As Jude drove Grae home, they talked about the damage and what information Jude could provide for Henry to pass along to the affected families.

Jude turned into the driveway at Grae's apartment building. "Remember to think more about my suggestion. I need your decision soon, okay?"

"About Melissa's tombstone?"

"Yes."

"I don't need to think about it. It's the right thing to do. I'll meet her parents, and I'll offer to make a new one at no charge to them. I'll pay for any materials needed, whatever they select."

Jude shook his head. "You don't have to buy it. I'll donate the slab. You do the work."

"No, that's not right. It should all be on me."

Jude put the truck in park and turned to face Grae. His expression was as serious as she'd ever seen it. "I need you to listen to me, okay? Every moment of every day since the morning Melissa died has taken a terrible toll on you. No amount of money could ever come close to the price you've already paid. Just like no amount of money could ever express how I feel about what you did for me and Ezra. So, a slab of granite is nothing. You're doing the right thing. Let me help you. It means a lot to me."

Grae's eyes filled with tears, and she tried to smile. "You're my hero, you know."

"And you're mine. Now get out. I've got places to be. Elaine's waiting supper on me."

Grae hopped out of the truck and watched Jude leave. He rubbed his sleeve across his face as he drove off. She dried her eyes on her coat sleeve, too. *It'll be our little secret.*

When Grae entered her apartment, her heart overflowed with happiness as Kendall greeted her. For a moment she dared to imagine a future where this would be routine—coming home and finding Kendall there. Then she pushed the thought aside and threw herself into Kendall's open arms.

Kendall smiled. "Wow, that's the best hello I've gotten all day."

"Are you sure? Because you seemed to really appreciate the way I said good morning."

Kendall's head tilted back as she laughed. "I don't know what got into your Wheaties, woman, but I like it." She bent her head and kissed Grae soundly. "I love you."

Grae sobered and laced her arms around Kendall's neck. "I love you, too. I'm sorry I took so long to tell you."

Kendall's eyes brightened with unshed tears. "No need to be sorry. It was worth waiting for. What a wonderful start to the year."

"It is, isn't it?"

❦

Grae wiped her palms on her trouser legs for the third time.

Jude glanced at her. "Are you all right?"

"Just a little nervous. I've rehearsed what I want to say to the Salishes, but actually saying it is going to be a whole other thing. What if I mess this up? I don't want to make things harder for them."

"You won't. Nothing will ever be worse than losing their daughter. What you're doing now is offering a kindness."

"That they wouldn't need if not for me."

Jude smacked Grae's shoulder. "Uh-uh. What did we talk about?"

"I'm not to take responsibility for Melissa's death in front of her parents. It would only add to their burden."

"Also, because it isn't true, but I know you're still working on that realization."

Grae sighed. *What's taking Ashley so long to show them in?*

The door opened, and Ashley escorted Melissa's parents into the room. "Jude, this is Rodney and Doreen Salish. Mr. and Mrs. Salish, this is Jude Herzog, the owner of Stone Gardens, and Grae Jordan, one of his best craftsmen."

Ashley left after making the introductions.

Jude offered his hand. "Thank you very much for coming in. Won't you take a seat?"

Grae hung back and waited for Jude to take the lead. She would play her part soon enough. She studied the couple across the table. Doreen was much heavier than the last time Grae had seen her, but her hair was still the same colour as Melissa's. She sat with slumped shoulders and a distracted expression. Rodney Salish eyed Jude and Grae, his narrow face set in hard lines.

I wonder if he thinks we're trying to scam them. Grae shook off her musing as Jude opened his file.

"First, I want to offer my sympathies on the desecration of your daughter's monument. It was a contemptible thing to do," Jude said.

Rodney scowled. "I'd have liked to get my hands on those bastards."

Doreen laid a hand on her husband's arm. "They've caught them, Rod. Justice will be served."

"They think they've rounded up all of them, but I don't know. There was an awful lot of damage for just four men."

"Four drunken louts bent on destruction can wreak a lot of havoc in one night," Jude said. "But we're here to see how we can make things better. I know Mr. Zierling passed along information from us about repairs or replacement, as needed. However, your case is special, and that's why we asked you to come in."

Rodney cast a suspicious glance at Jude. "Special? How?"

"It's Melissa. Of course it's special," Doreen said.

Rodney shook his head. "Not to them. They didn't know her."

That was Grae's cue. "Actually, sir, I did know your daughter."

Doreen's head swivelled toward Grae. "You did?"

"Yes, ma'am. I was a senior at the U of C the year that Missy... Melissa, died."

Doreen pressed her hands together prayerfully. "You knew her? You truly knew her?"

"Yes, ma'am, I truly did." Grae took a deep breath. "In fact, I think I was the last to see her that morning. We'd shared breakfast, and—"

"What did she have?" Doreen leaned forward with an imploring expression.

Grae wondered what she hoped to hear, but chose to answer the question directly. "It's been a while." *Still, every detail is crystal clear.* "I think she brought coffee and cranberry almond muffins with cream cheese."

Doreen's face fell. "Oh, her favourite was blueberry."

"Yes, ma'am, it was, but cranberry almond was mine, and that's the way Missy was. She was always so considerate of people. It was just like her to bring my favourite instead of hers."

Doreen beamed. "She was like that since she was a little girl. She always wanted to make people happy. She used to pick dandelions in the spring time and bring me bouquets. Remember, Rod?"

Her husband nodded. Both he and Jude had sat back, and allowed the women the floor.

"Were you helping Missy with some of her courses? She was an excellent student in high school, but she did have some difficulty adjusting to her first year in university. I always thought maybe she'd fallen for some boy and couldn't keep her mind on her studies." Doreen shook her head and sighed. "Our Missy always had boys flocking around her in school, but she was such a scholar that she never dated, not once. It's always bothered me that she never experienced love, even young love that wouldn't last."

With a shock, Grae realized that Melissa hadn't had the inclination, or maybe just the right moment, to come out to her parents. She was going to have to tread very lightly. "I wasn't that much of a student myself, Mrs. Salish, but Missy and I had become friends. In fact, the night before, she offered to buy me dinner. I had an assignment due and couldn't go, unfortunately, so we were having breakfast together instead. It was after breakfast that...well, the accident happened. I'm so very, very sorry for your loss."

"Thank you. Could you tell me—was Missy involved with some boy that you know of?"

"Um, no, she never mentioned anyone. Why?"

Doreen stared at the table. "The autopsy results said there were signs of recent sexual activity. I've always been so afraid that she'd been raped, and that's why she ran into the road without looking."

Grae's eyes widened, and her mind flashed back to the toys they'd enthusiastically used that night. "Oh, no, ma'am! Absolutely not! Missy was so happy that morning. I was kind of grouchy because I hadn't gotten much sleep, but she was little Miss Sunshine."

"So maybe she'd met someone special. He must've been if Missy slept with him, because that wasn't like her at all." Doreen nodded decisively. "That must be it. I'm sure she'd have told us about him soon."

"I'm sure she would've, ma'am. She was definitely upbeat that morning. Our breakfast got interrupted and so did our conversation, so maybe she'd have told me about him later."

Doreen leaned forward and took Grae's hand. "Thank you so much. For eight years I've imagined the worst. You have no idea what it means to me to know that her last hours were so happy."

Grae choked on her welling emotions as she fought to hold back the tears. Despite her strenuous effort, several rolled down her face.

"Don't cry, dear. It's wonderful to know that Missy's friends still remember her so fondly after all this time."

"I'm so sorry I didn't come to you sooner. I never for a moment suspected you'd been thinking in that direction. If I'd known—" *I hope I'd have done the right thing far sooner.*

"There's no way you could've known, dear. I'm almost grateful that those hooligans broke Missy's headstone, just so I could get to meet you."

Grae glanced at Jude, who nodded. "About that. When I saw Missy's broken stone, I felt so badly that I wanted to do something. Both to make up for the New Year's desecration, and also to express the condolences I should've conveyed all those years ago."

Doreen tilted her head. "Why didn't you? You seem like such a nice person, and I can tell that Missy meant a lot to you. Mind you, I went through those weeks in a haze, so I may not remember everyone who spoke to us or wrote."

Grae trembled, and Jude shifted his arm so it lay next to hers. She took comfort from his warmth and subtle support. "I saw it happen. I saw the accident."

Doreen's eyebrows shot up. "Oh, you poor dear!"

"I was so horrified, that it traumatized me. I was a zombie for a long while. I ended up dropping out. I didn't graduate."

"Oh, no. Oh, no, no, no, no, no. Missy wouldn't have wanted that at all. Please tell me that you went back at some point and finished."

Grae shook her head. "No, actually I didn't. But I love my job, and I'm happy with where life has taken me."

Doreen squeezed and released Grae's hand. "I'm relieved to hear that. I take that as a great testament to my daughter. To have witnessed such a horrific accident—to have seen a friend killed—and still to rebound and love life. That is exactly what my Missy would want."

"You know, Mrs. Salish, I think you're right. That's exactly the kind of person she was. She wouldn't have wanted anyone to mourn the rest of their life away, would she?"

Grae's gaze locked with Doreen's, and they exchanged nods of understanding.

Doreen's smile seemed softer, more relaxed, as if she'd lost a long-held bitter edge. "So tell me, what have you got in mind for Melissa's headstone?"

"Well, I have some ideas, but it is all subject to what you and Mr. Salish would like. We can recreate Missy's monument just as it was, or give you an entirely new design. It's your choice."

"Are you going to do the work yourself?"

"I am, and Jude is donating the slab, so it won't cost you a thing."

Rod sat up straighter. "It won't?"

Grae glanced at him. "No, sir, it won't. I'll give this job priority, and once we settle on a design, we'll have Missy's memorial back in place in no time. I promise."

"Oh, Rod, maybe we can have a little commemorative service when they put the new stone in place. I'd like that."

Rod patted Doreen's hands. "We can do anything you want, hon. And I'm okay with whatever you decide about Missy's marker."

Doreen turned back to Grae. "Tell me your idea for a new design."

Grae opened her sketch book and turned it toward the Salishes. "I think we should keep the basic elements of the original one that you selected, so, the same words and an angel holding a child. But then I'd like to add something special. We can put a raised portrait of your favourite headshot of Melissa, so she is immortalized at the height of her youth and beauty."

Doreen inhaled sharply. "Oh, I love that. And I know just the picture I want to use. It was one her dad took of her at Christmas. She had such a sweet smile. I want everyone who sees her headstone to know that's who she was. That smile, that sweetness."

"Excellent," Jude said. "We can give you that. Grae will do most of the work. She has an exceptional touch with the stone, but she hasn't done bas relief yet, so I'll handle that part. If you can bring that photo in, we'll get started right away. Once the mould is done, you'll get to approve it, we'll cast it, and then we can finalize the monument from there."

"Oh, this is wonderful," Doreen said. "I do believe Missy herself sent you our way." She rose, came around the table, and hugged first Grae and then Jude. She took Grae's hands. "I would be so pleased if you could join us when we re-dedicate Missy's stone. Perhaps you could even say a few words. Things you remember about her. Maybe even how she was so happy her last day."

Grae bowed her head for a long moment, then she met Doreen's hopeful gaze. "I would be honoured."

Doreen clapped her hands together. "That's wonderful. Oh, I'm so happy to have met you."

She and Rod left the room, talking non-stop. Jude closed the door behind them.

"That was a mitzvah, my friend. Well done."

Grae shook her head. "She thinks Missy sent us to them. If she only knew…"

"Maybe Missy did send us. Levi would always remind me that the ways of God are unknowable. Maybe Melissa knew that both you and her mother were suffering terribly, and she wanted to give you two some peace."

"Through Dylan? Does God use demons?"

"I expect God uses whatever He has at hand to get the job done. There are a lot of cemeteries in this town, and Westview's got a lot of acreage. Do you think it was just coincidence that Dylan and his cronies decided to party in exactly the spot where Melissa is buried?"

Grae peered at Jude and tried to decide if he was pulling her leg. He returned her gaze steadily. "You seriously think that's possible?"

"I do. And I know Levi would back me up on that."

"Huh. Well, who knows? I've always wondered how it was I was in that alley at just the right time to meet Marcus. That turned out to be a little miracle, so I know they can happen."

Jude smiled. "They can indeed. And one more thing. This *is* your redemption, Grae. I know you weren't comfortable misleading Mrs. Salish about the nature of your relationship with Melissa, but you did the right thing and you did it for the right reason. Today you gave her peace. Today, you must accept that peace for yourself, as well."

"Levi's advice?"

Jude shook his head. "Mine."

"That's good enough for me."

Chapter 32

Jude donated a gorgeous slab of polished pink granite, and Melissa's monument was shaping up beautifully. The Salishes had approved the bas relief mould of Melissa's smiling visage, and Jude would have it ready to affix once Grae was finished with the main stone.

Grae had checked and rechecked the computer-assisted design before she'd used the sand blaster on the monument, which was now nearing completion. She had been labouring over the last of the precision work all day.

Jude poked his head into the shop. "Everyone else is gone, and I'm heading home. Are you just about done?"

Grae didn't lift her head or her tools. "Almost."

"You know the world won't end if you don't finish it until tomorrow, right?"

"Uh-huh."

"I can see that you're paying absolute attention to my every utterance."

The dryness of Jude's tone finally sunk in and Grae lifted her head. "I'm sorry. What did you say?"

He sighed. "Lock up when you're done."

"Okay."

The door hadn't swung shut on Jude's departure when Grae returned to work. She couldn't quit until Melissa's marker was finished. She carved the channel between the angel and child deeper. Every detail had to be as perfect as possible.

She looked it over with a critical eye. "Missy, I don't want to sound boastful, but this is the best work I've ever done. I can't wait to show it to your parents."

The emotion of Doreen's visit to approve the bas relief the previous week washed through her again. When she'd seen Jude's handiwork, Doreen had cried and Grae had wept with her.

"You know, I'm not sure if I buy into Jude's notion—well, he'd say Levi's notion, that you might've brought your mom and me together. But if you did, thank you. When we cried together, it felt like...I don't know...like the tears were washing me clean of guilt for the first time in a lot of years. So if you did have anything to do with that, thank you."

Grae jumped as she heard the sand blaster roar to life. "What the hell?" She hurried to the back of the shop and cautiously peered into the blasting alcove. The machine was running. "I know I turned that off."

She hastened to power it down, and then stepped back to stare. In all the months she'd worked there, she'd never experienced an unprompted start-up. "Well, that's bloody weird."

She left the sandblasting room, after casting one last glance at the silent machine, and resumed her seat in front of the bench to pick up where she'd left off her carving.

Grae stopped suddenly. "You don't think... Nah, that's crazy."

She closed her eyes, and for just a moment she could see Melissa's smile, the smile that had blazed so brightly that last afternoon in the library. Her eyes snapped open.

"Jesus. Are you here, Missy?"

Nothing happened. The sand blaster remained mute, and no ethereal phantasm coalesced into human form in front of her. Grae laughed at her flight of imagination. Still, it was comforting to visualize Melissa, happy and whole, seated on a cloud as she watched Grae create a new monument for her.

"Don't tell anyone that I'm talking to thin air, okay? But if you are here, I want to tell you something. I would give anything in the world not to have treated you so miserably. I was callous and ignorant, and you deserved so much better. You were such a great person—sweet, kind, attentive, thoughtful...everything I wasn't. You should've had a partner who was all those things back to you. And that sure wasn't me."

It is now.

Grae blinked. Where had that thought popped in from? "Missy?"

Echoes of laughter filled her mind.

"Wow, freaky. I hope I am all that now. It's what I want to be for Kendall." Grae moved on to improve a tip on the angel's wing. "I don't think I'll ever know what you saw in me, I really don't. But then I mostly don't know what Kendall sees in me now, either, and she loves me."

Grae's hands stilled, and she smiled. "Kendall loves me. And I love her, too, Missy. I wish you'd lived long enough to experience the real thing for yourself. We had fun that night, your last night, but something like that doesn't hold a candle to the real thing. If you've been peeking in on my life, you probably know things aren't perfect between me and Kendall, at least not in the bedroom, but I'm working on that. Jo and Jude think I'm punishing myself for what happened to you. I never really thought of that before they brought it up, but they might be right. If so, it's only fair, right? You're dead because of me."

Her fingers trembled as they traced the engraved date of death. "You'd be twenty-seven now if you hadn't had the horrible bad luck to fall for me. I know your mom spends a lot of time thinking about who you would be today if you were still with her. Would you be married? Would you have given her grandchildren by now? 'Course she thinks you'd have married a guy, but we know better, don't we?"

Memories of the night they'd spent together floated through Grae's mind. Whatever Doreen thought, her daughter had been gay. A smile teased her lips. *Definitely gay.*

"She wouldn't have cared, Missy. You know that, right? Your mom loves you so much, you could've given her three-headed grandchildren and she'd still have thought you were perfect. That's the way our moms love us. God, look what my mom went through. Scratch that. Look what I put my mother through these last eight years. And she still loves me. I forgot that for a long time, but I won't forget it again."

Grae finished the final touches on the wing tip and sat back. Even just laid out on the bench, the monument was magnificent. And when Jude added the bas relief, it would be the most beautiful commemorative she'd ever worked on.

"I hope you like it, Missy. I know your parents will."

A light scent of lilac wafted in the air. Grae looked around. There were no air fresheners in sight, and nothing that would account for the lovely aroma.

"Huh. That's strange."

Grae stood, and brushed the grit and dust from her clothes. She studied the stone pensively. "Missy? I can't change what happened to you. I wish I could. But I want you to know that I'll never forget you, or stop feeling sorrow for my part in your death. But I have to leave that behind now. I've hurt too many people for too many years. And I regret that almost as much as I regret treating you as an irrelevant one night stand."

Grae took a short step back, and then another. "Something your mom said really stuck in my head. She said you wouldn't have wanted me to go through what I brought on myself all this time. She insisted that wasn't who you were. She said you'd want me to rebound from your death and love life again. She's right." She took a deep breath. "So, after all these years, I'm asking for your forgiveness. I never did that before, you know? And if you'll give it to me, I'm going to make you a promise. The woman you thought I was then? The one you thought you were in love with, rose-coloured glasses and all? I'm going to do my damndest to honour your life by being that woman. You idealized me, and I wasn't worth it. I haven't been worth it in all the years since you died, either. But I will be from now on. I swear."

A sense of peace, so deep and pervasive that Grae had never felt anything akin to it, settled over her. Tears ran down her cheeks, but they were healing tears that ran in trails around the curve of her smile.

She stood quietly for a long time as serenity filled every atom of her being. And when the sensation receded, it left behind it a new resolve: She would never again shut out the people who loved her. She would never again retreat into a morass of despair, no matter the provocation.

On that, I give you my word, Missy.

Grae got off the bus and looked around the neighbourhood. She'd never been there, though she had known Kendall's address for some time. Kendall had issued a standing invitation to visit, whether for a few hours or overnight. So far, she'd not taken up the offer, and Kendall hadn't pressed her.

For an instant, Grae reconsidered her impromptu decision. It was a weeknight, and they both had to work in the morning. Maybe it was a stupid idea to drop in unannounced. Still, it felt like the right thing to do, and she was going to trust her instincts. She pulled her phone out to text Marcus.

Won't be home tonight. At K's if you need me. Don't need me!

Within seconds, Marcus' response came back. *You go, girl! Promise not to need you. May not need you until next week, if you're up to it.*

Grae laughed and returned a single word. *Idiot.*

True, but your idiot.

She smiled fondly and turned off her phone. She didn't want any interruptions, not tonight.

Grae walked up the sidewalk to Kendall's elegant townhouse and rang the doorbell. Then she leaned against one of the pillars that fronted the landing. Though her heart was pounding, she affected a casual pose with her hands in her pant pockets.

Kendall opened the door, and her face broke into a grin. "Well, isn't this an unexpected pleasure. I thought you were going to be working all evening. You should've called. I'd have come to pick you up."

"You know, the city has a pretty decent public transit system. I can get around on my own."

Kendall mirrored Grae's pose, leaning against the door jamb. "You can do lots of things on your own, but I've heard that they're more fun with a friend."

"Have you? What about with a loved one?"

Kendall smiled and her eyes shone. "I have it on good authority that's best of all."

"Interesting." Grae glanced down at her clothes. "So, I came right from work, and I really need a shower. Do you happen to know anyone who could spare some soap and hot water?"

Kendall tapped her chin thoughtfully. "I might. You can come in, and I could make some calls for you."

Grae pushed herself away from the pillar and crossed the landing. She stopped just short of Kendall. Kendall's nostrils flared, but she didn't reach for Grae and Grae didn't reach for her. A delicious tension enveloped them.

Kendall stepped aside and pushed the inner door further open. "Won't you come...in?"

Grae grinned. "I'd be delighted."

They entered, and Kendall took Grae's work coat. Her trembling hands hung it in the hall closet. When she turned and studied Grae, her pupils were large and dark.

They still hadn't touched.

Kendall cleared her throat twice. "So, um, were you just in search of hot water, or are you planning to stay the night?"

"If you'll let me."

"Let you? I'd have rolled out the red carpet and sprinkled rose petals if I'd known you were coming."

Grae smiled. "Rose petals would probably be a plus. I really am in need of a shower. I didn't want to stop at the shop. I just wanted to get to you."

"I'm so glad. Follow me." Kendall led the way upstairs. She passed a bedroom and bath, entered the master bedroom, and directed Grae to the en suite. "Clean towels in the cupboard, and I think anything else you might need is in the shower."

Grae faced Kendall and their gazes locked. Grae could barely stand up in the face of the fiery desire in Kendall's eyes. She tried to speak, then shook her head. Words could wait; the shower couldn't. She tore her dusty clothes off, dropped them in a heap on the bathroom floor, and kicked them under the pedestal sink. She wouldn't need them until the morning. She bent over to turn on the spigot and adjust the water temperature.

Kendall moved behind her, close enough so Grae could feel her heat, but still not touching. "Mind if I join you?"

Still bent, Grae wriggled back a couple of inches and ran into very soft, very naked flesh. "Looks like there might be room for two."

Kendall clasped Grae's hips and exhaled a low moan. "You're killing me."

Grae pushed the curtain back, stepped into the fall of water, and extended her hand. Kendall took it and allowed Grae to pull her close. Grae slowly, deliberately placed Kendall's hand on her breast. She took Kendall's other hand and slipped it between her legs.

Kendall's gaze held hunger and hesitancy in equal measure. "Are you sure?"

"I am. I love you, and I want you to make love to me."

Kendall's gaze dropped to the hand that rested between Grae's legs. "I...if you want me to— If you need me to stop—"

"I won't." Grae leaned back and let the hot water sluice over her. Her hips moved as she encouraged Kendall to believe in her desire and determination. "Touch me any way you want, because that's what I want, too."

A brilliant smile blossomed on Kendall's lips. "It is, isn't it?"

"Yes."

"I'll ask you why later, but right now, there's something I've wanted to do for a very long time."

Kendall lowered her head to Grae's breasts as her hand began to move between Grae's legs. Suddenly it was if all restraints had been lifted. Kendall's mouth was everywhere. Her fingers grew confident, exploring and exciting Grae.

For one frantic moment Grae feared she'd forgotten how to orgasm. The wave of sensations Kendall's touch had brought to life took her higher and higher, but she couldn't climax. Until she focused on the deep intimacy of Kendall's fingers stroking her inside and out, and of Kendall's mouth teasing her breasts until her nipples felt as if they would burst.

The explosion made Grae's knees buckle.

Kendall held her close. "I've got you. I've got you."

Her limbs like rubber, Grae sagged against Kendall. "Oh, my God."

Kendall laughed softly. "No kidding. Please tell me I can do that to you again."

"Anytime."

Kendall turned Grae so she faced the tile, and then pressed her body firmly against Grae's back. "Then hang on to the bar, love. We're not done yet."

Grae fumbled blindly for the grab bar. She shut her eyes against the water and simply allowed herself to feel. Kendall's body supported hers; Kendall's hands stroked her from breasts to thighs and back; Kendall drove her crazy by avoiding her clit until it screamed for attention.

She finally grabbed Kendall's hand and guided it to her pubis. "Please?"

Kendall wrapped one arm beneath Grae's breasts, pressed herself rhythmically against Grae's ass, and stroked her with a sure hand. The second orgasm wasn't as powerful, but it lasted longer—much longer. Her whole body shuddered against Kendall's, until she stood panting, her forehead braced against the wall.

"Once more?" Kendall asked.

"It has to be your turn by now." Even though Grae wasn't certain she had enough energy to back up her words.

"I've had my turn many times."

"I don't know if I can."

"Shall we see?"

Somehow Grae summoned the wherewithal to turn in Kendall's embrace. She revelled in the love and triumph on Kendall's face. She opened her mouth, intending to suggest they move to Kendall's bed. "Yes." *Okay, wasn't expecting that.*

Kendall's eyebrows shot up. "Yes?"

"I'm not guaranteeing success, but yes. Your touch is addictive."

Joy blazed across Kendall's face before she sank to her knees and delicately parted Grae's labia. Her tongue was soft and slow, but Grae flinched at the touch on her tender flesh.

I'm so not going to be able to walk tomorrow.

Kendall stopped and looked up at Grae. Water hit her face, and she coughed.

Grae pushed her pelvis forward. "Please?"

"Are you sure, love? I don't want to hurt you."

"You're not. Please don't stop."

Kendall resumed the tender strokes. She lifted Grae slowly to a gentle, undulating peak, a sweet coda to the furious passion that had driven them before. When the waves ebbed, Kendall rose and picked up a bar of soap. She bathed Grae carefully, and Grae felt her love in each touch. When she was done, she shampooed Grae's hair, then turned off the shower and directed her to stand on the bathmat. Kendall towelled Grae dry, then quickly dried herself before leading Grae to her bed and steering her between the sheets.

Utter exhaustion washed over Grae. She was vaguely aware that Kendall had gotten into bed and was spooning her. She tried to rouse herself.

"Shh, just go to sleep, love."

Kendall's whisper tickled Grae's ear. "But I have to—"

"You don't have to do a thing. Seriously." Kendall gave a low chuckle. "The second time? I came too."

"You did?"

"Uh-huh."

"Damn, I'm good." Grae drifted off to sleep, and Kendall's laughter echoed in her dreams.

❀

Grae and Kendall joined the small group of people clustered around Melissa's grave. Grae only knew Missy's parents, but the half dozen strangers, including a priest, nodded and smiled in greeting.

It was the kind of February day that tantalized with the promise of spring, though it was still two months away. The air was crisp, but lacked the raw power of mid-winter. The sky was a deep, vibrant blue, with only the tiniest wisps of white clouds. A gentle breeze lifted a lock of Kendall's hair, and Grae smiled at the sight.

At the end of the brief, formal service, Doreen gestured Grae forward. "I want to introduce all of you to Grae Jordan. She was a friend of Missy's in university, and designed and created this gorgeous testament to Missy's far too short life. I've asked her to say a few words. Grae?"

Grae glanced at Kendall, and got a warm smile of encouragement. She took a deep breath. "I wish I could say I knew Melissa better than I did. We were casual friends who greeted each other in the hall and saw each other in the library. But I didn't have to know Melissa well to know the young woman she was—kind, but persistent; shy, but determined. She was absolutely beautiful, inside and out. I've wondered what Melissa might've become had not she taken those fateful last steps. She had a true gift to offer. She might not have been someone who changed the whole world, but I firmly believe she'd have been someone who made the world around her better. That's what she showed me—with her smile, her generosity, and her thoughtfulness. Rod and Doreen raised a beautiful human being, and that is who we celebrate today. I spent years haunted by her death. Now I am uplifted by her life. Not long ago, I made her a promise. I told Missy I would honour her by being the woman I knew she would've been—loyal, loving, devoted to family and friends. I will keep that promise as my tribute to her."

Grae took a step back and looked at Kendall again. Tears filled her lover's eyes as she mouthed, "Well done."

Grae was the final speaker, and after the priest offered a blessing, people began to drift away. Doreen approached Grae and Kendall.

"Thank you so much, Grae. That was lovely. I'm so pleased that you came. And I'm so happy that I met you. I don't know why, but I have been feeling more at peace lately."

"I'm glad," Grae said. She started to tell Doreen that it was an honour to have created Melissa's monument, when suddenly the aroma of lilacs surrounded her. She blinked and looked around. "I know it's not the season, but can you smell lilacs?"

"Oh, that would be me," Doreen said. "Lilacs were Missy's favourite, so I wore a lilac fragrance today in her honour."

"It's very nice."

"Thank you." Doreen leaned in, and Grae returned her hug. "We're having a small reception at our home if you'd like to come."

"Thanks, but we've promised to meet family and friends for supper."

"All right. Promise you'll stay in touch, though?" Doreen asked.

Grae nodded. "I will."

Doreen turned, and joined Rod and another couple, who were waiting for her near their car.

Kendall faced Grae. "Are you all right, love?"

"I am. I truly am."

"The others should be arriving at Halligan's about now. Are you ready?"

"Uh-huh." Grae knew that the unspoken reason for the change in schedule of their bi-monthly meet-up was so she would be surrounded by her loved ones on this, of all days. She appreciated their concern and support, but the serenity that descended over her the night she'd finished Melissa's stone had never left her.

Grae took Kendall's hand, and they walked to where Kendall had parked the car. The breeze blew a bit harder as they mounted the crest of a hill, but Grae smiled.

Even the wind couldn't dispel the lingering scent of lilacs.

Chapter 33

By the time Grae and Kendall arrived at Halligan's, everyone except Thea was already present. Marcus had saved a couple of seats between him and Ciara. Jo sat at one end of the table, and Virgil was at the other end. There was an open seat between Carter and Jude, so Grae assumed that her mother would be joining them soon. She was also pleased to see Elaine, who had proven to be a welcome addition to their meet-ups with her quiet good humour and cheerful disposition.

They made the circuit around the table and hugged everyone. When Grae got to Virgil, he pulled her head closer and whispered, "Ciara lost her job today. She's had a few drinks, so I just wanted to give you a heads up."

Grae resisted the urge to stare at Ciara. She hugged her brother. "Thanks, Virg."

After they finished greeting everyone, Grae and Kendall took their seats.

Kendall leaned around Grae. "So, Marcus, how does it feel to have the cast off?"

"It feels fabulous, but now my arm is all skinny and white."

Grae chuckled. "So, in other words, it coordinates well with the rest of you."

The others laughed, and Marcus rolled his eyes. He looked at Kendall. "I did want to thank you."

"You got the job?"

"I did. I start on Monday."

Kendall and Marcus high-fived behind Grae's head.

Grae hugged Marcus. "That's wonderful, bud, but don't forget your studies, okay? You're so close to achieving your GED."

"I won't. Hey, did you know that Billie and her husband actually own the Blue Moon?"

Kendall and Grae both stared at Marcus.

"Seriously?" Kendall asked. "I've been eating at the diner for three years, and Billie never mentioned a word."

"I know. When you told me they had an opening for a short-order cook, I figured the owner would interview me. But it was Billie who put me through my paces and made me demonstrate that I could handle the job. I worked with her the whole afternoon. I kept wondering when the boss would show up. Then her husband came in before the dinner rush, and they told me I had the job."

Kendall shook her head. "You actually met her husband? From all the stories Billie told me, I'd started calling him Mythical Jim. He seemed too good to be true."

Marcus shook his head. "No, he's real. And he's a super nice guy. So is Billie, for that matter. It's only minimum wage to start, but I think I'm going to like it there."

"A lot better than Magellan's, eh?" Grae was startled at the flash of sadness across Marcus' face. She leaned closer. "Is everything all right?"

He shook his head and lowered his voice. "Me and Freddie broke up, but we'll talk later at home, okay?"

Grae hugged Marcus again. "Aw, shit. I'm so sorry. Yeah, for sure. We'll talk later."

"So, Kendall, Grae tells me you're giving the keynote address at a conference in Ottawa day after tomorrow," Jude said.

Kendall nodded. "I am. I fly out tomorrow at zero-dark-thirty. I'm a bit nervous about it. Angels Unawares is one of a number of national charitable organizations competing for federal dollars, so there's a lot riding on my speech. The room is going to be filled with high level bureaucrats, not to mention representatives of all the other organizations vying for the same funding."

Grae smiled at Kendall. "Your speech is brilliant and funny...just like you."

"You might be slightly biased, love, but thank you. Hopefully it will go over well. We'd like to expand beyond Calgary and Edmonton, into some of the smaller towns in Alberta, so funding is critical."

Thea entered the pub, and Grae waved her mother over. She took the seat next to Carter as everyone greeted her. "Sorry I'm late. It was a busy day on the bench."

Jo nodded at Thea, but said nothing. Thea gave her a tight smile.

Their waiter came over to take orders.

Marcus leaned close to Grae. "If you don't mind, I'm going to cut out early. I'll see you at home."

"Are you sure? I'd be happy to buy you dinner, bud."

"No, thanks. I'm not really hungry."

Marcus squeezed Grae's shoulders and dropped a kiss on her hair before he left. Grae watched him go, saddened by his air of defeat. His shoulders were slumped and his head was down. He barely reacted when a couple of boisterous young men entering the pub bumped into him at the door.

Before she could say anything to Kendall, Ciara slid into Marcus' abandoned seat. "So, how's it going, little sister?"

"Pretty good. And you?" Grae wasn't sure if she should mention Ciara's employment status, or lack thereof.

"Not the best day of my life. I was laid off, along with twenty percent of my colleagues."

"Oh, Ci, I'm sorry. What rotten luck."

Ciara shrugged. "We're a boom and bust business. I knew that plummeting oil prices would mean lean times ahead, but I didn't know head office would order such draconian cutbacks."

"What are you going to do?"

"Well, I won't be looking for another job in the oil industry, that's for sure. I'm tired of the roller coaster. But hey, I'm in a lot better position than some of the guys who have wives who don't work and children to put through school. Bai won't lose his job. They never fire top-notch thoracic surgeons, so we'll still be able to put bread on the table. Besides, I'm confident I'll find a good job again. I always land on my feet, right? But enough about me. How are you really? Mom told me you were going to a funeral for an old friend today."

Grae glanced at Kendall, who was regarding her closely. She shot her a reassuring smile and looked back at Ciara. "Melissa actually died eight years ago. Well, it'll be nine years next month. It was a rededication of her memorial."

"She died nine years ago?"

Grae could almost see the wheels turn in Ciara's mind. Her sister had always had a knack for numbers. "Yes. I saw her killed. She was hit by a truck right in front of me."

Ciara's eyes widened. "Jesus. So…nine years ago— That was pretty close to the time you dropped out."

"It was exactly when I dropped out."

"Was that why?"

Grae's mind reflexively filled with the sights and sounds of that dreadful morning, but this time the memory lacked the emotional sway it had always held over her. "Yes. I felt responsible for her death, and had a tough time handling it."

"What? Why on earth would you think you were responsible?"

"Because we'd slept together the previous night, then argued in the morning. Because she was upset with me, she ran out into the street without looking. I was a Grade A jerk, and Melissa paid the price."

Everyone at the table had fallen silent and was watching her.

"But it was an accident," Ciara said. "You didn't push her in front of that truck."

"For many years I believed I had. Not literally, of course, but figuratively." Grae looked at Kendall, whose gaze was soft with love and compassion. "Now I accept that it was just a tragic accident."

Ciara slung an arm around Grae's shoulders. "Good. It's about time you forgave yourself."

"And you? Do you forgive me, Ci? "

Ciara knuckled Grae's head. "I suppose, but if you drop out again, I'm going to come find you and kick your ass."

Grae grinned, then looked across the table at her mom and dad and Virgil. "And you guys? Do you forgive me, too?"

Thea, her eyes bright with unshed tears, reached for Grae's hand. "Always."

Carter and Virgil murmured agreement.

"I'm really sorry, Mom. I never meant to hurt you…any of you. I was just so deep in my own misery that I couldn't think about anything or anyone else. By the time I met Marcus and finally started turning my life around, I figured I'd burned my bridges for good. I didn't know if I'd ever see you again. I definitely didn't think you'd want to see me."

"You were wrong." Thea squeezed Grae's hand.

Grae was reminded of Doreen. "I was unbelievably wrong. Thanks for giving me another chance." Grae glanced at Jo. "And thanks for sending me to someone who's helped more than I can say."

Jo gave a half-smile and nodded.

"But hey, this is meant to be a celebration of Melissa's life, at least for me. How about I buy a round?"

A chorus of cheers went up, and Grae signalled their waiter. Kendall laced her fingers through Grae's, and they exchanged loving glances. Ciara looked at their interlocked hands, which rested on the table.

"So are you two officially a couple now?"

Kendall laughed and raised their hands to her lips. "Do you want to field that question, or shall I?"

Grae grinned and winked. "I suspect Ciara already has her answer." She looked at her sister with a raised eyebrow.

"Awesome. So have you rented the flatbed yet?"

Grae cocked her head. "Flatbed?"

"Yes. Isn't that what lesbians traditionally do? Rent a flatbed trailer and move in with each other?"

Grae broke out laughing. "A U-Haul, Ciara. A U-Haul, not a flatbed. And no, we haven't reserved a flatbed or a U-Haul."

"Well, when you do, I volunteer my help and Bai's, unless it compromises his hands. We need those to feed us for the foreseeable future."

Grae leaned close to whisper in Kendall's ear, "And I need a certain someone's hands for so much more than that."

Kendall's eyes widened, and she whispered back, "Oh, that is so not fair. You know I can't come over tonight. I have to be out at the airport at four a.m. God, I can't believe I won't see you for four days."

"But only three nights. And there's always Skype."

Kendall grinned. "Did you just present a challenge?"

"Could be."

Grae was relieved when the waiter returned with their drinks. As fun as it was to tease Kendall, it never proved to be a zero sum game. They delighted in arousing each other by text, e-mail, or phone when they were apart, and brazen flirting when they were together. But if gratification was going to be delayed for several days, Grae would be frenzied by the time Kendall returned. And she was quite sure her mother would not approve of the two of them disappearing into the ladies room for a spontaneous farewell.

For a moment Grae considered going home with Kendall for the evening, but then she remembered Marcus' admission. It was so tempting to spend a few hours with Kendall before she left, but tonight she had to find out what had happened between Marcus and Freddie, and offer what consolation she could.

Kendall stroked the inside of Grae's wrist with a familiar rhythm, and Grae glared at her.

"Stop it, you. Behave."

Kendall grinned mischievously, but obediently turned to talk to Jude.

Grae filled her glass. Ciara was talking to Virgil, but held out hers out for a refill as well. Grae did so, and then pushed the latest pitcher of beer across the table to her father.

With lively conversations flowing around her, Grae surreptitiously watched her parents. Carter was talking with Virgil and Ciara, while Thea chatted with Elaine. Each leaned away from the other. When Thea turned to Carter to clarify what day they had tickets to the Vertigo Theatre, Carter responded promptly and politely, but continued his conversation, as did Thea.

They don't love each other. The thought didn't startle or sadden Grae. It was a simple distillation of her observations since she'd re-entered her parents' lives and learned of their mutual adultery in years past. They seemed fond of each other, and considerate, but it was as if they were quite content to remain on the periphery of each other's emotions. Grae had always chalked their reserve up to disdain for public displays of affection, but now she wondered if they'd ever loved each other. *They must've once...or maybe it was the modern day equivalent of a marriage of convenience. Still, they seemed happy enough.*

Grae glanced at Jo out of the corner of her eye and almost dropped her beer. Jo was looking at Thea, and for a stark instant, profound love, longing, and loss was evident in her eyes. Then Jude asked her a question, and it was as if a veil dropped over her emotions. She broadcast only her normal cool interest as she answered him, and her gaze focused solely on Jude as they discussed the upcoming provincial election.

Grae's hand shook as she set her beer on the table. *Well, that answers that question.* She tried to analyze how she felt. Despite Jo's protestations, it was clear that what had happened decades ago was as fresh to her as if she and Thea had parted yesterday. *What about Mom?*

Grae studied her mother. Nothing in her demeanour gave away any hint of her feelings, but Grae couldn't shake the memory of Thea coming to her apartment to confess her past infidelity with Jo. That night had shattered the myth of the judge's dispassionate veneer.

She shook her head. It was none of her business. Grae didn't relish the thought of her parents breaking up. But when she looked at Kendall, and a powerful rush of love made her momentarily dizzy, she wished the whole world, including their parents, could feel this same magic.

Kendall glanced at Grae, and did a double-take. "Are you all right?"

Grae smiled. "I am. Just thinking of all the ways to say hello to you when you get home."

Kendall's eyes widened. "You are a cruel wench, Ms. Jordan."

"And despite that, you love me."

"I do. I definitely do."

Grae and Kendall's leave-taking in the underground garage got heated enough that Grae had to button buttons before she could exit the car.

"You're going to get me arrested...again!"

Kendall was also rearranging clothing. "Excuse me, but I believe a certain someone who is not me is the one who started this. I was just a helpless innocent, swept along on the tides of desire."

Grae paused in zipping her fly. "Helpless innocent? Tides of desire? What kind of Purple Prose have you been reading lately?"

"Nothing but your incendiary texts…and my prep materials for the conference."

Grae laughed as she stuffed her shirt into her trousers. "Must be the conference papers then. Who knew they would rev your libido to such heights? Is it even safe to let you go to Ottawa alone?"

"Probably not. You should come along. I'll just tell anyone who raises an eyebrow that I don't go anywhere without the sultry vixen who seduced me to the Dark Side."

"Sultry? Seduction? The Dark Side? That does it. I'm checking your bedtime reading the next time I'm at your place."

Kendall slid a hand up the inside of Grae's thigh. "Oh, trust me, love, the next time you're over, we won't be reading."

Grae squeezed her thighs together, trapping Kendall's hand. "Damn, woman, you'd better get going or you're going to have to make a mercy trip to my bedroom."

"That could be arranged."

It took all of Grae's willpower to shake her head. "God, I wish I could, but I have to talk to Marcus."

Kendall instantly grew serious and pulled her hand away. "What do you think happened between them?"

"I don't know. At a guess, I'd say Freddie initiated the break-up, but they're both pretty young. They certainly weren't ready to settle down. Eighteen's way too immature, and Marcus has a lot of growing and living to do."

Kendall cupped Grae's face and kissed her softly. "Spoken like a true mother. Go look after your boy. I'll see you in a few days."

"Let me know when you get to Ottawa, okay?"

"Look for me. I'll be the naked woman Skyping you with a briefcase full of lascivious suggestions. I plan to compose them while I fly across Canada."

Grae laughed and kissed Kendall one last time. "Guess I'd better work on some suggestions of my own then."

"You do that." Grae got out of the car, very conscious of Kendall's gaze on her as she crossed the garage to the elevator. She turned and waved. She was tempted to flash her breasts, but the security camera near the elevator put a damper on that thought, so she contented herself with blowing a kiss. Kendall blew one back, then started her car and backed out. Grae watched her exit the garage as she waited for the elevator. The smile on her face lingered until she arrived on the fourth floor.

Grae smelled popcorn before she unlocked the door. She doffed her coat and followed the scent to the living room, where Marcus was curled up on the couch. A huge, half-empty bowl rested in the crook of his arm. His eyes were red and swollen.

Grae's heart broke. "Aw, shit. I'm so sorry, bud."

He put the bowl on the floor and, when she sat next to him, burrowed into her embrace.

"Shhh, it's okay. Damn Freddie for breaking your heart."

Marcus shook his head. "It wasn't Freddie's fault. I broke up with him."

Grae blinked. "You did? But I thought...you really cared for him. What happened?"

Marcus' arms tightened around Grae. "I cheated."

"Holy crap! You cheated on him? And you broke up with him? I don't get it. Were you breaking up with him before he could break up with you? Talk to me, bud. What's going on?"

Marcus sat up and dried his eyes on his sleeve. Grae handed him a tissue, and he blew his nose. She waited as he collected himself.

"I really screwed up, Grae. Do you remember me talking about a cute guy at the library I was flirting with last fall? Long before I met Freddie?"

"Vaguely."

"Well, I ran into him in the library again, and this time I got up the courage to talk to him. One thing led to another, and I went back to his apartment."

"Okay. And did that make you realize you weren't in love with Freddie?"

"It made me realize I didn't want to settle down. Freddie is the sweetest guy I've ever met. I may never do better than him. I'm so grateful to have had him in my life. But I don't want to be the kind of guy who screws around behind his boyfriend's back, so I confessed and we broke up."

"Wow. How he'd take it?"

"He was hurt, but I think relieved too. I don't think he's any more ready to be tied down at twenty-two than I am at eighteen. Things were pretty chilly between us when I left, but Freddie wasn't throwing pots at my head or anything."

"That's good, I guess."

"It is. There was another reason, too."

Grae ruffled Marcus' hair. "What's that?"

"You know I quit Magellan's after Domokos' thugs beat me up."

"Yeah."

"It always bothered me that Freddie didn't. He said all the right things, but it felt like a betrayal when he kept working for that asshole. I think that's when things started breaking down for us. And seeing you and Kendall together— That's the kind of relationship I want for myself someday. I know it won't be for a lot of years, but if you'd been in my shoes and Kendall was in Freddie's shoes, she'd have walked the moment she found out about Domokos, no matter how good the tips are."

Grae snorted. "She'd have bashed him over the head with a frying pan and then walked."

"That's what I mean. I want someone, someday, who will put me first—always. That isn't asking too much, is it?"

"No, bud, it sure isn't."

Marcus sighed heavily. "I just don't get it. Freddie works in the flagship Magellan's now, which means he has to see Domokos all the time. How can he stand being around that vicious hypocrite? I told him everything about Domokos. Hell, Freddie saw me get beat up because of Domokos, but it didn't matter. Only the money mattered."

Grae sighed. "That's often the way of the world. Integrity is mute, while money talks. Men like Domokos buy or bludgeon their way out of trouble. There's nothing we can do about it."

"Do you think he'll ever get what's coming to him?"

"No, I don't. I wish I could tell you different, but Domokos is far smarter, far richer, and far more connected than Dylan. Dylan's an opportunist, and not a very bright one. He'll pick a fight without thinking twice. Domokos is the kind of smarmy villain who'll fuck a kid behind a dumpster with one hand, and grease a politician's palm with the other. He'll always put layers and layers of plausible deniability between him and any consequences. If I'd thought through what he's really like, I'd never have confronted him. I'm so sorry I didn't."

Marcus shrugged. "I know you are. You've told me a thousand times, and I've told you a thousand times that I know you had the best intentions. I just hate that Domokos gets away with all this shit."

"Me, too."

"I don't suppose our budget would stretch far enough to hire a hitman, eh?"

Grae laughed at Marcus' wry tone. "Sorry, bud. Our budget is spoken for. Everything extra goes into your education fund. But I do have an idea."

"Yeah? What?"

"Don't pay any more heed to that fat, filthy pederast. Someday, maybe, you'll have your own five-star restaurant that makes Magellan's look like a McDonald's. The best revenge of all would be to live well."

Marcus grinned and held his hand up in a Vulcan salute. "And prosper."

"I think that was 'live long and prosper,' but you've got the right idea."

"Is that what you're going to do?"

Grae raised an eyebrow. "What? Live long and prosper?"

"Well, that too. But I meant live well. You always said you didn't dream. I got it, because we were struggling to survive day to day. But life's pretty darned good now, right? So do you dream now?"

Grae considered the question. What would she dream of? She had a woman she loved, who loved her. She had a job she could hardly wait to get to every morning. She shared a warm, clean, snug home with Marcus. All of this was more than she'd dared to imagine only seven or eight months ago.

"You know what, bud? I don't know if I can dream, but I do know that I don't need to dream. I couldn't be happier with reality. What more could I ask for?"

"A car. A house. A lottery win. That's the wonderful thing about dreams, Grae—the sky's the limit."

"Maybe, but I already feel like I've broken through to the stratosphere in the past year. Why limit myself to just the sky?"

"Huh." Marcus picked up the popcorn bowl and offered some to Grae.

She shook her head.

He popped a handful into his mouth and chewed thoughtfully. "Still, winning a lottery would be nice, like getting three wishes from a genie and then using one of them to ask for an endless supply of wishes."

Grae smiled, certain that he was picturing the animated version of *Aladdin*.

"If we had all the money and wishes in the world, you wouldn't have to work anymore," Marcus said.

"I love my job."

"We could start a restaurant together."

Grae laughed. "And what would I do in our restaurant, since I can barely boil water."

"You'd count our money."

"And what would we do with that money?"

Marcus looked her up and down, and shook his head. "Get you a new wardrobe, for one thing."

Grae looked at herself. "What's wrong with what I'm wearing?"

"For one thing, your shirt isn't buttoned correctly."

Whoops. Grae corrected the misalignment.

"You know, with money and wishes, you could take Kendall on an exotic vacation. You could go to some tropical island where gorgeous, semi-clad women would bring you fancy drinks with little umbrellas while you lounge on the beach. You'd only return to your luxury hut to make love while warm, ocean breezes blew through open windows."

"Hmmm, that's the best idea you've come up with so far."

Marcus sat up straight. "Yeah? Well what if when you came home, you returned to a fabulous mansion where all the servants were beautiful women?"

"Half-clad?"

"This is Canada. That would be cruel."

Grae pretended to consider the idea. "Would you live there too?"

"Of course, but I'd have a separate wing, where all the servants were gorgeous half-clad men."

"Hey! Why are your servants half-clad and mine aren't?"

"If you're not going to dream, you don't get to set the scene."

Marcus continued spinning wilder and wilder fantasies, until he'd finally put the two of them in charge of a whole country where everyone was beautiful, gay, and semi-clad at all times. Grae watched him with a smile. If she could, she would give Marcus anything, though she was content to see him dream the dreams she couldn't, as of yet. But she was on her way. One day she, too, would dream again.

She touched her lips, still bruised from Kendall's fervent farewell kisses.

And the best part was, she wouldn't dream alone.

Epilogue

GRAE PAUSED IN HER WALK up the cobblestones to Jo's door. The June rains and July heat had turned Jo's gardens into a verdant oasis bursting with brilliant colours. What Grae knew about horticulture wouldn't fill a dozen lines of a gardening book, but she appreciated the beauty that was the result of Jo's passion.

Jo came out of the house to greet her. Grae shifted the small but heavy box she carried, and waved.

"Hi, Jo. Gorgeous evening, isn't it?"

"It is, indeed. Very fitting for our final session."

Grae covered the last of the distance between them and handed Jo the box. "This is for you. Careful, it's heavy." She supported the bottom of the box while Jo opened it, and thrilled to Jo's delight as she extracted the gift.

"Oh, my goodness. It's Maddie, isn't it?"

"It is, at least as accurately as I could depict her. It's a stone deco for your garden."

Jo beamed. "And I know just the place to put it. Follow me."

Jo led Grae around the side of the house to the large backyard. Two wooden Adirondack chairs were placed in the shade of a tall weeping birch tree. Jo placed the stone cat so it appeared to be curled up and napping between the chairs.

"It's beautiful, Grae. And you made it? You're turning into quite the artist."

"Thanks, but I have to give most of the credit to the CAD software. I'm glad you like it, though."

"I do indeed." Jo took a seat and gestured Grae to the other chair. "It's such a nice day, why don't we have our last session out here?"

Grae sat down too. "So, no notebook?"

Jo smiled. "Not today. I really only wanted this final session to check in on how you're feeling about this past year. A lot has changed for you."

"I was thinking about that on the way over. When Mom first gave me her ultimatum—that I had to see you until you deemed me ready to be a productive member of society, I was pissed. I was ready to boot her out of our skanky apartment."

"You were very angry during our first session."

"Yeah, I was. If Mom hadn't bribed me with legal help and a better place for me and Marcus to live, I wouldn't have agreed to her terms. It scares me how close I came to missing all this."

"All what?"

"You, Kendall, Jude, my family…everyone and everything that has changed my life for the better."

Jo's gaze was as steady as ever. "Tell me how you've changed."

"I was so scared back then, you know?"

"Because of the attack on you and Marcus?"

Grae shook her head. "Not just that. I was scared every day. How was I going to provide for us? How were we going to get through another day without going hungry or losing a job? How could I ensure a decent future for Marcus?"

Jo tilted her head. "And what if the world ever discovered how scared you were?"

"Yeah, that too."

"You hid behind the persona you'd created."

Grae nodded. "I did. And every time I got some new ink or another piercing, I knew I was making it harder on myself, but I couldn't stop. I just couldn't stop."

"How were you making it harder on yourself?"

"Two crappy jobs equalled one lousy income, and I made sure no decent employer would look at me twice. God, where was my mind?"

Jo gazed at Grae with the same compassion she'd seen so often in Kendall's eyes. "I would say your mind was stuck in the past, on the morning that Melissa died."

"You're right. It was. There wasn't a day I didn't wake up that she wasn't at least second or third in my thoughts, right after 'what the hell do we have in the place to eat?'"

"And now?"

"I still think of her from time to time, but often weeks go by that she never crosses my mind."

"May I ask a question?"

"Of course. Why stop now?"

Jo smiled. "This is something of a philosophical question. You went through immense pain and grief in the years after Melissa's death. I look at you now, and you are not even remotely the angry, scared, defiant woman who first walked in my front door. You're happy, gentle, kind, and madly in love with my daughter. So knowing all that you know now, knowing that everything you've endured has brought you to this moment, what would you change?"

Grae contemplated Jo's question for a long moment. "You probably expect me to say that I'd change Melissa's dying. After all, it was the catalyst for my fall from grace."

"Is that what you're saying?"

"Maybe this will sound terrible, but no. I hate that Melissa died. I hate that the accident was partly my fault. But I'm where I am today because the cruelty I exhibited then, and the horror of Melissa's death, turned out to be gifts of a sort."

"Explain, please."

"I wouldn't wish those eight years after her death on my worst enemy. But without them, I wouldn't have a fraction of the love that is now in my life. And I'm not just talking about Kendall. I'm closer to my family than I ever imagined possible. And life without Marcus and Jude, or you, is unthinkable." Grae tapped the stone cat. "When I first thought of making this, it was because I wanted to say thank you for all that you've done for me. I know you were just doing your job, and that you took on that job despite a lot of reservations. But you did something truly amazing. You got me to believe that I was worth loving. Accepting that to be true was the hardest battle I'll probably ever fight in my life. It was also the most important. When I go over to Kendall's and she opens the door with that great big smile that's just for me; when I sit down with my family for Sunday dinner and I'm one of them again;

when Jude pats me on the back because I've done a damn fine job and he's proud of me, I know that every moment of agony was worth it, because I love who I am in their eyes."

"And Marcus?"

"I saved his life, Jo."

"You did indeed."

"The only thing that still terrifies me is the thought of what would've happened to him if we hadn't connected in that damned alley. Would he even be alive today?"

"Sadly, it's a strong possibility that he would not. And now look. Top marks on his GED and accepted into SAIT's professional cooking program."

"Which is already paid for, thanks to the unintended generosity of Rick and Dylan."

Jo laughed. "I'm not sure generosity is the right word, but they certainly hastened to settle out of court once they saw that video."

Grae grinned. "Virgil told me Rick was so pissed at Dylan that he was ready to kill him."

"I'm not surprised."

"Me neither. But I'm also glad I'll never have to see either of them again."

Maddie strolled over and wound herself around Jo's legs. Jo scooped the cat into her lap. "And now the time has come that you don't have to see me again either, at least in my professional capacity. I confess that thought saddens me a little. It's been a true joy to have been part of your journey back to health and happiness."

"Thanks, Jo. That means a lot to me. But you know, it's not all bad. You might not be my therapist anymore, but what would you think about being my mother-in-law one of these days?"

Jo's head snapped around. "Are you serious? Are you and Kendall—?"

"We've talked about it, and we both want the same thing, but until Marcus graduates and launches his own career, I'm not ready to desert him."

"You never would."

"No, you're right. I wouldn't. But even though I'm over at Kendall's most nights, I'll pay the rent on our apartment until he can take over the payments himself. Or move. But he does love his home."

"How long is his course?"

"Two years, and they have a one hundred percent employment rate for their graduates. Of course Marcus could end up working somewhere outside of Calgary. But at least while he's in school, I'm going to ensure he's got a stable home life and no fears for where he's going to hang his hat."

"I've heard of engagements much longer than two years."

Grae raised an eyebrow at Jo's patently innocent expression and laughed. "Joann Reaves, are you playing matchmaker?"

Jo smiled and handed Maddie to Grae. "Every mother wants her child to be happy. And I've never seen Kendall as happy as in the last few months."

Grae snuggled and caressed Maddie. The cat's purrs rumbled against her chest. "So you're saying you wouldn't object if I popped the question?"

"I certainly would not."

"Good to know."

"I'm going to have lemonade. Would you like a glass?" Jo asked.

"Yes, please."

Grae lavished attention on Maddie while Jo was gone and drifted into reverie. When Maddie wanted down, Grae set her on the grass and picked up the stone cat. She studied it. It was a lovely work of art, but cold and hard. Her gaze drifted across the gardens that lined Jo's backyard. They, too, were beautiful, dappled with the evening light and lush with life and growth. They complemented each other—the stone and the gardens; when the harsh winds of winter returned and the plants withered and died, the stone cat would still stand its post. She drifted on that thought for a moment.

Slowly, Grae's reverie turned to dreams—of rings and romance, of the family she had formed with Marcus, the birth family who had welcomed her home, and the family she would create with Kendall. And when her future mother-in-law stepped out of the back door with two tall glasses in hand, Grae smiled. She didn't need to dream of a life filled with more love than she ever could have imagined.

It was already hers.

About Lois Cloarec Hart

Born and raised in British Columbia, Canada, Lois Cloarec Hart grew up as an avid reader but didn't begin writing until much later in life. Several years after joining the Canadian Armed Forces, she received a degree in Honours History from Royal Military College and on graduation switched occupations from air traffic control to military intelligence. Having married a CAF fighter pilot while in college, Lois went on to spend another five years as an Intelligence Officer before leaving the military to care for her husband, who was ill with chronic progressive Multiple Sclerosis and passed away in 2001. She began writing while caring for her husband in his final years and had her first book, *Coming Home*, published in 2001. It was through that initial publishing process that Lois met the woman she would marry in April 2007. She now commutes annually between her northern home in Calgary and her wife's southern home in Atlanta.

Lois is the author of five novels, *Coming Home*, *Broken Faith*, *Kicker's Journey*, *Walking the Labyrinth*, *Bitter Fruit*, and a collection of short stories, *Assorted Flavours*. Her novel *Kicker's Journey* won the 2010 Independent Publisher Book Award bronze medal, 2010 Golden Crown Literary Awards, 2010 Rainbow Romance Writer's Award for Excellence, and 2009 Lesbian Fiction Readers Choice Award for historical fiction.

Connect with Lois:
Website: loiscloarechart.com
E-mail: eljae1@shaw.ca

Other Books From Ylva Publishing

www.ylva-publishing.com

Bitter Fruit

Lois Cloarec Hart

ISBN: 978-3-95533-216-7
Length: 244 pages (50,000 words)

Jac accepts an unusual wager from her best friend. Jac has one month to seduce a young woman she's never met. Though Lauren is straight and engaged, Jac begins her campaign confident that she'll win the bet. But Jac's forgotten that if you sow an onion seed, you won't harvest a peach. When her plan goes awry, will she reap the bitter fruit of her deception? Or will Lauren turn the tables on her?

Cast Me Gently

Caren J. Werlinger

ISBN: 978-3-95533-391-1
Length: 353 pages (100,000 words)

Teresa and Ellie couldn't be more different. Teresa still lives at home with her Italian family, while Ellie has been on her own for years. When they meet and fall in love, their worlds clash. Ellie would love to be part of Teresa's family, but they both know that will never happen. Sooner or later, Teresa will have to choose between the two halves of her heart—Ellie or her family.

Getting Back

Cindy Rizzo

ISBN: 978-3-95533-395-9
Length: 239 pages (73,000 words)

At her 30th college reunion, Elizabeth must face Ruth, her first love who bowed to family pressure long ago. As they try to reconcile the past, Elizabeth must decide whether she is more distrustful of Ruth or of herself. Is she headed for another fall or does she want to be the one who walks away this time? It's not easy to know the difference between getting back together and getting back.

The Return

Ana Matics

ISBN: 978-3-95533-234-1
Length: 300 pages (85,000 words)

Near Haven is like any other fishing village dotting the Maine coastline—a crusty remnant of an industry long gone, mired in sadness and longing.

Liza thought she'd gotten out, escaped on a basketball scholarship, but a series of bad decisions has her returning home after a decade. She struggles to accept her place in this small town, making amends to people she's wronged and rebuilding her life.

Coming From Ylva Publishing In Winter 2015/2016

www.ylva-publishing.com

Stowe Away

Blythe Rippon

Brilliant, awkward Samantha Latham couldn't wait to leave rural Stowe for an illustrious career in medicine. But when an unexpected call from a hospital forces Sam to move back home to care for her ailing mother, a life of boredom and isolation seems imminent—until a charming restaurant owner named Maria inspires Sam to rethink everything she knows about Stowe, success, and above all, love.

Rewriting the Ending

hp tune

A chance meeting in an airport lounge and a shared flight itinerary leaves Juliet and Mia connected. But how do you stay connected when you've only known each other for twenty four hours, are destined for different continents and each have a past to reconcile?

Stone Gardens
© by Lois Cloarec Hart

ISBN: 978-3-95533-541-0

Also available as e-book.

Published by Ylva Publishing, legal entity of Ylva Verlag, e.Kfr.

Ylva Verlag, e.Kfr.
Owner: Astrid Ohletz
Am Kirschgarten 2
65830 Kriftel
Germany

www.ylva-publishing.com

First edition: December 2015

No part of this book may be reproduced, scanned, or distributed in any printed or electronic form without permission. Please do not participate in or encourage piracy of copyrighted materials in violation of the author's rights. Thank you for respecting the hard work of this author.

This is a work of fiction. Names, characters, places, and incidents either are a product of the author's imagination or are used fictitiously, and any resemblance to locales, events, business establishments, or actual persons—living or dead—is entirely coincidental.

Credits
Edited by Alissa McGowan
Proofread by Marion Dries
Cover Design and Print Layout by Streetlight Graphics

CPSIA information can be obtained at www.ICGtesting.com
Printed in the USA
LVOW07s1631100316

478630LV00001B/229/P